The sensation of being in danger rose again.

Emily looked behind her, but there was only a blue van, two white cars and a small bus. Trepidation poured over her now like a dark syrup. She was afraid to look behind her again, afraid that she would finally see what was following them. She closed her eyes, and images of her father appeared. Emily grimaced, but she let the memory come. She knew Daddy, and he wasn't a monster.

Mommy called him that once. She called him that when Emily told her what Daddy had tried to do to her. Daddy had scared her so much, had touched her in a bad way. Mommy and Daddy had had a big, big fight. Then they went to a place called court, then a nice lady talked to Emily and made her show on a doll what Daddy tried to do to her, then the judge told Daddy he had to STAY AWAY forever. . . .

Emily covered her ears as if that could block out her thoughts. Mommy promised Daddy would never hurt her again. Mommy said they were going to live in a nice place called Pinebridge, Vermont. Mommy was going to teach there. Daddy couldn't hurt her now. Daddy was far, far away! He wasn't a monster. He was . . . he was . . .

. . . *right behind them.*

Tor Books by Clare McNally

Good Night, Sweet Angel
Somebody Come and Play
Stage Fright
There He Keeps Them Very Well

Good Night, Sweet Angel

Clare McNally

TOR ®

A TOM DOHERTY ASSOCIATES BOOK
NEW YORK

This is a work of fiction. All the characters and events portrayed in this book are fictitious, and any resemblance to real people or events is purely coincidental.

GOOD NIGHT, SWEET ANGEL

Copyright © 1996 by Clare McNally

Cover art by Paul Stinson and Tony Meyers

A Tor Book
Published by Tom Doherty Associates, Inc.
175 Fifth Avenue
New York, NY 10010

Tor Books on the World Wide Web:
http://www.tor.com

Tor® is a registered trademark of Tom Doherty Associates, Inc.

ISBN: 0-812-55103-6

First edition: May 1996

Printed in the United States of America

0 9 8 7 6 5 4 3 2 1

To my other mother, Marta Pastore, with love

one

For the past thirty miles, four-year-old Emily Galbraith had been certain something terrible was following her mother's car. Sometimes the feeling was so strong that she'd wriggle in her seat to look out at the road behind them, the road they'd been driving on for hours and hours. But there were no monsters on the road, only a lot of boring old cars.

"Emily, stop fidgeting," her mother admonished.

"There's nothing to do."

"How about your dinosaur tape?"

As Jenn groped for the tape player, Emily studied her mother's fingernails. They weren't long and red like Mimi Jackson's mommy's, or squarish with a jewel in the pinky like Emily's old babysitter. Mommy's nails were raggy looking, and sometimes they bled a little. She chewed on her nails a lot. Emily had tried it once, found she didn't like it, and stopped.

Mommy's hand brushed against the magnet Emily had made for her in school. "JENN" was spelled out in dried beans. Her real name was Jennifer, but everyone called her "Jenn." Except Daddy . . .

The sensation of being in danger rose again. Emily looked behind her, but there was only a blue van, two white cars, and a small bus.

"That tape's boring now," she said at last. "I heard it a million times."

Jenn made a *hmm* noise. " 'I see something red'? That's a nice game."

"There's nothing to see," Emily complained. "Nothing but green, green, green, green, GREEN!"

She opened and shut the glove compartment, fidgeted with the window button, then turned to look at her mother.

"If all the mountains are green," she said, "and Vermont means 'green mountain,' then how come we aren't in Vermont yet?"

Jenn laughed. "It *is* a long way from Buffalo to Pinebridge, isn't it? Maybe we can stop in a little while and stretch our legs."

Emily didn't reply. Trepidation poured over her now like a dark syrup. She was afraid to look behind her, afraid that she would finally see what was following them. She closed her eyes, and images of her father appeared. Emily grimaced, but she let the memory come. She knew Daddy, and he wasn't a monster.

Mommy called him that once. She called him that when Emily told her what Daddy had tried to do to her. Daddy had scared her so much, had touched her in a bad way. Mommy and Daddy had had a big, big fight. Then they went to a place called court, then a nice lady talked to Emily and made her show on a doll what Daddy tried to do to her, then the judge told Daddy he had to STAY AWAY forever . . .

Emily covered her ears as if that could block out her thoughts. Mommy promised Daddy would never hurt her again. Mommy said they were going to live in a nice place called Pinebridge, Vermont. Mommy was going to teach there. Daddy couldn't hurt her now. Daddy was far, far away. He wasn't a monster. He was . . . he was . . .

. . . *right behind them.*

Fear overcame Emily with such force that she threw up.

"Oh, Emily!" Jenn cried. "Why didn't you tell Mommy you were sick?"

Jenn looked for a way off the road. Emily began to cry.

"Don't stop, Mommy! Please don't stop!"

"I have to clean you up, dollbaby," Jenn said.

"NO!" Emily cried. "Daddy will get us! Daddy will get us!"

"Emily! Daddy is miles away!"

"He's back there! He's following us!"

Reflexively, Jenn looked in her rearview mirror. Her heart leaped into her throat when she saw the pickup that was tailgating them. There was a worn-out old baby doll, dressed in a hideous leather outfit, wired to the grille. She knew at once it belonged to Evan.

My God, she thought. *Has he been following us all this way? Why didn't I see him before?*

She stepped on the gas and tried to put some distance between them. He honked wildly, speeding up. The truck tapped the rear bumper of Jenn's car. Emily screamed.

Jenn changed lanes, still speeding. Evan kept up with her. When she dared to glance in her rearview mirror, she could just make out the malevolent grin on his face.

He'd vowed, back in the courtroom, that he'd get even with her, speaking low enough so that only she would

hear. She now held an Order of Protection. As soon as she
let the police know he was harassing her, he'd be arrested.

Emily was screaming.

"It's okay, dollbaby!" Jenn said reassuringly, although
she was terrified herself. "I'm going to look for an exit.
We'll drive to the police station in the next town."

She didn't tell her daughter how frightened she was that
there might not be a town for miles and miles. She'd
driven this road once before, when she'd interviewed at
Pinebridge College. There was a long stretch of nothing
but mountains in this area.

Evan hit her car again. Jenn swerved. Emily screamed.

Why was the road so deserted? Where the hell were the
other cars?

Jenn pushed on the accelerator pedal and shot forward.

Evan managed to keep up with her.

This time, when he hit her, he forced her car toward the
side of the mountain. Jenn gripped the steering wheel, her
knuckles white, her teeth clenched. The car began to shake
in protest.

There was a curve up ahead. Jenn put all her concentration into staying on the road, praying that they'd be safe
until they finally reached the next town. Evan pulled back,
then revved once more to ram her. She jerked the car to
the right, slamming herself and her daughter against their
seatbelts. The pickup swung around without making contact.

Jenn dared to catch her breath. Emily sat crying, covering her face.

"Don't let him get us, Mommy," she begged.

Hearing the child's plea gave Jenn strength. Somehow
she had to keep ahead of Evan. There was no place to turn
off the road, as it wound between two stretches of mountains. She could only speed ahead, grateful she'd filled the
gas tank at the last rest stop.

Suddenly there was another curve, heading right for a drop-off.

"Hang on!" Jenn ordered Emily, slowing down to take the curve.

Evan caught up. Honking wildly, he hit the gas with all his might. Jenn actually heard his engine revving. Before she could react, Evan's pickup hit her little sedan with great force.

Both Jenn and Emily screamed in horror as their car crashed into the guardrail.

They were flying through the air. Green and brown and blue shot wildly around them as the sky and earth mixed together in a wild swirl.

A moment before impact, Jenn saw Evan's pickup sail past. She had an instant to be surprised before the car slammed headfirst into the trees below. Jenn's airbag inflated, but the impact knocked her unconscious. Emily, cushioned in her car seat, might have been safe, had it not been for a loose can of soup that dislodged from a box in the back seat. At high speed, the can flew up and hit the back of Emily's head, knocking her deep into darkness.

A hundred yards away, Evan Parsons's pickup truck burst into flames, devouring him and all his hatred for his wife and daughter.

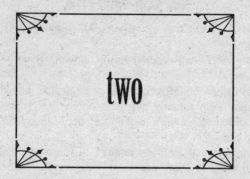

two

When she woke up several hours later, Jenn's world was an unfocused blur of pale green and white. She glimpsed a flash of bright colors before painkillers carried her down into sleep again. It wasn't until she came fully awake, later than evening, that she realized she was in a hospital bed. The bright colors were two vases of flowers that sat next to her bed. She tried to reach for them, but found she couldn't move her arm. Pain shot through her shoulder, and she cried out.

A dark-haired nurse with a round face and an even rounder body came into the room. Jenn blinked at her.

"Hi," the nurse said. "I'm Rita. Do you want some more medication? Are you in pain?"

"My ... my shoulder," Jenn choked. Her mouth felt pasty, her throat dry.

"The doctor will be in to talk to you in a little while,"

Rita said. "You can have some Demerol now, if you'd like."

Demerol. The word reminded Jenn of Emily's birth, when she'd been given the same medication to help her through labor.

Emily . . .

"Oh, my God," Jenn moaned, trying to pull herself up awkwardly with her good arm.

Rita put a firm hand on her.

"Emily," Jenn said. "My little girl! What happened to my little girl?"

She was becoming more awake by the moment, concern for Emily surpassing her pain. Her wide blue eyes must have told Rita what was on her mind, because the woman smiled.

"She's alive," Rita said.

"Where is she?"

"That's all I can tell you," Rita said. "Dr. Emerson's the pediatrician on her case. I'll send him in as soon as I can. In the meantime, do you want the Demerol?"

Jenn shook her head. The action made her suddenly nauseous. In a flash, Rita had a kidney-shaped pan under Jenn's chin. She choked up a little bile, then grimaced at the taste in her mouth.

"I'll get you something to rinse with," Rita said.

Before Jenn could speak, Rita was back again with a paper cup and a foil packet of mouthwash. While Jenn used it, the nurse explained how to use the call button on the bed and how to turn on the television. She finally talked Jenn into taking something for her pain, and by the time she left Jenn was falling asleep.

Voices woke her up again in the night, and she opened her eyes to see a man in a green scrub suit carefully examining the bandage around her shoulder. He was slightly built, almost lost in the loose-fitting outfit, with a ring of pale yellow hair around his head. When he smiled, the expression lit up his hazel eyes.

"Hello, Ms. Galbraith," he said. "I'm Doctor Petri. How ya feelin'?"

Jenn frowned at him.

"I hurt," she said. "How do you know my name? Where is this place?"

"The police ID'ed you from your wallet," Petri explained. "And this is St. Michael's hospital. We're about thirty miles from Pinebridge."

Thirty miles? She'd actually gotten that close to her destination? She closed her eyes and shuddered to think how fast she'd been going.

"What's wrong with my shoulder?" she asked.

"Dislocated," Petri told her. "You've got an airbag to thank for your life. That, and the fact that the trees broke your car's impact. It's a miracle, really. All you've got otherwise are a few scratches and contusions."

But Jenn didn't care about herself.

"What about my daughter?" she asked. "When can I see Emily?"

"If you're up to it," Petri said, "I can have someone wheel you up there right now."

"Up there?" Jenn asked. "Pedriatics is upstairs?"

"No, peds is down here," the doctor said, pronouncing the word with a long *e*. He sighed. "I'm afraid your little girl is in ICU."

"But . . . but she was in a car seat!" Jenn protested.

Panic began to rise in her. The Intensive Care Unit was where dangerous cases were taken! Where her mother had been in the days before she'd died.

"I'll get a wheelchair for you," Dr. Petri said, seeing how distraught she was. "You'll be with your little girl in a minute."

It wasn't Rita who returned with the chair, but a young

nurse's aide named Kathy. Kathy had sun-bleached blonde hair and a pretty face that was still freckled from days on the beach.

"Hi!" she said cheerily. "Going to pay a visit?"

Jenn was in no mood for chatter. Her heart was turning flip-flops, and her stomach felt sour again. She fought the urge to be sick, telling herself that she wouldn't do Emily a bit of good then. She let Kathy help her into the wheelchair, then gripped the armrests until her knuckles turned white. Upstairs, Kathy wheeled Jenn through a pair of automatic doors, where they were greeted by a young man with skin and hair so pale he seemed as sterile as the surroundings. He gave Jenn a sympathetic smile and held out his hand.

"I'm Rick," he said. "I'll be taking care of Emily tonight."

He dismissed Kathy and took the wheelchair himself.

"What have you been told?" he asked.

"Nothing at all," Jenn replied

"Well, Dr. Emerson is gone for the night," Rick said. "But his associate, Dr. Hargety, is on duty. She's with Emily right now."

Dr. Hargety greeted them at the entrance to Emily's room. She was a petite black woman whose small nose, large brown eyes, and soft curls gave her the look of an elf. Only the gray in her hair and the firmness of her handshake made her seem like someone to be respected.

She pulled aside pale green curtains to reveal Emily's bed. For a moment, Jenn couldn't see her daughter. All she saw were wires protruding from a mound of blankets. Her eyes followed a plastic tube and she saw that cold oxygen was being gently sprayed at her baby's tiny face. IV lines dripped fluids into the child's arm. She gasped, the hand of her good arm coming to her mouth. She bit hard on the corner of one nail.

"Oh, God," she whimpered, tears coming to her eyes. "She's so small! I didn't even see her in the bed!"

"She's a little one," Rick said. He brushed a gentle hand over Emily's forehead.

"Emily suffered a severe concussion," Dr. Hargety explained. "As far as the police could tell, something came loose and hit her in the back of the head. We've CAT-scanned her, and we've done an EEG. Both came up abnormal."

Jenn's head jerked around so fast that pain shot through her shoulder. She grimaced at the same time she echoed:

"Abnormal?"

"Don't hurt yourself," Rick said.

"We expect readings like this in a head injury," Dr. Hargety told her. "At this point, it's cause for concern but not great worry. We have to monitor her progress over the next days."

Jenn looked back at Emily. Although the child was a fair-skinned blonde, she looked gray now. Soft ice crystals formed on the tiny hairs of her chin, the oxygen giving her a beard of frost. Jenn carefully wiped it away.

"What else?" she asked. "What else is wrong with her?"

"The concussion is our main concern," the doctor replied. "There are some bruises and scratches, but luckily no broken bones. I'm afraid I can't tell you how long she'll be here. These are things we deal with on a day-to-day basis."

"Can I spend the night with her?"

"If it's all right with your doctor," Dr. Hargety said. "But Emily won't even know you're at her side. Why don't you spend this first night in your own bed? Then, when you're stronger, a cot can be wheeled in here."

"But . . . what if she wakes up? Will she wake up?"

"She might," was the reply. "These things can go either

way. She can be wide awake and talking by morning, or she could be like this for a while."

"You've been through quite a lot today," Rick said. "You must be exhausted."

Jenn nodded slowly. She *was* tired, and it wasn't just the vestiges of the Demerol. She asked if she could be alone with Emily for a while, and the others left. She took Emily's small hand in her own and bent to kiss it. It felt so cold to her.

"Emily, do you hear me? It's Mommy. Can you open your eyes, dollbaby?"

Emily did not respond. Jenn stared at her for a long time, feeling tears coming back. Tears—and something more. Anger.

"Evan," she growled through her teeth. "You bastard. If you're alive, I'm going to kill you!"

If he was alive, she hoped he was suffering twice as much as Emily. Three times as much.

Rick entered the room carrying a chart.

"Time for her vitals," he said. He took Emily's temperature and blood pressure. As Jenn watched, he peeled back both her eyelids and shone a light in them.

"Why are you doing that?" Jenn asked.

"Look at her pupils," Rick said, doing it again. "Do you see how they react to light? That's a very good sign."

For the first time, Jenn felt hopeful.

"Really? Then she's going to be okay?"

"I can't say that," Rick replied. "But she isn't as bad as she could have been. Watch this."

He prodded the bottom of Emily's foot with a pen. The little girl jerked back her leg without even opening her eyes.

"Baseline reactions," Rick said. "Another good sign. Here, let me explain about all this equipment. The IVs are

feeding her medication, as well as dextrose and electro-
lytes ..."

By the time he finished, Jenn had a basic understanding
of the monitors connected to Emily. The room didn't seem
so frightening now, and she realized she'd have to take
Emily's condition one step at a time or she'd go crazy. She
also realized that she was in too much pain herself to sit
up all night in a chair. She told Rick she wanted to go
downstairs again. Kathy appeared a short time later to
wheel her back.

They had nearly reached her room when a uniformed
police officer approached, introducing himself as Lieutenant Bill Mifflin.

Jenn wasn't surprised to see him. "Is Evan in jail?" she
asked as the lieutenant followed her into her room.

"Evan Parsons was killed in the accident," Bill told her.
"His truck blew up on impact. We thought you might be
able to tell us what happened."

Jenn let Kathy help her into the bed, then told her story.
Lieutenant Mifflin took a few notes, then left. There was
no one to arrest. As far as the police were concerned, the
case was closed.

An RN came in to give Jenn another dose of medicine,
and soon she slept.

In the morning, Jenn was surprised to see a familiar face
setting up her breakfast tray. Simone Trenton was a math
teacher who had recently retired from Pinebridge. Jenn
was going to take over her position. She and Emily would
live in the Trentons' house while Simone and her husband,
Joel, did some traveling.

Simone's eyes were bright blue in a soft-featured face,
dancing eyes that beckoned others to smile whether they
wanted to or not. Jenn found her own lips twitching. She
had met Simone only briefly, introduced to her by Dean

Kimberly Stone, but the older woman had expressed such concern for Jenn's welfare that she'd felt very comfortable with her. Now, Simone wheeled the tray to her and adjusted it while Jenn pulled herself up.

"How are you, *cherie*?" Simone asked in a faint French accent. Like many people in this part of Vermont, she was French-American.

"A little better," Jenn said. "What brings you here?"

"You, of course!" Simone replied. "Did you like the flowers?"

"The . . . Oh!" Jenn turned to look at them. The roses had started to open. "You sent those? I didn't even have a chance to look at the card. They're so beautiful."

"The yellow roses are from the staff," Simone explained. "And your sister wired the daisy arrangement as soon as we told her what happened."

Jenn took the plastic lid off the cup in front of her.

"It's just plain hot water," Simone said. "I didn't know if you liked coffee, or tea, or even hot chocolate. So I got a little of each. Do you know they were going to give you broth and Jell-O? I put a stop to that nonsense!"

"Coffee's fine," Jenn said. She lifted the cap off her plate to find scrambled eggs and an English muffin. "Thanks. But how did you find out about the accident? How did you get in touch with my sister?"

"Nick Hasken is the head of our science department," Simone said, leaning closer and lowering her voice. "He's a bit strange. He listens to his police-band radio all day and night, whenever he's not teaching. He heard about your accident and told Dean Stone. She called your sister at once, using the information you'd left on your job application."

Jenn had listed Rosalie as her next of kin.

"Is Rosalie coming up here?"

Simone shook her head, her pure white hair bouncing.

"No, she simply can't, *cherie*," she said. "But she'll call you this afternoon."

"She's got three kids," Jenn said in understanding. In a way, she was glad Rosalie wasn't going to show up. Her older sister had a way of taking charge of things that was just slightly short of intrusive.

"What time is it?" Jenn asked as she buttered her muffin.

"Nearly nine," was the reply. "I tried to go upstairs to see Emily, but they wouldn't allow it. It was hard enough to get in here before visiting hours. I told them I was your aunt, your only relative in the area."

Jenn couldn't help laughing. She wondered if she'd be as assertive as Simone when she reached sixty-two. She told Simone about how Evan had attacked her and Emily, and that he was dead. Her fury made her voice shake.

"You're right," Simone said. "It's almost a shame Evan isn't alive to suffer for what he did. What an evil, twisted man! To think he followed you all that distance!"

Jenn stared into her cup for a moment, then sighed. When her shoulders heaved, they didn't hurt quite as much as they had the night before.

"Nothing about Evan surprises me," she said with resignation.

"You're lucky to be rid of him," Simone said. "But I can't understand how a nice, intelligent woman like yourself ended up with his kind."

Simone's manner was so warm and inviting that Jenn found herself opening up. She hadn't really talked to anyone about Evan; not even her sister Rosalie.

"Evan wasn't always this way," she began. "When I first met him, he was teaching English at a small community college in Buffalo, where I had my first assignment as a college math teacher. Oh, he was so handsome then! And he had the best sense of humor—sharper and faster than anyone I've ever met. He was like one of those radio 'shock jocks,' except around me, of course. He never made fun of me or hurt my feelings. We got married, and at first we were very happy. Then he started using drugs, and he changed."

Simone looked concerned. "Why did he turn to drugs if he was so happy?"

"I don't know," Jenn said with a shake of her head. "I think the pressure got to be too much for him. You see, he started moonlighting to bring in more money. I didn't care about money, but it meant a lot to him. Maybe it was the stress, or maybe it was because the crowd from his night-time job was a bad one. He got mixed up with crack, and it turned him into a Mr. Hyde. Now he *did* start insulting me. He was so cruel. I tried to stick by him and it cost me my job."

She opened her cup of orange juice, took a sip, and found it had grown warm.

"Then Emily came along," Jenn said. "Evan vowed things would be different."

Simone made a snorting noise. "Famous last words!"

"Well, they were, at first," Jenn said. "He really adored Emily, did everything for her. Then I saw that he was deliberately defying everything I said or did when it came to our daughter. He was trying to turn Emily against me! But Emily is so bright, she didn't really buy it even when she was a toddler. She whispered to me one day, a year ago, that Daddy scared her. I went to a lawyer, and after a long, hard time we were finally free of Evan. That was six months ago. He should have been out of our lives forever. And now she's up there in ICU because he tried to kill her!"

The last few words were choked out, as Jenn began crying again. Simone narrowed her eyes in disgust, shaking her head. She got up, pushed the tray aside, and sat on the edge of the bed to hold the younger woman in a warm, motherly hug. She assured her again and again that things really would be okay.

Neither woman was aware that, at that moment, the staff of ICU was doing its best to keep Emily alive.

three

The clouds were so pretty. Pink and lavender and pale green; they reminded Emily of the cotton candy her mother had bought at a fair earlier this summer. She tried to reach out and grab a piece, imagining it melting and sweet in her mouth, disappearing the moment it touched her warm tongue. But the clouds were just too far away.

She heard music just then, a happy tune, and turned to find its source. Instead she saw the most brilliant, beautiful light she'd ever seen. It was as bright as the sun, but it didn't hurt her eyes one bit to look at. Somehow, she just knew there was a wonderful place beyond the light, full of fun and good things. She started to run toward it.

Suddenly, another girl stepped into her path. Emily stopped short and stared at her, wondering where she had come from. She held tightly to Emily's hand and stared at

her with huge, scared eyes. She had long curls that were
kind of red and brown mixed together, her face was milky
colored, and her eyes were big and brown. Emily thought
she was pretty. If she was pretty, then maybe she was nice,
too. And maybe she could tell her about the light.

"What's your name?" the girl asked. The blue dress she
wore, as pale as the clouds, billowed softly around her thin
legs.

"Emily Janine Galbraith," the four-year-old revealed. "It
used to be Emily Janine Parsons, but Mommy made that
name change."

"My name is Tara," the other girl said. "I'm glad you're
here. I thought I was all alone, and I was so scared!"

Scared? Tara's words surprised Emily. How could she
be scared of that beautiful, wonderful light? She looked
longingly toward the brilliance. For the first time, she noticed the silhouettes of people milling about in the distance.

"Who are they?" she asked.

Tara followed her gaze, her own eyes full of worry.

"Other people waiting," she answered. "They're not
scared of the light. They keep trying to get me to come in,
but I don't want to."

"I want to play in the light," Emily said. In truth, the
far-off figures held no more interest for her than strangers
on a crowded street.

Tara wrapped her arms around herself.

"The light means you never see your mama again. Not
ever. No more Mama."

Emily considered this, momentarily torn between the
joy the light promised and the need to be with her beloved
mother again. She held the light in complete awe, almost
as complete as her love for her mother. The awe was
growing stronger by the moment.

"I want to go back where I was," Tara said in a small voice. "I don't want the light."

"But it's so pretty . . ."

"You go in the light, and you never come back," Tara said. Tears began to spill from her eyes. "I don't care if the light is beautiful! I don't care if it's the best place that ever was on the other side! I don't want to stay!"

"Can't I just take a look?" Emily asked. She wanted that light, and whatever was behind it! It was the best thing ever, she was certain. She just couldn't understand why Tara seemed so scared.

But Tara was bigger, and older. That meant she had to be smarter, too, as far as Emily was concerned. Maybe she knew something Emily didn't.

Tara gasped, her eyes growing huge as she stared at the distant figures. Emily could see now that a few were coming closer. She still couldn't make out their faces, but somehow, they scared her. If a big girl like Tara was afraid, then something must be bad about them.

And yet, in a funny way, they made her feel happy, too. She bit her lip and chewed thoughtfully. What was the right way to feel?

Tara's face contorted now, and she cried even harder.

"NO! I don't want the light!"

Emily could see faces now, glowing and liquid. It was hard to make out what anyone looked like, but she could tell they were saying something.

"How come I can't hear them?" she asked.

Tara, caught in her own terror, didn't hear her.

"Leave me alone! I want my mama! I want my mama!"

Her fear was infectious, for now Emily looked at the light with new-found doubt. Maybe it was a trick. Maybe it was like the Wicked Queen in *Snow White*, the way she pretended to be a sweet old lady selling apples, and then Snow White had been poisoned.

Quickly, Emily turned away from the light, afraid to
look at it.

"I want my mommy, too," she said in a soft voice, too
soft to be heard over Tara's cries.

With shaking hands, she covered her own ears to block
out the screaming.

Simone had wheeled Jenn upstairs in time to see people
moving swiftly in and out of Emily's room. She quickened
he pace, but a nurse stopped them in the hall.

"What is happening?" Simone demanded, her accent
thicker than usual.

"Your little girl is very sick," the nurse, Marie, reported,
looking directly at Jenn. "Please, stay out here for a minute."

"Wait!" Jenn cried.

But Marie was already back in the room. Jenn looked
up at Simone, who put a firm, supportive hand on her
shoulder.

"Why won't they let me see her?"

Jenn realized her knees were shaking, almost knocking
together. She began to chew at the corner of her thumb-
nail. Something was wrong with Emily, something so bad
that they didn't want her to see.

"Oh, Simone, what if she's dying?"

"No, *cherie*," Simone insisted. "Don't talk like that.
Look at your thumb," she said. "You've made yourself
bleed."

A handsome, gray-haired older man stepped out of
Emily's room, wiping his forehead. He crouched down by
Jenn's wheelchair.

"Ms. Galbraith?"

Jenn nodded. "What's wrong with Emily?"

"I'm Dr. Emerson," he said. He spoke in quiet, no-
nonsense tones. "I'm afraid your little girl had a very close

call this morning." Jenn gasped. "She's all right now," Emerson continued. "But we've got to keep a close watch on her. I'm going to have her under constant surveillance for a few days. I don't like that head injury at all."

Jenn watched, chewing the cuticle that was already bleeding, as a parade of medical personnel exited her daughter's room. At last, Simone was able to wheel her inside. Marie gave the woman a disapproving stare.

"Only one visitor at a time," the nurse said.

"All right," Simone said. She looked at Jenn. "Do you want me to wait outside?"

Jenn shook her head. "I'm going to stay as long as I can."

"If you're certain, *cherie*," Simone said. "You've had a terrible scare . . ."

"I'll be okay," Jenn said. In truth, she really wanted to be alone with her little girl. She managed a smile for Simone. "Thanks."

Simone gave her a kiss on the cheek and departed. After she left, the doctor pulled up a chair. He flipped over a few pages on a clipboard and clicked open his pen.

"What . . . what exactly happened?" Jenn asked. Her knees were still shaking slightly, and she was glad she was seated.

"Her blood pressure dropped to a dangerous level," Emerson said, "and her heart stopped. I don't believe in pulling any punches, especially when it comes to talking to parents about their children. Emily is very sick, Ms. Galbraith. She almost died this morning."

"Oh, no . . ."

"I've stabilized her," Emerson said. "She's sleeping comfortably now. I'd like to ask you some questions about her medical history."

Jenn nodded.

* * *

Jenn was released from the hospital the next morning. As soon as she was able, she went back upstairs to the ICU. Over the next days, Jenn stayed at Emily's bedside almost constantly. A convertible chair was brought in for her, and she slept there at night, tucked between Emily's bed and the sink cabinet. She tried to bring a touch of cheer to the room by placing the vases of flowers sent to her by her fellow teachers on the windowsill.

Emily began to speak, incoherently at first—garbled protests when tests were done on her, "STOP THAT!" when a needle was administered. She mumbled strange phrases, like: "No light now," and "Get away, Tara." Jenn couldn't recall anyone named Tara and guessed Emily might be referring to a classmate from her old nursery school.

Rick, Marie, and the other nurses had nothing but encouraging words for Jenn. Both Dr. Emerson and Dr. Hargety were pleased with Emily's progress. It helped Jenn get through the next days, when the fear of the unknown haunted her dreams. Would Emily be brain-damaged? Would there be adverse physical effects from the accident?

When would she finally wake up?

Simone dropped by on a daily basis, and in her motherly way suggested that Jenn take it one step at a time. It was good advice. The fact that there were no more relapses, and that Emily grew stronger with each passing day, helped Jenn keep her spirits up.

Dean Kim Stone, as well as a few other teachers, also paid visits. As none of these people was permitted in the ICU (Simone's one visit there had been an oversight), Jenn would sit with them in the cafeteria and offer progress reports over lunch or coffee.

Rosalie called every other day. When Jenn tried to tell her Emily was getting better, she insisted that Jenn was just trying to keep bad news from her. That was Rosalie's way, always worrying, but Jenn didn't let it get to her. It was more important that she concentrate on Emily.

Over the next week, Emily's room grew more and more crowded with balloons, stuffed animals, and flowers. One day, while having a cup of coffee and watching the morning news, Jenn heard a soft, babyish whisper.

"Hi, Mommy."

Jenn nearly dropped the cup.

"Oh, hi, dollbaby!" she cried. She put the cup on the sink next to her and hurried to give Emily a kiss. She took the child in her arms awkwardly, IV tubes twisting. Her happiness made her deaf to the frantic beeping of an alarm, indicating an IV had been yanked out.

"You came back to Mommy," Jenn said, tears coming to her eyes. She'd cried so much over the past days that she wondered how her body could produce more water. But these were tears of joy. Her baby was back!

"I came back," Emily said softly. "But Tara didn't. Those shadowy people near the light wouldn't let Tara come back."

Jenn didn't wonder about Tara. The only thing that mattered was Emily's recovery.

Rick, ending his night shift, came into the room to check the alarm.

"Well, look who's up!" he said cheerfully.

Emily regarded this fair-skinned man, almost as pale as the spirits she'd seen, and hugged her mother closely.

"How do you feel, kid?"

"Okay," Emily said tentatively. She wasn't so sure about this stranger.

Jenn looked up. "I'm sorry. The IV came out."

"Doesn't look like she'll be needing it," Rick said. "Are you hungry, Emily? Do you want some breakfast?"

"I want a hot dog."

Rick laughed. "I'll see what I can do."

The rest of that morning moved at a delightful pace, and Jenn felt higher than she had in weeks. Dr. Emerson had Emily moved to pediatrics that same day. Jenn met a whole new set of nurses, but she hardly heard their names. Her full attention was given to Emily. The little girl was ravenously hungry, and didn't complain when she was given clear broth and Jell-O instead of a hot dog.

She was siting up, using the coloring book and crayons sent in by a teacher named Noreen Kane, when Simone arrived. She was accompanied by a bald-headed man with sparkling green eyes and a big smile that showed large, white teeth.

"Well, you must be that pretty girl everyone's talking about," he said.

"This is my husband, Joel," Simone introduced. "Oh, *cherie*! It's so good to see her awake!"

Emily gazed at them in wonder, frowning. There were so many strangers in this place. It was a little scary . . .

Then Joel placed a pink teddy bear on the bed. Emily's eyes lit up. She took it in her arms and hugged it tightly.

The grown-ups began talking, and Emily went back to her coloring. She heard everything they said and understood a lot. She was very sick, she knew, and she had almost died. But she was going to be okay, and pretty soon Mommy would take her to live at Simone and Joel's house. Simone and Joel talked in a different way, a little like Pepe La Pew from Looney Toons. Simone called Emily *"petite chou."*

"What does that mean?" Emily asked.

Joel laughed. "She's calling you a little cabbage."

"A little cream puff," Simone corrected. "You know that's what it's supposed to mean, Joel. Cream puffs look like cabbages."

"I'm not a cabbage," Emily protested. "And I'm not a cream puff, either. My name is Emily."

"Emily!" Jenn cried.

The French-American couple only laughed.

"She's a smart kid, n'est-ce pas?" Joel asked. "I like you, Emily. Do you want to come to Europe with Simone and myself?"

"No," was Emily's simple reply.

She couldn't understand why the Trentons were laughing at her, but she decided she liked them. They came to visit a few more times over the next several days, and Simone even stayed with her one afternoon when Mommy had to go to the college and do some work.

At last, almost two weeks after the accident, Emily was declared well enough to go home. By now her bruises had faded, and there were only a few scratches left unhealed. Jenn herself no longer wore a sling, and she had been able to drive a rented car for a few days. Emily sat in a wheelchair and held fast to the pink teddy bear as a nurse wheeled her out of the hospital. They waited by the curb while her mother went to get the coupe. Emily stared at the car, a little brown car, nothing like her mother's own car, the one that had gone over the hill, the one that had crashed, the—

"Dollbaby, you're shaking like a leaf!" Jenn said, cutting into her frantic thoughts. "It's okay, really. I'm a good driver. Nothing is going to happen to you."

"Daddy ..."

Jenn gave her a tight hug.

"Daddy is gone now," she said. "He was killed in the accident. I already explained that, Emily. You don't have to be afraid.

Emily stiffened in her arms, but somehow Jenn managed to get Emily in the car and buckled in. The child stared down at her pink teddy bear.

"Listen, I bought you a new tape," Jenn said, popping it into the cassette player. "It's about a little dinosaur who moves to a new home."

Emily hardly heard the tape as it played. She was clutching the pink teddy for dear life, trying to pretend the car wasn't pulling away from the curb. But over the next miles, she began to relax. She started paying attention to the tape, closing her eyes and imagining the dinosaur, a girl stegosaurus named Stephanie. Stephanie's world was full of volcanoes and strange creatures. But for reasons Emily didn't try to understand, all the clouds were pastel-colored like cotton candy.

When the tape came to an end, Jenn spoke up.

"You're just going to love our new home," she said. "Simone fixed up a little bedroom for you. It's so pretty."

Emily began to feel strange. Not the sick, shaky feeling she had had when she knew Daddy was following them. Just a weird, empty feeling.

"Our new home is gone now," she said quietly.

"What do you mean?" Jenn asked.

But before Emily could reply, two big fire engines roared by them along the highway. Jenn saw smoke rising from the direction of the college and forgot Emily's strange statement.

"It looks like there's a fire on campus," she said.

Following directions she'd gotten from the dean a few months earlier, Jenn turned onto an exit ramp. As she approached the street leading toward the Trenton home, the smell of burning wood wafted through the vents. It grew stronger, and in a moment bits of charred debris floated before the car. Jenn found her access cut off by a police car set horizontally across the road.

"Our home is gone," Emily said again, her voice small and sad.

"Emily, it may not be the Trentons' house," Jenn said.

But deep inside, she had a sick feeling that Emily was right. When she'd been up here before, she'd noticed there were no other cottages along this road. It was filled mostly with the trees, balsam and fir, that surrounded the entire campus. Maybe it was a forest fire. Jenn was still worried, though, that the fire might spread to her new home.

She opened the door, wanting to question a cop she saw standing near the police car.

"Stay in here," she told her daughter, then called to the cop. "Excuse me!"

When he turned, she recognized Lieutenant Bill Mifflin. She hurried up to him.

"What's happening?"

He squinted at her, then his face relaxed with recognition.

"Hi," Lieutenant Mifflin said. He looked back over his shoulder. "One of the campus homes is on fire. It isn't safe to go up this way."

Jenn felt sickened. She couldn't see the house from this bend in the road, but she could see the black smoke billowing up to the sky. She shivered.

"It's the Trentons' place, isn't it?"

"I didn't get the name," Mifflin admitted. "You know them?"

"Yes," Jenn said, thinking how close she'd become to the French-American couple in such a short time. "Please, I have to know if they're okay!"

Mifflin picked up his hat, ran a hand through his hair, and put it on again before speaking.

"An ambulance drove off a few minutes ago," he said. "I think your best bet is to talk to the dean about—"

He cut himself off suddenly and broke into a run.

"HEY, KID!"

Confused, Jenn glanced back at her car just long enough to see that Emily's door was open, and that she was gone.

She turned and went after the cop. He was running as fast as he could, calling out. As they came around the bend, they could see the inferno that had once been the Trentons' little cottage. It was a good fifty yards away, but somehow Emily had already managed to cross half that distance.

"Emily!" Jenn screamed. "Get away from there!"

Her voice seemed drowned out by the roar of the flames, but an alert firefighter saw the child and grabbed her. Emily screamed and struggled, reaching toward the house. She seemed completely unaware of the intense heat. She was yelling something that Jenn couldn't hear, crying hysterically. It was as if she could see something in the red and orange flames that shot out of the windows, in the dark smoke that billowed toward the sky.

When Jenn reached her, breathless, she heard Emily at last:

"Tara! Tara's in there!"

"Honey, we got everyone out," the firefighter who was holding her said.

Jenn took her daughter into her arms.

"Mommy! Tara's in there! I saw her face!"

Mifflin looked up at the blaze. "My God, is there someone else trapped?"

The firefighter shook his head. "Definitely not. We got through the whole house before it went up completely."

Jenn held Emily tightly and rocked her back and forth.

"I'm ... I'm sorry," she choked, smoke burning her throat. "She had a head injury. She sometimes talks about a child named Tara."

"You sure?" Mifflin asked, still worried someone was trapped inside.

Jenn nodded. "Sure."

She looked at the firefighter. "Please, did you get Joel and Simone out in time?"

"Are you a relative?"

"I was supposed to move in here today," Jenn said.

The firefighter sighed. "We got them out, but they were in bad shape."

Jenn didn't want to hear more. She took her daughter's hand.

"Come on, Emily."

"Where's Tara?" Emily whimpered.

"She isn't here," Jenn said.

She carried the child to her car and buckled her into her seat. As she drove toward the administration building, she tried to ask her daughter what had happened.

"Emily, just who is Tara?"

"My new friend," Emily said. "I met her at the hospital. She's pretty."

Emily wriggled until one leg was tucked underneath her. She began to dance the pink teddy on the seat between them. The hysterical child who had been carried by the firefighter was gone now.

"What made you think she was at the fire?"

"She called to me," Emily said. "I went there and I saw her."

Worry crept into Jenn's mind. Was Emily hallucinating? Was this a result of her head injury? The thought was more terrifying than the fire she'd just witnessed.

She recalled now that Emily had known about the fire before they even saw smoke. What had she said?

"Emily, why did you say our new home was gone?"

"Tara told me," she said.

She cuddled the pink teddy close to her and turned to stare out the window. Jenn knew she wouldn't get any more answers out of the child. She didn't want to wear her out by pressing the matter.

They reached the administration building, a large brick and stone structure on the opposite side of the campus. Somehow, she wasn't surprised when Kim Stone greeted her as she exited the car.

"Please, come into my office," Kim said. "I'm afraid there's terrible, terrible news."

When Jenn had first met Kim, on her interview, she'd been impressed by the confidence the woman radiated. The squareness of her broad shoulders and the tilt to her sharp chin gave her a military air. This was a woman who would never let a husband's sharp wit destroy her self-esteem. And yet there was a softness in her light brown eyes, set close together in an angular face, that made her approachable in spite of her no-nonsense manner. A pair of dolphin-shaped earrings and a starfish lapel pin were a stark contrast to her simple brown suit and bow-tied blouse. This was a woman who knew when to be serious, and when not to be.

Right now, she was dead serious.

Jenn followed her inside, holding Emily by the hand. Once in the dean's office, Kim gave the little girl some paper and a red pen to draw with. Then she took Jenn aside.

"I can hardly believe this," she said, speaking softly.

"Neither can I," Jenn said. "I heard about the fire when I drove up the road. Do you know anything? Are Simone and Joel all right?"

Kim took a deep breath, square shoulders moving only slightly. "The fire began about three hours ago. Since it was only eight in the morning, it's possible Simone and Joel were sleeping."

"Oh . . ." Jenn knew what was coming.

"They're dead," Kim confirmed. "I'm so sorry you have

to arrive to such bad news, Ms. Galbraith, especially after your own troubles."

Jenn resisted an urge to start chewing her nails. The whole atmosphere of the dean's office made her want to be as professional as possible, even in a stressful situation. She looked out at the campus grounds, beautiful in their late summer finery. Copses of birch and maple dotted the grass between the brick buildings. Mountains of balsam and fir stretched up behind the campus, reaching into the clear, blue sky. There was no sign of the devastation that was taking place on the opposite side of the campus. Students who had arrived early to settle in before first day hurried about as if unaware of the tragedy that had taken place this morning.

Jenn didn't cry. She'd seen so much death and destruction recently that, for the moment, she was simply too numb.

"You'll need a new place to stay," Kim said quietly, business-as-usual. "I've got an extra room that will do for tonight." ·

Jenn hardly heard her. She was looking at Emily, who sat drawing houses with flames coming out of them.

Dean Stone made arrangements for Jenn and Emily to stay in an empty dorm room, the only space available on campus, until Jenn could find an apartment. Emily insisted on staying in her mother's bed, and Jenn was only too glad to keep the child close to her. Cuddled into the crisp, cool sheets and fluffy comforter, Emily had fallen asleep almost at once. But Jenn lay wide awake, thinking about Emily's strange words in recent weeks. She'd known Evan was behind them even before Jenn saw him. She'd known their new home was on fire. And who was Tara? Jenn didn't recall meeting her, either back in Buffalo or at the hospital.

Emily was an exceptional child, much more intelligent

than most four-year-olds. She would get up to answer the
doorbell before it rang, sometimes knew the next commer-
cial on television. Her teacher at nursery school said she
was insightful, and very sensitive to her surroundings. She
had suggested that, perhaps, Emily should be placed in a
program for advanced students. This was one of the reasons Jenn had chosen Pinebridge College. Its on-campus
day-care center had a program for gifted children.

Gifted, that was all. Not strange. Not clairvoyant, for
God's sake. Smart people just noticed more than the rest
of the world.

Emily had noticed Evan when she turned around and
looked.

She had seen the fire engines, the smoke, and made a
lucky guess.

Nothing more than that.

"But that doesn't explain Tara," Jenn whispered to herself.

Emily suddenly bolted upright with a scream. Jenn
grabbed her and hugged her, trying to soothe her out of
her nightmare.

"Daddy was coming out of a big fire," Emily wailed.
"He was coming with a great big ugly pizza cutter and he
was going to slice me up with it!"

"Oh, dollbaby," Jenn cooed, "that was just a horrible,
terrible nightmare. Daddy's gone now. He can't hurt you
again."

"There was fire everywhere! And Tara came and chased
Daddy away, and she said it was a bad house, and we
couldn't live there, and . . ."

"Shhh . . ."

After a long time of being rocked and cooed to, Emily
fell asleep once more. But now she'd given Jenn something else to think about. The fire in the dream didn't surprise her—Emily had seen two fires recently. But the pizza

cutter was something she hadn't mentioned in over a year. Evan had done something to their daughter with that kitchen tool, something Emily refused to discuss. It had been so terrifying to her that Jenn had had to throw out her own cutting wheel. Now she used a knife to cut pizza. What had triggered that memory in her daughter?

Would Emily ever get over her fears of the monster disguised as her father?

It was a long time before Jenn was able to fall asleep, loving arms locked protectively around her daughter.

four

Jenn had left some of her boxes in the car, and the next morning she and Emily brought them inside. She felt a little strange moving into a dorm. Not a few students turned to look at her, wondering what this woman and child were doing here. The room Kim Stone had offered, with apologies, was a small suite with two bedrooms and a half bath. Normally, Kim had explained, each bedroom would be occupied by two students. But these particular rooms were not filled this year. The only setback, Jenn thought, was having to share a communal shower room with students.

Well, it was good incentive to hit the local real estate agents as soon as possible.

Emily helped her carry their belongings inside, taking charge of her own toys. As they made trips back and forth, Jenn began to wonder how they ever fit so much in her car, let alone repacking it into this smaller rental. Emily hobbled along with a box in her small arms, the pink and still-nameless teddy perched on top. She peered around the corner of the box, following close behind her mother.

Emily heard a soft *thump-thump-thump*.

"Mommy, my teddy fell!"

"I've got him," came a voice from behind them.

Jenn went up to the landing, then turned to see Emily watching a young woman ascending the staircase. The newcomer smiled at Emily as she put the bear back on top of the box.

"Say, can I carry that for you?" she asked.

"Okay," Emily said. "It weighs a ton."

The girl took the box and pretended to heave it with a big groan. Emily laughed, aware the older girl was only teasing.

"What's your name?" Emily inquired.

"Michelle Wallace," came the reply. "How about you?"

"Emily Janine Galbraith," Emily said.

"Say, Emily, is that the 'Future Fighters' on your sweatshirt?" Michelle inquired. It was a popular afternoon television show. "My little brother is crazy about them, especially the one who wears black and yellow."

"That's Patrick," Emily said. "I like Tammi. She wears gold."

She pulled Michelle by the hand until they reached the spot where Jenn was working.

"This is my mommy. She's a teacher."

Michelle's eyes widened, round pools of chocolate in a round, freckled face.

"Ms. Galbraith?" she asked. "The new math teacher?"

"Guilty."

They turned into a doorway and headed for Jenn's room.

"I'm Michelle Wallace," the girl said. "I've got you for trig. But . . . ?"

She hesitated, as if trying to find a polite way to ask a rude question.

"What's a nice teacher like me doing in a place like this?" Jenn asked for her.

"Well, yes," Michelle said with a laugh. "I thought . . . Oh! Oh, I'm sorry. You were probably going to live in the Trenton's house, weren't you? Isn't it terrible, what happened to them. I cried all day when I heard. Mrs. Trenton was so very nice."

They entered Jenn's room.

"Emily, you can take those into your room and unpack them," Jenn instructed.

When the child was gone, Jenn turned to Michelle.

"Are the kids talking about it much?"

"Only the ones who are already here," Michelle said. "And really just those who knew the Trentons. Mrs. Trenton was one of my favorite teachers. See, I'm really a French major. I've been studying since my sophomore year in high school. I hope to become an ambassador, or a delegate to the UN, or something like that. Mrs. Trenton would talk to me in French even though she wasn't really my French teacher. I was going to miss her now that she'd retired. And Mr. Trenton, too. He taught American literature, you know. Nice guy, I guess. I didn't really know him . . ."

Jenn had lost much of what Michelle was saying, her ears tuning in for important words among all the chatter. What she mostly understood was that Simone and Joe Trenton were well liked. It didn't surprise her.

"Well, it'll take us some time to adjust, I suppose," she said, cutting Michelle off midsentence. She was afraid the student would go on talking forever. "Thanks for helping Emily."

"Oh, you're welcome," Michelle said. "If I can help in any way else, let me now. I'm just downstairs." She started for the door. "See you Tuesday ..."

Michelle was half into the hall when Jenn had an idea and called the girl back.

"Are you busy this afternoon?"

"Not really," Michelle said. "See, I've already unpacked. Now my roomie is—"

"Would you like to make some money?" Jenn asked. "Would you baby-sit for me? I've got a staff meeting for the math department, and it would be easier to go alone."

"Sure," Michelle said. "I love kids."

Emily came running from her bedroom whooping.

"Yay! Yay! What're we gonna do?"

"Emily, you were eavesdropping," Jenn scolded. She looked at Michelle. "I saw a playground just off campus. Can you take her there?"

Jenn opted for a public park instead of the play area at the campus's on-site day-care center because, although it was off the grounds, the playground was actually closer to the dorms.

A short time later, Emily was flying into the air, begging Michelle to push her higher and higher. The air flew through her long blonde hair, her giggles filled the air. Everything moved far from her, then closer to her, in a dizzying blur.

And then, in the midst of the swift-moving scenery, Emily's eyes were drawn to a little girl on the monkey bars. She seemed brighter than anyone else around, as if the sun was favoring her with special rays. Recognition was instantaneous, and delight completely filled Emily. She skated her heels into the wood chips below the swing and brought herself to a stop.

"Had enough?" Michelle asked.

"I wanna go on the monkey bars!" Emily said. "I see my friend Tara there!"

Michelle looked at the monkey bars.

"You're a silly kid," she said. "I don't see anyone there at all."

"I do!" Emily insisted, and took off as Michelle headed for a bench.

Michelle couldn't see the young girl who was sitting on the highest level of the monkey bars.

"Tara, Tara!" Emily cried as she climbed up. "Did you come to play with me?"

"Yes," Tara said. "Those people on the other side—the ones waiting to go into the light—tried to keep me away, but I wouldn't listen to them. I had to see you. You're my special friend."

Emily grinned. "You're my special friend, too. Tara, did you get hurt? Did you get hurt in the light?"

"I'm okay," Tara said. She hooked her legs over the bars and swung down. The pale blue dress she was wearing, caught behind her knees, didn't flip down over her face. Emily saw her body pass right through the steel pipe, but didn't register surprise. As bright as Emily was, she was still a preschooler, at an age where reality and fantasy blended into one. If cartoon characters could fall from cliffs and walk away, little girls could pass through monkey bars.

Emily swung upside-down herself, but her head came to rest against the bar below. She looked at Tara.

"We're like two bats," Tara said.

"Yuck," Emily replied. "I hate bats. Mommy says they carry rabies."

"My mama said so, too," Tara replied. "My mama was always real careful. She took good care of me. She loved me. Does your mama love you?"

Emily frowned. "Of course. She's my *mommy*."

"My mama would love you better," Tara said.

Emily stuck out her tongue and blew a raspberry at her. Then she swung around, jumped to the ground, and ran to the nearby group of riding animals. All were occupied except for a whale, perched on top of a heavy spring that would allow a child to rock back and forth. A moment before Emily reached it, another boy cut in front of her and stuck out his tongue in triumph.

"Hey, no fair!" Emily wailed.

Michelle, who had seen what happened, started toward her charge. Suddenly the little boy went flying from the whale, slamming down into the wood-chip-covered sand. He began to cry, chubby cheeks turning bright red.

"She pushed me! Mommy! Mommy!"

"I did not!" Emily protested.

Michelle reached the scene at the same time as the mother.

"She pushed me!"

"Did not!"

"She didn't," Michelle said. "I saw the whole thing. You jumped off."

The little boy screamed loudly.

"Shh, Freddy," the mother said. Her eyes shot daggers at Emily. "Why don't you keep your hands to yourself?"

"I . . ."

"Not her, Mommy! The other girl! The other girl!"

"There is no other girl," the mother insisted.

"My arm HURTS!"

"She didn't do it," Michelle said in a firm voice.

The mother shoved up the sleeve of Freddy's jacket. An ugly red mark promising to become a nasty bruise had formed on his upper arm.

"Then explain this," she snapped.

Michelle looked down at Emily, who seemed both bewildered and annoyed. Then she looked at Freddy. He had to be nearly twice Emily's weight and much taller. There was no way Emily could have knocked him down.

"You jumped," she said again. "You hit your arm when you fell. Come on, Emily. Play someplace else."

"Brat!" the woman called after them.

"Bitch," Michelle growled.

Emily giggled.

"Don't you tell your mother I said that," Michelle warned. "Okay?"

"Mommy says *bitch*," Emily replied.

"Never mind. Why don't you try the slide?"

Emily headed for it, but Tara cut her off.

"That boy was mean," she said, her eyes thin.

"Yeah. Tara, did you push him?"

"You bet I did," Tara said. "Nobody gets away with hurting my best friend! If he tries it again, I'll break his arm. I can do that now, you know. I can break somebody's arm."

The idea of a bone sticking out of flesh sent a chill through Emily. She made a face.

"Don't say that," she begged. "Gross! Tara, do you want to go on the swings? I want to go on them again."

The subject was changed that quickly. They ran to the swings, hand in hand. Emily scrambled onto hers, while Tara seemed to float into her seat with all the gracefulness of a ballerina.

"You didn't tell me you could swing by yourself!" Michelle called from the bench.

"That's 'cause you didn't ask me!"

Michelle laughed. A moment later, she was surprised to see the empty swing next to Emily's start moving. She looked around at the trees, but there was no wind at all. A chill ran down her spine.

"She's staring at us," Tara said, stopping her swing.

Michelle saw the swing was still and concluded that Emily had simply given it a push. But she still had the weird, creepy feeling that someone had just walked on her grave.

"Michelle's nice," Emily said.

"Mama's nice, too," Tara replied. "You'd like her. You'd like to live with her."

"I live in a little room with my mommy," Emily told her friend. "Our new house got burned up."

"I know," Tara said. "Maybe you could live in Mama's house. Mama's house is very, very big."

Emily smiled. "That'd be great! Then we could be like real sisters. I'll tell my mommy about it."

"I'd like you to live with me," Tara said. "I'd like us to be friends forever and . . ." Suddenly, Tara blinked a few times, then closed her eyes and covered her ears. *"No! You can't come over here! She's mine!"*

"Tara, what's the matter?"

Tara's eyes snapped open. They were glassy and wild. She grabbed Emily's arm so hard that the smaller child cried out in pain.

"He's looking for you! He's over there in the trees and he's looking for you!"

Emily wrenched her arm free and turned to the woods. At once, her knees seemed to turn to jelly. She saw something more horrible than any demon emerging from the nearby beech trees.

It was her father, holding up a gleaming pizza cutter that was bigger and sharper than any Emily had ever seen before. He was looking around, searching for her, planning to cut her up in little pieces. She just knew it!

"Run!" Tara cried. "You've got to run away before he

gets you! Hurry! I'll ... I'll get his attention so he doesn't see you!"

But Michelle was already there, lifting her off the swing. Emily squirmed and wailed in terror.

"Daddy! Daddy's coming!"

"Emily, I thought ..."

"He's in the woods! Tara saw him!"

Gripping Emily as tightly as she could, Michelle turned to look at the trees. There was no one there at all.

"Come on," she said, "I'm taking you home."

"He's coming to kill me!"

Emily clung to Michelle with all her strength, her eyes darting here and there in search of her father. Where was he now? Where was Tara? Was he hurting her friend?

As Jenn walked down the hall to the staff meeting in the math building, she was met by another teacher, a woman of about her own age.

"I'm Noreen Kane," the woman said, extending a hand. "Sophomore trig. I'll bet you're Jenn Galbraith."

"Yes," Jenn said. "Nice to meet you."

Noreen's heels tapped along the floor as they walked together. They made her about three inches taller than Jenn, and her fluffy brown hair added even more height. The double row of gold buttons that ran down either side of her blue dress caught the lights overhead and seemed to call attention to her curvaceous figure. Jenn was thinking Noreen was absolutely gorgeous when the woman said:

"I hear you're living in the dorm."

"It's only temporary," Jenn replied. "Until we can find a new place. We were supposed to live—"

"In the Trentons' house," Noreen finished. "I know. We're all sick about what happened."

Jenn, worried that thoughts of the Trentons would

darken her mood for this important gathering, changed the subject quickly.

"You wouldn't happen to know of a place, would you?"

Noreen gave her a crooked smile. Jenn noticed that one of her front teeth slightly overlapped the other and realized this perfect-looking woman wasn't so perfect after all. She had to admit it was a catty thing to consider, but she also realized it made her like Noreen even more.

"I'll keep my eyes and ears open for you," Noreen said.

They entered the meeting room. The long table at the center had been covered with a yellow paper tablecloth strewn with colorful leaves. There was a cornucopia at the center, brimming with candies. Noreen took her around and introduced her to everyone. She took in the names as best she could—William Perry, Marta D'Achille, Rosie something-or-other. It was easy to remember Steve Kirby, with his snow-white hair and matching teeth. She'd never seen anyone who grinned so much. And of course she had to make it a point to fix Herb Cole's name in her mind. The head of the department pumped her hand warmly in his own big one.

"Welcome, Ms. Galbraith," he said. "I'm sorry you had to start under these terrible circumstances."

Jenn didn't know what to say, but managed a weary smile.

"Simone had so many good things to say about you," Marta put in. "You come highly recommended."

"Simone was a wonderful person," Jenn said. "I wish I could have gotten to know her, and Joel, better."

"We all loved them," Rosie agreed.

Steve appeared with two glasses of champagne. He handed one to Jenn. Then, as if eager to drop the subject of the Trentons, he said cheerily:

"Let's make a toast. To a new friend and a new year!"

"Hear! Hear!" the others agreed.

Glasses were raised and champagne was sipped. William offered a tray of hors d'oeuvres, Marta asked about Emily, Steve wondered if Jenn was nervous. Jenn fielded the questions as best she could, feeling comfortable around these friendly people. She was beginning to realize how much she was going to enjoy working here.

She was telling Mr. Cole (out of respect, he was the only one she referred to in this formal way) about her plans for the year when they heard the sound of a child crying.

"Who's that?" Steve asked around a bite of stuffed mushroom.

Noreen went to open the door and look down the hall.

"Jenn, it's Emily!" she said. "Michelle is carrying her in."

Jenn hurried out of the room and down the hall. Emily was struggling in Michelle's arms, but as soon as Jenn took her she settled down. She buried her face in the crook of Jenn's neck.

"I don't understand what happened," Michelle said. "She was swinging very nicely, then all of a sudden she stopped and started screaming. She says someone named Tara saw her father. Is that Tara an imaginary playmate? I had one when I was a kid, and . . ."

The others had come into the hall.

"I thought I heard the father was dead," Jenn heard Rosie whisper to someone.

Jenn ignored the others.

"Michelle, thanks for bringing her to me," she said. "I'll take care of her now."

She handed her a folded bill. Understanding she was no longer needed, Michelle left. Jenn knelt down and held Emily at arm's length, her hands firmly on the child's upper arms.

"What's this all about, dollbaby?"

Emily cried for a few minutes, unable to answer.

"Oh, the poor little thing is terrified," Marta said.

"What happened, honey?" Steve asked gently.

Emily looked up at him and started crying harder. Her body heaved so much that it jerked Jenn's own arms up and down.

"Emily, tell Mommy what's wrong!" Jenn urged.

"Daddy was . . . was . . . coming af-af-after me!"

"Emily, you know you couldn't have seen Daddy," Jenn said in a calm voice. "Daddy's dead. Maybe you fell asleep on the swing and had a bad dream. Do you remember how we talked about dreams? How they never come true?"

"Tara saw Daddy, too!" Emily cried. "She saw Daddy and he scared her! He had a big pizza cutter and he was going to cut me up!"

Jenn heard someone repeat the words *pizza cutter*? in a questioning whisper.

"No, dollbaby. Daddy's not here. He died in the car accident and he'll never hurt you again."

"Tara saw him! She saw him!"

Jenn gazed at her daughter for a moment, thinking. She finally decided she should take Emily back to their room, where she could deal with this in private.

"I'm sorry," she said to the others as she picked the child up again.

"Don't be," Herb said. "You just go home and take care of her."

"She's just a baby," Jenn said, still feeling the need to apologize for this interruption.

"Most of us here have children," William said, as if to show her it was all right.

Jenn smiled a thanks and walked away.

"Hope she feels better!" Noreen called.

Back in the dorm room, Jenn did her best to divert Emily's attention.

"Emily, why don't you tell me about Tara?"

"Tara saw Daddy."

"I know," Jenn said. "But what does Tara look like? What kind of kid is she?"

"She's n-nice," Emily stammered. "She's pretty, and she's a little bigger than me. Like a big sister."

Poor kid is probably starving for a sibling.

Jenn pushed aside those old only-child worries.

"Does she make you happy?"

Emily nodded. She seemed to be calming down at last. "You know what, Mommy? She says her mama has a great big house. She says maybe we can come live with them."

"I'd like to meet Tara and her mama someday," Jenn said, humoring the child.

Emily yawned. Her tantrum had worn her out, and now her eyelids began to flutter. Jenn stood up and lifted her into her arms.

"I think you need a little nap," she said. "You've had such a busy morning."

"Don't need a nap," Emily mumbled, her head resting on her mother's shoulder.

But the moment she was in the bed and under the covers, she was asleep.

"Great," Jenn mumbled. "Bad enough to be traumatized by Evan in life, but now your father's even scaring you in death. And then you make up a story about a good mother and a sister and a big house."

She looked around at the tiny, cramped dorm room.

"No wonder," she mumbled.

But Jenn was confused. She bit the corner of a nail as

she thought about this. She understood the part about the sister and the house well enough. But where did Evan fit in? What had made Emily imagine him? And what was the pizza cutter all about?

Someday, she vowed, she would find out what the hell Evan had done with that thing.

five

Searches for both a new home and a used car kept Jenn very busy over the next few days, but not so busy that she didn't pay close attention to Emily. She was pleased that the little girl didn't dwell on the incident in the park. By the time the first day of classes arrived, Emily was so excited about her new nursery school that it was the only subject that interested her.

"Do you think they have puzzles there?" Emily asked.

"I'm sure they do," Jenn said.

They were walking along a twisting path that cut through the campus, leading toward the small white building that housed Emily's school. Students, excited about the first day of class, scurried past them like busy squirrels, holding books instead of nuts. Jenn looked down at her tiny daughter and tried to imagine her as a coed someday, dressed in jeans and a school sweatshirt instead of the corduroy pants and sweatshirt, decorated with a group picture of her favorite TV characters, the Future Fighters, that she'd selected for the first day of school.

"Do you think they have mazes, too? I like mazes the best."

"I got a peek at the center when I came up here for my interview," Jenn said. "It looks very bright and fun."

The Pinebridge Center for Gifted Children was more than just bright. The cubbies were each painted in a cheerful primary color, and toys and games were stored in lively purple crates. But that was where the center's similarity to an ordinary preschool ended. There were few posters of cartoon characters on the walls. Instead, the children were treated to reproductions of different famous paintings, all chosen for their interest and appeal. In the ABC frieze that ran along the wall, "A" was for "Asteroid." Jenn knew that Emily's day would be a mix of familiar activities, like clay and dress-up, and special programs geared to children like her daughter. The moment she entered the room, Emily made a mad dash for the stack of puzzles set out on one table. She ignored the smaller ones for a challenging three-hundred piece depiction of a field of huge daisies.

"Emily, maybe you'd better wait," Jenn said.

"Oh, it's okay," said a woman. "I'm glad she's excited. Some kids don't become motivated for several days."

"Motivation isn't one of Emily's problems," Jenn said. She smiled and introduced herself.

"I'm Dee Crowley," said the teacher, holding out a hand.

There wasn't a gray hair in Dee's brown locks, which were tied back in a big, yellow bow. Her face was smooth, her brown eyes clear. Unconsciously touching the spot where she'd thought she'd seen a wrinkle that morning, Jenn guessed that Dee was much younger than Jenn's own age of thirty-seven.

"This is Emily," she said. "Emily Galbraith."

Dee nodded. "Yes. Dean Stone told me about you. She looks great, the poor little kid, considering what happened to her. How is she now?"

"Physically, she's fine," Jenn said. "We're due to go back to the neurologist in a few weeks for a follow-up. But ..."

She paused. Should she tell this younger woman about Emily's fears? It might cause her to prejudge Emily, to push her into a niche and force her to stay there. Labels could be so damaging, Jenn knew from experience. She'd always been the "shy one," so no one in school ever gave her a chance to speak out. She didn't want the same thing to happen to Emily.

"Ms. Galbraith?" Dee prompted.

Jenn looked across the room at Emily, who had already finished separating the outside pieces from the others. She didn't want Emily labeled. But Mrs. Crowley should be aware there was a problem, just in case the little girl started talking about her father again ...

Sighing, Jenn filled her in. Dee's eyes rounded in surprise and pity.

"It must have been a nightmare for both of you," Dee said.

"Sometimes Emily imagines her father is coming after her," Jenn found herself revealing. "If that happens, if she gets too upset to handle, you can send for me."

Dee looked over at Emily and smiled. Emily looked up, grinned back, then returned her attentions to her jigsaw puzzle.

"Don't worry," the teacher said. "I'll keep close watch on her. And we'll keep her so busy she won't have time to think about bad things!"

Jenn thanked her and left. Armed with a briefcase in one hand and a large book in the other, she headed to her first class. She was filled with a mix of emotions—excitement, a sense of apprehension. She hadn't actually taught in years, not since before Emily was born. Could she do it? Would the kids like her, and more important, would they actually learn something? What if she goofed up?

Stop it, she told herself firmly. *That's Evan talking to you. And you don't listen to him now, right?*

"Well, you certainly look intense," a voice said. "Are you nervous about your first day?"

Jenn looked up to see Noreen Kane. Jenn realized she must have had a thoughtful look on her face. What had Noreen said? She looked intense. Well, thinking about Evan could make anyone intense.

But she couldn't tell her problems to this virtual stranger. As friendly as the teachers had been at the staff meeting, she wasn't ready to spill her heart out to any of them.

"A little," she said, smiling through the lie. In truth, she was very excited.

"You don't have to be," Noreen said. "These are a great group of kids. I had a lot of them myself two years ago."

They started up the steps together and entered the brick building. They passed Marta D'Achille, who gave them a friendly, but quick, greeting before disappearing into a classroom. Then they ran into Steve Kirby. He flashed his snow-white grin at them and wished Jenn luck on her first day. When he left, Noreen sighed.

"I'll bet he was gorgeous in his day," she said. "Sometimes I wonder why all the nice ones are too old, or already married."

Jenn laughed. She stopped, having reached the door to her classroom.

"Good luck," Noreen said. "And if you need anything, I'm two doors down."

Jenn thanked her and entered her room, thinking Noreen had never even answered the question about living space.

It was early, but there were already a few kids in her class. She gave them a friendly greeting without introducing herself, then started to set up her desk. When she had it the way she wanted it, she turned to write TRIGONOMETRY on the blackboard. By the time she finished, the class had filled up.

"Hi," Jenn said, turning to the sea of eager young faces. "I'm Ms. Galbraith, and this is Trig 103."

A few kids who had apparently confused her class with another got up and left. Jenn told the remaining kids to open their books.

It was a good, enthusiastic group, as was the second class. During the long break that followed, Jenn decided to check in on Emily. It might be fun to take her out to a burger place for a first-day-of-school treat.

As she was straightening up her desk, she heard a male voice ask:

"How'd it go?"

She straightened up to look at a man who stood just a little taller than she. He was a bit overweight, but not unpleasant looking with light brown hair and hazel eyes. He held out a hand. When Jenn shook it, she noticed the blue stains of some kind of chemical.

"I'm Nick Hasken," he said. "I heard about your accident on the police-band radio."

"You told Dean Stone," Jenn said. "Thanks for that. She was able to contact my sister."

"Is everything okay? You look okay."

"I'm fine," Jenn said. "I had a dislocated shoulder, but it's fine now."

"And your little girl?"

"She's fine," was Jenn's simple reply. "I'm going to pick her up for lunch, in fact."

Nick looked disappointed, but if there was something on his mind he didn't say so.

"Well, see you around," he said, and walked away.

She felt a tap on her shoulder.

"He's a sweet guy," Noreen said. "A little eccentric, but that's the way with scientists, isn't it? I thought about dating him myself, but he's not my type."

"He seems nice," Jenn agreed, although she wouldn't admit she'd already forgotten his name.

"I think he'd like to ask you out," Noreen said. "He's seen you around campus, but he's too nice a guy to jump at you your first day of teaching."

"Oh?" Jenn feigned interest. The last thing she cared about now was a date, but to say so would mean going into a speech about how turned off she was to men after what Evan had done. Instead, she looked at her watch.

"I've got to pick up my daughter," she said. "I don't want to be late on the first day. Talk to you later, Noreen!"

With that, she left her colleague. Emily was reluctant to leave the center until Jenn promised to buy her a meal that came with a toy. Throughout lunch, Emily kept Jenn amused with stories of what she'd done that morning. It seemed that Evan was the farthest thing from her mind.

Jenn returned Emily to the center after lunch and headed to her afternoon class. When Michelle Wallace arrived, she stopped at Jenn's desk to inquire after Emily. Jenn reassured her that Emily was just fine. But when class was over, Jenn took Michelle aside to elaborate.

"I didn't get a chance to ask about you," she said. "Did Emily give you a scare?"

"Oh, I wasn't upset at all," Michelle insisted. "I was just worried about Emily. I'm sorry, Ms. Galbraith, but I gotta run to my next class!"

She turned to hurry away, Jenn called after her.

"Michelle!"

"Yeah?" The teenager lingered in the doorway.

"Can you baby-sit again this weekend?"

"So long as you don't give me too much homework!"

Jenn laughed, and Michelle waved good-bye.

It was a good first day, an excellent promise for a good year.

Jenn spent the rare free time she had during the rest of the week visiting real estate agents. She was exhausted and discouraged, finding the apartments she was shown either too small or too expensive or both. Some were so worn-down she wouldn't dream of bringing Emily to live in them. One good thing did come of the search. One of the agents was selling a four-year-old Saturn at a price Jenn could afford. The insurance she'd collected on her wrecked car was just enough to buy the new one. Now if only she could be as lucky in finding a home!

Noreen saw her drive up in the new/used car, and was full of questions about it. She showed great interest in Jenn's search for a home, and even tried asking around herself. The two women found they had breaks three days a week, and they shared bag lunches on the grounds. Sometimes they were joined by Steve Kirby or Marta D'Achille, but for the most part it was the two of them. Noreen was the kind of person who wore her heart on her sleeve, and by the end of the first week Jenn thought she knew the woman's entire life story. She herself was reticent, only giving the minimal amount of information. She just didn't want to talk about her bad marriage, her divorce, the ex-husband who'd tried to murder her and her daughter. Noreen didn't seem to notice this and genuinely enjoyed Jenn's company. Jenn could see she had a new friend.

The week passed quickly, school taking up much of Jenn and Emily's time. In the afternoons, Emily amused herself with toys or watched her favorite show, "The Future Fighters," as Jenn corrected papers.

Saturday afternoon, Jenn's papers and books were vying for space on a small table with Emily's tea set and the pink teddy bear. Seeing the toy made Jenn think about the Trentons' house. Emily would have enjoyed it there. Jenn thought she'd seen some children in the area who could have been playmates for the little girl. It didn't really bother her that Emily had no friends here—as a child who was head and shoulders above most kids her age in intelligence, she was a bit of a loner—but it would have been nice to give Emily the chance to make friends beyond preschool class.

Someone was knocking at the door, and Emily was bounding from couch to chair as she ran to answer it. Michelle came in, dressed in jeans and a Fair Isle sweater. A turtleneck made her round cheeks look even chubbier. Emily took her by the hand.

"Do you want me to take her to the park again?" Michelle asked. "I mean, do you think it's okay? I could take her to the burger stand, y'know. They've got that indoor play area with all those plastic balls you can jump in. If you think it might be better ..."

But Emily didn't seem the least bit worried. "The park! The park! Maybe I can see Tara again."

"The park is fine," Jenn said, pleased by Emily's enthusiasm.

Without further discussion, Michelle and Emily left.

It was a short walk to the park, and on this clear, crisp fall day, it was crowded with families. Emily made a beeline for the swings, while Michelle sat with a novel she was reading for her French literature class.

She looked up every page or so to check on her charge, but Emily seemed fine. Then, at the end of a chapter, Michelle noticed that the little girl was talking to her-

self—or, more likely, to her pretend playmate—and that
the swing beside her was moving by itself. Recalling her
own imaginary friend, Michelle smiled. Though she'd
never gone so far as to move objects, she was certain
Emily had set the swing in motion, pretending "Tara" was
sitting next to her.

She couldn't resist the urge to ask Emily about Tara.
The little girl was so much like herself as a kid! Michelle
put her book aside, dog-earring the page to mark it. As she
stood up to approach Emily, a strong, icy wind blew in her
face and brought tears to her eyes. It seemed to be pushing
her back.

A nor'easter, she thought. *We must be in for an early
snow.*

Michelle didn't notice that the wind ruffled her hair
alone, or that the pages of her book, lying open on the
bench, remained perfectly still.

A man appeared before her so abruptly that she cried
out. He'd seemed to materialize out of thin air. If he'd
jumped from either side, she hadn't seen him just seconds
ago. Annoyed that she'd been startled, Michelle tried to
move around him. He moved with her. A sickening, acrid
odor wafted from his clothes.

"Get away from me!" Michelle said, firmly, trying to
push ahead.

He blocked her path.

"I said, get away!"

His arm shot out so fast that she didn't see it coming.
A large, sinewy hand closed around her upper arm,
squeezing as tightly and painfully as a bear trap.

"What are you doing here?" he demanded. "I thought
this was the right door. You aren't supposed to be here—
Emily is!"

Michelle jerked her head away. His breath was even
more offensive than his body odor.

"Keep away from Emily," she choked. God, who was this pervert? And why wasn't anyone helping her?

The man's grip twisted, tightening her sweater around her neck.

"You talk to Jennifer," he growled. "You tell her I'm gonna find the right door, then I'm gonna make her pay for taking E.J. from me."

"NO!"

Michelle forced out the word, pushing the fear away. She had to take control! She cried out in anger, expecting any one of a dozen people nearby to come to her aid. But no one moved.

"What's wrong with you?" she demanded. "Help me!"

She looked toward Emily, who swung high and low, oblivious. How could she not see Michelle and the stranger—they were only a few feet away!

The man pulled Michelle even closer to him.

"You tell her I got the pizza cutter ready."

A running dog, a ball gripped in its teeth, skidded to a halt right near Michelle and the man. Its hackles went up, and a feral growl rumbled in the back of its throat. The man stomped one foot, and the dog went away with its tail tucked between its legs. The two boys who had been playing with it wondered aloud at its strange behavior.

Michelle realized that no one—no person, anyway—could see what was happening.

But how was this possible?

She turned to the man, ready to demand some answers in spite of her fears. But as she opened her mouth to speak, his face changed horribly. His features twisted and melted until they formed a totally new visage: that of a little girl. She was beautiful, but her smile was full of evil.

"It gets worse," she whispered. *"And I'm the only one who can stop him."*

Michelle fell to the ground, as if the earth had opened up to suck her into a deep chasm.

And then she was lying down on the bench, her book still clutched in her hand. A classmate, Roy Javier, was patting her hand.

"Michelle! Michelle, are you okay?"

Michelle blinked at him, then began to frantically look around for the man who had attacked her. He was gone. A few people were milling about, looking concerned. Michelle wanted to scream at them, to demand to know why they hadn't helped her before.

"Michelle, are you having an attack?" Roy asked. "Do you need some gum? Maybe one of the moms here has apple juice or orange juice."

"I'm . . . I'm okay," Michelle said wearily, sitting up.

"It isn't okay when a diabetic passes out," Roy insisted.

"Are you a med student or a French major?" Michelle asked.

She'd meant it to be friendly teasing, but it came out abruptly. Her smile felt more like a smirk.

"C'mon," Roy said. "I'll walk you back to the dorm. Unless you want to go to the infirmary . . ."

"No," Michelle said. "I've got Ms. Galbraith's little girl with me."

Emily had noticed the crowd around her babysitter. She approached slowly, worry on her face. When she saw Michelle smile, the child ran to her and gave her a hug.

"Tara said Daddy was going to hurt you," she said. "I'm so glad he didn't!"

Michelle felt a chill rush through her. Emily's daddy—could he be the stranger? He'd left a message with her but she couldn't recall it.

"Let's go home," she said.

Roy walked her all the way to Jenn's door, where he explained about Michelle's collapse.

Michelle sat on the small couch, staring down at her lap. Her hair, brushed so beautifully just a short while earlier, hung in tangles over the bulky shoulders of her sweater. She was so pale that Jenn reached out in a motherly way to feel her forehead. It was ice cold.

"Mommy, Tara said that Daddy was going to hurt Michelle. But he didn't, did he?"

Before Jenn could respond to her daughter, Michelle looked up at her. Her eyes were glassy, and her voice seemed to belong to someone else:

"He's coming for you. As soon as he finds the door that leads to E.J., he's going to make you pay."

Jenn's reply was a soft breath: "What?"

"He's got the pizza cutter ready."

"It's Daddy! It's Daddy!" Emily screamed, running to hug her mother's legs.

Jenn lifted her up.

"What do you mean?" she asked Michelle. "Why would you say such a terrible thing?"

Michelle was staring at her lap again, and said nothing more.

"Who told you my husband used to call Emily 'E.J.'?"

Still no response.

"I don't get it," Roy said.

"It's . . . it's a long story," Jenn said. She could see that Michelle was sick. "Roy, take her to the nurse, whether she likes it or not."

Roy nodded and led the unresisting Michelle from the room. Once the teenagers were gone, Jenn sat down with Emily and hugged her tightly.

"Mommy, I'm so scared," Emily said. "Tara saw Daddy trying to hurt Michelle. What if he finds me?"

"Emily, your father is dead," Jenn said firmly. "He can't hurt you. Michelle was talking that way because she's sick. You remember how strangely Great-Aunt Millie used to act sometimes? That was when her body needed sugar."

"Dye-a-beet-ees," Emily pronounced carefully. "Does Michelle have that?"

"Yes," Jenn said. "She didn't mean what she said."

"But Tara told me . . ."

"Forget about Tara," Jenn insisted. "She doesn't know everything. Your daddy can never hurt you again. I won't let anyone, anyone at all, hurt you."

Emily snuggled close to her.

"I love you, Mommy," she said.

"I love you, too, dollbaby."

Jenn held her daughter close, her mind full of questions. How had Michelle known about the nickname "E.J."? Or about the pizza cutter? As soon as she could, Jenn planned to get some answers. Someone had filled the young woman's head with this information. All she had to do was find out who, and ask why they'd do such a cruel thing to a four-year-old baby.

That evening, she was sharing a delivery of Chinese food with Emily when she heard an ambulance pull up in front of the dorm. Curious, she went to the window to look out. Emily climbed on a chair for her own view, and when she saw the figure on the stretcher she cried out:

"Mommy! That's Michelle!"

It was. Jenn took Emily by the hand, and they hurried downstairs and outside. The dorm advisor, a fifty-year-old woman named Jessica Bradford, stood with a group of frantic students.

"What happened?" Jenn asked.

Jessica looked at her. She was dressed in a quilted robe and was holding it shut.

"She had a diabetic reaction," she said. "The poor thing just collapsed! I don't understand it, she was always so careful with her insulin!"

Jenn couldn't help wondering if the day's strange incident had anything to do with this. Emily tugged at her. She picked up the child and hugged her as the ambulance drove away.

"Is Michelle gonna be all right?" Emily asked worriedly.

"I hope so," Jenn said.

She continued hugging the child tightly, overcome by an inexplicable need to keep very, very careful watch on her tonight.

SIX

The protective instinct in Jenn made her reluctant to leave Emily at the center the next day. If someone was cruel enough to feed Michelle private information that would scare Emily, that person might try to hurt Emily herself. She'd spent the night trying to figure out who it could be, but no one came to mind. She hardly knew anyone in the area well enough to be a friend, let alone an enemy.

Emily's enthusiasm when they arrived at the preschool pushed away all Jenn's doubts. The girl ran toward a group of children playing at a water table, and in no time she, too, was splashing and giggling. This place was a safe haven, Jenn thought. In spite of her youth, Dee Crowley kept careful watch over all her charges. No one could get at Emily here.

Jenn went off to class and immersed herself in the world

of numbers. Thoughts of Emily would sneak in, but she forced herself to trust Dee's caregiving skills. In spite of her best efforts, however, she was on her way to the center the moment her last class ended for the day.

Emily gave her a big hug and asked if they could go to the park.

"Really?" Jenn asked, surprised Emily would want to go there after two separate incidents had frightened her.

"I like the park," Emily said. "That's where I can play with Tara."

When they arrived, Emily climbed onto the swings. Jenn gave her a few hard pushes, and soon Emily was pumping her legs. Jenn went back to a bench to sit down, planning to mark a few test papers. She wondered if Michelle had been sitting on this bench when someone told her about Evan. Jenn looked around, half expecting to see someone watching her. There was no one there at all but mothers and children.

When she looked back at Emily, she saw her daughter talking to thin air. She smiled slightly to think of her carrying on a one-sided conversation with an imaginary playmate. But the smile faded quickly. What would an intelligent child like Emily need with a make-believe friend? She seemed to get along well enough with the kids at school.

"And how many of them live on campus?" she whispered to herself. "Jenn, you've got to find a new place to live!"

Somehow, she had a feeling Tara filled more than a need for friendship. She had first shown up at the hospital, hadn't she? Did she have something to do with the trauma Emily had experienced at the hands of her father?

At that moment, Emily gave a happy cry and jumped from the swings. She didn't seem to be dwelling on the terrible things that had happened to her. Typical kid, Jenn thought, wishing she herself could push fear aside so easily.

She saw Emily climbing up the ladder of the slide.

"Be careful, Emily!" she called. The slide seemed far too big for a child Emily's size.

"Don't worry, Mommy! Tara's gonna help me!"

Jenn was about to get up, but held herself back. Her worries might scare Emily. She had to stop being the overprotective mother.

Emily paused at the top of the ladder. She tilted her head to one side, as if listening to someone. She turned to look behind her . . .

. . . and slipped.

"Emily!"

Time seemed to switch into slow-motion. Jenn saw that the tie on Emily's hood had caught the top corner of the ladder. She ran toward her, calling out. Others who saw the little girl hanging from her jacket, turning blue, also came to the rescue. One woman was up the ladder in a flash, and in seconds—to Jenn it seemed like hours—she had Emily free. One of the fathers took hold of her and carried her to Jenn.

"Oh, Emily," Jenn said, her voice shrill and her body shaking, "Dollbaby, what happened? Are you okay?"

"Tara got mad," Emily said with a pout. "She pushed me."

Jenn hugged her even tighter. She wasn't about to try to understand the psychological implications of an imaginary playmate who would hurt someone.

"I hope she's okay," said the woman who had rescued her. Her bright green eyes seemed to sparkle as she held up a small pair of scissors.

"I was doing needlework when I heard her yell," she said. "I just cut the string."

"Thank God you were here," Jenn said, standing. "Thank you so much."

"I'm just glad I had my embroidery scissors," the woman said. She held out a hand, and Jenn took it. "I'm Laura Bayless."

"I'm Jenn Galbraith," came the reply.

Not to be ignored, Emily tugged the pants of her mother's suit. "I'm Emily Janine Galbraith. And I'm hungry, too."

Both women laughed.

"So am I," Jenn said. "Can I treat you to lunch, Laura? It's the least I can do."

"Sounds good," Laura said.

Over chicken sandwiches and salads at a nearby diner, Laura explained that she'd been out admiring the fall foliage.

"I live about forty miles from here," she said. "I come to Pinebridge once in a while to shop. The park is a nice place to relax after a long drive."

"It's a pretty place," Jenn agreed. "I like Pinebridge a lot. We're originally from Buffalo."

"Buffalo, New York?" Laura said. "I took my son to Niagara Falls just a year ago."

"I went there," Emily put in. She emptied the bowl of sugar packets, then started to replace them neatly. "I got all wet."

She poured extra ketchup on her plate, took a loud bite of her pickle, and snatched the decorated toothpick from her mother's plate. Laura smiled at her.

"Active, isn't she?"

"She's a great kid," Jenn said. "I just wish she had more room to play. Unfortunately, we're stuck living in the dorm for a while."

"The dorm!" Laura echoed in surprise. "Why would a teacher live in the dorm?"

Jenn explained what had happened, her voice growing soft as she spoke of the Trentons. Laura expressed sympathy.

"I understand how you can feel close to someone after just meeting them," she said. "Some people are like that."

"Simone Trenton certainly was," Jenn said.

Laura took a long sip of her diet cola. "Are they doing an investigation?"

"I haven't heard much," Jenn said. "But I haven't heard it was an accident, either."

The thought that the Trentons might have been murdered sent chills through her. And that thought led to new thoughts of the stranger who had accosted Michelle.

Emily piped up, "Can we go to Laura's house?"

Thoughts of the stranger flew from Jenn's mind.

"No, not today," Jenn said. "We've got things to do at home."

"Wait," Laura said. "Why not? Why not come to my house, to live? I live on a huge farm, and there's a small cottage there that was once a groundskeeper's quarters. I've been thinking about renting it out."

Jenn thought a moment. Visions of the crowded, impersonal dorm came to mind.

"Guess it wouldn't hurt to take a look," she said. "How about tomorrow?"

"Fine," Laura said.

They went on talking in that friendly way. And although no deep information was exchanged, Jenn had a very good feeling about Laura. By the time lunch was over, she'd made a new friend.

As soon as classes ended the following day, Jenn and Emily piled into the car. Following Laura's directions, they drove about thirty miles, then started a series of turns that took them deep into the woods. Jenn thought that Laura's home couldn't have been more isolated, and was reminded of an old New England saying: "You can't get there from here." There was certainly no way she could have found Laura's farm without instructions.

When she came out of the trees, Laura's huge white house loomed in the middle of a large stretch of land. She parked near a run-down barn, turned off the ignition, and helped Emily out of her seatbelt.

"It's smelly here," Emily said when they got out of the car, her nose wrinkling.

"Don't say that out loud," Jenn warned, "it's rude. But I think that smell is hay—it must be rotting in the fields."

"Gross."

Jenn suddenly felt depressed. She began to understand why as she took a better look at her surroundings. The whole place was worn out, not just the barn. Grass had grown nearly two-feet deep around a tractor, the barn door hung askew from a broken hinge. Leaves and bits of hay littered the yard, even though Jenn could see a rake leaning up against a fence that was badly in need of whitewashing. An aging mutt was lying on the porch. It lifted its head and gave a halfhearted bark before falling asleep again.

The condition of the property surprised Jenn as much as her sudden feeling of melancholy. She had only met Laura yesterday, but the woman had been so nicely dressed and so friendly it didn't seem possible she could live in a place like this. It made Jenn think that appearances were deceiving—Laura might have as many problems as she had.

Emily took her hand. "Something bad happened here, Mommy."

"Oh, it's just a little neglected, Emily," Jenn said, although she was surprised at her daughter's astute feelings.

"Well, hello! You found us!"

Laura had opened the front door and was coming down the porch steps. Unlike her property, her appearance was neat and stylish. Her short, gamine haircut looked even prettier as the breeze tousled it gently. She came up to them where they stood near the barn and held out a hand. Jenn squeezed it.

"Your directions were great," Jenn said, pushing aside her worrisome thoughts. "And the drive was much faster than I expected."

"As long as the weather holds up," Laura said, "you can make great time between here and Pinebridge College. And if it snows, you probably wouldn't be teaching, anyway."

Emily had wandered off and was trying to climb over the fence.

"Emily!" Jenn called.

"Oh, honey, don't do that!" Laura said. She looked at Jenn. "That fence is so old. Ever since my husband . . . Well, I haven't felt much like keeping up with the place. My husband passed away last year."

"I'm so sorry," Jenn offered, moving toward Emily. "He must have been young."

"Forty-three," Laura said. "It was a heart attack, very sudden. I know the place is a shambles, but it was always Walt who kept it up so nicely."

Jenn had reached Emily, who was now trying to scramble onto the seat of the tractor. She grabbed her daughter.

"I wanna see if there's any animals!" Emily cried out.

Suddenly the crooked barn door squeaked open, and a teenaged boy emerged. He scowled at the newcomers. Jenn put Emily down and looked at him with inquiry in her eyes.

"Mommy, where are the animals?" Emily pressed.

"There aren't any animals," he said darkly. "They're all dead."

Jenn felt Emily move behind her, her grip tightening around her legs.

Laura hurried up to them.

"For heaven's sake, Peter," she said, "do you have to be so melodramatic?"

She looked down at Emily with a smile.

"He means we sold them all," she said. "They were just too much work without a man around the house. And I think it will be a while before Peter has the skill with animals my husband had."

Peter stared down at the puddles his baggy jeans made around his sneakers.

"Peter's thirteen," Laura said, as if that explained his whole surly personality.

"Hi, Peter," Emily said.

Peter gave her a quick, sorrowful look and stalked away.

"Well!" Laura said brightly, as if nothing had happened. "Ready to see the cottage?"

All Jenn's uneasiness flew away the moment she entered the little cottage at the other side of the property. It was as neat and clean as the grounds were untidy, a perfect little doll's house from the braided rug on the floor to the asters set in the middle of the round table.

"This is your bedroom, over here," Laura said, leading the way.

There was a chenille spread on the bed, white as if it had just been washed. The place had the fresh pine scent of a recent scrub-down. The furniture gleamed with polish, and there were fresh asters in here, too, atop the dresser.

"You can see the house from your window," Laura said. "It's . . . Oh, listen to me. I'm acting as if you've already decided to move in."

Jenn smiled at her. "It's adorable."

They heard a series of cabinet doors open and close. Emily was busy investigating the kitchen.

"There's food in here, Mommy," she said.

"Just a few things," Laura said. She gave a little shrug. "I thought you might need them. I mean, if you move in."

Before Jenn could say a word, Emily ran into the bedroom and pulled on Laura's arm.

"Where's my room? Do I get a room?"

"You betcha!" Laura escorted them to the second bedroom.

Emily squealed in delight and took a dive on top of the bed that jutted away from the room's single window. It was decorated with a Sunbonnet Sue quilt of pastel colors. The curtains were sheer yellow and the rug was a soft rose. There was an empty bookshelf on one wall, and a four-drawer dresser.

"My grandmother made that quilt," Laura said.

"It's lovely," Jenn said. There were Besse Pease Guttman prints of pretty, almost ethereal children on the walls. Had Laura put these up since yesterday? "You certainly went to a lot of trouble."

"Not for nothing," Laura said hopefully.

Jenn didn't reply. She walked back into the living area and gazed at the green and maroon plaid couch for a few minutes. The house was darling, just perfect. But there was that feeling she'd had a while ago, and Emily's strange statement that something bad had happened here . . .

"Mommy, do we hafta go back to the dorm tonight?"

Jenn took a deep breath. She was being silly, of course. This was a wonderful opportunity to bring Emily up in a nice, quiet place. The dorm wasn't the right environment for a child! There was a perfectly logical explanation for her feelings, too. Any worn-out old place makes a person feel bad. And this place was worn out simply because of the tragedy that had occurred here a year ago. Poor Laura! Jenn had often wished Evan dead, but Laura had seemed to love her husband.

"All right," she blurted out, not giving it another moment's thought. "All right, how much are you asking?"

When Laura told her, Jenn had to have her repeat the figure.

"But that hardly seems enough!" she said. "If you heard the prices they were asking in Pinebridge . . ."

"This isn't Pinebridge," Laura reminded her. "I don't have college kids competing to move in. I'm tired of the place sitting empty. Even a little will help!"

"Well, it's an incredible offer . . ." Jenn thought a moment, then sighed with resignation. "We'll move in tomorrow."

"Wonderful!"

Emily looked disappointed. "I gotta sleep in the dumb old noisy dorm again, huh?"

"Just another night," Jenn said, giving her a hug. "By the time we get back there, it'll be too late to return."

"Could she stay with me?" Laura asked. "I wouldn't mind."

Emily jumped up and down. "Please! Please!"

"I'm sorry," Jenn said. "I don't think it's a good idea." She looked at Laura. "She's only four, you know."

"I'm four and a half," Emily reminded her with indignation. "I'll be five in January, Mommy."

"I know, dollbaby," Jenn said. "But the answer is still no."

Before Emily could argue further, Jenn started to the door.

"I only have one class tomorrow," she said, "and then I want to visit a student who was taken to the hospital."

"Nothing serious, I hope."

"Diabetic coma," Jenn said. "I'm really worried about

her. Anyway, I'll be back in the early afternoon, if that's okay."

Laura smiled. "It's fine, just fine."

That night, neither Jenn nor Emily slept much. Emily was bubbling with excitement, talking about her pretty new room and all that space to run around outside. Jenn was worried, wondering if she'd made the right decision.

She was asking herself this for the umpteenth time that night when a group of boys wandering the grounds outside her window let out a series of loud curses. That clinched it for her—at least she was certain Emily wouldn't be exposed to that!

Jenn left Emily at the center the next day while she paid a visit to Michelle. She was staying at St. Michael's, and some of the staff recognized Jenn as she walked down the hall. A nurse walked toward her; it was Rita, one of the nurses who had cared for her after the accident.

"Well, hello," Rita said. "How are you? How's Emily? I certainly hope you aren't back here to stay with us again."

"No, no, we're both just fine," Jenn said. "Emily's in school now. I'm here to visit Michelle Wallace."

Rita's face fell. She gave her head a shake.

"That poor thing," she said. "She's so pretty, isn't she? Her mother has been at her side night and day."

"Mrs. Wallace is here?"

"Not at the moment," Rita said. "She's gone to have her lunch. But you can take a peek at Michelle."

A monitor beeped softly, reminding Jenn of the days Emily had been lying here in the same eerily quiet manner. Michelle was very pale, and it appeared she had lost some weight. She didn't even seem like the same extroverted person who had talked Jenn's ears off just a few days ago.

"Hi, Michelle," she said. "It's Ms. Galbraith. I just

came to say hi." She thought a moment, searching for words, then continued, "We're all thinking about you. Sorry, but you missed a killer trig exam today."

The joke fell flat without the sound of Michelle's laughter. Jenn could see there was nothing more for her to do. Promising to visit again, she said good-bye and left.

Back at the dorm, she was thoughtful as she packed, recalling how Michelle had helped Emily carry boxes upstairs just a few weeks ago. Emily sensed her mother's despondency and took care of her own things without much chatter. Soon they were ready to leave. Nick Hasken was riding a bike down the sidewalk as they filled the back of the car. He stopped to watch.

"Found a place?"

Jenn looked up at him. The conservative dark brown suit that Nick wore was a sharp contrast to his tie, printed with an image of Curly from the Three Stooges. The autumn wind tousled his light brown hair, and he brushed it away from his eyes.

"Yes, we did," Jenn said. "It's a little cottage on a farm about thirty miles from here."

Nick nodded. "That's great."

Jenn didn't reply. Nick didn't have to be head of the science department to understand she wasn't in the mood to talk. He simply said: "Well, best of luck!" and pedaled off.

"He's real nice, Mommy," Emily said.

"Yep," was all Jenn would say, maneuvering a box to fit in a suitcase.

To herself, she thought: *Nick seems like a nice guy. Okay, maybe he's got a little bit of a paunch, and maybe he's always got some kind of chemical staining his fingers. But can a guy who wears comic-book ties be all bad?*

She cut her reverie short, reminding herself she had better things to think about. Besides, Simone had said Nick was "strange," and that was warning enough for her. She had had a bad enough experience with Evan—who was handsome and strong at first—without getting involved with another potential loser. And to Jenn, that meant every man on earth.

Jenn stood back. "Well, that's it. I just have to drop off the room key, and we're on our way."

She left the key with Kim Stone's secretary, then drove off campus. She was still thinking about Michelle, and those thoughts stayed with her all the way to Laura's place. She hoped the excitement of moving would change her mood, but somehow it seemed to grow darker as she approached the big white house.

But Laura was too cheerful to even notice Jenn's mood. She was smiling broadly as she approached the car, saying: "Chocolate chip cookies."

She held out a small white basket lined with a red checkered cloth. "A welcome gift."

"My favorite!" Emily cried.

"Then you can take them into your new house," Laura said, handing her the basket. She gave Jenn a key.

"Welcome home," she said.

"Thanks," Jen replied, her disposition beginning to change. Laura was just too nice, she thought.

"You didn't have to bake for us," she said.

"It's no problem," Laura replied. "I bake for a local gourmet shop, and I just made an extra batch."

"That's interesting," Jenn said. "Do you get much work from them?"

"Every day," Laura said. "My pies are famous around here. People driving through stop at the Mixing Bowl. Tourists are willing to pay a premium for a home-baked goodie."

She gave a shrug. "It brings in a little extra money. Walt's life insurance helps maintain things, but I like to have pocket money, too."

Jenn was glad when they entered the house. Somehow she felt uncomfortable discussing something as private as another woman's financial situation. Inside, she put her suitcase on her bed and left boxes in the middle of the table.

"Now, listen," Laura said. "No cooking on your first night. You're both invited up to the house for clam chowder and pan-fried trout. Peter caught them this morning, before he went to school."

"It sounds delicious," Jenn said, suddenly realizing she was hungry. She had been so worried about Michelle that she'd skipped lunch.

Dinner *was* excellent, made no less so by Peter's refusal to talk in more than one-syllable words. He hunched over his bowl of chowder as if afraid someone would snatch it from him. Once in a while, Jenn saw him staring at Emily. She smiled when Emily stuck out her tongue. If she'd been afraid of Peter yesterday, she sure wasn't now!

Jenn decided once and for all that this move was the right choice. With a private home and healthy country surroundings, she was certain good things would happen from now on.

seven

While the grown-ups were talking, Emily had gone into another room to watch television. She draped herself sideways in a big armchair, one foot bopping up and down as she flicked the channels with a remote. After three times around, Peter snatched the changer from her.

"Quit channel surfing," he said.

"I can't find anything to watch," Emily complained.

Peter tossed the remote onto the couch.

"Yeah, well, we don't get cable up here in the sticks."

Emily looked around.

"Is your house made of sticks?"

"For a smart kid," Peter said with a curl to his lip, "you're a little pea-brain."

Emily jumped from the chair.

"You wanna play?"

"No way," Peter said, his voice registering disgust at the very thought of entertaining a four-year-old.

He crouched down near the television and opened a cabinet. He ran a finger along a neatly ordered row of video games, making a choice. Emily ran up behind him.

"Wow!" she cried. "You've got as many games as a store! Do you have Future Fighters game? I love the Future Fighters, especially Tammi."

"No, I don't have Future Fighters," Peter said. "And keep your little mitts off my games. I like them the way they are. See? You know what alphabetical order is?"

Emily clicked her tongue. "Sure I do. I am NOT a pea-brain."

"Just keep your little paws to yourself," Peter said, closing the door again.

He fed a game into his Sega Genesis system, then settled back to massacre aliens. Emily watched him for a while, grew bored, and went to an end table to pick up a small statue of an angel.

"Put that down," Peter said without turning.

Emily traded it for a china pig. She studied its painted floral design for a moment, then lost interest, put it down, and turned to the mantel. The brass candlesticks and photos in old frames were much too high to reach. With a sigh, she shambled toward the door.

"I'm goin' home," she said. "This place is boring. I sure wish Tara was here to play with me."

Peter stood up. "Say, listen, you wanna see something?"

"Yeah?" Emily asked warily, her eyes thinning. "Is it something gross? Gary Michaels showed me a bug yesterday. Don't you be showing me any bugs, 'cause I hate bugs."

"Just shut up and follow me," Peter said. "It's upstairs, in a bedroom."

"I bet it's bugs," Emily said, but she followed him anyway.

"You've got to swear you won't tell the grown-ups," Peter said.

"About what?"

"Swear!"

"Okay!" Emily said impatiently. "I swear."

She wasn't sure about Peter. He seemed so mean, but so sad, too. Then she remembered that his daddy had died. Maybe his daddy wasn't mean, like hers, and maybe Peter missed him a lot.

Peter opened a door, and Emily squealed in delight to see Tara sitting on the edge of a stripped-down bed. It was the only piece of furniture in the room, but Emily didn't notice.

"Tara! You came to play with me!"

"Hi, Emily," Tara said. She gave Peter a smile. "Told you I'd get her here."

"Huh?" Emily was confused. No one else had ever seen Tara.

"Forget it, Emily," Tara said. "Let's play. Peter, what should we do?"

Peter shifted from one foot to the other and looked up at the ceiling. "Oh, right," he said sarcastically. "I'm going to play with little girls."

Suddenly he doubled over with a cry of pain.

"Hey!" Emily said. "What's the matter?"

Tara walked over to Peter, ignoring Emily.

"Don't piss me off," she said grimly.

Emily approached him warily, as afraid of hurting him as she was of the angry look on his face. She reached out a hand, but Peter pushed it away.

"Peter, are you hurt bad?" the little girl asked.

He ignored her.

"All right, you little jerk," Peter growled at Tara. "I'll

play anything you want. You . . . you want me to get the old Chutes and Ladders game down?"

Tara answered with a shrug of her shoulders.

"Do you have Scrabble?" Emily asked. "I like Scrabble. I can spell."

"Fine, I'll get Scrabble," Peter said, leaving the room.

Tara came nearer to Emily and put an arm around her shoulder.

"I'm so glad you're here," she said. "Now I can visit you whenever I like."

"Do you live right here?" Emily asked.

Tara shook her head. "Nope. I live . . . close to here. But you won't have to go to the park to see me. And you know what?"

"What?" Emily asked eagerly.

"The best part is that your daddy doesn't even know you're here," Tara said. "He can't find you, and you'll be safe."

Emily grinned. She *did* feel safe here. All those scary thoughts she'd had the first day, that something bad had happened here, had somehow vanished.

"I like my new home," she said.

"Good," Tara said, "cause I hope you're gonna live here forever."

Downstairs, the conversation had somehow turned to husbands. Laura painted hers as a saint, the perfect husband and father. Jenn was almost embarrassed to say how stupid she'd been to marry a guy like Evan. But, somehow, Laura brought it out of her. Even though they'd only met, Jenn was beginning to feel close to her. She found she could talk to Laura in a way she could never talk to her real sister. Rosalie would just pass judgment on her; all Laura did was listen.

"You couldn't have known how he'd change," she said.

"Oh, there must have been hints," Jenn said. "He was a smart-ass from day one, only he never directed it at me. I always teased that he should become a radio shockjock."

She sighed, toying with the half-eaten cookie on her dessert plate.

"I never knew a human could be so full of evil," she said, "so full of hatred. I knew he hated me, but how could he try to kill Emily, too?"

"Old story," Laura said. "If he couldn't have her, neither could you."

Jenn finished her cookie and found a way to change the subject. "These are the best chocolate chip cookies I've ever eaten. There's something different about them . . ."

"Almond extract," Laura said. "It's my secret ingredient. I'll make more when you run out."

"Thanks," Jenn said. "I'm not much of a baker. I can multiply three-digit numbers in my head, but I can't bake a pie to save my life."

Laura laughed, then stood up to clear the table. She waved away Jenn's efforts to help.

"You're a guest," she said. "More coffee?"

"No, thanks," Jenn said. "In fact, I think I'd better look for Emily. It's awfully quiet down the hall."

She got up to investigate. When she got to the den, though, it was empty. A colorful but undefinable scene filled the TV screen, broken in the middle by the word PAUSE.

"Emily?" No reply. Jenn guessed that her daughter couldn't be nearby, or she would have answered at once. On her way back to the kitchen, she looked in the other rooms, but they were all dark.

"I can't find Emily," she said. "Mind if I look around for her?"

"Feel free," Laura said. "And if you see Peter, tell him I need him in here."

Jenn walked through the downstairs, calling to her daughter. Guessing she might be playing a game, she turned on lights to see if Emily was hiding. Each room was unoccupied, and as she moved through them she began to realize what a beautiful home Laura had. It was huge, probably three times bigger than any home Jenn had lived in. Jenn didn't know much about architecture, but she was certain homes hadn't been built with this kind of detail in many, many decades. The molding around the ceilings was elaborately carved, the doors seemed to be solid wood. Appropriately, all the furniture was either antique, or made to look that way.

"Must be nice to have money," Jenn said, feeling a twinge of jealousy. She had forgotten Laura had to bake cookies and pies to supplement her husband's insurance.

Nice husband, big house, and she could cook, too. It seemed to her that Laura had been pretty lucky. Sure, her husband had died of a heart attack. But at least he hadn't tried to murder her.

Jenn climbed a huge staircase that led straight up from the front foyer. The hallway wrapped around either side of it. Surely, Emily could hear her call from here. She wouldn't have to look in any more rooms, making herself even more depressed. Laura probably had antique four-posters or brass beds in all the rooms.

"With a handmade quilt by her little old granny on every bed," she growled.

She stopped at the top of the stairs.

"Emily?"

No answer.

"EMILY!"

She waited for one of the doors to open, but nothing happened. Emily *must* have heard her! Why didn't she answer? Was she trying to trick her mother, to scare her?

She started down the hall.

"Emily, answer me! It's time to go home!"

"I'm in here Mommy!" came a muffled reply.

"Well, we'll just see about you ignoring me," Jenn said in a harsh tone, striding angrily toward the sound of her daughter's voice. She had an overwhelming desire to slap the child.

She stopped just short of the door. She ran her fingers through her long blonde hair and shook her head. What the hell was she thinking about? She'd never laid a hand on Emily in her life! Surely, Emily hadn't been ignoring her! She simply hadn't heard through the door.

"What is wrong with you?" she asked herself. "First you act jealous of a widow, then you think about hurting your kid! Lighten up, Jenn!"

It was the move, of course. She was simply exhausted. She told herself that having bad thoughts didn't make bad things happen, and tried to change her mood. It would be wrong to frighten Emily for no good reason.

With a deep sigh, she reached for the doorknob. She heard Emily say something, then Peter. And then, to her surprise, a third voice—a girl's voice. Curious, she opened the door.

Two faces turned up to her. Emily put down the game piece she was holding and ran to her mother with a grin.

"Who were you guys talking to?"

"Nobody," Peter said, hurrying from the room with his chin tucked into his chest.

"Are we going home?" Emily asked.

"Yes," Jenn said, looking around the room. She was sure she had heard a third voice, but maybe it was only her tired mind. She took Emily by the hand and they left.

"You know, Peter's very sad," Emily said.

"Peter is a grouch," Jenn replied.

"I like him," Emily said. "Tara likes him, too. She came to play with us tonight."

Jenn thought of the third voice, then shook the idea away. Tara was an imaginary playmate.

"Really?"

"She helped me with some big words for Scrabble," Emily said. She giggled. "I beat Peter and he got really mad."

You could probably beat that juvenile neanderthal on your own.

"You're my smart dollbaby," Jenn said proudly.

They passed through the kitchen, where they exchanged good nights and thank-yous as they put on their coats. A cold rush of wind blew into the kitchen when Jenn opened the back door.

"Winter's coming too fast," Laura commented, looking up at the starry sky. "It gets very dark and cold here at night. I don't like it much."

She shivered dramatically. Jenn picked up Emily, said good night again, and left. As she walked, she held her daughter so that Emily's back was to the wind. That was a strange thing for Laura to say, she thought, especially in front of a small child. Fortunately, Emily wasn't saying much about the shadows cast by the full moon, or the cold. She was just hugging her mother tightly.

Although it was only a short distance to the cottage, across a field strewn with wildflowers that bent to the wind, the darkness made it seem like miles. Jenn's legs began to ache, and she realized there was a slight incline up toward her home.

She was thinking she ought to get out and exercise more when Emily suddenly screamed.

"Daddy! DADDY!"

"Emily, what is it?"

Jenn paused, trying to put the child down, but Emily clung to her like a barnacle to a rock, screaming.

"It's Daddy! Oh, Mommy, he found me! He found me!"

Jenn hugged her daughter and swung around to see what had frightened her. She gasped to see a figure moving out of the shadows, only a silhouette in the moonlight.

Evan . . .

Then the figure turned to them. Jenn saw an old man, carrying a log. He tossed it onto the woodpile, then twisted back to stare at them. For a moment, Jenn was unable to speak. Even in the darkness, she could tell he was studying them. His stare made her uneasy.

"It's okay, Emily," she whispered. "It's just an old man. Probably works for Mrs. Bayless."

Then again, what kind of worker would let the farm run down like this? Even an old guy could push an electric mower!

She had a funny feeling he didn't belong here. The feeling became worry, and she quickened her pace toward the cottage, certain she could feel the old man's stare boring into her back.

Because it was her first day traveling to campus over such a long distance, Jenn left early the next morning to give herself extra time for the drive. She ended up arriving too early, when the campus was quiet and virtually deserted. Fortunately, Dee Crowley was at the center and said it would be no bother to take Emily in. Jenn herself headed to the cafeteria, where she'd wait out the extra time over coffee and a pastry.

"Glad to see another early bird," a cheerful voice said.

Jenn looked up to see Noreen Kane.

"I left too early," Jenn said. "I overestimated how long it would take to get here from my new home."

"You found a place? Great! Where is it?"

Jenn told her.

"Hmm," Noreen said, stirring her coffee with a little

red-and-white straw. "Laura Bayless—where have I heard that name before?"

She shook her head. "Who knows? Forget that. Jenn, have you heard anything more about the Wallace girl?"

"Nothing's changed," Jenn said with a sad shake of her head. "I saw her yesterday. It doesn't even look like the same kid."

"Diabetes is a horrible illness," Noreen said. "My mother had it. She had trouble with her legs and her eyes all her life. She had trouble walking up and down stairs because she couldn't feel the bottoms of her feet."

At that moment, Nick Hasken appeared with a tray. Noreen nodded at him. Jenn blinked at his brightly colored tie, a distorted image of the Periodic Table of the Elements.

"Have a seat," Noreen invited.

He settled in next to Jenn.

"Good morning. I heard you mention Michelle Wallace. She's that kid with the dark hair who talks a lot, right?"

The women nodded.

"She's in my biology class," Nick said. "My students are very worried about her."

"We all are," Noreen said. "I've been remembering her in my prayers and I went to a novena for her."

Abruptly, Nick changed the subject.

"Will you be going to the welcome back tea at Dean Stone's place?" he asked.

Neither woman answered at first, but Jenn quickly realized Nick was looking right at her when he asked.

"Oh, I forgot about it," she admitted. She'd received the invitation, but had been in a hurry to get to class and had tucked it in a book. "Of course I'll be going. Is this an annual event?"

"A little party Kim throws to help us all get reacquainted," Noreen said. "And to introduce newcomers like yourself."

The conversation went on in that friendly way, with Noreen doing most of the talking. Jenn felt a little uncomfortable around Nick, although she couldn't have explained why. She recalled that Simone Trenton had said Nick Hasken was "strange." Why? He seemed like a nice guy.

Then again, anyone could be considered nice when compared with her ex-husband. She had to learn not to compare all men she met with Evan!

She was glad when it was finally time to go to classes.

Class went smoothly. This was Jenn's domain, the one place she had complete confidence in herself. She never worried, never bit a nail while teaching. Getting back to teaching was the best thing she could have done. Evan had tried to take this ability from her, but he hadn't succeeded in the long run. She was good at this, and she knew it.

After classes, though, she passed a group of students crowded around Herb Cole. They were talking to the department head about Michelle, and she was flooded with her old worries. She thought of the strange words Michelle had spoken before her collapse. Once more, she wondered how Michelle could have known Evan's nickname for Emily: "E.J."

When Jenn picked Emily up at the center, the girl showed off a painting, which Jenn made a fuss over. During the drive home, Emily chattered on about her day, leaving Jenn almost no time to worry about Michelle.

"You know what?" Emily asked. "Andy LaMont's daddy saw a panther last weekend!"

Jenn laughed. "There are no panthers in Vermont, Emily."

"He saw one!" Emily insisted, bouncing on the seat. "He really did! Miss Dee says the last panther was shot a long time ago. I think she said when the century turned around."

"The turn of the century," Jenn corrected. "About the year nineteen hundred. You're kidding, aren't you? I can't believe there were ever panthers in this part of the country."

"Miss Dee said so," Emily replied. "But she doesn't believe Andy's daddy, either. Except she heard someone else say they saw a panther, too."

"Just so long as we don't see one around our place," Jenn said, humoring her daughter.

Emily went on talking, her words an aural blur. As much as Jenn wanted to give her daughter her full attention, thoughts of Michelle had begun to creep into her mind again. She drove with one hand, chewing at a nail on the other.

Emily saw the gesture and stopped talking at once. By the time they drove onto the farm, her head was hanging.

Caught in her own thoughts, it took Jenn a while to notice the change in Emily. She parked the car and took the keys out before asking.

"What's wrong, dollbaby?"

"I dunno," Emily said. "I feel sad."

"I do, too," Jenn said. "I was thinking about Michelle."

"I wasn't," Emily said. "I just feel sad."

In the house, Emily went into her room and changed quietly into play clothes. She asked permission to ride her Big Wheel trike, then went outside.

Jenn went into the kitchen for an after-school snack. She pulled lettuce, carrots, and Italian dressing from the refrigerator. There was a half-eaten can of pineapple chunks on the bottom shelf, leftover from the previous day, and some ricotta cheese. Between all of it, Jenn planned to make a nice snack for herself and Emily. She washed the lettuce, shook out the water, and started to tear it up.

"Have you seen E.J.? Do you know where her door is?"

The voice was so loud, so clear, that Jenn dropped the pieces of lettuce she was holding.

It had sounded just like Evan.

"No!"

She took in a deep breath. Of course it wasn't Evan! What was she doing, making up things just like her daughter? Next thing, she'd have an imaginary playmate, too!

She grabbed a carrot and started scraping, oblivious to the little pieces of orange that were flying in all directions. She gripped hard at the knife, as if the carrot was a whetstone and she was sharpening it for the kill.

"E.J.! E.J., I'm calling you! Answer me! Open your door for me!"

Light giggling.

Jenn swung around in time to see a black shadow slip around the half-wall between the kitchen and dining room.

More giggling.

"Emily?"

Had her daughter come in without her hearing?

"E.J., answer me, damn you! Open the door!"

Oh, God, that was Evan! He wasn't really dead! It had all been a trick and now he was after Emily!

Without stopping to put on her coat, Jenn ran for the front door. As she jerked it open, she saw the black shadow again, moving across the yard like a low-flying rain cloud. And then, before her turned eyes, it began to roll and twist and solidify. A hand shot out from inside of it, human at first, then feline. It was black, sleek, clawed. A roar sounded so loudly that Jenn had to cover her ears. Then, suddenly, she found herself staring across the yard at a panther!

She screamed, but the animal didn't turn. Instead, it began to run toward the barn. Jenn raced after it. She didn't think what she'd do when she caught up with the thing. Her only concern was getting to Emily.

"Emily! Emily, a panther!"

Her scream carried across the wind, but it didn't seem loud enough. She crashed into the barn, still calling her daughter's name.

Emily looked up, confused. She was sitting on a pile of hay with a kitten pressed to her shirt.

"Mommy?"

"Emily, sit quietly," Jenn said softly, looking around.

"Why?"

"Don't move!" Jenn warned. "There's a panther in here. We have to be careful!"

"A panther! Cool! Wait 'til I tell Andy!"

The barn seemed empty. A big animal like that couldn't hide in the shadow, could it? But where had it gone?

"Emily, did you see it?"

"Nope," Emily said.

Jenn stopped herself, made herself think. Had it been here at all? Or had it only been her imagination? She covered her face and tried to review the past few minutes. She'd been standing at the kitchen counter. She'd heard Evan . . .

"Oh, God," she said. "I must be going crazy."

Of course there was no panther at all. No Evan. It had all been an illusion, a daydream.

She felt a hand on her leg.

"Mommy, what's wrong?"

Jenn sighed. "I'm sorry, dollbaby. I guess I was having a dream."

Emily studied her for a few minutes. "Sometimes I walk when I dream, too."

"I know," Jenn said with a tired smile. "I guess the long drive home and thinking about Michelle just got to me."

Emily held up the kitten and spoke as if she hadn't heard her mother mention Michelle.

"Isn't this one cute?" she asked. "It has a little black spot under its nose like a mustache. There's six kittens in the hay. Tara told me about them."

"Tara?"

"She went away when you came," Emily said. "She said Daddy was nearby and she had to make him go away before he found me. Tara protects me, y'know. She says Daddy's looking for a door to get to me. Everybody has her own door, she says."

Jenn felt herself grow cold inside. "Tara" had said Daddy was nearby . . .

It was just coincidence. Tara wasn't real, and Evan was dead and gone!

And the panther was nothing more than a trick of light, shadow, and weariness.

Right, Jenn, she thought. *Tired people always hallucinate.*

Maybe she needed to talk to someone. Maybe counseling would help her understand what was happening.

She pushed the thought aside at once. There was no telling how long she could keep sessions with a shrink secret. Of course Dean Stone wouldn't fire her just for seeking counseling, but it might tarnish the woman's opinion of her.

Jenn took a deep sigh, determined to get through her problems on her own.

"Come into the house, Emily," she said quietly. "I . . . I was making pineapple and ricotta cream . . ."

Emily put the kitten back in the hay and followed obediently. Neither knew that Tara was still there, invisible, watching them carefully.

Another spirit, infinitely more malevolent, watched Tara, wishing he knew how he could make her tell where to find E.J. The little bitch knew the right door, but he didn't have the power to scare her the way he could frighten Emily. All he could do was follow her around and hope she'd show him the way.

For he knew Emily was close, oh so close, and it was only a matter of time before he found her.

eight

Jenn, who usually woke up in a good mood, dragged herself out of bed the next day feeling as if she hadn't slept at all. She ached all over, as if little demons had been biting her all night. She was tired, too. When Emily started making a fuss over breakfast, Jenn hardly had the strength to deal with her.

"If you poured milk on that cereal," she said, "you have to eat it, Emily."

"I hate Cheerios!"

"Sure you do," Jenn said with blasé sarcasm.

The smell of coffee wafting up from the pot was all she could concentrate on right now. She fixed herself a cup and shuffled over to the table.

"I'm so tired this morning," she said with a yawn.

"Me, too," Emily said. "I want to stay home."

Jenn reached across the table to feel Emily's forehead.

"No fever," she said. "You're not sick."

"I'm not sick," Emily agreed. "But I want to stay home."

"Can't," Jenn said, sipping her coffee. Like a miracle drug, it was already starting to make her feel better. "I've got four classes today."

Emily turned over the salt shaker and sprinkled its contents on the table.

"Emily, clean that up!"

Emily's way of cleaning was to blow the salt onto the floor. She took a few very loud bites of cereal, growling as she ate.

"I'm a panther!" she declared.

"You're gonna be a panther in big trouble if you don't cut it out," Jenn said. She finished her coffee and got up.

"It's time to get dressed," she declared.

Emily ran to her room and returned a moment later in shorts and a T-shirt. Jenn laughed.

"You can't wear that, Emily,' she said. "The thermometer on the window says it's only fifty degrees out."

"I want to!"

"Don't be silly," Jenn said. "Go into your room and find something warmer."

"Please."

"No!"

Emily burst into tears. Exasperated, Jenn threw up her hands.

"Okay, wear whatever you want, you little brat! I hope you freeze!"

Just before they left, Jenn quietly grabbed a sweater and jeans and tucked them under her arm. She handed these to Dee when they arrived at the center and whispered:

"Emily wanted to dress herself this morning."

Dee winked. "Gotcha. Don't worry—I'll get warmer clothes on her before recess!"

Somehow, as Jenn left Emily in Dee's care, she began to feel better. In fact, she felt a little guilty. Sure, Emily was acting bratty this morning, but was that any excuse for her own bad temper?

"You're an adult!" she said out loud. "How could you let a four-year-old get the better of you?"

"Excuse me?"

Jenn swung around to see Nick Hasken close behind her, riding his bike along the curb. He wore a navy blue corduroy jacket and a tie with Einstein's portrait. She gave him a slight smile.

"Just thinking out loud," she said. "Do you have kids, Nick?"

"Not married," Nick said. "Why? Is something up with Emily?"

Jenn shrugged, turning away from him. Why should she share family secrets with him?

"Can I make a suggestion?"

From someone who doesn't have kids?

"Sure."

"There's a special thing going on at Burger Barn tonight," he said. "One of the Future Fighters is appearing Brianna Dali—my assistant—mentioned that she was taking her own kids."

Emily *loved* "The Future Fighters," an action/adventure show on television.

She smiled at Nick. "I'll think about it."

Nick gave her a quick wave and pedaled off. Standing in the middle of the sidewalk, Jenn watched him for a moment. It surprised her that a man, especially one without children, would come up with such a good idea. Treating Emily to the fast-food restaurant tonight would make up for their bad morning, wouldn't it? And it was a great way to break the tensions brought on by the move. Nick was such a nice guy to suggest it . . .

Jenn pushed thoughts of Nick aside and went on to her class. During lunch, she told Noreen about Nick's suggestion.

"Sounds like something Nick would do," Noreen said. "I told you he was a sweetheart. He'd make a great daddy."

With her spoonful of fruit halfway to her mouth, Jenn looked at her friend with hooded eyes.

"Is that a suggestion?"

Noreen shrugged. "Whatever you think. But Nick is a great guy."

"So, go out with him."

"He's not my type," Noreen said. "I told you that."

"What type is he?"

"The kind you stay married to forever," Noreen said. "The kind of guy who likes mowing the lawn on weekends and taking two-week vacations with his family every summer."

"What's wrong with that?"

"I already told you," Noreen said. "I only want a man long enough to have babies. Men tie you down. Even the nice ones. I like my independence. I don't want to share my paycheck with anyone."

"Except a bunch of kids."

They both laughed, and Jenn managed to turn the subject from Nick to an anecdote about class that day. By the time lunch ended, she was in a very good mood. It carried through the afternoon, and she was still feeling light when she went to pick up Emily.

As Jenn leaned against the fence at the center, watching children at play, Emily appeared out of the bottom of a big yellow tube. She ran to her mother with a big smile on her face. Jenn was grateful to see that her mood had improved, too, and that Dee had gotten the long pants and sweater on her.

"Hi, Mommy!"

"Hi," Jenn said. She took her daughter's hand and led her to the car. "Guess what? I have a special treat for you. Guess where we're going?"

"Where? Where?"

When Jenn told her, Emily squealed with delight. She chattered happily the whole way to Burger Barn. Jenn felt relieved. This was nothing like the grumpy brat she'd faced that morning.

The restaurant was crowded, but Emily managed to get up to Tammi the Future Fighter to shake her hand. Jenn laughed. If there really was a Cloud 9, Emily was on it the whole way home. The experience was all she talked about for thirty miles.

But the moment they turned onto the Bayless farm, Emily clammed up. She stared out the window with her lips pressed together. Jenn felt a strange depression washing over her, too. But she wouldn't let it take hold. It was just a run-down old farm, nothing to be sad about! All she had to do was remind herself of the crowded, noisy dorm, and the farm began to look like paradise. Still, there was a sense of melancholy . . .

She snapped off those thoughts at once.

"You know," she said, "it might be a nice idea to help Laura fix this place up. She hasn't been able to, you know."

"It's a sad place," Emily said.

"I know," Jenn said, parking the car.

Thoughts of fixing the place up made her think of the man she'd seen the other night. Who had he been? Laura hadn't mentioned a helper of any kind. If he worked here, he certainly did a lousy job. Jenn decided she would ask Laura about the man when she saw her again, but the big house was dark and it seemed Laura and Peter were out.

The rest of the evening passed eventfully. The next

morning, Emily was much more like her pleasant and co-operative self. In fact, she was so quiet that Jenn was worried she might be sick.

"You okay, dollbaby?"

Emily grinned, milk dripping off her lower lip. She wiped it away. The bowl of Cheerios was finished, once more a favorite breakfast food.

"Yep," Emily said. "I'm gonna get dressed now."

It was the longest sentence she'd spoken all morning.

She returned in pink corduroy pants and a pastel-colored sweater. Jenn helped her into her coat and they grabbed their things and left. A few miles down the road, Emily began to talk like her usual, animated self. In fact, she was so energetic that Jenn actually felt a little worn out when she dropped her at the center.

It was a good day, and Jenn was happy enough at the end to give Emily another surprise. She'd take her out to get a Halloween costume.

"I'm gonna be Tammi!" Emily announced. "I want her silver costume!"

Jenn, who had heard that Future Fighter costumes were a rare commodity these days, felt worried that disappointment would put Emily in a bad mood.

"Emily, we might not be able to find it," she warned carefully.

"We will, too!" Emily insisted. "I wanna be Tammi!"

Oh, God, we're starting up again. Maybe this wasn't such a good idea . . .

By some miracle, there happened to be a Tammi costume in Emily's size, tucked in behind bags of other costumes. Jenn suggested it had been tossed aside because some of the silver lace was hanging and a few beads were missing. It bothered her to pay that much money for something so poorly made, but the delight in Emily's eyes was enough to placate her.

At home, Emily laid the costume out on the bed. She climbed up next to it, gingerly touching the beads with a small hand. To Emily, it was the most beautiful thing she'd ever seen.

"I like gold better than silver."

Emily gasped, and turned to see Tara standing near her door. She jumped from the bed. She was happy to see her friend and didn't wonder for a moment how she'd gotten in.

"Hi!" Emily said, smiling.

Tara regarded her coolly.

"Is that your Halloween costume?"

"Yep," Emily said. "Tammi is my favorite. I'm going to be Tammi for Halloween."

"Halloween's better over here," Tara said.

"Over where?"

Tara ignored the question. "You know who I saw today? I saw your daddy, and boy, is he mad!"

Emily's eyes rounded, and her heart began to pound in her chest.

"He's mad at me?" she asked in a tiny voice.

Tara only shrugged, indifferent to the smaller girl's fears. "Don't worry. He doesn't know where you are."

She fingered the costume.

"I sure won't tell him," she singsonged.

She pulled off a bead. Emily gasped and yanked the costume away.

"I like Courtney myself," Tara said. "Her gold costume is much better. Tammi's costume is geeky-looking."

"It is not!" Emily said. "What would you know, anyway? You wear the same dress all the time. Don't you have any other clothes?"

Tara looked down at her blue frock.

"I like this dress," she said. "But I hate your costume!"

The door began to open, and Tara vanished. Jenn peeked inside.

"I heard you talking, Emily," she said. "Did you try your costume on yet?"

Emily pouted. "I don't want to. I don't want the silver costume anymore. It's geeky-looking."

"Oh, Emily," Jenn sighed. "It just needs a little sewing . . ."

Emily threw it on the floor. "It's dumb! I hate it!"

Jenn could see another argument brewing and bit her tongue to prevent herself from yelling.

"Fine," she said. "Then don't trick-or-treat this year."

She shut the door. From inside her room, Emily listened to the sound of slamming cabinet doors and crashing pots. When Tara appeared again, she frowned at her.

"You made Mommy mad at me," she said.

"Your mommy is mean," Tara said. "My mama never gets mad."

Abruptly, as if nothing was wrong at all, she changed the subject.

"Let's play with your tea set and dishes . . ."

Out in the kitchen, Jenn was tearing open a box of spaghetti when suddenly she began to cry. She didn't understand why, but she couldn't stop, either. What was happening here? Why was she so tense, and Emily so bratty, lately? With Evan gone, life should be perfect. Why wasn't it?

Neither mother nor daughter spoke during dinner. Jenn left the dishes in the sink, too tired to wash them. She tried to busy herself correcting papers, but when she marked the same correct answer wrong on three different tests, she knew she had to put them aside. Instead, she pushed back her chair and went to check on Emily.

* * *

The little girl was already in her pajamas and sound asleep. Guilt washed over Jenn as she thought of the fights they'd had recently. She would have to try harder. Feeling deep love for this towheaded child, she bent to kiss her. Emily grimaced in her sleep and tightened her grip around her pink teddy bear, as if to shield herself from something.

"Sweet dreams, dollbaby," Jenn whispered.

Jenn went to bed early. Sometime in the night, she was awakened by the sound of a horrible scream. She bolted up in bed, her heart pounding, her ears keenly attuned to the noises around her. Had that been Emily? Or was it only part of a dream?

The scream sounded again, but this time she realized it wasn't a scream at all. It was the terrified whinny of a horse. Jenn pushed her covers aside, got up, and pulled on her robe. She looked out her window, but all she could see was the darkness of the night. For a few moments, everything was quiet.

"Some poor animal must have wandered onto the farm," she said out loud. "It must be stuck somewhere."

She put on her coat and boots. She'd find out where the horse was, then she'd call Laura to get some help.

When she opened the front door, she was met with such a cacophony of noises that she jumped back. An incredible racket of moos, neighs, honks, and barks filled the air. It was as if she was trapped in the lower decks of Noah's ark, surrounded by dozens of animals.

Footsteps thundered past, but when she turned to see what had made them, there was nothing there. Frantic wings fluttered by her ears, so close she could feel wind against her cheeks. But there were no birds.

There wasn't an animal in sight.

Slowly, Jenn walked outside. She was so tense that she didn't even feel the iciness of the night air.

A dog yelped as if being beaten.

A cat yowled.

What is going on here, she wondered. Perhaps the sounds were from a neighboring farm. Was there one nearby? Jenn didn't know.

Thinking Laura might have an explanation, she went to the phone to dial her number. After two rings, there was a whir and a click, and Laura's answering-machine voice said: "Hello. Sorry we can't take your call, but we're not here right now. We were never here. We're all dead."

Jenn hung up quickly. What the hell kind of message was that? She waited a moment, then picked up the phone to dial again. But very abruptly the animal noises came to a sudden halt. Jenn listened for a long time, phone receiver in hand. The night was still.

The stress of being rudely awakened in the middle of the night hit her just then, and she decided she just didn't want to know. She'd ask Laura about it in the morning, and about the odd message on her answering machine.

The very last thing she thought of before drifting off to sleep again was how strange it was that Emily, who was a light sleeper, hadn't been awakened by the noises.

The next morning she saw Laura loading a box in the back of her station wagon.

"Glad I caught you before I had to leave," Laura said. "I've got some pies and cookies to deliver to the Mixing Bowl."

Jenn didn't care about that at the moment.

"Did you hear those animals?" she asked.

"Animals?" Laura's expression was guileless.

Jenn explained how she'd been awakened by a horrible racket.

"I don't understand," Laura said. "The nearest farm is half a mile away, and those animals have never wandered through the woods. At least, not as many as you were hearing! Could you have been dreaming?"

"I'm sure I was awake," Jenn said. "I called you, too. Laura, that's a strange message on your answering machine."

Laura laughed. "What answering machine? There, you see? You were dreaming, Jenn. I don't even *own* one!"

Jenn frowned. Was it possible it was only a dream? It had seemed very real to her. But Emily hadn't heard a thing, and Laura claimed not to have an answering machine. She sighed.

"I guess you're right," she said. "But that was the most realistic dream I've ever had!"

"It's the quiet country life," Laura said. "It gives your mind room to imagine things."

Jenn, recalling the panther she'd thought she'd seen the other day, couldn't have agreed more. She also recalled the strange man, whom Emily had mistaken for her father.

"I saw someone here the other night," she said "An older man, carrying a log."

"That's René DeLorris," Laura said. "He lives on the next farm over and sometimes stops by to lend me a hand. He's a good man, but a little unsociable."

Jenn thought that a great understatement.

"Well, now that you're here," Laura said, "I'd like to invite you for breakfast tomorrow morning. Can you come?"

"Sure," Jenn said. "I'll see you then."

She headed back to the cottage. As she opened the door, she didn't notice the bloodied goose feather that floated on the wind just behind her. It swung back and forth lazily, then finally landed on the ground next to the front step, right beside the imprint of a horse's hoof.

nine

Rain was pouring down when Jenn and Emily walked up to the big house the next morning. Emily was a bright spot in a gloomy day with her hot-pink slicker and flowered umbrella. She enthusiastically tried her boots in each and every puddle, so that by the time they knocked at Laura's door the boots were full of mud.

"Take those off here by the door," Jenn said.

"Don't worry about it," Laura insisted. "A little mud never hurt anyone."

Emily took off her boots, anyway. She and Jenn hung their coats on brass hooks that Jenn thought might be antiques. As soon as she turned, she was struck by a variety of delicious smells: bacon, coffee, something sweet . . .

"Are those muffins?"

"Cranberry," Laura said with a smile.

"They smell wonderful," Jenn said.

In fact, the whole atmosphere of the kitchen was wonderful. It was warm and cozy, the perfect country kitchen. Jenn felt a little jealous, thinking she could never match Laura's culinary and decorating prowess. As if reading her mind, Laura said:

"I don't have to get up early to drive to school every day. Besides, I don't usually cook like this, unless I'm baking for the Mixing Bowl. It's just for company. Right, Peter?"

Peter simply shrugged and poured syrup over his pancakes. Emily sat in the chair next to him. When Laura filled a plate for her, she picked up the syrup jug.

"Don't use it all up," Peter said.

"Peter!" Laura said sharply.

Peter ignored his mother. He shot Emily a dirty look, but she seemed unaware of it. Jenn watched the children as she ate her own breakfast, almost glad to see Laura had the same problems with Peter that she had with Emily. But then again, Peter was an adolescent—in a way, he was supposed to act like this. Emily, on the other hand, had always been sweet and cooperative before.

Peter finished his breakfast and carried his dish to the sink, where he rinsed and washed it. Well, Jenn thought, Laura had taught him some things right. But she was even more surprised when he looked at Emily and said:

"I brought some colored pencils home from art class. You want to try them?"

"Sure!" Emily said with delight, jumping from her chair.

"Thanks, Peter," Jenn said, a little flabbergasted. "It's nice of you to entertain her."

"She's okay," Peter said quietly, not looking at Jenn.

Emily ran after him as he left the kitchen.

"Wow," Jenn said, turning to look at Laura.

Laura was beaming. The way she stood at the stove

with a cup of coffee in her hand, wearing a white apron embroidered with sunflowers over a green dress, she looked like an old magazine advertisement. Jenn half expected her to launch into a sales pitch for a new dishwasher, circa 1958.

"He's some kid," Laura said. "I'm so proud of Peter. It hasn't been easy for him, losing his father."

"I can't imagine," Jenn said.

Maybe she had misunderstood Peter. Was his surly act his way of showing grief? Was there a decent human being under the spikes of hair that fell over his hooded eyes?

At that moment, the boy in question was leading Emily toward the attic door.

"I've got something to show you," he said. "It's up in the attic."

"The colored pencils?"

"There aren't any," Peter admitted. "I just said that to get you out of the kitchen. But it's a secret, and you have to promise you won't tell anyone."

"Cross my heart and hope to die," Emily said solemnly. She remembered that the last time Peter had a secret, Tara had come to play with her.

She followed him through a door and up a small flight of stairs. In the attic, he pulled an overhead switch and led her to a big box marked TOYS. It was filled with playthings for a little girl. Emily squealed with delight as she pulled out a doll.

"Wow!"

"You can play with them for a little while," Peter said. "They used to belong to a kid who lived her once. But you have to promise not to tell about them."

"I already did," Emily reminded, taking out a Chinese checkers game. She looked up at him and found he was staring at her with an eye that wasn't hidden behind his bangs. He looked sad, like he needed a friend.

"Peter, how come you're being so nice to me?" she wanted to know.

He shrugged. "You're okay, I guess. You've got worries, like me."

"What kind of worries do you have?' Emily asked, amazed that a big boy like Peter could be worried about anything. She suddenly wanted to be nice to him.

"You wanna play with me?"

"Not a chance," Peter said. "And I'm not going to stick around until she makes me, either!'

He turned and hurried down the stairs. Before Emily could catch up to him, he shut and latched the door. Emily knocked on it.

"Hey!" she yelled.

Peter didn't answer her. Emily turned back up the stairs. She didn't really feel scared, because she knew her mommy would come looking for her soon enough. And she wanted to play with those toys. Who did they belong to, she wondered?

Reaching the top of the stairs again, she noticed a white bed that sat just under a small window. Curious, Emily climbed up on the mattress and looked out the rain-speckled window. The yard stretched for a long distance below, reaching up a gently sloping hill to woods of birch and pine. The grass had turned a golden-brown color, and deciduous leaves had given up their green for reds, oranges, and yellows. It looked very pretty to Emily, who decided she might prefer to play outside instead, even if it was damp and muddy.

A flash of white appeared through the soft curtain of rain. Emily watched as an ugly white dog struggled through the grass, limping on twisted legs. A moment later, a woman appeared out of the woods, holding a shotgun. To her dismay, Emily realized it was Laura.

"That was a bad dog," she heard Tara say.

She looked at her friend, kneeling on the bed beside her now.

"Is she going to shoot it?" Emily asked. "Is Laura gonna shoot the dog?"

"My mama isn't going to shoot anything!" Tara insisted. "It's not her down there, it's your daddy. He's looking for the door to you, Emily. He thinks the dog knows the way."

"No!"

"Look! Look out the window!"

Emily couldn't resist. She turned back to the window and looked out. This time, it was a man chasing the dog. Terror, familiar after the abuse she'd suffered at her father's hands, washed over her. Trepidation iced her small joints and twisted her stomach. Her body began to shiver, but she couldn't turn away from the scene below. Her small hands clamped the windowsill until they turned pale and her eyes rounded.

Once, a long time ago, she had a little puppy. Mommy had found it and brought it home. But Daddy had told her to "GET RID OF IT," or he would "BLOW ITS BRAINS OUT." Emily didn't know what that meant, but it scared her. She didn't want the puppy to get hurt. She cried and cried, because she liked the puppy so much, but she was glad when Mommy took it away the next morning. It was safe now.

Now Daddy was back again, and he wasn't holding a gun any longer. He was holding a huge, sharp, pizza cutter, all ready to slice her in half. He seemed to be looking around, trying to find something.

Emily opened her mouth to scream, but instead felt herself being pulled away from the window.

"He's trying to find the door to you," Tara said again.

"What door? There's no door outside!"

"Not that kind of door," Tara replied. "You can't see it." She tilted her head, listening.

"He's gone now," Tara said. "Look."

"No!"

Tara shot her such a mean look that Emily was frightened into obedience. She climbed back on the mattress and looked out. The yard below was empty. No man, no dog.

"What . . . what was wrong with that dog?" Emily wanted to know.

"It was a bad dog," Tara said. "Mama killed it. She killed everything."

"You said your mommy didn't shoot anything," Emily reminded her.

Tara didn't reply. Instead she jumped from the bed and pulled more toys from the box.

"Forget it," Tara said. "He's gone for now. I just want to play."

Emily's underlying fears were gone now, and she felt safe again. She didn't want to think about her father, or ugly old dogs, so she turned her attention to a doll. Soon the little girls were playing games, thoughts of Emily's father for the moment abandoned.

And then, someone was pounding on the door below. Though it seemed only moments had gone by, in truth, Emily had been in the attic for nearly an hour.

"Emily?"

Her mother's voice made her jump. She looked at Tara with worry in her eyes.

"That's Mommy," she said. "She sounds mad."

"Oh, she's always mad," Tara said. "Don't answer. I still want to to play with you."

Emily stood up. "I have to. Mommy gets mad a lot, and it's really scary when she does. I don't want her to yell at me!"

Before Tara could say a word, Emily raced down the stairs. She reached the door just as it opened. Her mother stood there with Laura, who had a key in her hand. Emily bowed her head and waited for her mother to start yelling at her. Instead, Jenn picked her up and hugged her.

"You poor thing!" Jenn said. "You must have been terrified!"

"I'm ... I'm so sorry," Laura said. "I don't know why he did this! Peter's never pulled a stunt like this before."

Emily was confused. Why were the grown-ups so upset? She wiggled until her mother put her down again.

"What did Peter do?"

"Locked you in that dirty old attic!" Jenn said. "Are you okay?"

"Sure," Emily said. She didn't want to get Peter into trouble, even in he had locked the door on purpose. Peter had helped her find Tara again. "But he didn't mean to lock the door, Mommy. It was an accident! And I wasn't scared at all."

She bit her lower lip and stared thoughtfully at the pattern on the hall rug.

"Except when I saw the dog," she said finally. "Laura was chasing it with a gun."

"She must have been dreaming," Laura said quietly.

"Then it was Daddy chasing the dog," Emily went on. "He had a gun, and then he had a pizza cutter. He looked right up at me!"

Jenn knelt beside her.

"Dollbaby, you must have been dreaming," she said. "Laura was with me the whole time, and you know Daddy isn't here."

"Oh, no," Emily insisted. "Tara saw him, too. But she said it was okay. She said he doesn't know where I am. Tara keeps Daddy away from me, y'know."

"Good for Tara," Jenn mumbled.

"You won't let Daddy get me with the pizza cutter, will you?"

"Never!"

Emily put her arms around her mother's neck.

"I ... I'll go have a talk with Peter," Laura said softly. "I'll warn him to be more careful."

She walked away. Jenn stood up and took Emily by the hand, heading toward the stairs. A moment later, they could hear the muffled sounds of an argument.

"Peter didn't mean it," Emily said again.

A loud pop sounded over their heads, and bits of glass rained down on them. Emily let out a little scream. They both looked up to see the broken remains of a shattered ceiling light.

"How did ... ?"

At the bottom of the stairs, another bulb imploded.

Emily began to feel cold all over. Something was going to happen. Someone was going to hurt her ...

She heard glass shattering through the house, and in moments the place was dark. Laura and Peter came hurrying down the hall just as the last bulb, one in the bathroom, imploded.

"This is crazy," Peter said, looking around. "It's like someone shot them out with a gun."

A gun. Daddy had a gun when he came out of the woods. Daddy was here ...

"Must have been a power surge," Laura guessed. "I've never seen anything like it."

"A power surge," Jenn asked. "You didn't have that many lights on, Laura. And the storm isn't that bad."

"There has to be some explanation for ..."

Emily fainted.

"Emily!"

Jenn knelt to take her daughter into her arms.

Suddenly filled with an overwhelming sense that she had to get out of there, Jenn scooped up the child and hurried away. Laura followed, making futile efforts to help. At the door, she put a hand on Jenn's arm.

"Please, let me call a doctor!"

"I'll handle it myself!"

Jenn threw their coats over Emily and rushed outside, oblivious to the fine drops of cold rain that pelted her. The rain had the effect of a stimulant, and Emily opened her eyes. She began to cry.

"Daddy . . ."

"Daddy's not here," Jenn insisted. "You're safe with me."

When they got inside the cottage, Jenn settled Emily on the couch. Emily got up on her knees and looked over the back, as if expecting something to jump out at her. The look of terror on her face tore Jenn apart inside.

"Daddy had a gun," Emily whispered.

"It wasn't Daddy," Jenn insisted.

Emily ran to the window and looked out. The rain was falling harder again, making the house in the distance seem like part of a dream. Emily felt dizzy, sick. Her knees were shaking.

But, somehow, she also had a sense that she was safe again. Her father was gone.

He couldn't catch her as long as Mommy was with her.

As long as Tara kept watch over her.

ten

Jenn needed to clear her head. More than that, she
needed to get away from the farm for a while. She bun-
dled Emily back into her raincoat, and they drove off.

"Where are we going, Mommy?" Emily asked. She
looked around nervously.

Jenn wondered what her daughter was looking for. All
she saw was the play of shadows and light as the sun tried
to peek out from behind the clouds, illuminating the
woods for a moment, then disappearing. It was as if light
was fighting with dark, and dark was winning.

"I don't know," Jenn said. "Just for a ride."

She really didn't know where she was going, but when
the sign for Mapletree Mall appeared through the falling
rain, she turned into its parking lot. Mall walking had
never been one of her pastimes, but today it seemed like

a good way to blow off steam. It was a place to be out of the rain, at the very least.

Emily was fascinated by all the sounds, smells, and colors. She insisted on looking at every window, watching a TV in one video store, giggling as a woman dressed a mannequin in a boutique. She pulled Jenn into a toy store, where Jenn promised her again and again that she could "have that for Christmas." A play area in one children's clothing boutique kept Emily occupied so long that guilt made Jenn buy her something. Just a pair of socks, about all her budget could afford.

She stood there at the rack trying to choose between green socks with polka dots and pink socks with pearly lace. Then she started to laugh. An hour ago, she was agonizing over strange, almost supernatural events at Laura's house. Now her biggest worry was choosing a pair of socks!

"Why are you laughing, Mommy?"

Jenn stopped herself, realizing she must sound like a crazy woman. She felt a little crazy. She brought a thumb to her mouth to bit at the nail, but put her hand down again. She couldn't stand here chewing her fingers in a public place, could she?

"I'm . . . it's nothing, dollbaby," Jenn said. "I'm okay. Which socks do you like?"

Emily studied the two pairs in her hands, shrugged, and took down a pair with yellow and blue stripes. Jenn started to laugh again.

"Mommy!" Emily said with impatience.

"Sorry," Jenn said.

It was nervous laughter, she knew, relief after the tension of the morning. When she calmed down, she told herself things were going to be okay. Maybe Peter really had locked Emily up by accident. Maybe there was a perfectly logical explanation for those bulbs breaking. After all, when did she go to MIT to get her degree in electrical engineering?

She paid for the socks and they left the store. By now, Emily's abundant energy was beginning to take its toll. She decided to buy dinner from a kiosk—baskets of chicken and fries and two colas. They sat at a white plastic table.

"Do you like our new home so far?" Jenn asked.

"It's okay," Emily said. "Except for when I see Daddy."

"Emily, those are just bad dreams," Jenn said. "You know Daddy was killed in the accident. He can never, ever come back again."

"Tara says he's looking for me," Emily told her. She bunched a handful of fries together and bit the ends off all at once.

Although logic told Jenn that Tara didn't exist beyond Emily's imagination, it bothered her that this pretend playmate was putting frightening suggestions into Emily's head. There were probably volumes written on the psychiatric implications of this—Emily's continued fear of her father, her inability to accept his death, her reaction to the upheavals in her life.

"That's a mean thing for Tara to say," she answered. "She doesn't sound like much of a friend."

"She's my best friend!" Emily insisted. "She keeps Daddy away!"

Jenn decided to change the subject. It was just too depressing.

"So, do you think you'll get a lot of candy this year when you go trick-or-treating?"

Emily grinned, nodded, and started talking about her favorite kinds of candy. Then she kept Jenn busy through the remainder of dinner asking about the costumes she'd worn over previous years. She made no mention of the silver

Tammi costume, and Jenn hoped it meant she was willing to wear it after all.

As much as she wanted to stay out, the day was getting long, and it was finally time to head home again. But as they passed the campus, Jenn remembered something.

"Oh, I've got to see if I can get into the math building," she said. "I just remembered that I left a book there, and I need it to prepare a test for next week."

She could very well have waited a day or two to get the book, but she didn't care. It was as if her subconscious had given her another chance to delay their return to the farm.

She parked the car in her usual space, and she and Emily got out. Emily ran on ahead, up the stairs of the brick building. Dry leaves crunched beneath her sneakers. The bulbs in the lampposts, which came on automatically as the sun went down, cast yellowish light over the child. She laughed and danced and waved her arms to make shadows that sprayed out in different directions from different lamps.

This part of the campus was dark, cold, and deserted at this hour.

Jenn realized she'd been silly to think she'd be able to get the book.

She was about to call Emily back, to return to the car, when Emily screamed.

Jenn looked beyond her daughter to see the dark silhouette of a figure on the other side of the building's translucent glass doors.

"Daddy!" Emily screamed, and jumped over all three steps in her hurry to get away.

"Of course it isn't," Jenn insisted. But her own heart was pounding as she felt empathy for the child. In this dark, cold loneliness, the figure was unnerving.

Emily hugged her tightly. The door opened. Emily buried her face in her mother's coat.

The figure stepped into the light.

"Ms. Galbraith," Herb Cole said. "What brings you here at this hour?"

Jenn patted her daughter. "It's only Mr. Cole, dollbaby."

The older man stared at the child as if trying to figure something out. Jenn realized that Emily had thrown a fit the two times he'd seen her. But she made no attempt to apologize.

"I . . . I forgot a book," she said. "I thought I might get into the building. Would you mind?"

"Not at all," Herb said, and opened the door again to let her inside.

He followed them.

"It's a lucky coincidence you came back," he said. "I was working late here myself, and I've received a disturbing call. I was able to get all my other staff, but you were out."

They walked together, their shoes sounding oddly hollow in the long, empty corridor.

"What's wrong?" Jenn asked.

Herb sighed deeply. "It's the Wallace girl, I'm afraid. Her mother called Dean Stone, who began to relay the information. Michelle's taken a turn for the worse. I'm not sure she'll last the night."

"Oh, my God!"

"I'm going there myself in a few minutes," Herb said. "There have been some other visitors, but I think the family prefers to be alone."

Jenn's book was suddenly forgotten once more. She shook her head.

"I've got to check on her," she said. She looked at Herb. "She's only nineteen, for God's sake. Maybe she'll pull through. Maybe she'll be all right."

"There's always hope," Herb said.

"I'm sure she'll be all right," Jenn babbled as she took

Emily by the hand and hurried from the building. In her worried state, she didn't say good-bye to her superior.

But she wasn't sure at all, and as she drove to the hospital, she became more and more fearful. Emily was quiet during the entire ride, as if she understood this was no time for play or chatter. Jenn sat her down in the lobby and made her promise not to move.

"I'll be out in a few minutes," she said. She found a book on a table and gave it to her daughter. "You can read this until I get back."

Emily held the book in her lap and watched her mother's retreating figure. When she disappeared into an elevator, Emily turned around to kneel on the cushion, her arms resting across the back of the chair as she observed her surroundings. The hospital lobby was a bustling place, filled with people with too much on their minds to pay much attention to one small girl. Emily sort of remembered being in the hospital, but it was an unhappy memory that she had pushed to the back of her mind. This was a place for sick people, even people who died. The only good thing about it was that she'd met Tara here.

Determining that nothing exciting was going to happen, she turned back around and bounced until she was comfortably seated. She opened the book and started to read. So many people had been surprised that she could read at such a young age. To Emily, it was nothing special. She'd been doing it since she was two, ever since she picked up a picture book and stunned her mother by rattling off the words under each photograph. The book she held now was a Berenstain Bears edition.

"That's a baby book," she heard Tara say. "How come Brother and Sister don't have real names?"

"I like it," Emily said. She put the book aside and smiled at her friend. "Hi, Tara! Did you come here to play with me?"

Tara nodded. "There's a girl named Michelle here who's talking about you all the time."

"Michelle!" Emily cried out, so loud that an old woman seated on the couch across from her looked up from her copy of *Reader's Digest*.

"Quiet!" Tara hushed her. "You want everyone to hear us?"

"You saw Michelle?" Emily whispered.

"Yeah, she's here now," Tara said matter-of-factly. "I don't like her. She's a snob. She told me to leave you alone."

"Michelle's nice!"

Tara sighed with resignation, leaning back in the chair.

"I've got everyone fighting to keep me from seeing you," she said. "First your daddy, now this Michelle person . . ."

"My daddy?" Emily repeated in a small voice.

Tara looked at her, eyes solemn.

"He's not here now," she said. "But he's getting stronger. I don't know how much longer I can keep you a secret from him."

She covered her ears and closed her eyes, as if to block out sights and sounds that Emily couldn't sense.

"He's so big, and so mean! I'm afraid of him, Emily! I'm afraid he's going to kill you, and your mother, and then he's going to hurt me, too! Just 'cause I helped you!"

A movement, slow and liquidy, caught the corner of Emily's eyes. She looked across the lobby at a bronze statue. It looked like nothing more than a blob at first, but when you got close up to it you realized each protrusion was a human figure, reaching out for help. And the flowerlike shape cupped up around all of them was a hand. "The Hand of Caring," it was called. Now those figures began to move, mouths crying out words Emily couldn't understand. A few of them screamed. Emily watched in fascination, unaware that she was the only one seeing this spectacle. She turned to Tara, who still had her eyes closed.

"Tara, look at that!"

"He's full of evil," Tara whispered. "Emily, you just aren't safe."

"Stop it!" Emily cried. "You're doing it, right? You're making the statue move!"

"Emily, Emily! You've got to come with me! It's the only way I can save you. Come with me, now!"

"I can't!"

Tara's eyes popped open. Instantly, the statue was a solid, lifeless piece of bronze again.

"What do you mean you can't? Why not?"

"I told Mommy I wouldn't move!"

Tara sneered at her. "You're stupid. You don't even know how much fun I have over here. But you'll come over when it gets too scary! When he tries to kill you all, you'll be yelling for me to help you. But I won't! I won't!"

Tara vanished. At the same time, the book Emily had been reading flew across the lobby and knocked the old woman's *Reader's Digest* out of her hands. She stood up abruptly and strode over to the child.

"Now, you listen to me! I've had about enough ..."

Suddenly, Emily felt herself being lifted up. She turned in surprise to see her mother, and hugged her tightly.

"Oh, leave her alone!" Jenn snapped. "She's just a baby!"

Ignoring the woman's protests, Jenn carried Emily to the front door. She stopped just long enough to help her with her jacket. Emily reached out and touched her mother's wet cheeks.

"What's wrong, Mommy? Why are you crying?"

"Michelle died, dollbaby," was her mother's simple reply.

Emily smiled and gave her mother a hug around the neck that caused Jenn to gasp.

"It's okay, Mommy," she said. "Tara saw her. She's gone into the light. I know the light is fun, and Michelle will be happy there."

Jenn grabbed up her daughter and held her tightly, sobbing.

"Don't cry, Mommy," Emily begged.

"I just . . . I can't stop thinking about Michelle's parents," Jenn said. She put her daughter down and held her hand as they walked out to the car. "They've lost their little girl."

"Michelle was a big girl."

"She'll always be their baby," Jenn said knowingly.

Emily smiled up at her mother, filled with understanding far beyond her years. She knew her mother was glad that she hadn't lost Emily, even though Emily was in the hospital even longer than Michelle.

"I'm not going to get hurt, Mommy," she said, squeezing Jenn's hand. "Tara is going to keep me safe. Maybe Michelle will help me, too."

"Maybe she will," Jenn whispered.

They said nothing more during the drive home. The rain had let up, but the sky was still full of clouds and the night was cold and dark. Driving along the twisting mountain roads was hazardous and made doubly so by the tears that blurred Jenn's vision. By the time she reached the Bayless property and pulled up to their little cottage, tears were spilling down her cheeks.

"Let's get inside, dollbaby," she choked. She just wanted to be alone with her thoughts.

She got out of the car and came around to help her daughter. A movement caused her to turn and look toward the woods. Someone was standing in the trees, half hidden so that only part of a dark blue jacket showed. But even from this distance, Jenn had a feeling they were being watched.

Emily had it, too. She took her mother's hand and squeezed tightly.

"Is that Daddy, Mommy?" she asked in a tiny, frightened voice.

"No," Jenn said simply. "I think it's Laura's neighbor. She told me that he sometimes comes to help."

"He's scary," Emily said.

"Let's go inside," Jenn replied, feeling eerie.

Once inside, though, she couldn't stop thinking about Michelle, wondering how a nineteen-year-old could die. Her heart went out to the girl's parents. She just didn't know what she'd do if she'd lost Emily in that accident. Once again, her hatred for Evan floated to the surface of her mind. She pushed it down with hateful thoughts, not wanting him to take up any of her time. Her reflections today would be for Michelle.

And for Emily. She looked at her daughter watching a video of the Future Fighters and wondered how she could take the news so well. Was it because she was only a baby? Really, how much of a concept of death could a four-year-old have? As intelligent as Emily was, she was still immature in some ways. Well, that was fine with Jenn. At least Emily wasn't dwelling on Michelle's death the way she seemed to dwell on Evan's.

Jenn felt an inner chill, recalling how Michelle had said Evan spoke to her. That was only her sickness talking, of course.

But how did she know about E.J.?

The chill stayed with her as she sat down and tried to do paperwork. Thoughts of Michelle kept interfering, and she finally put the papers aside. She decided a fire might be a nice idea. Not only would it warm up the place, but it might help change the mood. They needed a diversion, anyway.

"Come on, Emily," Jenn said. "I want you to help me carry in some firewood."

"A fireplace fire!" Emily cried. "Like at Grandma Galbraith's!"

It had been over a year since Emily was at her grandmother's, but she liked the fireplace so much she never forgot it. Jenn was glad she had a few fond memories of her grandmother. The fireplace had offered much more warmth than the woman.

Jenn hauled in a log, while Emily carried kindling.

"This is gonna be neat," Emily said, kneeling down to throw in the kindling.

"Do you remember the most important thing about using a fireplace?"

"Let a grown-up handle the matches."

Jenn laughed. "Okay, the second most important thing."

Emily held up her hands and tilted her head.

"You have to open the flue," Jenn said. "If you don't, you'll have smoke all over the house."

She knelt down and reached up into the darkness, her hand seeking the latch. Her fingers grabbed hold of it, and with a great yank she pulled it open. Instantly, a big, dusty cloud poured into the room.

"Smoke! Smoke!" Emily yelled.

Jenn coughed and moved away from the fireplace.

"Not smoke," she gagged. "Dust—no, old bird's nests!"

An avalanche of nests had tumbled out of the chimney, sending bits of dried twigs and leaves floating in the air.

"There must not be a cap on the chimney," Jenn said, batting at the dirty air. "Birds must have been building nests for—"

Emily's scream interrupted her. In a flash, the little girl was scrambling up a chair and onto the table. She jumped up and down, pointing at the floor, knocking over a vase of asters.

"Spiders, Mommy! Spiders!"

Jenn looked down at the floor, then jumped back herself. There were hundreds, perhaps thousands, of tiny red spiders scurrying in all directions. They took over the polished wood floor and the braided rug in seconds. With a cry of horror, Jenn grabbed Emily and ran from the house. She was grateful they were still wearing their coats from bringing in firewood, because a light snow had begun to fall. They raced through the darkness toward the big house, where Jenn pounded on the door. She was breathless when Laura pulled it open.

"We've got a problem," Jenn gasped.

Laura let her in, and Jenn told her what had happened. Immediately, Laura went to the phone to make a call. Then she sat Emily down at the table and quickly gave her milk and cookies to calm her down. Emily couldn't stop shaking, and Jenn knew it had nothing to do with the cold. The little girl was terrified of insects and spiders. Jenn wasn't bothered by just a few, but thousands of them . . .

She shivered herself.

"René DeLorris will be here in a little while," Laura said. "He's the best we can do to help us on a Saturday night. I doubt I'll be able to find an exterminator until Monday. In the meantime, let's see what a spray can can do."

She pulled on her coat, then tilted her head into the doorway. "Peter!"

Her son looked out from the den.

"Look after Emily. I'll be back in a minute."

Peter rolled his eyes, but said nothing.

"You wait here, honey," Laura said to Emily.

Her reply was so quiet they had to lean closer to hear her.

"I don't wanna sleep in that house."

"We'll talk about it," Jenn said.

The two women walked back to the little cottage in silence. Jenn hesitated at the door, then burst inside. Laura had the can aimed at the floor.

There wasn't a spider in sight. The nests were scattered in front of the hearth, but they were clean and dry.

"Where did they go?" Jenn asked in wonder.

She moved closer to the braided rug, but there wasn't a single spider to be found.

"I . . . I don't understand," Jenn said.

"Those little creeps move very fast," Laura said. "They probably crawled back into the fireplace."

With that, she began to spray the hearth.

"All of them?" Jenn asked. "There must have been thousands!"

"Nature is pretty amazing," Laura said, as if this were the most natural thing that ever happened. She put her hands on her hips and surveyed the mess. "Well, it might help to get rid of these nests."

Working together, the women cleaned up the floor. They were almost finished when they heard a knock. Laura let in a big bear of a man and introduced him to Jenn.

"This is René DeLorris," she said. "He's an old family friend—exterminator, handyman, and all-around helper. René, this is my new tenant, Jenn Galbraith. I'm afraid she's had a terrible scare."

Jenn instantly recognized the man who had been staring at her from the woods. It should have made her relax to meet René in person, but there was something creepy about his deep, dark eyes when he pulled back his hood to reveal a face grizzled with a day's growth of beard. He simply nodded at her and carried his big canister toward the fireplace. As he sprayed, Jenn said:

"It's more for my daughter than me. She hates spiders."

René said nothing until he was finished. Then he looked at Laura and said:

"Shouldn't have any more problems. I'll come back in the morning and cap the chimney. Repair those cracks, too . . ."

"Thanks," Jenn said.

René gave her another silent nod.

Laura put a hand on his arm.

"Come up to the house, René," she said. "I've made oatmeal raisin cookies, and there's a pot of coffee on the stove."

She turned to Jenn. "Do you think Emily could sleep at my place tonight? It might be better for her, after such a terrible fright."

Jenn had to agree. "All right. I appreciate it. And I need a little time alone after . . ."

She realized she hadn't told Laura about Michelle Wallace. But why should she? Laura probably didn't know Michelle, anyway. And this didn't seem the right time to talk about that tragedy.

"I'll have her back in the morning," Laura promised. "Don't worry. She'll be just fine with me."

She watched Laura and René as they walked up to the big house. A strange, worried feeling came over her. She realized she was still cold and was reminded that the flue was open. As she reached up to close it, a strong shudder racked her whole body.

"Stop it!" she told herself. "You're just upset about Michelle, and worried about Emily spending the night at a stranger's."

But she couldn't stop the uneasy feeling.

She went into the kitchen to make herself a cup of tea.

As she was sitting at the table, holding the cup close to her nose so that she'd smell cinnamon and rosehips instead of insecticide, a thought occurred to her.

Why hadn't Laura invited *her* to sleep over?"

"I guess she isn't such a good neighbor, after all," Jenn growled. "She doesn't give a damn that I'm choking on insecticide fumes!"

She felt herself growing more and more angry at Laura, her hands gripping the coffee mug. When she looked down to see that her knuckles had turned white, she forced herself to take a few deep breaths. Wasn't it more important that Emily was safe and sound tonight? Maybe Laura didn't feel right about having an adult as a houseguest. What right did Jenn have to criticize her?

"God, why am I so emotional lately?" Jenn asked out loud.

Self-analyzing, she decided that it was stress from all the things that had happened. She was projecting her anger at Evan toward a woman she hardly knew, she was grieving for Michelle . . .

"No more," she whispered, suddenly very tired.

She got up and walked slowly to her room, wanting nothing more than sleep right now. It didn't matter that there were papers to correct, or housework to catch up with. It only mattered that she was completely overcome with emotion, and only sleep would calm her down.

eleven

Up at the house, René stayed just long enough for a half cup of coffee. Then Laura walked him to the back door, where they stood talking quietly for a few moments. Emily watched the adults from her seat at the kitchen table, where she sipped a cup of hot chocolate. She wished she could hear what they were saying. She *could*, however, get a sense of their emotions. The old man had a grumpy look on his face, but Emily knew he was worried about something. Maybe it was the spiders. Maybe he was worried the spiders wouldn't die from his poison.

She shuddered. Taking a long sip of chocolate to warm herself, she turned her attention to Laura. Laura didn't seem worried at all. In fact, she seemed happy. She was even smiling as she gave René a bag of cookies and sent him on his way. Maybe that was a good thing. Maybe the spiders really were gone, or else Laura wouldn't seem so happy.

Emily returned Laura's smile when the woman came over to the table.

"Are the spiders gone?"

"Far, far away," Laura promised. "René took good care of them. Do you want more hot cocoa?"

"Mommy doesn't let me have cocoa at night," Emily said. "She says it will keep me awake.

Laura smiled at her the way a friend smiles when sharing a secret.

"I think tonight's different," she said. "If you want another, that's perfectly okay."

Emily thought about this. It was a big treat, and yet, she didn't really want any more.

"No thanks," she said.

"I've got some Disney tapes," Laura suggested. "You want to watch one?"

"Really?" Emily asked. "I'm not allowed to watched t.v. on a school night."

"Well, your mommy certainly has a lot of rules, doesn't she?" Laura commented. "Don't worry, it's just for tonight. And a video tape isn't really like t.v."

Emily didn't understand this, but she accepted it as great good fortune. She followed Laura into the den, where she sat in a brown leather recliner while Laura set up the VCR. Then Laura tucked an afghan around her.

"Cozy?"

Emily nodded, smiling, playing with a crocheted flower.

"I'll bring back a snack in a little while," Laura said.

She left the room. A moment later, Emily heard her talking with Peter. She shut out the voices by concentrating on the animated feature. She'd already seen this movie a few times, back when she lived in Buffalo. Emily knew the words by heart, and sang the songs loudly as they came on.

Laura didn't come back with a snack, but Emily hardly noticed she was so engrossed in the movie. Towards the end, the long day began to take its toll, and her eyelids began to flutter. She felt so warm and cuddly, so safe ...

A pair of bluebirds were twittering in the film.

"Emily ..."

Emily shifted a little, but couldn't seem to open her eyes.

"E.J., look at me!"

The sound of her nickname jerked her wide-awake. The pretty cartoon was gone, replaced by a screen full of fire. As Emily sat mesmerized by fear, a face appeared. It was watery at first, twisted and ugly. But when the features solidified, they were more horrible than any monster face.

Daddy was staring at her from the t.v. screen.

"I know you're out there, E.J. Why don't you open the door for me?"

Trained to be obedient, Emily couldn't help answering. "What door?"

The only door she saw was the entrance to the den, and it wasn't closed. What was her father talking about?"

"You've been a bad girl, and you're going to get it when I find you! You and that bitch mother of yours!"

Emily threw the afghan over her head and began to scream.

In a few moments, she felt the blanket being yanked from her. She kept her hands over her head, still screaming, waiting for her father's hand to grab her.

"What's the matter with you?" she heard Peter demand.

She dared to look up. Peter was frowning at her.

"Are you okay, kid?" he asked.

"Peter, for God's sake, move!" Laura practically shoved Peter out of the way, picked up the terrified child. She clucked and cooed and rocked her soothingly. Emily clung to her crying.

"What made her freak out like that?" Peter demanded.

"I don't know," Laura said. "Go on upstairs now, Peter. It's getting late."

With a groan, Peter left. Laura carried Emily up the stairs and into a bedroom.

"What happened, sweetie?" Laura asked as she laid Emily down on the bed.

"Daddy was on the t.v.," Emily choked out. "He was coming to get me. He's looking for a door."

Laura brushed back a tear-soaked lock of blonde hair from Emily's reddened face.

"A door!" Laura asked. Emily could see she didn't understand. "Your mommy told me that your daddy won't ever come back. You're safe."

"He was in the t.v. set," Emily insisted. "He was looking out."

"It was just a dream," Laura insisted

She stroked Emily's hair gently. Before long, the child's eyelids began to flutter.

"I forgot my nightie," Emily mumbled.

"Your sweatshirt will do for tonight," Laura replied, taking off Emily's pants and shoes and socks. She tucked the girl into the bed, then bent and kissed her.

"Goodnight, Sweet Angel," she whispered.

"Mommy calls me Dollbaby," Emily mumbled before falling asleep.

Laura left the door open a little so that some of the hall light could enter the room. She didn't see the other child who had suddenly appeared from the shadow.

Tara stared at Emily. Her jaw was set hard with anger. *Laura had called this other child 'Sweet Angel.'*

Then her face relaxed. A sardonic smile pulled at her lips. She, too, bent down to give Emily a kiss.

And Emily began to dream.

She was back home, at the apartment in Buffalo, standing outside the bathroom door. Everything looked bigger to her, and her underpants felt damp. She needed to be changed like a baby.

She saw herself in the mirror that backed the bathroom door. She was a baby. A baby with wet underpants and a bottle in one hand. But she could think just like a big girl. She could understand the mean, terrible things her parents were screaming at each other.

"I WANT OUT, EVAN! I WANT TO GET AWAY FROM YOU!"

"THEN YOU'LL GO WITHOUT EMILY. SHE'S MINE!!!"

Emily didn't want to be Daddy's. Daddy hurt her.

She reached up for their doorknob and turned it.

"Mommy, I'm wet . . ."

There was no bed in the room, only a huge spider web strung from one wall to the other. Mommy was caught in the middle, screaming and fighting.

"Hello E.J.," Daddy said. "Welcome to my parlor . . ."

It was a big, red spider that spoke to her. A spider with Daddy's head and eight eyes that looked just like his.

Emily woke up screaming. Instantly, a cold hand clamped over her mouth.

"Be quiet!" Tara commanded. "You'll wake Laura!"

Emily struggled, but Tara was stronger.

"You gonna be quiet?"

Emily nodded, and Tara moved her hand away.

"What're you scared of, anyway?"

"Daddy," Emily choked out, tears streaming down her face. "Daddy was an ugly spider and he was going to kill me and Mommy."

Tara stared at her.

"You want me to stay?" she asked. "Those people waiting on the other side don't like it when I come, but I can stay. I don't care what they like."

"Okay." Emily said in a small voice. Somehow, she felt safer when her friend was here. She settled back on her pillow.

"So, what was wrong with your daddy?" Tara asked. "Was he really, really mean?"

"He hurt me," Emily said. She turned her head away. "I'm tired."

"So go to sleep," Tara said. "I'll stay."

But the moment Emily's eyes were closed, Tara vanished. Emily fell asleep without knowing her friend had abandoned her.

As horrible as it had been, the nightmare faded over the course of Emily's sleep, and she woke up with only a vague memory of it. She did, however, recall seeing Tara, and was disappointed her friend had left. She thought that Tara probably had to go home to her own mommy, and then to school.

Thoughts of the Center made her happy, and she hurried downstairs to the kitchen with a smile on her face.

"Good morning!" Laura said cheerfully.

"Hi," said Emily. "Do you have cereal? I like Cheerios."

"I just happen to have Cheerios," said Laura, taking down the box. She began to fill a bowl. "Did you sleep okay, honey?"

"Yep." Emily said. She climbed onto a chair and leaned across the kitchen table to smell the fresh bouquet of mums at its center. Then she sat down and turned so her legs were straddling the chair. She put her arms across the back and rested her chin in her elbows.

"Is Tara gonna come back?"

Laura paused, holding a container of milk.

"Who?"

"Tara, my friend," Emily said. "Is she gonna come back today? She came last night to play with me."

"I don't know, honey," Laura said, setting the cereal bowl in front of her. "Eat up!"

Emily turned around and ate. Laura stood behind her, playing with her hair.

"You have the most beautiful hair," she said. "So silky and yellow. You and your mother should have been models."

Milk dripped from Emily's lower lip. She wiped it away as she spoke.

"Don't wanna be a model," she said. "I'm gonna teach trickanomady just like Mommy."

Laura laughed. "Trigonometry."

"That's what I said."

"Do you ever do special things with your hair?" Laura asked. "Do you ever curl it or braid it?"

Emily made a face. "Braids hurt."

"Oh, but I think you'd look especially pretty," Laura said. "There's a style called a 'rope' that doesn't pull at all. Can I try it on you?"

Emily shrugged, more interested in her breakfast.

Laura left the room, then returned with a comb and elastic band. As Emily finished her cereal, she brushed and roped her hair. Unlike a braid, where a strand went between the other two, a rope involved putting it across both of them. The result was a long, pretty twist. She finished it off with the elastic band.

"I wish I had a ribbon," she said. "Come on, take a look at how pretty you are today.

Emily dropped her spoon into the empty bowl and followed Laura from the room. In the bathroom Laura lifted her up to stand on the counter. Emily pulled the cord of hair sideways.

"Cool!" she said. She got on her knees and climbed down. "I wanna show Mommy. Can I go home now?"

"Sure, as soon as you're dressed." Laura said. "Do you want me to help you?"

Emily gave her an impatient look. "I'm not a baby. I can even tie my shoes!"

"Good for you!"

A short time later, they were walking through the front door of the cottage. Jenn picked Emily up to hug her.

"I missed you, Dollbaby," she said. "Did you sleep good?"

"I dunno," Emily said. "Look at my hair, Mommy!"

She turned around proudly.

"Very pretty," Jenn said. "That was nice of Laura."

"It wasn't anything," Laura said. She leaned closer to Jenn. "Any more of them?"

"Not a one, thank God," Jenn whispered. Louder, she said: "Emily, you have to change for school."

Emily ran into her room to dress.

"I really appreciate what you did last night," Jenn told Laura. "You didn't have to take Emily in. We hardly know each other."

"She was a delight," Laura said. "She's welcome back any time."

"I hope she won't need to," Jenn said. "I really missed her when I woke up this morning." She sighed. "But then, it was a good time for me to be alone. I had a lot on my mind."

"Anything I can help with?" Laura asked, looking concerned.

"No," Jenn said sadly. "One of my students died yesterday."

"Oh, no!"

"Her name was Michelle Wallace," Jenn said. "She was only 19 years old. I'm surprised Emily didn't mention her. She was very fond of Michelle, but she's hardly reacted to the news at all."

Except to say Michelle was happy in 'the light.' She ignored the thought. Laura would think she was crazy if she mentioned it.

"Well, she's only four," Laura said. "Children accept death much more easily than we do. Perhaps she thinks Michelle simply went away."

"Perhaps," Jenn said with a shrug.

Emily came back out, dressed in a blue jogging suit with a big yellow cat on the shirt. She'd traded her play sneakers for nicer school ones. As she wriggled into her coat, Laura reached for her backpack. But Jenn was faster, and in a moment she had it around her daughter's shoulders.

"Well, thanks again, Laura," Jenn said. "We'll see you later."

As usual both mother and daughter enjoyed their days at their respective schools. Emily was a typical chatterbox on the way home, but not once did she mention Michelle. Jenn tried to remember Laura's suggestion that children take things differently than adults. If only she could be as accepting as Emily—but she could never simply accept the death of a nineteen-year-old!

As they were driving up the road leading to the cottage, Emily fell abruptly silent.

"What's wrong, Dollbaby?"

"I feel sad again," Emily said. "How come I always feel sad when we come home?"

Jenn frowned. Was it true? Did this place make them

sad? Their moods certainly seemed to change when they arrived here.

But that was ridiculous. A place couldn't make you sad. Sure, it was run-down and the woods made it too dark, but that couldn't make much of a difference.

"We just have to get used to this place," she said. "It's nothing like any of our old homes."

They got out of the car. Jenn pointed to a doll left on the grass, and Emily picked it up. She was pouting as they entered the house, swinging the doll by its hair. She stopped in the doorway and gazed worriedly at the floor.

"They're all gone," Jenn said, understanding. "Mr. DeLorris did a good job."

Slowly Emily entered the house.

"Can I sleep at Laura's again?" she asked.

"No, Emily," Jenn said. "I want you here tonight, in your own room."

"But the spiders, Mommy! What if they come back?"

"They won't." Jenn said. "Mr. DeLorris got rid of them."

She could see that Emily needed a diversion.

"Come on and sit with me on the couch," she said. "Maybe I can tell you a story. What do you want to hear? Goldilocks? Red Riding Hood?"

"The traveler and the old man!"

Jenn laughed. "Okay, then. You comfortable?"

Emily nodded, resting her head in her mother's lap. Jenn stroked her hair as she spoke.

"One day," she began," a traveler met an old man walking along the road. Suddenly, the traveler pointed to a bush and cried out."

Emily interrupted her. "There's a monster in that bush!"

"That's right," said Jenn. "And the old man said: "Don't be silly. There is no monster in that bush. The traveler replied: " 'Yes, there is! It's a monster with green fangs, orange hair and purple eyes!' "

The old man insisted it wasn't there.

"Take a look for yourself," said the traveler. "A monster with green fangs, orange hair and purple eyes is hiding in that bush!"

" 'Very well,' said the old man."

Jenn looked down at Emily, who was smiling in anticipation of the story's end.

"The old man went up to the bush, then turned back to the traveler."

" 'Your monster isn't here.' "

" 'Are you sure?' asks the traveler. 'I'm certain I saw a monster with green fangs, orange hair and purple eyes in that bush!' "

Emily laughed out loud.

" 'Oh, there is a monster, all right.' " Jenn continued. " 'But this one has green fangs, orange hair and . . .' "

"RED EYES!" Emily howled. She turned on her back and giggled.

"You never get tired of that story," Jenn said, tickling her. "You're just too silly!"

Emily's blue eyes were shining as she looked up at her mother with a smile.

"I love you, Mommy," she said.

"I love you, too, Emily."

The little girl pulled herself up and hugged her mother so tightly it seemed she didn't want to let go.

"Be my Mommy forever, okay?"

"Emily?" Jenn asked, taken aback. It was an unusual question. "What's this about?"

"I don't think Tara is allowed to be with her Mama," Emily said.

"Well, no one's going to tell me I can't be with you," Jenn reassured.

Emily kissed her all over her face.

"I love you. I love you, I love you!"

Jenn gave her daughter one last hug and kiss, then pried her away.

"I love you, too Dollbaby," she said. "But you know what? I've really got to get some work done now."

"Tell me another story!"

"Later," Jenn said. "There's a whole pile of papers on that table that I have to correct before dinner . . ."

Emily giggled and kissed her again. This time, Jenn managed to put the child off her lap. She loved it when Emily was affectionate, but there was something more here. Why was she suddenly acting so *clingy?*

"Go on and play in your room for a while," Jenn said. "Mommy needs some quiet time."

Emily walked away grumbling, her good mood suddenly broken.

"Wish I could go to Laura's," she said. "She'd tell me two stories!"

Jenn sighed impatiently, but turned her attention to her paperwork. She rubbed her neck surprised to find that it actually ached where Emily had embraced her. A half hour later she heard Emily talking out loud. She went to investigate, and as she reached for the door she heard a second voice. It sounded just like the child she'd heard the other night, when Peter and Emily were playing together.

When she opened the door, however, only Emily looked up at her.

Of course only Emily. Who else did you expect? Tara?

"Hi, Mommy."

"Hi, Emily," Jenn said. "It's time to get ready for bed."

"Okay," Emily said, putting aside a book.

Of course—she was just doing voices for her characters.

"It would be fun to sleep at Laura's again."

"No more of that," Jenn warned. "You're acting bratty. Come out and kiss me goodnight when you're dressed."

Fifteen minutes later, when Emily hadn't come out, Jenn went to check on her. She found Emily tucked into bed, fast asleep. A feeling of disappointment washed over her.

It was the first time Emily had ever gone to sleep without kissing her goodnight.

twelve

Although she hated the rituals surrounding death, Jenn knew it was only right to attend Michelle's wake. Laura was happy to baby-sit Emily, and before Jenn was even out the door she had the child seated at a table with a slice of pumpkin pie and a glass of cider.

"You be good, dollbaby," Jenn said.

"She's always an angel," Laura replied.

Emily kissed her mother good-bye, finished her pie, then reached into the bag she'd brought and pulled out a jigsaw puzzle.

"Can I do this here?" she asked.

Laura picked it up. Her eyebrows disappeared under her dark bangs.

"Three hundred pieces?" she asked. "You can do this?"

"I can do five hundred pieces," Emily said proudly. "But I like this picture. I like the teddy bears."

"Well, why don't you take it into the den?" Laura asked. "I have to clean up the kitchen."

Emily hurried off. She sat down on the floor between the couch and the coffee table and opened the puzzle. As she was searching for outside pieces, Tara appeared at her side.

"Hi," she said.

"Hi, Tara," Emily replied. "You want to do a puzzle with me?"

"Laura makes good pies, doesn't she?"

"Yep." Emily said, not looking up from her task.

"They don't have pies over here," Tara said, her voice wistful.

"That's dumb," Emily said. "I hope I don't ever go there."

Tara picked up a puzzle piece and studied it.

"You will," Tara said. "Your daddy wants you here right now."

Emily froze.

"Don't worry," Tara said. "I won't tell him where to find you." She stood up. "Let's go up to the attic."

"I can't do that," Emily said. "I'm not allowed."

"Says who?" Tara replied with a click of her tongue. "There's something really neat up there. I want to show it to you."

"What?"

"You gotta come see!"

"I don't want to get in trouble," Emily protested.

But Tara was pulling her to her feet, and Tara was a lot stronger.

"Okay," Emily relented. "But we better hurry. I don't want Laura to get mad."

"Laura doesn't get too mad," Tara promised. "Not like your mother."

Emily followed her up to the attic. At Tara's command,

she climbed up onto the white bed and looked out the window. Moonlight shone over the yard, trees casting shadows like grabbing arms. The view was cold and dark and ugly. Emily shivered.

"I don't see anything, Tara."

"Keep looking," Tara said. "Over there, that big black spot in the grass."

Emily stretched her gaze as far as possible, until she saw the spot Tara was talking about.

"What's that?"

"A pond," Tara said. "Keep watching."

Emily crossed her arms over the windowsill and put her chin down. What was so exciting about a pond?

"Watch," Tara whispered.

Suddenly a figure stepped out of the shadows. For a moment, Emily was terrified that it was her father. Then she saw Michelle looking up at her! Michelle looked strange, as if she was made of a cloud. Her voice was no louder than the wind that carried it, yet Emily could hear her clearly through the glass. Michelle held her arms up toward the window.

"Get away, Emily! Get away!"

"Michelle?" Emily called.

"No!" Tara snapped. "Not now!"

She yanked Emily away from the window, Emily swung around to yell at her, but suddenly she felt a sharp pain in her stomach. Prickles of ice started working their way up Emily's arms. Her heartbeat quickened, and her mouth went dry.

Something bad was going to happen. That's why Michelle had told her to get away! She began to shake. She wanted to jump off the bed, to run downstairs, to go home to Mommy so Mommy could make the bad feeling GO AWAY!

"Oh, good, she's gone," Tara said. "She's such a pain!"

She tugged at Emily, pulling her up with amazing strength and forcing Emily to look out the window again. She searched the grounds for Michelle, but the girl had vanished. Thunder rumbled, and for a moment Emily glanced at the sky. It was full of stars, cloudless.

"It's not going to rain, silly," Tara said, reading her mind. "That isn't thunder. It's a horse. Look!"

Emily followed the direction of Tara's pointed finger. A large black horse was galloping across the grass, heading toward the pond. Emily straightened herself up, her mouth open in wonder. She was still afraid, but her curiosity was just a little stronger. Where had the horse come from?

As it came close to the pond, it reared up, legs scrambling through the air. A sharp, terrifying whinny sounded through the night, loud enough to be heard up in the attic. Tears welled up in Emily's eyes. She knew the horse was frightened, too, and there was nothing she could do to help it.

The horse's forelegs crashed down into the pond. Then, to Emily's horror, the edges of the pond seemed to move in and out. As if the earth was a monster, and the pond its mouth, the edges of the ground swelled up. They grew like impossible little mountains, taller and taller.

Suddenly, the earth snapped shut around the horse, devouring it.

Emily screamed, throwing herself down on the bed and covering her head.

Tara stroked her hair for a few moments, not speaking. Then she said: "You can look now, it's gone away."

"What . . . what happened to the horse? Why did the ground eat the horse?"

"It was a bad horse. Mama had to cut it all up."

"Why?"

"Look outside, Emily, It's okay now. The horse is gone, and we can play together now."

"I won't look! I won't! I WON'T!"

"Emily?" This wasn't Tara's voice. Emily went silent, but sobs still racked her small body.

"Emily, how did you get up here?"

It was Laura. Where had Tara gone? Slowly, Emily sat up and looked around. Tara always disappeared when there was trouble. Emily wasn't supposed to be in the attic, and now Laura would be angry. Tara had gotten Emily into trouble again!

"I . . . I don't know," Emily lied.

"Poor thing," Laura said. "Come on, I'll take you downstairs."

Obediently, Emily took her hand and walked downstairs with her. She wondered if she should ask about the horse, but then she'd have to say that Tara had brought up here. Then she'd catch it for lying, she was sure.

But Laura didn't seem angry. Instead she brought Emily back into the den and sat down on the couch with her.

"Why don't we finish this together?" she suggested.

Emily felt a little disoriented, but the puzzle looked like enough fun to distract her from the fright she'd seen through the attic window. Still, she asked, "Laura, do you have a horse?"

"We used to," Laura said. "But I sold it along with my other animals."

It was a bad horse.

"Did you like it? Was it a good horse?"

"Phoenix was a lovely animal," Laura said. "Why do you ask?"

Emily shoved a puzzle piece into place.

"I dunno," she said.

Mommy had to cut it all up.

"If it was a bad horse, would you kill it?"

"Emily!" Laura cried. "What kind of question is that? I'd never hurt . . ."

She paused, and Emily turned to look up at her. There was sympathy in her eyes and she held open her arms.

"I know what this is about," Laura said. "You probably had a bad dream in the attic. Maybe you're sad because your friend Michelle is gone now."

Emily wanted to tell her about seeing Michelle in the yard. But then she'd have to talk about Tara, and explain about the horse, and then Laura would know she was wide awake when she went up to the attic. But then, maybe Laura wouldn't be mad. Maybe Laura could help her understand things. She was really nice. She never yelled, not the way Mommy yelled sometimes. But what if she was just pretending to be nice? What if . . .

Emily was so confused that she burst into tears.

"Oh, you poor, sweet angel," Laura cooed, lifting the small child onto her lap. "It's okay. Don't you worry. It's okay to cry about Michelle."

Emily just went on crying, not for Michelle, not for any reason she really understood.

Michelle's wake brought back the questions Jenn had pushed from her mind. She sat at the end of a row of teachers. Noreen sat to one side, dabbing her eyes with a lace-trimmed hankie. Herb Cole was on her other side, chewing his lip. In the row of students behind Jenn, Roy Javier sat wearing sunglasses that Jenn was certain hid tears. Michelle's roommates cried openly. Most of the kids sat stony-faced, some with silent tears streaming down their faces.

Because this was the last night of the wake, there was a small ceremony. Jenn watched the minister as he spoke, but she hardly heard him. She couldn't help thinking about Michelle's strange warning. How had she known to call Emily "E.J."? She'd racked her brain but couldn't remember ever mentioning that nickname. She'd never used it herself, because it really upset Emily. If only she could talk to Michelle once again!

At the wake's end, Noreen hooked an arm through her elbow and they walked out together.

"The funeral's tomorrow," she said. "Two funerals, and this is only the start of the school year."

"It can't continue like this," Jenn insisted. She bit a nail. "It just can't."

"They say death—"

"Don't!" Jenn snapped. The last thing she needed to hear was that old adage that "death comes in threes."

When they reached Jenn's car, Noreen gave her a hug. "You want to stop for coffee? To talk things over?"

Jenn shook her head. Noreen started to say something, but seemed to understand that Jenn just wanted to be alone.

Jenn drove home after the service with a strange feeling inside. Maybe she should have told Noreen what was on her mind. Discussing it with another adult might help make sense of it all. Emily had known Michelle was dead even before Jenn mentioned it. She'd spoken of Michelle being in "the light." Tara had told her so. Then again, premonitions and unseen children sounded too much like the supernatural, something Jenn didn't accept. Noreen would probably laugh at her and insist that Tara was nothing more than a stage.

"I wish Tara would go away and leave us alone," Jenn growled, pretending Tara was a real person and not just an imaginary playmate. She supposed she had to be grateful for the fact that Emily hadn't mentioned her in a few days.

Emily was solemn when Jenn retrieved her from Laura's house.

"I think she had a bad dream," Laura whispered. "Maybe you'd better talk to her about Michelle."

Jenn nodded, agreeing. She thanked Laura for baby-sitting, then walked hand in hand to the cottage with her daughter. Inside, she took her to the couch and sat down with her in her lap.

"Do you want to talk a little while?" she asked.

Emily shook her head.

"Laura says you had a bad dream. Was it about Michelle?"

"It was about a horse," Emily said. "The ground ate it up. Michelle was there, but she went away."

Jenn didn't understand the significance of the horse, but she thought it must symbolize something.

"I went to a special place to say prayers for Michelle," she said. "All her friends were there."

"I wasn't."

"I know, dollbaby," Jenn said. "I meant, all her big friends. They all miss her very much. I think she must know that."

Emily took a lock of her mother's hair and began to play with it.

"Maybe she didn't hear them," she said, "because she was here. But she went away before the horse got ate up."

"Eaten up," Jenn corrected. Then she felt stupid—as if grammar mattered at a time like this!

Emily climbed off her lap.

"I'm hungry," she announced and went into the kitchen.

As they shared a snack neither one mentioned Michelle. Jenn watched Emily almost constantly, but if the child was grieving for Michelle, she didn't show it. She played and ate as usual, except she never smiled or laughed even once.

At bedtime, Jenn asked if Emily wanted a story.

"No thanks, Mommy."

"All right, then," Jenn said, leaning forward to kiss her. "Sleep well, dollbaby."

Jenn went to her own room. Although the solemnity of

the day had curbed much physical activity, mental stress had rendered her exhausted. She soon fell asleep. When she entered her first dream cycle of the night, her mind produced something that was more memory than dream.

It was years earlier, back in the days when she and Evan were newlyweds living in an apartment in Buffalo. Evan had been so handsome then, so full of hope for the future.

"Maybe I'll write a play. Maybe a comedy."

"You can be very funny, Evan. I think that's a great idea."

But then there had been budget cutbacks as the governor decided to cut school aid. Neither Jenn nor Evan was tenured, but it was Evan who lost his job. He couldn't find another, and it upset him greatly.

"What about that play? It might be a good time to start it."

"Yeah, and I'll call it The Big-Mouthed Wife."

By then there were so many cutting remarks, so many nights when Evan came home drunk. But Jenn had stuck by him, still loving him. He'd get through this—*they'd* get through this.

"I'm just trying to help, Evan. I love you."

Puppy-dog eyes. Tears of sorrow.

"Oh, God, Jenn. I'm sorry. I love you, too! I hate myself when I hurt you like that!"

And he'd shown it. It was probably the last time she'd felt good making love to him. His problems with drugs started soon after that night. But for the moment, in the memory and in the dream, his touch was sweet and gentle.

Suddenly, he grabbed her thigh and squeezed as hard as he could. Jenn yelped and flipped onto her back. The young, handsome Evan was gone, replaced by a crazed drug addict. His hair was a mess, his eyes red, his beard untrimmed.

"Let me go!"

"I will when you show me which door is Emily's," he offered, his voice crackling like burning wood. *"There are millions of doors, doors to the living. But I can't find Emily's!"*

He smelled as if he hadn't bathed in weeks. Jenn struggled to get out from under him, but it seemed he weighed several hundred pounds.

"Get away from me, Evan! You're a pig! A PIG!"

And suddenly she was awake. She lay in bed breathing fast and hard, once more in the little cottage in Vermont. Evan was dead and gone now. She was safe, alone.

No—not alone.

She had the feeling there was another presence in the bed. At first, it was just a sensation, and then it was a smell. Something like . . .

She thought a moment.

Something like a butcher shop.

Slowly, she reached for the lamp and turned it on.

Slowly, she turned and looked . . .

. . . and went into fast-forward when she saw the pig. She jumped from the bed, screaming. The huge thing lay there like a dead lover. The head was cracked and bloodied. Its mouth hung open, sharp teeth surrounding a silent squeal.

Sickened, Jenn ran from the room. She had to get Emily and get out of here!

To her horror, Emily wasn't in her bed.

"EMILY?"

"Mommy?" The voice was small, far away.

Jenn swung around. The bathroom light was on. She went to the open door and looked in, but again she didn't find her daughter.

She realized that Emily must have gone into her room in search of her.

"Oh, Emily!" she called. "Emily, wait!"

Jenn moved as fast as she could, nearly crashing into Emily's small body as she entered her room. Emily was standing at the foot of the bed. She looked up at her mother with hooded, sleepy eyes.

"Where'd you go?" she asked in a babyish voice, yawning.

Jenn couldn't answer her. Slowly, she bent down and picked up her daughter. Her eyes were focused on the bed the whole time.

She would have sworn she was wide awake over the past few minutes. She would have sworn the pig was real.

But if it had existed, there was no sign of it now. Not even blood.

"Let's sleep in your bed tonight," Jenn whispered. "Won't that be fun?"

Emily didn't answer. She had fallen asleep against Jenn's shoulder.

Jenn looked back into the room just before shutting her door, half expecting the pig to rematerialize. Then she went into Emily's room and laid down on the bed. It was only a twin-size, and crowded. But there was no way in hell she would return to her own room until morning.

thirteen

Jenn was awake half the night, too full of worries to sleep. She had seen a panther a few days ago, when none was there. She had awakened to find a pig in her bed, but the pig didn't exist. And both times she'd heard Evan as clearly as if he were alive. Were they dreams, or hallucinations? If they were hallucinations, she was in trouble. She needed someone to help her understand why she was imagining such vivid images. Had she been hurt more in the accident than she realized? But Emily had had the head injury, not her!

And Emily sometimes heard Evan, too . . .

Jenn didn't know what to do. Would Pinebridge College accept a teacher with mental problems? Would they worry she might harm the students? Jenn knew in her heart that would never happen, but if things got worse, could she herself be completely sure of that?

Was she going crazy?

The next morning, the phone rang while they were eating breakfast. Emily answered it and announced with delight that Aunt Rosalie was on the line.

"Hi, Jenn!" Rosalie said cheerfully. "I'm glad I caught you before you left."

"What's up?" Jenn asked. "Is something wrong?"

Rosalie never called her during the week, let alone this early in the morning. Something terrible must have happened! Jenn gripped the phone wire, twisting it.

"Oh, I know it's early to call," Rosalie said. "But I was just so excited about Travis's idea. He thought it might be fun if we drove up there to visit you during Thanksgiving vacation. What do you think?"

Jenn's laugh was short and nervous. That terrible dream last night had made her paranoid! The news was good—perfect. The idea of family visiting lifted her spirits at once.

"Oh, it would be wonderful," she said. "You know how much Emily enjoys her cousins."

The two sisters made plans. They chatted just a little longer, until it was time for Jenn to leave for work. Jenn said good-bye to her sister, then packed a lunch for Emily.

"Your cousins are coming this Thanksgiving," she said. "Won't that be fun?"

Emily jumped up and down, clapping.

Jenn felt elated herself. Maybe she didn't need counseling at all. Maybe she just needed the support of family. After all, she had no relatives and few friends up here. Loneliness could do things to a person, she decided.

Emily tugged at her pants leg.

"What about Halloween? How come they can't come for Halloween?"

"Because Halloween isn't enough time for that long a

trip," Jenn said. "Besides, it's just around the corner. Aunt Rosalie and Uncle Travis have to make plans."

"Just around the corner?" Emily echoed. "You mean, in a few days?"

"That's right," Jenn said with a smile, glad to have something pleasant to think about instead of funerals and nightmares. "It'll be here before you know it."

But Halloween didn't come fast enough for Emily, and when it finally did she was a bundle of energy. She woke up early in the morning and came bounding into the kitchen with a smile on her face.

"We're having a party and a parade at school!" she announced.

Halloween had come far too fast for Jenn. She'd been so busy that she had never exchanged Emily's costume She dreaded a confrontation.

"That's nice," she said. "I'm going to come see the parade and take pictures of you in your nice silver costume."

Make it sound appealing, and maybe Emily will forget she hates it.

But Emily had forgotten nothing. She stamped her foot and pouted.

"I don't want to be Tammi!" she cried. "Tammi is a geek! I want the gold costume!"

Jenn looked Emily straight in the eye and said calmly: "Fine. Don't wear the costume. Don't march in the parade. Don't trick-or-treat."

A look of horror came over Emily's face.

"But . . . but it's geeky," she whispered, uncertain.

"Do what you want to do."

Emily was quiet through breakfast, thinking. Jenn found herself staring at the child, wondering if "Tara" would show up and influence Emily's decision. When her daughter was through eating, she went into her room and noiselessly dressed in her school clothes. She put on her favorite jogging suit and her new sneakers, then came out to retrieve the lunch box and bookbag her mother had packed for her. She didn't say a word.

"Are you okay, dollbaby?" Jenn asked.

"Yep," Emily said softly, opening the front door.

Jenn packed a camera in her purse, then went into her daughter's bedroom and located the costume. She tossed it into the back seat, ever hopeful, and drove off to Pinebridge College. Somehow she wasn't surprised that Emily did a complete 180 when they entered the center. It seemed all she had to do was see the other kids in their costumes. She even beamed proudly when little girls came up to admire her as Jenn helped her into her costume.

"You have to wait outside the fence, Mommy," Emily told her. "That's where mommies watch the parade."

"Okay," Jenn said, giving her a kiss.

As she stood near the fence, Jenn listened to other mothers chatting with each other. She realized she had never taken the time to get to know any of them. Well, she reasoned, she was very busy between teaching and traveling back and forth from the farm. But it still bothered her that none of the mothers offered her more than a perfunctory greeting.

These thoughts flew away when the door opened and the children came marching out. They sang a Halloween song to the tune of "Frere Jacques." Emily was so cute that Jenn used up a whole roll of film taking her picture. When the parade was over, her daughter ran up to the fence and whispered:

"Tara says silver is a nice color, now."

Jenn was pulling into her parking space just as Nick Hasken was chaining up his bike. He smiled and waved to her. Jenn took a deep breath, trying to decide if she was in the mood for him today. But there was no getting away, since he was walking in the same direction.

"Happy Halloween, Jenn," he said. "I'll bet Emily's really excited."

Well, there was no point in being rude.

"She sure is," Jenn said. "They're having a party at school this morning."

Nick nodded in response. They walked along without speaking for a few moments. Jenn found herself looking around, hoping to see someone else.

"I was wondering," Nick said. "Would you like to join me for lunch? I'm getting tired of the cafeteria, and there's a nice little coffee shop in town."

Jenn turned to him with a surprised look on her face. Was he asking her on a date?

Don't be an idiot, Jenn. Lunch is not a date!

"I . . . um . . ."

"We have breaks at the same time today," Nick pointed out. "We can get back in plenty of time."

He smiled.

"They have the best cream pie this side of Boston," he tempted.

Jenn had to admit that it was nice to be attractive to someone. Nick didn't seem to be anything like Evan, although she couldn't be sure about this.

"Well, I usually have lunch with Noreen," she said, hesitant.

His face fell. "Oh. I wouldn't want to interrupt your plans. I'll catch you later, Jenn."

He started to walk away. Something leaped in Jenn's heart, and she found herself changing her mind. She took a deep breath for courage.

"I suppose Noreen won't mind if I break our routine," she said. "I think Marta D'Achille's going to join her, anyway."

Nick stopped and turned around, looking hopeful. She couldn't help smiling at him.

"And I love cream pie."

Nick's smile widened into a triumphant grin.

"Great! I'll meet you at the math building at 11:45," he said.

They reached the science building and parted company. Jenn was surprised that she felt excited, not nervous, as she walked on to her own classes. And when students looked at her and started to laugh behind their hands, she realized she was smiling broadly.

Well, maybe I'm just happy that, for once, something nice is happening to me.

She met Noreen between classes and explained the situation.

"I knew you two would hit it off!" Noreen said, delighted.

"We aren't hitting anything, Noreen," Jenn said. "This is just a friendly meal shared by two colleagues."

"Sure it is," Noreen said in a droll way.

When lunchtime arrived, Nick met her as promised and they walked to her car together. They talked about trivial, friendly things all the way to the coffee shop. It was housed in a little saltbox-style building tucked between a grocery and a hardware store, a place out of time.

"I don't think I've ever seen this building," Jenn admitted as they pushed open the sky-blue front door. "The Cornucopia—what a cute name."

"It's easy to pass by," Nick said. "The stores to either side overwhelm it. It's just a shame they have to build on every available piece of land."

As Nick asked for a table, Jenn looked up at a sign over the entrance to the dining room.

"It's been here since 1789," she said, charmed by the rustic surroundings of dark wood and simple furnishings.

A waitress in colonial garb led them to a table and handed them menus. Jenn chose a New England boiled dinner. For a moment she wondered if her selection was a subconscious attempt to influence this luncheon, to keep it bland and safe. She shook off the idea, reasoning she was no psychiatrist, and closed her menu. Nick was still making his selection. He wasn't what she'd call a handsome man—more the "regular guy" type. Well, Evan had been handsome and hadn't proved to be worth much. Nick was losing some of his light brown hair and could probably stand to lose fifteen pounds. But there was a warm glow in his eyes when he closed his menu and looked across the table at her. And as lunch progressed, she realized he was looking straight at her when she spoke, really listening. Evan had always been easily distracted, even before his troubles.

But Simone Trenton had said Nick was "strange."

She pushed the thought aside. Whatever Simone's reasons for thinking that way, Jenn had the right to form her own opinion.

And her opinion was that Nick was a nice guy.

"Are you going to take Emily trick-or-treating around your house?" he asked.

"We're going to walk through town," Jenn said. "It's a half mile to the next farm, so we can't go around our own neighborhood."

Nick cut into his Yankee pot roast and savored a bite before speaking again.

"Where is that, exactly?" he asked. "I know you have a long commute."

Jenn told him, and explained the circumstances that had led to her meeting Laura Bayless.

"Laura Bayless," Nick said. "Why does that name sound familiar?"

"I have no idea," Jenn admitted. "But I suppose you're

bound to hear and remember a lot of names in an area with a small population like this one."

Nick was thoughtful as he continued to eat.

"Probably," he said at last. "It's just that it seems I should know that name. Well, anyway, I'm glad she was there for Emily. It gives me chills to think what might have happened."

"I think Emily's guardian angel was there that day," Jenn said.

"Well, guardian angel or not," Nick said, "they ought to be more careful about their playground equipment. They shouldn't have a toy that a kid's jacket string can catch on so easily."

Jenn had never thought of that.

"You're right," she said. "I'll have to write to the parks department about it."

Conversation continued in that safe, friendly vein. There was a brief altercation over Nick's paying the bill, but Jenn finally made him understand that his paying in full made her nervous. They agreed to split the tab.

As they were driving back to the school, he brought up a topic they'd both been avoiding.

"It was a nice turnout for Michelle's wake, wasn't it?" he said.

"I felt a lot of love there," Jenn agreed.

And something else, right, Jenn? Questions and worries . . .

"School's been in session barely seven weeks," Nick said, "and we've had two funerals already. I keep thinking about Simone and Joe. I still can't believe what happened to them. Did you hear that the fire department finally ruled out arson?"

Jenn was startled. She had only skimmed over the newspaper in recent days and had missed that story.

"I didn't even know the fire was suspicious," she said. "I thought the furnace blew up."

"Kim Stone authorized new burners to be put in a few houses last spring," Nick said. "The Trentons had one of them. The fire department still can't figure out exactly what caused it to blow, but they've just about concluded it was a manufacturing error."

Jenn closed her eyes in disgust but opened them quickly to watch the road.

"Whatever happened," she said, "it was senseless. Were you friends with the Trentons?"

Nick laughed as if recalling fond memories.

"Simone got me my job here," he said. "We were always joking with each other. She called me the 'mad scientist,' and I called her a 'numbers nerd.' Simone was a great person. So was Joe, in his own way. A quiet guy, with a head filled with facts. The kids really liked both of them."

"So I gathered," Jenn said.

They'd reached the college. After she parked the car and they got out, Jenn thanked Nick for a nice time. As nervous as she'd been, lunch had been a thoroughly enjoyable experience. Maybe there was hope for the men in the world, after all. They couldn't all be like Evan, could they?

At least now she understood why Simone had said Nick was "strange." It had been meant in a joking way. Nick Hasken, Jenn thought, was about as normal and straight as anyone she'd ever met.

It would be nice to get to know a guy like that. Nice for her, and nice for Emily.

But something kept her from mentioning Nick to Emily when Jenn picked her up later that day.

"Are we going trick-or-treating now, Mommy?" Emily asked.

"You bet," Jenn said. "But first I have to drop off this film."

There was a one-hour developing store in town, and Jenn made arrangements to pick up the film after she and Emily had finished trick-or-treating. The town's shops were all offering free goodies. They were greeted by friendly people who passed out everything from candy and apples to stickers and Pogs. In the bakery, the owner told Emily she could pick out any big cookie she wanted, then chatted with Jenn while Emily made her decision.

"You're Miss Galbraith, aren't you?" the baker asked in a French accent.

"Why, yes," Jenn said, surprised to be recognized "How . . . ?"

"I'm Marie Guillaume," the woman said with a smile that showed large, rectangular teeth. She stood half a head taller than Jenn. "My son, David, is in your class. He showed me your picture in the school paper. He talks of you fondly. You must be a good teacher."

"I like to think so," Jenn said, flattered.

"You're new around her, n'est-ce pas?"

"I moved in just before school began," Jenn said, "from Buffalo."

"How do you like New England?"

Jenn had to stop and think. How did she like it? It was so beautiful, with so many friendly people. And yet, all these bad things had happened lately . . .

"Just fine," she said quickly. "I was lucky enough to get a little cottage on a farm about thirty miles from here. Laura Bayless, my landlady—"

Marie interrupted her. "Laura Bayless? How is she doing?"

Jenn frowned. This was the second person in a day who knew Laura's name. Did it mean something?

"All right, I guess," she said.

"It was a terrible tragedy over there," Marie said with a shake of her head.

Jenn nodded, guessing Marie had heard of the death of Laura's young husband. She noticed that Marie was gazing at Emily with a strange look on her face. It was as if she was trying to hold something back.

"I want this one, please," Emily said, pointing to a cookie shaped and iced like a colorful clown.

Marie bagged the cookie for her and wished the Galbraiths a good day. If she had anything more to say about Laura, she was keeping it to herself. Jenn liked the idea of a town where people didn't spread gossip.

Emily continued trick-or-treating until her plastic pumpkin was near overflowing. Worried she'd fill up on junk food instead of a proper dinner, Jenn decided they would eat early that day. She found a place that sold hero sandwiches and ordered tuna for Emily, a BLT for herself. Over dinner, Emily talked excitedly about her day.

"I wish Tara was here," she said. "She told me Halloween was better where she is, so I guess she just stayed there."

"Where's that?"

"Where the light is," Emily replied. "Where Michelle is now. Mommy, do you think Michelle is trick-or-treating? Do you think big kids get to trick-or-treat in heaven?"

A chill rushed through Jenn, and her sandwich suddenly lost its flavor. She mumbled an answer and quickly changed the subject. "So who had the best costume today?" she asked, steering Emily away from the topic of Michelle's death.

Emily answered easily. "Oh, I liked Jaclyn Parks's fairy costume. It had sparkles all over it!"

They talked on, in the way that mothers and little children do. After dinner, Jenn picked up her pictures. In the car, on the way back to the farm, she heard the rustling of plastic and realized Emily was opening her candy.

"I have to check that first," she said.

"But I want to taste some maple-sugar candy," Emily said. "Please?"

"I'm sure it's okay," Jenn said, "but I always like to check the candy to be certain. Don't you remember how that little boy cut his tongue on a razor-blade last Halloween?"

"Gross," Emily mumbled.

But she stopped opening the package. At her request, Jenn played one of her story tapes, and Emily listened to it quietly on the way home. Then, just as they were turning onto the property, she started to open a candy bar.

"Emily, what did I tell you?" Jenn asked sternly.

"I'm hungry!"

"We'll be at the house in a minute," Jenn said. "You can wait."

"I want a bite now!" Emily whined.

Jenn sighed deeply. Then she reached across the seat, never taking her eyes from the driveway, and moved the pumpkin to the other side of her.

Emily began to wail.

"Oh, Emily, knock it off," Jenn said wearily.

"NO FAIR!"

"Quiet down or no candy at all tonight," Jenn said, making her voice firmer.

What had happened to their nice day?

Jenn answered herself with another question: *Since when does a four-year-old have to be patient? She's over-excited, Jenn. Stay cool.*

She parked the car. When she got out, she handed Emily the bakery cookie. It seemed to placate the child, because she was quiet as they walked up to their door. They stopped to look toward the Bayless house, which was elab-

orately decorated with ghosts and bats and other Halloween paraphernalia. A scarecrow made of old stuffed
clothes, with a painted basketball for a head, sat on the
porch. "Blood" dripped down its forehead. Its arm was
raised, and it was holding an ax. Below it, another stuffed
scarecrow had been positioned in a cowering pose.

"Sick," Jenn said. "Must have been Peter's idea."

Lighten up, Jenn! It's Halloween!

In the house, she made a quick but careful check of
Emily's candy, then put a handful back into the pumpkin.
The rest would be saved, to be rationed out over the next
week. Jenn sent Emily to her room with orders not to de-
vour the candy all at once.

"I won't, Mommy," Emily promised.

At last, Jenn sat down with her snapshots. The first few,
of Emily mugging for the camera, were enough to make
her laugh out loud. Emily was wonderfully photogenic.

"Cute kid, and brains, too," Jenn said fondly. "She's going to be something else when she grows up."

Halfway through the pack, something made her stop and
pause. She tilted the picture to get a better look, unsure
what she was seeing. There was a strange shadow next to
Emily as she marched in the parade. It was a little taller
than Emily, almost human-shaped, a gray mist nearly ob-
literating the background. Jenn guessed it was a double exposure.

All the remaining pictures were like it.

"But how can you get a double exposure from simple
110 film?" she wondered aloud.

Well, she was no photographer. Maybe the man in the
shop could explain this phenomenon to her.

Emily came into the room with a candy bar. She handed
it to Jenn with a smile.

"This is for you, Mommy," she said.

"Thank you, dollbaby," Jenn replied. "That's nice of you. It's my favorite kind, too."

"Tara told me to give it to you."

She ran back to her room before Jenn could say a word. Putting the pictures away, Jenn opened the candy bar and went to turn on the news. She sat down and took a bite. It had a creamy peanut butter center. Delicious.

She took another bite, and tasted something other than peanut butter and chocolate.

Blood.

Confused, she put a hand to her lip and drew back a finger coated with blood. She got up and ran to the bathroom to look in the mirror. She was bleeding profusely from her lower lip, and now it was beginning to sting. She pressed a wet, cold washcloth against the wound and went back to check the candy bar. Closer inspection revealed a small sliver of metal. But how could that be? Jenn had checked every piece, and nothing looked tampered with! Surely she would have seen a cut in the wrapper where this was inserted . . .

She realized Emily had come out of the room again. She was staring at her mother, her eyes glazed over and her cheeks flushed, like she'd just wakened.

"Mommy," she said in a quiet, distant voice, "Tara wants to know if you like the trick she left in your treat."

fourteen

Saturday was such a pleasant day that Jenn shooed Emily out of the house right after breakfast. Emily found a doll she'd dropped on the grass and put it in her toy carriage. She circled the house twice, then stopped and reached into her pocket for a piece of the candy she'd tucked in their earlier. It was wrapped in orange waxed paper, the last of six pieces of licorice she'd found in a little paper bag with a ghost printed on the front. Some were in black wrappers, some in orange like this one. They were all delicious.

Don't eat that!

"Huh?"

Emily looked around. Who had said that? She looked down at her doll, but the plastic baby lay there sleeping.

"Janine Emily, are you teasing your mommy?" she asked.

A single leaf, blown by the wind, whirled around her head like a bat.

She opened the wrapper. Instead of a piece of black licorice, she found a black millipede, legs scrambling hideously. With a scream, she threw it as far as she could.

"Yuck!"

She heard giggles behind her and turned around, looking for her friend. "Tara?"

"I told you not to eat it."

Emily turned again. Tara was beside the carriage, holding the doll in her arms.

"You leave my baby alone," Emily said. "And my candy, too! That was mean—just like the way you hurt my mommy."

"So what?" Tara asked. "I did you a favor. If your mama gets sick, you get to stay at Laura's house. Don't you want to come back again?"

"Yeah . . ." Emily said dubiously. She wanted to go, but she didn't want Tara to do anything to hurt Mommy.

"Don't worry," Tara said. "I won't hurt you—or your mother. And you'll get to come to lunch. You'll see."

Emily took the doll and put her back in the carriage. "You want to play something?"

"Okay," Tara said. "Let's play explorer."

"You mean like Columbus?" Emily asked, tucking a little pink blanket around the doll. "We read about Columbus in school."

"Yeah, except we aren't going across the ocean," Tara said. "We just arrived here, and we're a couple of scouts who have to explore the woods."

Emily looked toward the woods. Even with the sun shining, they seemed dark and scary. Maybe there were animals in there. Maybe a coyote, or even a panther. Mommy saw a panther the other day . . .

But Mommy said it was her imagination, and Miss Dee said there were no panthers here.

But what if there is and it eats me up?

"Well, do you want to play or not?" Tara asked impatiently.

"Do we hafta go in the woods?"

"Just a little," Tara said. "There's a neat place I want to show you. It's called Copperhead Hill."

"'Cause there's copper in it?"

"No, 'cause it's named after copperhead snakes."

Emily took a few steps back, pulling the carriage with her.

"No way! I'm not going to anyplace with snakes! I hate snakes!"

"You hate snakes, you hate bugs," Tara said with disgust. "What a baby!"

"Am not!"

"Are too!"

"Am not!"

"Then come into the woods and see the hill."

"Oh, okay!" Emily said angrily. "I'll see your dumb hill. But I don't want to see any snakes there."

"No snakes," Tara promised. "They named the hill hundreds of years ago. Peter told me. We don't have poisonous snakes around here now."

"Really?"

"Come on, I'll show you."

Emily followed her, leaving the safety of the warm sunlight to her doll.

Jenn sat on the couch; the photographs were spread over the coffee able. She hadn't been able to get back to the photo shop until today, but it had been a futile trip, anyway. The man there had said he'd never seen anything like this. The fault wasn't in the film, he believed. Had there been a light source she was accidentally aiming at? But it had been outside, and the only light source was the sun overhead.

Jenn picked up a picture and studied it for the hundredth time. The blur looked more human-shaped every time she saw it. Of course, she knew it was just a mistake. Despite what the photographer said, she was sure there was a logical explanation.

Then why did she feel so uneasy that the shadows fell so close to Emily?

Like the spectre of death . . .

Someone was ringing the doorbell. Jenn answered it and greeted Noreen. The other teacher was dressed in gray wool slacks, her down jacket opened to reveal a pink-and-gray plaid flannel shirt.

"Hi!" Noreen said, holding back a fluff of brown hair that the wind tried to tousle. "I was going to the mall and thought you might like to come out shopping."

Jenn looked down at her own Ohio State sweatshirt, jeans, and sneakers and shook her head.

"I'm hardly dressed for it," she said, backing up to let her friend in. Noreen looked around and nodded approvingly.

"What a cute place," she said. "It's perfect for you and Emily, isn't it?"

"I like it," Jenn said. "We were lucky to find it."

Noreen tilted her head in the direction of the big house. "What's your landlady like? She seems kind of nosy."

"What do you mean?" Jenn was genuinely puzzled.

"She was standing on her porch, staring at my car as I drove up here. She had something in her hands, too. It looked like a plate of brownies or cookies."

Jenn guessed that Laura had intended to come to the cottage with another plate of goodies. It bothered her, but she didn't understand why.

"Laura's always bringing treats here," Jenn said. "She bakes for a shop in a nearby town. I think it's called the Mixing Bowl."

"I've heard of it," Noreen said. "Pricey, touristy stuff. But forget about that. How did your date with Nick go?"

"I told you before, Noreen," Jenn said. "It wasn't a date."

She hadn't seen Nick in several days, since Halloween.

"But I'll bet he was pleasant company," Noreen pressed.

Jenn rolled her eyes.

"Noreen!" she cried in protest. "It was only lunch. Nick is a nice guy, but I'm not ready for a commitment yet. I still have nightmares about my ex, for God's sake."

The vision of the pig was still clear enough in her mind to make her shudder.

"That's right," Noreen said with a sad look and a nod of understanding. "You haven't been divorced all that long, have you?"

"A little over a year," Jenn said. "And I was only able to stop his visitation rights with Emily early last summer. She has nightmares about him, too. So you can see how I just can't push a strange man at her."

Noreen was thoughtful for a few moments before speaking again.

"I heard he tried to murder the two of you," she said.

Jenn, who hadn't made the accident common knowledge around campus, said:

"Who told you that?"

"I heard it from Mary Young," she said. "I think she heard it from one of her students."

"Mary Young? From the art department? I don't even know her! I don't think I like the idea of people discussing my private affairs."

"Better get used to it," Noreen said. "Gossip travels fast in a small place like Pinebridge. But is it true?"

Jenn scowled. "It's true. The bastard's dead, and Emily's still scared shitless of him, even now."

Noreen waited for Jenn to go on, but instead Jenn turned to her coffee table and started straightening up a pile of magazines. It was time to change the subject.

"So, do you want to go shopping?"

"Well, I'll have to put on something decent," Jenn said. "I can get an early start on Christmas. Just give me a few minutes to put on some makeup and locate Emily."

She indicated the living room, where Noreen took a seat. She leaned forward and glanced at the rows of photographs.

"Halloween pictures?" she called toward Jenn's room.

"Take a look," Jenn called back through her opened door.

Noreen picked up each picture, and paused just as Jenn had done when she saw the strange shadows. When Jenn returned, Noreen asked: "What happened here?"

"I have no idea," Jenn admitted. "Even the developer can't figure it out."

Noreen studied the photograph in her hand.

"If I didn't know better," she said, "I'd think you captured a ghost. I've heard of this kind of thing."

"A ghost?" Jenn asked, her voice slightly more shrill than she meant it to be. "Don't be silly. There aren't any such things."

She remembered the phantom animal noises she'd heard, the panther, the pig in her bed, Emily's saying that Michelle was "in the light." She dismissed the images. It was all nonsense, of course!

"Some people swear there are," Noreen said. "I had an aunt who used to insist there was a banshee living in her attic. It followed her from Ireland in the hold of a ship about eighty years ago, and it's been screaming its head off up there the first Sunday of every month since then.

Some of my cousins swear they've heard it. But I'm not one of them."

She put the pictures down. "It's just a shame so many nice shots were ruined."

Jenn didn't answer. A flicker of shadow caused her to look out the window, but the yard was empty. Suddenly she had the overwhelming feeling that Emily was in danger.

"I have to find my daughter," she blurted, hurrying out the door.

"EMILY!"

She ran around the house, but her daughter was nowhere in sight. The doll carriage sat abandoned. She began to run toward Laura's house, her voice filling the autumn air.

"Emileeeeeee!!!!"

Emily could not hear her, although she was only a short distance away. Strange forces prevented Jenn's words from reaching the little girl. Emily was playing king of the hill with Tara, racing to the top of a mound that might have been, during some primeval era, home to poisonous snakes. Right now, it was nothing more than a high and smooth swelling in the middle of the forest.

"Look at me, Tara! Look at me! I'm king of the hill!"

"Not for long!" Tara cried, racing up to push her off.

It was a gentle push, and Emily rolled down with a delighted squeal. At the bottom, she got up and tried to scramble to the top again. But halfway there, she suddenly heard her mother's voice as clearly as if Jenn was right behind her. She froze, a frown pulling her eyebrows closer together.

"What's the matter?"

"Mommy's calling me," Emily replied. "I have to go now, Tara."

"No, you don't," Tara said. "She just wants you to stop having fun."

Emily turned around and started down the hill.

"I don't want Mommy to get mad," she said.

"No!" Tara cried. "You can't go! You can't leave me!"

Emily paid no attention to her. Her mother was calling, and she didn't want to get into trouble.

Tara grabbed her. "Emily, your daddy is over there! If you leave me, he'll see you! I'm the only one who can protect you!"

Emily began to cry, torn between obeying her mother and staying hidden from her father. But what if Tara was making it up, just to make her stay?

"I . . . don't believe you!" she stammered. "You're lying! You just want me to get in trouble!"

"It's true!" Tara insisted. She gasped, pointing. "There he is! Look! There he is!"

Emily dared to look, and to her shock saw her father standing only a short distance away. He had one hand up against a tree trunk. In the other hand, he held a pizza cutter. Emily's scream was cut off as Tara clapped a hand over her mouth.

"Shh!" Tara hissed. "He can't see you, yet. But he's very close to your door, and if you scream, he'll find it."

Emily wiggled out of her grip.

"What door?" she demanded in a small, shaking voice. "There aren't any doors in the woods!"

"It isn't that kind of door," Tara whispered. "It's a . . . a sort of light you walk into to get from where I am to where you are. There's a lot of different lights, different ways through."

"E.J.! I know you're here somewhere! Answer me!"

Emily cringed and covered her face. How could Daddy be so close and not see her?

"He can't see you because I'm protecting you," Tara said, reading her mind.

"I'm gonna get my mommy," Emily decided just then, and turned to run.

"Emily, don't!" Tara cried.

Emily had run only a few feet down the hill when she felt something slide across her ankle. Daring to look down, she let out a scream of terror.

"MOMMMMEEEE!!!!!"

This was something even more frightening than her father. Copperhead Hill, devoid of reptilian life for ages, was crawling with snakes. One of them was coiling around her small ankle. With a cry of disgust, Emily kicked out flinging the snake away.

"MOMMY! MOMMMMEEEEE!!!!"

"She isn't coming," Tara said calmly. "She can't hear you."

Emily swung around, too terrified to move. There were snakes everywhere she looked, hissing and writhing, ugly.

"Make them go away, Tara! Please make them go away!"

"I can't! I didn't do it! It was your daddy!"

Emily choked on a sob. The snakes had made her forget! She looked around frantically, but he was gone.

"Where . . . ?"

"Your daddy didn't find your special door, but he's getting closer!"

"But he saw me, Tara! He saw me!"

Tara shook her head. "No, he didn't. He's still looking. He won't stop until he finds you, Emily. That's why you have to do what I say, so I can help you!"

"I just want my Mommy!"

A snake reared up and hissed at her. Emily screamed again.

"Make them go away, Tara. *Make them go AWAY!*"

"I can't," Tara said grimly. "I'm sorry."

Emily kicked at another snake, then turned to look up at the top of the hill.

Tara was gone.

She heard her mother calling again: "EMILY! EMILY, WHERE ARE YOU?"

Emily found the courage to run down the hill through the tangle of serpents. As she reached the bottom, she tripped. A snake grabbed her ankle, sinking its teeth into her baby flesh. Another bit through the sleeve of her jacket, another at her thigh. She screamed and screamed.

Suddenly, someone picked her up.

"Mommy . . ." Emily said weakly.

"No, it's Laura," said a familiar voice. "I heard you screaming, sweet angel. What happened?"

Emily dared to open her eyes. The snakes were gone. There was nothing below her but dirt, stones, and dried grass. She threw her arms around Laura's neck and began to sob.

"There were snakes everywhere! Daddy made snakes come!"

"Shh, shh," Laura cooed, rocking her. "It's all right now. You're safe with me."

And then, Emily heard a more welcome voice. "Emily? Oh, my God, Emily!"

Emily tried to let go of Laura, to run to her mother. But for a moment, Laura held her too tightly. She struggled and broke loose.

"Mommy!"

"Emily, why didn't you answer me?" Jenn demanded angrily.

But her anger dissipated at once when she saw the spots of blood all over her daughter.

"What happened to her?" she demanded, lifting her child up into her arms.

Noreen stood at her side, watching the scene in wonder.

"She must have fallen down the hill," Laura said. "You shouldn't let her wander into these woods, Jenn. It isn't safe."

Jenn was put off by Laura's comment, but before she could say a word Emily cut in.

"It was snakes, Mommy! Daddy made snakes come and they bit me!"

"Snakes?" Noreen asked. "There aren't any snakes around here."

"I don't know what happened," Jenn said, turning to walk back to the cottage. She said nothing more to Laura, who watched her retreat. "But I'm going to have a doctor look at Emily's cuts."

"How about if I drive?" Noreen suggested.

Jenn agreed. She was too shaken up to feel safe behind the wheel. Jenn helped Emily into the backseat of Noreen's car and buckled her in. Then she climbed in beside her. She held her daughter close. No one spoke until they were five miles down the highway.

"God, I feel terrible," Jenn said. "Laura was there for Emily, and it should have been me."

"Don't start feeling guilty," Noreen cautioned. "She just happened to be there. And if you ask me, that remark about not letting Emily into the woods was a little self-righteous."

"But she was right . . ."

"Maybe," Noreen said, "but it wasn't her place to say so. Who does she think she is? Mother of the Year? God, did you see what she was wearing?"

"No."

"A white eyelet apron and a dress," Noreen said. "She didn't have her coat buttoned, and I saw. Who the hell wears something like that on a Saturday?"

"Laura Bayless does," Jenn replied softly. She looked down at Emily, who had laid her head in Jenn's lap.

"That woman is caught in the fifties," Noreen said. "I bet she irons her underwear."

Emily giggled.

"Hear that? Emily knows a joke when she hears one."

But Jenn wasn't laughing. She said nothing more until they arrived at the hospital. She was delighted to see Dr. Emerson on duty. When he heard that Emily had seen snakes, as well as her father, a look of concern came over his face. He sat down and spoke to the child at length, then took Jenn to the side.

"I'm going to order an EEG," he said. "I don't like the idea that she's hallucinating, especially considering the head injury occurred only two months ago."

"But she's been fine," Jenn protested, fearing the worst. "We were due for a follow-up visit on Monday, but it was just routine."

The doctor smiled reassuringly. "It's just to make certain."

Jenn tried to grasp at something she could understand, something beyond the mysteries of the brain.

"What . . . what about those cuts on her arms and legs?"

Emerson shook his head.

"I'm not sure," he said. "They do look like snake bites, two small dots together. Is it possible there was a snake there, perhaps a pet that had escaped?"

Jenn's mouth dropped open. Was it possible Peter had a snake that got loose and was lost in the woods?

"I . . . I'm not sure," she admitted.

"I'll have samples taken," Emerson said.

Emily, quiet all this time, spoke up at last.

"Am I gonna sleep here again? Daddy can't get me here, can he?"

"No, darling," the doctor said with a smile. "I promise

your daddy can't get you, no matter where you are. Mommy will see to that."

Jenn nodded, not sure what to think. What on earth had made Emily hallucinate like this? What frightening thing had happened to make her think Evan was there?"

"Come on, Emily," the doctor said. "We'll have you out of here in no time."

It actually took the entire afternoon to run all the desired tests. Jenn apologized to Noreen, but her fellow teacher wouldn't hear of it.

"You're keeping me from spending money I don't have," she said.

"But it's so boring here," Jenn said.

"Are you kidding?" Noreen asked. "How can I be bored with so many cute doctors walking around? Hell, I'll settle for slightly-less-than-cute."

Jenn couldn't help a laugh.

"I saw a little fat guy in scrubs when we were walking in," she teased.

"She can still joke!" Noreen cried, as if this were miraculous.

Jenn needed Noreen's good sense of humor to get her through the next hours. And she needed Noreen to hold her hand when Dr. Emerson came back with the results.

"She's great," he said, smiling. "The EEG came up fine, and her blood is normal. I still can't explain those marks on her, but she'll be okay."

"Thanks," Jenn said, her shoulders relaxing visibly.

"I'd like to suggest counseling, however," Emerson continued. "It's obvious Emily hasn't accepted what her father did, or that he's paid the price. Therapy might help both of you."

"I'll think about it," Jenn said halfheartedly.

Noreen squeezed her hand as the nurse brought Emily out to her.

"But the only thing wrong with this little lady right now," said Dr. Emerson, more brightly, "is that she's half starved. Be sure to get her something special tonight, Mommy."

Jenn smiled, relief showing in every facial muscle.

"You bet I will," she said.

She knelt down to give Emily a big hug. She felt safe now, but in a way she was frightened, too. Frightened that the strange incident in the woods wasn't the last of the troubles she and Emily would face.

You're going to cause trouble for us even now, aren't you, Evan?

Noreen volunteered to drive them all to a family-style restaurant that specialized in roast chickens. In the back seat, Emily played with a puzzle book the nurses had given her; Jenn sat up front with Noreen. They chatted, keeping their conversation away from the day's events.

But Jenn's worries were strong, and while Noreen was talking about something that didn't interest her, Jenn was struck by a new thought.

Laura had reached the woods before her. Why hadn't Jenn seen her walking across the farmyard?

fifteen

On Sunday, Jenn took Emily to the movies, followed by a trip to the Ice Cream Cottage for a sundae and some maple sugar candy. In a way, she wanted to make up for the fright Emily had had. It bothered her that Laura had been there first for Emily the day before. And it bothered her that Laura had turned up at Jenn's door Saturday night with a gift for Emily, acting as if she hadn't made any nasty remarks. Jenn had tried to ask, in a casual way, what she'd been doing in the woods. She thought the woman might have been spying on them, but Laura had had a legitimate answer.

"Looking for pinecones," she had said. "I'm making a door wreath for Christmas."

So much for the spying theory. But that didn't make Jenn stop wondering if Laura was watching her, judging her. It didn't matter that Laura's own child was nothing to brag about. She was always there for Peter. Was Jenn always there for Emily?

Guilt, guilt, guilt . . .

Guilt slightly alleviated by a Steven Speilberg movie and a handful of video game tokens. But it wasn't enough.

"You love me, dollbaby?" Jenn asked as they drove home.

"Yep," Emily said.

"Do you love Laura?"

Emily giggled.

"I can't love her," she said. "She isn't you, Mommy. I just sort of like her. She's nice."

Jenn breathed a deep sigh. Emily only thought Laura was "nice." Laura wouldn't usurp the child's love anytime soon.

But Laura had been there to comfort her after the incident on Copperhead Hill. Laura, not Jenn.

Guilt . . .

"Mommy, look! Puppies!"

They stopped at a red light. Two boys sitting on a bench held a box in their arms marked with the legend: FREE PUPPIES!

"Oh, Emily, I don't know . . ."

"Mommy, can we look? Can we just look? Please?"

Jenn felt the guilt tugging at her again. Looking wasn't so much to ask, was it?

She found a parking space and they got out. As it happened, looking was just enough to convince her to take one of the dogs. It was a female, black with brown markings. It had the big, clumsy paws that often promise a large dog.

"I'll bet she'll be a good watchdog when she grows up," she said, trying to justify her moment of weakness. "I think there's some rottweiler in there."

"I just think she's cute," Emily said.

The little animal helped raise Jenn's mood, and the delight she saw on Emily's face erased any doubts she had about her daughter's happiness. Emily was in heaven.

They made a quick stop for pet supplies, then headed home again. Emily unzipped her jacket and tucked the puppy inside, its little head poking out. She zipped it up again and began to sing softly as she petted it. The puppy closed its eyes and fell asleep.

"What are you going to name her?" Jenn asked.

"I don't know," Emily said. "I hafta think."

She stroked the dog gently.

"She has a spot on her forehead like a Hershey's Kiss," Emily said. "But I think Hershey's a silly name for a dog, don't you?"

"It might work," Jenn said.

"Nope," Emily said. "And I can't call her 'Kiss,' either."

She thought hard, staring out the window at the road ahead.

"Baci," she said.

"Huh?"

"Baci," Emily said again. "Miss Dee says it means 'kiss' in Italian. I'm going to name her Baci."

"Bocce Ball," Jenn teased.

"Not Bocce Ball!" Emily said. "Just *Bah*-chee!"

Keeping her eyes on the road, Jenn reached across the seat to pet the little dog.

"Baci's a perfect name," she said.

They drove on, Jenn watching the road, Emily singing a doggie lullaby she made up herself. Then, when they were turning onto the Bayless property, Emily suddenly said:

"Mommy, Baci's shaking!"

"Really?" Jenn asked. "Maybe she doesn't like the car ride."

Emily cooed at the dog. Now Jenn could hear the animal whimpering, as if it was afraid of something.

"Easy, girl," she said. "Easy. We're almost home, Baci."

"Mommy, she peed on me!"

Jenn couldn't help a laugh.

"That's what puppies do, Emily," she said.

But now the little animal was yelping loudly, her voice full of fear.

"Mommy, what's *wrong* with her?" Emily demanded, frantic.

"I don't know, dollbaby," Jenn said, growing worried herself. "We'll take her inside and give her something to eat and drink. She's probably just lonely for her littermates."

The moment the car stopped and the door opened, though, the dog jumped from Emily's arms and ran off.

"Mommy, catch her!"

"I've never seen a puppy move so fast," Jenn said in wonder. "Look, she's gone into the barn. You can probably catch her in there. But be careful. You don't want to scare her. I'll go inside and get her dinner ready."

Calling to the dog, Emily ran for the barn. She was heading around the corner when she bumped into Peter.

"Watch it!" he cried.

"Did you see my puppy?" Emily asked. "She ran away and . . ."

She sniffed the air and made a face.

"Gross, were you smoking?"

"None of your business," Peter said. "What puppy?"

Emily told him about her new dog.

"Well, I didn't see her," Peter said. "But if you want, I can help you look for her."

"Okay," Emily said. "She ran away when we got here, like she was scared of something."

"Maybe she was," Peter mumbled.

"Huh?"

"I'll check the woods," he said. "You, uh, you look around here."

He turned and headed toward the trees. For a moment, Emily stood wondering why he was helping her. Sometimes, Peter could be very mean. And sometimes he could be nice.

"Peter's weird," she decided.

She headed toward the front of the barn. The door hung askew, and she slipped inside. It was dark in here, but Emily was too intent on finding the puppy to be scared. She called to it. "Baci! Here, girl! Baci!"

Hearing soft whimpering, she headed toward the sound. The barn was cold and it smelled bad. Emily recalled that Mommy once had said the hay was rotting. Emily hoped Baci wouldn't end up smelling like this place. Could she give a puppy a bath? She recalled that her Uncle Travis had given one of his hounds a bath after a run-in with a skunk. Pokey had *hated* that. Emily didn't want Baci to hate her.

"Baci! I won't give you a bath! I promise!"

"I see you, E.J."

Emily stopped just short of the piles of hay.

"Baci?"

Did her puppy say something to her? Dogs in movies could talk; so could cartoon dogs. She had never heard a real dog talk before, but . . .

Come here, E.J. Be a good girl and come to me . . ."

That wasn't Baci! It was Daddy! Daddy had found her! Maybe he was hiding behind the hay, holding Baci prisoner! Maybe he was up in the loft and he was going to jump down on her!

Frantic, she turned to run to the door. It seemed impossibly far away, the darkness and cold and her own imagination stretching the distance for miles.

Then she heard the sound. It was strange, something like a bird fluttering around in a cage. She froze. Daddy was going to get her. He had wings because he was dead now and when you died you got wings. Only he wasn't an angel, he was bad, and he probably had black wings like a bat.

The sound grew louder.

Emily ran screaming.

The fluttering became a frantic beating of wings now, hundreds of wings overhead. Emily dared to look up just before struggling through the opening in the door.

The ceiling was black and moving.

Forgetting the dog, Emily ran to her house. Jenn had heard her cries and was racing with open arms. She swooped her daughter up.

"Emily! What's wrong?"

"Daddy's in the barn!" Emily cried. "He found me! Mommy, he found me!"

"Dollbaby, that can't be true," Jenn insisted.

"Keep him away from me!" Emily screamed.

Jenn put her down. Emily wasn't just making this up. *Something* had frightened her. Anger rose within her as she strode toward the barn to investigate.

"No, Mommy! Daddy will get you!"

"No, he won't, Emily," Jenn insisted. In her anger, she was invincible. And she knew it wasn't Evan in there. It was probably Peter, playing a mean trick. She'd seen him come out from behind the barn a while ago, just a few moments before Emily herself appeared. When she got hold of him she'd—

She yanked the barn door open. A great rush of blackness shot out, knocking her to the ground. With a scream, Jenn rolled over and threw up her arms to protect the back of her neck. Emily stood near their cottage, watching in horror. Bats! Hundreds and hundreds of bats were flying out of the barn! The beat of their wings was near deafening, their screeches like the cries of pure evil.

"EMILY! GET IN THE HOUSE!"

Emily obeyed at once. Safe behind a window, she watched as Laura ran toward the barn, waving a broom. Peter appeared from the woods. He hooked up the hose and turned on a spray of water. In a few moments, all the animals had taken to the sky.

Emily dared to come back out again, to run to her mother and hug her.

"I've never seen anything like this," Laura said.

"We only had one or two bats in there," Peter insisted. "Where did they all come from?"

Jenn wanted to say they came from Hell itself, but she couldn't say a word for fright. When Laura helped her to her feet and led her up to the house, she didn't protest.

"I've already called René," Laura said.

It wasn't until Laura had gotten a cup of coffee into Jenn, and cocoa into Emily, that Jenn spoke.

"I've had enough!" she said. "Spiders and bats! I'm sorry, Laura, but this place is just too 'country' for me. We're going to have to find a new place to live."

"Oh, please don't," Laura said. "I'll lower your rent! René will take care of the bats. There's no need to leave!"

"I don't want to leave," Emily said. "I want to stay with Tara."

Jenn sighed, her voice shaking. "It's getting on my nerves. I'm a wreck lately, Laura."

The back door opened, and Peter announced that René had arrived. The women went outside. Emily looked up at the sky, waiting for the bats to return. Laura went to speak with René.

"Mommy, do we really have to leave?" Emily asked.

"Emily, this place is dangerous." Jenn whispered so that Laura couldn't hear. "I think the way Laura has left it uncared for is attracting vermin. Those bats could carry rabies! Thank God none of us was bit!"

She watched as René went into the barn. A few minutes later, he came out again. For a moment, he stared across the yard at Jenn. He seemed about to say something to her when Laura spoke up.

"Well? What did you find?"

"Nothing," he said. "I don't understand. That many bats would leave droppings, and the barn is fairly clean."

"We all saw them," Peter insisted.

Ignoring the boy, René scratched at his beard.

"I'll seal the place up," he said. "And I'll fix the door. If they come back, they won't be able to get in. They'll have to find another place to live."

"Can't you just exterminate them?" Jenn asked.

René shook his head. "Illegal. Some bats are endangered species."

"Well, they can just be endangered someplace else," Laura said, a look of disgust on her face. "One or two bats are fine for catching bugs, but that many are horrible!"

She turned to Jenn. "Do you want to come up to the house?"

"No, thanks." She'd had enough of Laura's hospitality for one day.

She realized that thought made no sense. Was she still burning after the way Laura spoke yesterday? But the woman was being so nice today! Then again, she was always "Nice," wasn't she?

"No, thanks," Jenn said again, simply. "Come on, Emily. Let's go home."

"Can I watch Mr. DeLorris, Mommy?"

Jenn looked down at her. Emily's blue eyes were bright, curious. She seemed to have forgotten the spectre of her father—for now.

"All right," Jenn said, amazed at the child's resilience. "I'll call you when dinner's ready."

"I can walk her back to the cottage," Peter offered.

Jenn looked at him with surprise. She was about to compliment him on the nice gesture when Laura interrupted.

"You have homework, Peter. And chores."

Peter moaned, but went back into the house with his mother. Jenn watched him go, curious. The way he brooded all the time, the way he hung his head and never looked directly at you when he spoke—did he feel the way she did? Was he depressed by this place, too?

Well, she couldn't carry his burdens as well as her own. She had her own child to worry about. Let Laura deal with Peter's problems, Jenn decided as she headed back to the cottage.

Emily followed René into the barn. With the doors wide open, it was much brighter in here. But it still smelled awful. Emily held her nose.

René laughed. Emily had never seen him do that before. He was always so grumpy that he scared her. But now his face was sparkly like Santa's. Emily watched as he loaded hay into a wheelbarrow.

"I know," he said, "It is pretty bad in here. Poor Laura's just not able to deal with it, and that lazy son of hers is no help."

"You help Laura a lot," Emily stated.

René nodded. "Walter was a friend of mine. Thought I'd stick around to help out after he. . ."

He stopped himself. Emily guessed there was something he didn't want to say because she was only a kid. She hated when grown-ups did that, treating her like a stupid baby. But before she had a chance to protest, René suddenly cried out:

"Well, hello there!"

He pulled Baci out from behind the hay.

"Baci! Baci!"

Emily had been so frightened that she'd forgotten all about the new puppy.

"Here you go," René said, handing the dog to her. "She's a cute little thing. You call her Bah-chee?"

"It means 'kiss' in Italian," Emily said.

"Smart kid," René said. "Do you speak Italian?"

Emily giggled. "No. Miss Dee told me."

"That's your teacher?" René said as he continued to work. "I'll bet she's nice."

"She's real nice," Emily said. "Almost as nice as my mommy, and almost as nice as Laura."

"Nobody's ever nicer than your own mommy," René said.

Emily stroked the puppy. The little dog seemed to have calmed down now, and she licked Emily's face with a warm tongue.

"Tara says her mama is nicer than my mommy."

René stopped. He looked back over his shoulder.

"Tara?"

"My friend," Emily said. "Only, she's been kind of mean to me lately so I don't know if she's really my friend."

"You talk to Tara, huh?"

He went back to work, lifting the handles of the wheelbarrow and walking out of the barn. Emily followed close behind.

"Sometimes," she replied. "Can I have a ride in that?"

"On the way back," René said. "You don't want this stinky old stuff on your nice clothes, do you?"

"Yuck!"

He loaded the hay into the back of his pickup, then lifted Emily into the wheelbarrow.

"So, tell me about Tara," he said. "What mean things does she do?"

"She talks mean sometimes," Emily said. "And she put a razor in Mommy's candy at Halloween. Tara is mad all the time. I think it's because she's over in the light and she doesn't want to be there. But you know what? Tara keeps Daddy away from me."

René stopped and set the barrow down. He knelt to Emily's level, hands curled over the edge of the bucket.

"Emily, I want you to listen to me," he said. "I know why Tara's sad. And I think it's the kind of sad than can become mad. You know what I mean?"

Emily nodded. She'd seen enough "sad into mad" in her mother lately.

"That kind of mad can be dangerous," René said. "When Tara comes back, tell her you don't want to play with her anymore."

"But she's my friend! And she keeps Daddy from hurting me!"

"The good Lord keeps your daddy away," René insisted. "No one else has that kind of power. No matter what Tara says to you. You just be careful of that child."

Emily thought, and her confusion grew. Sometimes, Tara was mean. But sometimes she was nice, too. And she liked Emily. The other kids at school didn't like her.

"She's my friend," she said again.

She scrambled out of the wheelbarrow and ran to the cottage, carrying the puppy. When her mother tried to ask what was wrong, she refused to answer. She ran into her room and shut the door. A moment later, Jenn opened it.

"I saw you talking to René," she said. "Did he say something bad to you?"

Emily nodded. She saw her mother's shoulders stiffen and her eyes grow darker.

"What?" Jenn demanded.

"He said I should tell Tara to go away," she said.

To her surprise, her mother's shoulders relaxed again.

"Well, he's right," she said. "You're a big girl. And Tara is only make-believe. You're smart enough to know that, Emily."

Emily climbed onto her bed and turned away from her mother. The puppy jumped down from the bed and tore around Jenn's legs, yapping.

"Are you hungry, girl?" Jenn asked. "Come on, I've got dinner for you."

Before she left the room, she spoke to her daughter's back.

"Your dinner will be ready soon," she said and shut the door.

A moment later, Emily felt the bed sink as if someone had sat on it. She knew at once who it was.

"Go away, Tara," she growled, pulling the pink teddy close to hug it tightly. "You didn't make the snakes go away yesterday. Did you do the bats, too? Did you tell my daddy where to find me?"

"It wasn't me!" Tara insisted." Your daddy is just getting so much closer to your doorway! I wouldn't hurt you! I like you!"

"René says you're bad."

"René's a jerk," Tara said. "Are you gonna listen to that creepy old man?"

"He gave me a ride in the wheelbarrow."

There was a moment of silence. Curious, Emily finally turned to face her friend. Tara was sitting with her hands fisted, her lips set hard in anger.

"He used to give me rides. And Mama came and hugged you yesterday and she bought you a present. And sometimes she calls you 'sweet angel.' *I'm* 'sweet angel,' not you! It isn't fair!"

Emily glared at her. "Yes, it is."

"It's all supposed to be mine, not yours!" Tara said darkly. "And I'm going to make you pay for taking it from me!"

Emily sat up. "I didn't take anything from you."

"No, but you're going to give me something," Tara said, staring at her. "Soon. And then I'll have everything back again."

"What?"

"Can't tell you now," Tara said. "Close your eyes. I want to try something."

Though she was wary, Emily did as she was told. In a flash, she was filled with an image of a man lifting her up and swinging her around. She was laughing, but it wasn't her laugh. And when she looked in a mirror in her 'dream,' she saw Tara's face.

Her eyes snapped open.

"Stop that," she said, rubbing her head. "Stop walking around inside my brain."

Tara smiled. "Just wanted to see if I could do it."

The door opened. Emily's mother said, "It's time for dinner."

She looked right past Tara as if she didn't see her. When she shut the door, Tara stood up.

"I'll see you later," she said. "I've got to talk to René now."

She vanished.

When Emily entered the kitchen, Baci was sleeping soundly on an old towel Jenn had laid out for her. Jenn was at the table, serving up mashed potatoes, gravy, and chicken.

"We had quite a day, didn't we?"

"Those bats were scary," Emily said. "I sure hope they don't come back again.'"

"Me, too," Jenn agreed.

Baci whimpered and turned over in her sleep.

"Why was Baci so scared before?" Emily asked.

"I don't know, dollbaby," Jenn said.

Emily ate for a few moments, then spoke quietly.

"Sometimes I feel scared," she said.

"Really? Tell me about that"

"Sometimes I see Daddy, and—"

A terrified scream interrupted her, so shrill it seemed to cut through the glass of the windows. Mother and daughter jumped up to look outside. Laura was running away from the barn. Curious, Jenn put on her jacket and went outside.

"Laura?"

The woman didn't seem to hear Jenn as she raced into her house. Jenn went to the barn herself to investigate. René had taken off the broken door and set it to one side. Jenn looked into the opening. In the red light of the setting sun, she saw a horrible sight that made her stomach lurch. She turned away, but not quickly enough to keep an image from planting itself in her mind.

René DeLorris was lying against the remaining pile of hay, staring out the door. But he wasn't seeing anything. The pitchfork slammed into his chest made certain of that.

Jenn ran up to the house to be sick.

"Mommy?"

Emily pounded on the bathroom door, but Jenn didn't answer.

"It's okay now," she heard Tara say. "I took care of him. He won't be saying mean things about me anymore!"

Emily swung around. "What did you do?"

Tara laughed out loud.

"Go away!" Emily screamed. "GO AWAY! GO AWAY!"

Tara stopped laughing.

"I'm going," she said. "But don't blame me if your daddy shows up and kills you all!"

sixteen

Mike Hewlett was one of the police officers who came to the scene. When he finished his work, he spoke to the women. They had been watching the scene, side by side. Laura had been crying openly, but Jenn stood in stunned silence. Behind them, Peter scuffed his sneakers and stared down as if there was an answer in the dirt.

Now, as Mike approached them, Laura asked frantically:

"Is he gone? Is the killer gone?"

"There was no killer," Mike said. "Mr. DeLorris died in an unfortunate accident."

"What?" The women's question was gasped in unison.

"Here, come take a look."

They cautiously followed Mike into the barn. It was well lit now, illuminated with floodlights. Mike pointed toward the ceiling. Jenn looked up, squinting. Part of her worried that there might still be bats there, ready to swoop down and attack.

"We found his flashlight in the loft, still on," Mike said. "It looks like he slipped and fell."

"My God," Laura whispered. "He was sealing off the barn because we had bats."

Jenn had the sudden feeling of a malevolent presence in the room, someone hidden in the shadows. But there were no shadows.

I'm getting to be like Emily—too vivid an imagination.

Then she saw the bloodied pitchfork, leaning against the haystack. How much effort had it taken to yank the thing out of René's body?

Sickened, she hurried from the barn. Her knees were tense, the fear response of someone with an enemy in pursuit. She could see Emily watching from the kitchen window. Had she seen the large, black bag they'd put into the back of the coroner's van?

She was at the door of the cottage.

No one reached out to grab her.

Inside, she took Emily into her arms and hugged her.

"Tara did a bad thing, Mommy," Emily whispered.

"Did she?" Jenn asked, hardly hearing the child.

"She killed René, Mommy," Emily said. "She got mad at him 'cause he said I should make her go away, and she killed him."

"Shh," Jenn said. "Don't talk like that. Just don't."

And she hugged Emily all the tighter.

Sometime later, when Emily was fast asleep, she tucked her into bed and went to make herself a cup of coffee. She could see the barn through the kitchen window, and a shudder racked her. Jenn considered calling Laura to talk about what had happened, but dismissed the idea. Laura was already upset, not the strong person Jenn needed right now. Jenn had been there to soothe Emily's fears, but who did Jenn herself have?

Her sister's name came to mind next. But Rosalie had always been an overprotective mother hen. If she knew Jenn and Emily were living in a house where a murder was committed, she'd nag Jenn until they moved out.

"I know," Jenn said out loud. "I'll call Noreen."

Noreen had often indicated she was willing to listen to Jenn's problems. She dialed her friend's number. Noreen's voice was a little slurred when she answered.

"Oh, I woke you," Jenn apologized.

"Not at all," Noreen said. "I just got in. Had a date tonight, drank a little too much. What's up, Jenn?"

Jenn told her.

"Are you all right?" Noreen asked. The slur in her voice was completely gone now. "Oh, my God, Jenn! Did anything happen to Emily? Did she see it?"

"I don't think she saw anything much," Jenn said. "But all the police activity scared her. It was hard to get her settled down to sleep."

Jenn took a deep breath. Should she tell Noreen what Emily had said?

"Jenn?"

"Noreen, Emily said something strange," Jenn replied. "She said that Tara killed René."

"Who?"

"Her imaginary playmate," Jenn went on. "Emily was in the barn with René before he died. I think he told her to make Tara go away—not that I understand what he meant. It's almost as if he believed Tara was real, and a danger to Emily. Emily says that Tara got mad and killed him."

"Oh, boy," Noreen mumbled. Louder, she said: "Jenn, maybe she feels guilty because she was with him right before it happened. You know how little kids can twist things around. I'd stay on top of that, if I were you. Make sure she knows it wasn't her fault."

"You can bet I will," Jenn said. "But I'm getting tired of this Tara character. I wish Emily would drop her."

"She will, in time," Noreen reassured her. "Little kids go through stages. I've seen it in my nieces and nephews."

"I hope so."

The women talked a while longer, eventually turning from the murder to other topics. By the time she hung up, Jenn felt relatively better, although there was still a knot of fear in her stomach when she went to sleep that night.

To Jenn, it was a good thing Monday brought classes. The world of numbers and mathematical equations helped push thoughts of René from her mind. Noreen passed her once in the morning and asked how she was, and she insisted she was holding up okay. When lunchtime came, she put all her concentration into finding a new place to live. Accident or not, she had to get away from Laura's property. She didn't want Emily constantly reminded of René's death. Still, the horror of the weekend must have been stamped on her face, because she noticed people looking at her askance and frowning. Kim Stone passed her as she was walking to her car and said:

"Is everything all right?"

Jenn hadn't wanted to talk about the weekend. The troubles at the Bayless farm were something she wanted to leave there, not bring to work with her. But then, talking with Noreen hadn't completely alleviated her tension. What was a dean for, if not to support her teachers in time of trouble? She told Kim what had happened.

"Unbelievable," Kim said with a shake of her head. She straightened her broad shoulders and pointed her sharp chin up a little, like a captain taking charge of a bad situation. "Do you want a few days off? I would understand, after such a traumatic experience."

Jenn gazed for a moment at the cluster of gold and copper leaves on Kim's lapel, thoughtful. Then she looked the dean in the eye and said:

"Nothing would help me through this more than concentrating on my work."

Kim smiled her approval. "Great. But you know where my office is if you need to talk."

Jenn thanked her, and they parted. She tried to think of something else, but thoughts of the past weeks kept flooding her mind. It seemed that death was following her everywhere these days. First, Evan's death in the accident—but that was a relief to her, a dark wish come true. Then there were the Trentons, killed in a freak fire just before she and Emily were to move into their home. Michelle Wallace's death was of natural causes, if you could call a nineteen-year-old's dying "natural." Now René DeLorris, who had been watching her lately, as if ready to tell her about something. What could it have been?

Jenn found herself spending more and more time on campus. She and Emily were happier the less time they spent at the little cottage. Jenn took a bitter relief in the fact that Emily hardly talked about the murder; Noreen's theory of Emily feeling guilty seemed wrong, but Emily was more clingy than usual, more fearful. They often ate dinner out, or went to the movies, not coming home until Emily was so tired she couldn't keep her eyes open. Then Jenn would tuck her into her bed and kiss her good night and pray there wouldn't be any nightmares.

Emily crawled into bed with her almost every night now, whispering that she was afraid of Daddy. Jenn herself hardly slept, unable to stop thinking about what had happened. She still managed to do her job well, but she knew it was only a matter of time before frustration and exhaustion took their toll. It didn't take long for Noreen to see that something was very wrong.

"Jenn, what's going on?" she demanded. "You look like you haven't slept in days.

"I haven't," she admitted. "At least, not very well."

"Are you still thinking about that man that died?" Noreen asked. "Or about what Emily said?"

"That, and a lot of other things," Jenn said. "We're very unhappy at that house, but I just can't find another place to live! I've looked everywhere!"

Noreen gave an understanding nod. "And I've kept my eyes and ears open. The trouble is, Jenn, that by now all the affordable apartments have been snatched up by students who don't want to live in the dorms."

"I don't know what to do," Jenn said. "I've got to get Emily out of that place, but we could hardly afford to spend the next few months in a motel."

"I wish I could help," Noreen said. "But my apartment is so tiny . . ."

Jenn smiled gratefully at her friend's kindness.

"That's okay," she said. "I'll work it out somehow."

But she didn't work it out, not quickly. Emily grew more and more babyish, frightened by the littlest noise, insisting her father was after her. She made a terrible fuss at bedtime and would only settle down when Jenn crawled in with her. There was no private time to catch up on work and personal needs. Jenn was exhausted, worried—and resentful. She snapped at her little girl more than a few times, and when she saw the hurt in Emily's eyes she felt as if she could cut out her tongue.

The tiredness would hit her at odd times—standing at the blackboard, eating lunch. She always managed to fight it down, but one day it was so overwhelming that she plunked down on a campus bench and buried her face in her hands.

She had to do something. This was killing her.

"Jenn?"

The sound of her name pulled her head up. Nick was standing there, holding a large foam box marked: FRAGILE: SPECIMENS.

"Are you all right?" he asked.

Jenn suddenly felt like crying, but she bit her lip and nodded.

"Could you use a friend?"

There was so much genuine concern in his voice that she couldn't resist him. Surprised at herself, she said:

"I'd like to have someone to talk to."

Noreen had always been willing to listen to her, but something about Noreen's manner made Jenn feel like she was being interrogated. Noreen didn't mean to be that way, of course, but that was just the way she *was*. Nick, for some reason, seemed more likely to listen without passing judgment on Jenn's sanity. In a million years, she couldn't have explained why she thought that way, so she didn't even try. She simply nodded her head when he said:

"We could have lunch."

They set off to find a quiet, private place to talk, taking Nick's car this time. By mutual agreement, they chose the colonial restaurant where they'd first had a meal together. Jenn hardly touched her roast chicken and sweet potatoes as she spoke to Nick. She found herself telling him almost everything, from the fright of seeing Evan in her rearview mirror to the horror of finding René speared by that pitchfork. She only left out her worries about Emily's "premonitions." They were just too bizarre to discuss with anyone, even a man who genuinely seemed to like her.

"No wonder you looked upset," Nick said. "You've been through hell lately. But none of those deaths was your fault. It was just coincidence that those people were somehow connected to you."

"I don't know what to think," Jenn said.

She stared at the light that glistened on the facets of her red crystal water glass.

"There's something else," she said. "I didn't notice it at first. But every time Emily and I return to the Bayless property, we both take a real downswing in mood. No matter how our days go, we always feel—oh, I don't know ... I guess we feel a little down. Isn't that crazy? That a piece of property could be so depressing?"

"From what you told me of it," Nick said, "it seems so seedy that anyone would feel bad there. I don't think that's so unusual."

"I do," Jenn replied. "Run-down or not, it's still better than the apartment we had in Buffalo."

"It has to be better than living in the dorm," Nick said. "How did you manage, with all the noise?"

Jenn smiled at him. "It wasn't easy, believe me. But we ..." She squinted at him suspiciously. "Are you trying to change the subject?"

He grinned, all innocence. "Am I?"

"Well, it would be nice to think of something different for a change," Jenn said.

"Anything that would make you smile," Nick suggested. "You're very pretty when you smile, you know. Your eyes get very bright."

Jenn looked down and pretended to concentrate on her plate. Evan had been full of empty compliments, too.

"Jenn?"

But why did Nick's words have to be empty? Why did she project Evan's personality on this man, who was nothing at all like him?

"Damn," Nick said. "I'm sorry. I shouldn't have ..."

Jenn looked up again, smiling. "It's okay," she said.

"I . . . I'm just not used to hearing a man say something nice about me."

"I could do it on a regular basis," Nick suggested. "Lunch twice a week, with a minimum of five compliments."

Jenn studied him. It took her a moment to realize he was teasing. She laughed.

"I'm serious," Nick said. "Jenn, I could say nice things about you all day."

"Well, it'd be pleasant," Jenn said. "Better than feeling lousy, the way I have been."

They both fell silent, concentrating on their lunches. Finally, Nick spoke again.

"Did it ever occur to you that you might be feeling bad because you never really had a chance to deal with what your ex tried to do?"

Jenn frowned at him. "No, not really."

"Listen," Nick said, leaning forward. "You went from the hospital to teaching without any real break. I read once that we deal with trauma in a four-step process."

"I know," Jenn said, recalling hearing the same thing. "Anger, denial, sorrow, and acceptance. Not necessarily in that order. I was angry enough, I'll tell you. And I felt sad about what happened to Emily. But I'll never accept what Evan did."

"That's the denial part," Nick said. "You aren't supposed to accept something like that. It was a rotten thing to happen, especially to a little girl. But I think they mean just accepting that it *happened*, putting it aside, and getting on with life."

Jenn was thoughtful. Once more, Nick had shown himself to be quite astute. It made sense that some of her bad feelings were vestiges of anger over Evan's attempt at murdering her and Emily. The thought was so profound that she felt tears rising. They had been fighting to spill from her eyes for days now, and there was nothing she could do to stop them. Nick was so caring, so kind . . .

He was suddenly at her side, holding her in his arms. They had chosen a booth for privacy, and no one could see them. Jenn let herself cry, but after a moment she pulled away. Nick stared into her eyes. Jenn held her breath. This was the part where he was supposed to kiss her, right? One emotion exchanged for another? It always happened that way in the movies . . .

But Nick slid away a little. He seemed to sense she felt uneasy.

"I'm sorry," she said in a quiet voice. "I just couldn't . . ."

"It's okay," Nick said.

They sat awkwardly silent for a moment, side by side. Then Nick reached for the water pitcher and refilled both their goblets.

"I hope this doesn't sound too forward," he said, "but have you considered counseling?"

"No." It was a lie. Jenn had thought about it, but she was afraid word would get back to Dean Stone, and she'd lose her position.

"Maybe you should think about it," Nick said. "Glen Miniver, our school counselor, could help you sort through things. He's a great guy—we've been friends for years."

Jenn shifted uncomfortably. "I don't want my problems spread all over school."

"Glen would keep anything you say in strictest confidence," Nick said.

Jenn was about to point out that rumors had shot through the campus like wildfire after their first lunch. But Nick was suddenly looking at his watch.

"We've got to get going," he said. "My next class starts in half an hour."

They paid the check and left. When they arrived back at

school, Nick gave her another quick hug. This time, Jenn found herself returning it.

"Don't worry," he said. "I'm sure everything will work out in the long run."

"Thanks, Nick," Jenn said. "Thanks for everything."

She walked to the math building with a slight smile on her face, and a feeling that her burdens had been lifted, if only for a little while.

All of a sudden, it was Thanksgiving week. Jenn was grateful to have something else to think about, and she was determined that nothing would spoil her sister's visit. Maybe things could be okay, after all. It had been almost three weeks since René's death, and even Laura was back to her cheerful self. Jenn became as busy as a squirrel, decking out the cottage in the prettiest fall finery. Emily was delighted by the change in the house. Jenn hoped it wasn't just the silk leaves and acorns and cornucopias. Maybe the holidays could be a new beginning.

Laura came knocking at the door on the Tuesday before Thanksgiving. Emily gasped and jumped up and down with glee when the woman held up a child-sized fancy dress. It had a full skirt, big puffy sleeves, and a huge bow at the back. The fabric was gold, orange, red, and purple, a tumble of leaves printed on cotton. Gold lace trimmed the neck and cuffs.

"My Thanksgiving gift to you," Laura said. "Do you like it? I'm pretty sure I got the right size."

Jenn didn't know what to say. She had been shopping just a week earlier, and she knew how much a dress like this cost. She thought of the simple yellow corduroy jumper and acorn-printed blouse she'd bought for Emily to wear on Thanksgiving, and her heart sank.

"It's beautiful," she managed to say, feeling the old jealousy rising again. "But I've already bought her a Thanksgiving dress."

"Oh, Mommy!" Emily whined. "It's so beautiful!"

"Yes, but . . ."

Laura smiled at the little girl.

"You can wear it on Sunday," she said. "And you can wear the dress from Mommy on the holiday. Here, try it on."

Before her mother could say a word, Emily took the frock and ran into her room.

"Laura," Jenn said, the word coming out in a sigh, "I wish you wouldn't do things like that. It's just too much!"

Laura tossed a hand at her.

"Oh, it was my pleasure, believe me," she said.

Your pleasure to show me up in front of my daughter.

Jenn chewed a fingernail for a moment, as if that could keep a nasty remark from coming out. She realized she was just being mean-spirited, and tried to soften her words.

"All right," she said, "since it's a holiday. But please, don't be doing anything fancy for Christmas!"

Laura laughed and promised she wouldn't.

Jenn didn't laugh, and hoped she and her daughter would be gone when Christmas came.

The bedroom door opened, and Emily danced into the room. Jenn sighed fondly, thinking her little girl really *was* beautiful in the dress. And she ached a little to see the long, warm hug Emily gave Laura. All she'd gotten for the corduroy outfit was a peck on the cheek.

There was that jealousy again! Jenn told herself it was wrong, and that if she let it fester it would ruin the holidays.

"Well, I've got to go now," Laura said. "I've got bread baking."

After she left, Jenn helped Emily out of the dress and

hung it in the closet. She tried not to see how much fancier it was than the dresses that surrounded it.

The next day, she took Emily to the grocery store for some last-minute shopping, letting Emily pick out a few things. They spent the afternoon rolling out pie dough and cutting up apples. Emily ate too many green peels and felt sick enough to go to bed early.

That night, she ran into her mother's room in hysterics. Jenn pulled her under the covers and hugged her.

"Daddy was looking in my window!" Emily wailed. "He was looking for me, and he had the pizza cutter, and . . ."

She broke into tears. Jenn soothed her, cradling the small body to her own. Why had the nightmare come back tonight? Things had been going so well! Was it the stomachache? Maybe Dickens was right about spirits being nothing more than a bit of undigested beef. Maybe Emily would be back to her old, cheerful self by morning.

But just to be safe, Jenn prayed for a long time before falling asleep.

The sound of the doorbell woke them early the next morning. As if nothing at all had happened, Emily leaped from her mother's bed to answer it.

"Aunt Rosalie! Aunt Rosalie!" she cried.

Jenn shrugged into a robe and was tying it as she hurried after her daughter.

"This early?" she said with surprise.

Emily opened the door to see Laura.

"I baked too many loaves of cranberry-nut bread," she said, holding out two foil-clad packages that looked like silver bricks. "Can you use these for company?"

"Sure," Jenn said, taking them. They still felt warm. It didn't surprise her that Laura had been up early today, baking. "Thanks a lot. Do you want to come in for coffee?"

"Oh, no," Laura said. "I've got to get ready to go. Peter's spending Thanksgiving with a friend, and I'm heading into Boston to see an old classmate."

"That sounds wonderful," Jenn said.

"I'll be back Sunday night," Laura told her. "Have a nice Thanksgiving!"

She gave both Jenn and Emily a quick hug and kiss, then walked back to her house.

Jenn swung around. "Well, I have a turkey to get in the oven!"

Later, when the cottage was filled with delicious smells and Emily was engrossed in the billionth rerun of Laurel and Hardy's *March of the Wooden Soldiers*, Jenn heard the sound of a car pulling up to the house.

"They're here!" she announced.

Emily got to the door first, yanking it open. Jenn was right behind her, taking off her apron. She watched as Rosalie opened her door and got out. Her sister looked great, her blonde hair cut in a pageboy, bangs fluffed up over her forehead. She was a little heavier than Jenn, but the curves looked good on her, and even after hours on the road she wore her khaki trousers and turtleneck sweater very well. Her smile was all sunshine as she hurried up to hug her sister.

Then she stopped short, her smile turning to a look of concern.

"Jenn, have you been sick?" she asked softly.

My God, is it that obvious?

"Just a little worn out from running back and forth," Jenn replied.

"Well, give me a hug hello," Rosalie said, coming closer. "And we can talk about this later."

Jenn embraced her sister, a chorus of childish voices sounding in the background. Her brother-in-law Travis, who was a dead ringer for Bruce Willis except for having more hair, came up to kiss her hello.

"You look great, Jenn," he said. "It's nice to see you."

Jenn looked at her sister, who made a face as if to say: *Men! They never notice anything different in a woman, do they!*

Still, Jenn was glad her exhaustion wasn't obvious to *everyone*. Then again, Travis always had something nice to say.

"Must be this mountain air," she said, smiling.

"I could get used to New England," Travis said.

"Ha!" Rosalie said. "The first snowstorm, and you'd be running south!"

Travis laughed, then called his kids over. There was fifteen-year-old Danny, handsome and blond, who took Jenn's hand with a shy "hello." Sandy, eight years old, tugged her sleeve and pulled her down for a kiss. Jenn smiled at the little girl. Last time she'd seen Sandy, the child had sat in a corner sucking her thumb and staring. Sandy was autistic, but her enthusiastic manner made it obvious that her parents had been working very hard with her.

Someone was missing.

"Where's Merrie?" Jenn asked.

"Moping around," Danny said.

"She's a little carsick," Rosalie said. "She'll be out in a few minutes."

Emily took Sandy by the hand and led her into the house.

"Wanna see Baci?" Emily asked. "She's my puppy and she's *sooooo* cute!"

The others followed, all but Jenn. She wanted to greet her niece, sick or not. As she approached the van, she noticed Meredith's eyes flitting all around, as if she was expecting something to jump out at her at any moment.

Jenn felt her heartbeat quicken. She'd seen that same nervous look on Emily's face, especially when she'd just had a vision of her father. What would make Meredith so frightened?

"Merrie?"

The young girl screamed, jumping back in her seat. Then she put a hand on her chest and stared at Jenn wide eyed. Jenn climbed in next to her.

She is *afraid of something.*

"Sorry," Jenn said. "I didn't mean to startle you. Your mom says you're sick?"

"I have a stomachache," Meredith said, in a way that told Jenn it wasn't her stomach at all.

"I'm sorry to hear that," Jenn said. "Why don't you come inside and lie on my bed? It's warmer, and more comfortable. And I hate to leave you out here alone."

Jenn hadn't meant it as a warning, but the idea of being alone seemed to frighten her niece. Meredith followed her into the house. Jenn showed her to the bedroom, then left her. She would talk to Meredith later. How could this place have an effect on a thirteen-year-old who had never been here before?

Travis and Danny had already settled in front of the TV, watching football; Jenn could see the little girls through Emily's opened door, rolling around the floor with the puppy. She was surprised to find her sister in the kitchen.

"What needs to be done?" Rosalie volunteered.

"Nothing," Jenn insisted. "I've got everything set."

In truth, she was afraid that her sister would take over completely if given the chance. It would be as bad as having Laura here directing the kitchen.

Now where the hell did that thought come from, Jenn?

She opened the refrigerator and pulled out a tray of cut-up vegetables. Before Jenn could stop her, Rosalie had the lid off the cup at the center. It was Rosalie who carried the tray into the dining room and put it on the table. She grabbed a carrot, crowned it with dressing, and came back into the kitchen munching it.

"Mom's dip recipe," she said approvingly.

"It's always been a favorite," Jenn said.

Rosalie perched on one of the tall stools that lined the wall between the kitchen and dining area.

"Okay, time to talk," she said. "Jenn, you look *terrible*."

Jenn's eyes widened in mock insult, but she couldn't bring truth into her voice when she said: "Thanks. Nice way for a sister to talk."

Because what Rosalie had said was true.

"I'm saying it *because* I'm your sister, Jennifer," Rosalie said.

Jenn cringed. God, she sounded just like their mother when she used Jenn's formal name.

She ran a finger through her hair and heard her sister make a *tsk tsk* sound.

"Look at those nails," Rosalie said. "You haven't stopped biting them yet, have you?"

"Have you quit cracking your knuckles?" Jenn shot back.

For a moment it seemed they would fight the way they had long ago, when they shared a room.

Then Rosalie backed off, her shoulders sagging a little.

"Jenn, I'm concerned, that's all," she said. "I haven't seen you look like this since you divorced Evan. Have you been sleeping? Is there something going on here?"

Rosalie's straightforward approach to things had always made it hard for Jenn to ignore her. She'd always been the mother hen, even when their mother was alive and well. It was Rosalie, through phone calls and letters, who had helped Jenn get through the divorce.

Suddenly she found herself opening up. She told everything, from the people who had died to the strange pests that had been invading her home. Tears began to form in her eyes as she spoke of Emily's visions of Evan, and her own nightmares. The talk was a catharsis, and she didn't object when Rosalie came to put her arms around her.

"No wonder you're a wreck," Rosalie said. "Jenn, have you seen a counselor?"

"What for?" Jenn asked, pulling away. Nick had suggested the same thing. Did they think she was going crazy?

"What for!" Rosalie echoed with surprise. "To help you deal with all this, of course! Maybe you haven't yet come to terms with what Evan tried to do to you. Maybe Emily hasn't, either."

Jenn felt uncomfortable, remembering what the doctor had said the day Emily came in with phantom snakebites on her body.

The day she'd seen Evan in the forest.

"I just haven't had the time," she blurted. "I want to get through the holidays."

"Well, don't put it off too long," Rosalie said.

Merrie entered the kitchen. Jenn was glad to see her, to have a chance to change the subject. Her niece still looked a little wary, but at least there was a slight smile on her face.

"Can I stay in here with you guys?" she asked.

"Sure," Jenn said. "Open the fridge and get yourself a soda."

"Hey, can you bring me one?" Danny called from the couch.

Rosalie lifted herself up higher. "When did you become a cripple, Daniel Dubicki?"

With a groan, the teenager pulled himself from the couch and shuffled into the kitchen. Jenn handed him a soda, plus a beer for his father.

"Hold up," she said, and filled a bowl with popcorn.

Emily must have heard the kernels falling against ceramic, because she came bounding out of her room in search of a snack. Sandy and Baci were close behind. Baci was excited by all the company, and it was an effort to keep her from under everyone's feet. When her big tail swept across the coffee table and knocked the popcorn all over the floor, Jenn thought she might lose her temper. But when she saw the way everyone was laughing, even Merrie, she relaxed.

If that was the extent of the day's disasters, then Thanksgiving would go pretty well.

seventeen

Meredith tried to tell herself she was being silly. No-body feels afraid for no reason at all. She was thir-teen, for crying out loud. Too big to see monsters in shadows.

But still she had a vague sense that something bad was going to happen, a feeling that overcame her the moment they turned onto the road that led to Aunt Jenn's house. She had been tired from the long car ride, two days on the road, and the sensation was like waking up from—or wak-ing into—a terrible nightmare. She had doubled over, moaning, tears coming to her eyes. Sandy had poked her arm and said something unintelligible. Her parents had been concerned.

She couldn't tell them the truth, so she made up a lie about her stomach.

And now she couldn't tell them about the dream she'd just had, while lying on Aunt Jenn's bed.

She'd been kneeling beside a pond, flicking the water with her fingers to lure goldfish to the surface. The sun had been warm on her back—it was summer, and she was wearing a halter top. Meredith thought this was weird, because she didn't even own a halter top. Mom and Dad thought they were vulgar. She accepted it, though, in the dream. Just as she accepted the snuffling noises of a horse that stood just a few feet away.

That part of the dream had been nice. Then she'd heard the low, feral growling and turned to see an ugly, bent, white dog sauntering toward her. The rest of the dream ran in fast-motion: the dog leaping at the horse and biting, blood and spit flying an all directions; the horse rearing up, whinnying in pain; a scream that was not her own but came from her, and the horse's hooves slamming down toward her . . .

She'd awakened at that moment, trembling. It wasn't the first time she'd had a nightmare, and she tried to do what her father had taught her; say out loud how ridiculous it was. She didn't even own a horse, and she'd never seen a rabid dog.

It didn't work. The whole thing had seemed too real, like a memory. Merrie knew Danny would make fun of her if he heard about it, and the grown-ups would make an embarrassing fuss. It was just a dream, a nightmare, something crazy her brain made up.

She jumped from the bed, but stopped herself short of crashing through the door. She took a deep breath, fixed her hair with her fingers, and left the room with a falsely calm demeanor.

Now she was helping to carry dishes to the table, the Thanksgiving feast about to begin. It was nothing like the dinners Mom put on, with almost as many courses as there were people. This was a small affair, just the seven of them. She was safe here in this warm little house, and it was a holiday. She was going to be happy about it, no matter what. Because, after all, thirteen wasn't a baby.

The table was too small for all of them, so Jenn had set up the coffee table for the little girls. They all sat down, said grace at Rosalie's insistence, then began to eat. Meredith was surprised that the food tasted pretty good. Her mother had always said Aunt Jenn wasn't much of a cook.

Apparently, Sandy thought the same thing because now she was whining about something.

"No Mommy's stuffing," she said.

Meredith turned to look at her little sister. Sandy looked kind of cute in her cream and brown striped jumpsuit, even though the sleeves were too big for her thin arms and she had the collar crooked. Meredith loved her sister, really, but sometimes Sandy was a big pain. Like when she got a bug about something and wouldn't stop. Meredith steeled herself for just such a display right now. Sandy had that look on her face . . .

"Of course it isn't Mommy's stuffing, Sandy," Rosalie said. "Aunt Jenn did the cooking today. Isn't it delicious?"

"Yucky! Yucky stuffing!"

She pushed her plate away, and in the process knocked her glass of milk over. It spilled off the table and onto Emily's lap. Emily howled.

"My dress! You stupid dummy!"

"Emily!"

The little girl didn't pay attention to her mother, and gave Sandy a shove. Sandy grabbed one of Emily's pigtails and yanked, hard. In seconds, the two little girls were fighting, until Travis got up and tugged them apart.

"Stop it! Sandy, you behave!" His angry tone stopped Sandy cold. She cringed, tears spilling down her cheeks.

"Not Mommy's stuffing," she pouted.

"Oh, brother," Danny mumbled.

Rosalie stood up and took Sandy from her father.

"We'll have to separate them," Rosalie said.

Meredith stood up. "I'll sit with Emily. I don't mind." And she really didn't, because she thought the grown-ups were about to get into an argument. Even being a few feet away would help. She picked up her dish, waited until Jenn had cleaned up the spilled milk on both the table and Emily, then sat down and started eating again.

"I like your stuffing," she said, meaning it.

Aunt Jenn smiled at her.

Everyone calmed down, and there wasn't a fight, after all. They talked about Danny's high school football team, Meredith's flute lessons, and finally about some guy who seemed to like Aunt Jenn.

"I'm so glad," Rosalie said. "You deserve someone decent, after that creep you put up with for so many years."

"Well, we're just friends," Jenn insisted. "I like Nick, but . . ."

"Famous last words," Rosalie said.

Travis picked up his wineglass. "Well, I certainly wish you all the luck."

"Thanks, Travis," Jenn said with a smile.

"OW!"

Meredith looked up from the turkey she was cutting to see her brother holding his hand to his cheek. He spat something into his palm.

"I lost my crown," he said.

"Your new one?" Travis asked.

Danny nodded, a look of pain on his face. "There was a nutshell in the sweet potatoes."

"Really?" Jenn asked. "But I didn't use any nuts, only marshmallows."

Travis took his son's hand and displayed the nutshell, alongside the crown.

"I'm sorry," Jenn said, with a shake of her head. "I don't know how that happened. I didn't do any baking today."

"You should be more careful," Rosalie snapped.

Jenn's eyes widened. "Excuse me, but I had a lot to do. People make mistakes, you know!"

"That mistake pulled out an eight-hundred-dollar tooth!" Rosalie said.

"Maybe we can find a dentist . . ."

"Oh, right! On Thanksgiving!"

"Rosalie, it was an accident," Travis put in.

"Shut up!" Rosalie snapped.

"Mom, it's okay . . ." Danny offered.

"You shut up, too!" Rosalie said. "What kind of slob doesn't clean up her kitchen? If she cleaned it up, there wouldn't have been any nutshells, and—"

Meredith shot to her feet. "Oh, why don't *you* shut up, Mom?" she screamed.

She ran to the door, grabbing her coat on the way outside, just wanting to get away. The sun was going down now, and shadows drew demons along the ground. She ran without direction, the fear that had accosted her in the car rising again. But the unnamed fear, somehow, was easier to take for the moment than all that bickering inside the house.

The sound of the slamming door shocked everyone into silence. Jenn looked around, seeing the uncomfortable looks as they all tried to figure out what had set them off. Emily climbed into her lap and fidgeted with Jenn's necklace.

"Well," Travis whispered.

Rosalie's eyes were big. She blinked a few times, shaking her head.

"I'm sorry, Jenn," she said. "I don't know what made me act like that."

Jenn managed to smile, although her thoughts were bitter. *It's this place. It makes everyone mean.*

She looked at Danny. "Are you okay?"

"I guess so," Danny said, "Mom, we have to find a dentist by Monday. Dr. Borgman says the teeth around a crown start shifting in about forty-eight hours."

"We'll take care of it, Danny," Travis promised.

Jenn looked toward the door. "Shouldn't one of us check on Merrie?"

"Let her stew," Travis said. "She's been a grouch since we got here."

"That's not really true," Rosalie defended her daughter.

Jenn, who had seen the fear in Meredith's eyes earlier on, couldn't say anything on her niece's behalf. This place was getting to all of them, but if she said so, Rosalie would think she was crazy. She turned her attentions to Emily.

"Why don't you go in your room and play with Sandy?" Jenn suggested, lifting Emily off her lap.

"When are we gonna have dessert?" Emily asked.

The adults laughed.

"At least one of us is no worse for the wear," Travis said.

"How can you be hungry after all that food?" Danny asked.

Emily frowned at them. What was so funny about wanting dessert?

"Give us a little time to digest," Jenn said.

While Jenn and the others cleared the table, Emily took Sandy to her room to play. The dog followed close behind, and patiently allowed itself to be dressed up in a bonnet and a doll dress. The little girls giggled as Baci paraded around with her paws stuck through the dress sleeves and her tail flicking the lacy skirt.

Suddenly, she stopped and stared at an empty corner of the room. Her lips turned up in a snarl, and she growled softly.

Then Tara was standing there.

"Where you come from?" Sandy demanded.

"Tara!" Emily cried with delight. "You were gone for a long time! Do you want to play with me again?"

Over the past week, Emily had gradually forgotten that Tara said she was the one who killed René DeLorris. She was just happy to have her best friend back again.

"Sure," Tara said. "But I only want to play with you, not her."

She gave Sandy a mean look that made the other child back away. Sandy poked a thumb in her mouth.

"What a baby," Tara said.

"She is not!" Emily insisted. "Sandy's my best cousin!"

To prove a point, Emily put an arm around Sandy's shoulder.

"Then play without me," Tara said. "I don't need you, anyway."

Baci let out one angry bark. Tara stomped at him, and with a yelp the dog ran under the bed. Smiling wickedly at the other girls, Tara vanished.

"How she do that?" Sandy asked. "How she dis'pear?"

"That's just how she comes here," Emily said. She was worried that Tara was angry and might do something bad. She just couldn't understand why they couldn't all play together. Didn't Tara see how nice Sandy was?

Outside, Meredith sat against an old oak tree with her arms wrapped around her legs, thinking how much she wanted to go home. She would bet her best friend, Leliah Patterson, was having a great vacation. It was warmer down south, and not as dark and spooky. Everyone said New England was beautiful in the fall.

"Fat lot they know," Meredith grumbled. "I hate this place."

"I hate you," came a small voice.

Meredith looked around twisting to see behind the tree, but there was no one there at all. The wind picked up speed and blew leaves at her.

"Who's that?"

She heard giggling now. Strangely, it seemed to be coming from overhead. She looked up, but she could just barely make out the flecks of stars through the branches.

Something dropped on her head.

"Hey!"

Meredith stood up quickly. Something hit her shoulder. She bent to the ground to pick up an acorn.

"Sandy, is that you up there?" she asked, annoyed.

There was no reply. Meredith told herself it couldn't be Sandy, or Danny, or even Emily. She would have seen them come out of the cottage.

"Who is that?" she cried out, her tone more demanding.

"Go home," the unseen person said. "Go away and take your stupid retarded sister and your stupid family. Emily is *mine*."

The voice was childish, yet so full of malice that Meredith felt her heartbeat quicken.

"Why don't you come down here and say that?" she asked with false bravado. Part of her wanted to bolt into the house, but part of her needed to see who this nasty little brat was.

"If I do," the child said, "I'll have to hurt you."

Meredith rolled her eyes. Maybe this kid had a creepy voice, but she was nothing more than an obnoxious little jerk.

"I'm not afraid of you," Meredith insisted.

"Then I'll give you something else to be afraid of."

Meredith stood watching the tree, expecting the child to either come down or throw something at her. From this point of view, with the outside lights of the cottage behind her, she could see the tree more clearly. And yet, try as she might, she couldn't make out any kind of human form in the branches. How was the kid hiding so easily?

Moments passed. The wind had stopped blowing and the night went deadly silent. Meredith was certain she could hear her own heart beating.

"Just go inside and forget it," she whispered.

But she wasn't sure she wanted to face her angry family any more than this mysterious, threatening child. She opted for the child. She was thirteen; the kid sounded young. Certainly Meredith could handle her. Once she grabbed hold of her, she'd drag her inside and tell the grown-ups what had happened.

More time passed; in reality, only minutes, but to Meredith it seemed like forever. The night remained still, not a leaf turning. At last, with a sigh, she decided the kid had gone off someplace else. Meredith turned to walk back into the house.

A hideous ugly dog blocked her path, staring at her with wild eyes, foam dripping from its mouth as it let out a deep, feral growl. Meredith knew it was impossible, but this looked just like the dog in her dream. She didn't dare shout or move for fear of setting the creature off.

Stay calm, stay calm, don't move. Oh, God, Merrie, don't move. Maybe it'll go away. GO AWAY!

She shouted in her mind what she couldn't shout at the dog.

"But we want *you* to go away!"

Meredith couldn't help gasping and turning at the sound of the child's voice. As she did so, the dog flew up at her with an angry bark and sank its teeth hard into her arm.

Meredith screamed, falling to the ground, throwing her free arm over her face to protect it.

Then the dog was gone. She saw the child now, a little girl with auburn hair, wearing a pale blue dress. The child glared at her.

"I told you to leave this place," she said. "I want you all to go home and leave us alone!"

She vanished. Meredith lay in shock, blood pouring from her arm.

Inside the house, everyone heard the sound of Meredith's scream. Jenn, closest to the door, was the first to run outside and find the teenager lying on the ground. Rosalie and Travis were close behind.

"Merrie!" Jenn cried. "Merrie, what happened?"

"Oh, dear Lord, she's bleeding," Rosalie said.

"Dog," Meredith choked out. "Little girl."

She burst into tears and let her father pick her up as if she were a small child. He carried her into the house, the women following. "Danny, there's a first-aid kit under the bathroom sink," Jenn instructed.

As the boy went to get it, Jenn hurried to the kitchen and grabbed a roll of paper towels. Rosalie all but grabbed them from her and began to soak up the blood. Travis had pulled a handkerchief from his pocket and was making a tourniquet.

"She says a dog bit her," Travis said.

The little girls had come from the bedroom. Emily was holding Baci, still dressed up like a doll. She backed away at the look on her aunt's face. Jenn's eyes widened.

"Oh, Rosalie!" she cried. "You don't think that little puppy . . . ?"

"What other dog is there?" Rosalie demanded. "That dog has the look of rottweiler to it. He could be vicious even at this age!"

Travis had bandaged Meredith's arm, but the blood was already soaking through, despite the tourniquet.

"I'm going to call an ambulance," he said. "I want a doctor to look at this."

"I hope that dog has it shots," Rosalie demanded.

"She's just a baby," Jenn said.

"Emily hugged the dog so tightly the puppy yelped. "It wasn't Baci! It wasn't!'

Jenn went to her daughter and stroked the little dog. "I know, dollbaby. Baci was with you the whole time, wasn't she?"

Emily nodded.

"Maybe it was a stray," Danny suggested.

Travis came back to tell them the ambulance was on its way. Jenn knelt down beside her niece now. Meredith's eyes were closed as she tried to fight the pain. Softly, Jenn asked.

"Meredith, was it Baci? Did Baci attack you?"

"Mommy, it wasn't!" Emily insisted.

Jenn ignored her. "Merrie?"

The teenager shook her head.

"Can you tell us what happened?" Jenn pressed.

Meredith shook her head again.

"Why don't you leave her alone?" Rosalie snapped. "Can't you see she's scared to death?"

Jenn stood up and looked at her sister. "Of what? A stray dog? If there's one out there, we need to find it."

"The dog went away," Meredith whispered, her eyes still closed. "It disappeared. The little girl disappeared"

"She's delirious," Travis said. "Damn! Where's that ambulance?"

"I'm afraid it's a long way to the nearest hospital," Jenn apologized.

Rosalie sat on the edge of the couch and took her

daughter's hand. Patting it a little too hard and fast she said nervously:

"How can you stand living here, so far from everything? We would have had the police and an ambulance here inside of five minutes!"

Jenn didn't answer her. She simply helped Travis change the bandage two more times. No one said anything in the moments that followed, except to reassure Merrie. Jenn was afraid anything she said might set Rosalie off. She wanted to talk to Meredith in private, to find out what really happened. She had to find out what she meant when she said "the little girl disappeared."

But the ambulance was there at last, and the EMTs were tending to the wound. Police officer Mike Hewlett arrived again, too. He promised Jenn that he'd search the woods for the dog. They both knew it had to be found and tested for rabies, but neither one said so out loud.

Jenn had a strange feeling they were never going to find the dog.

eighteen

Jenn stood at the window and watched the ambulance drive away, her arms around the two little girls who flanked her. Rosalie had ridden in the ambulance with her daughter, and Danny and Travis had followed in the family car. Outside, a team searched the woods for the mysterious dog.

"Mommy?" Emily asked softly.

"Hmm?" Jenn's eyes were fixed on the retreating red light.

"Y'know when Merrie said there was a little girl?"

Now Jenn looked down at her. "She's a little mixed up right now, dollbaby. She didn't know what she was saying."

Emily's blue eyes were huge with worry. "It was Tara, Mommy. Tara was mad 'cause Sandy's here to play with me, so she hurt Merrie!"

"Oh, Emily," Jenn said with frustration.

"Mommy, I don't want Tara to be mad," Emily insisted. "She's the one who keeps Daddy away. She keeps Daddy from finding my special door!"

Jenn put both her hands on her daughter's shoulders. "Emily, there is no special door between us and those who've died. Daddy can't come back here."

"Yes, he can," Emily said, pouting. "I saw him . . ."

"Tara bad girl," Sandy said.

Jenn let go of Emily and turned to her niece, frowning. Had Sandy seen something, or was this the talk of a disturbed child?

Meredith said she saw a little girl . . .

"No," Jenn said out loud, firmly pushing the idea away. Tara was only a figment of Emily's imagination. Sandy was just picking up on Emily's words, and if Meredith saw someone, it wasn't that mysterious child.

"We'll ask Merrie about it when she comes back," Jenn offered. She knew there was no point in trying to argue with the little girls. It would only upset them further, and the day had been ruined enough already.

She gave them each a tight squeeze and changed the subject.

"Are you still hungry for dessert, Emily?" she asked.

"Yeah!"

"Sandy hungry!"

Jenn smiled down at them. "Then let's see about that pumpkin pie."

Emily followed her mother into the kitchen, saying proudly, "I helped bake it!"

A short while later, they were all sitting in front of the television, watching a Thanksgiving special. A knock sounded at the door, and Jenn put her plate down to answer it. Mike stood there, shaking his head.

"If that dog was here," he said, "it's long gone now.

Just be sure you don't let the kids wander into the woods tomorrow."

"Will you come back?" Jenn asked.

Mike nodded. "It might be easier to spot the animal in the daylight, but I doubt we'll find anything."

Jenn felt a chill rush through her as she realized Mike had echoed her own thoughts.

"Dogs can travel twenty miles in a day," Mike went on, explaining himself.

Of course, Jenn thought, he wouldn't think anything supernatural was going on.

"I'm just so worried for my niece," Jenn said. "I hate to think of her going through rabies treatment if it isn't absolutely necessary."

"Yeah, that's a lousy thing," Mike agreed. He looked back over his shoulder at the big house. With all the lights out, it was nothing more than a dark shadow. "I'll alert Mrs. Bayless about the situation. She might know something about the dog. And if she doesn't, her husband might. Or the kid—he's with his dad right now."

Jenn's heart seemed to stop beating for a moment. "Her husband?"

Mike gave Jenn a strange look. "Well, yeah—I mean, her ex-husband. They were divorced a while back. Len Bayless lives about fifty miles from here."

"Oh, yes," Jenn mumbled, "I suppose I forgot."

She didn't let Mike know that Laura had told her the man was dead.

"That's it, then," Mike said. "We'll be back in the morning."

He started to walk away. Jenn called to him:

"Would you like a piece of pie? You and your team?"

Mike laughed and patted his stomach. "My wife brought us all Thanksgiving dinner at the station. We're stuffed more than the turkey was!"

Jenn joined in his laughter, but the moment she closed the door she stopped. Confusion washed over her. Why had Laura lied about her husband, saying he was dead? Laura had even had to compound the lie by saying Peter was with a friend, not her husband.

She took a deep breath. There was no sense pondering the question right now, with Laura off in Boston. She'd ask her about it when she came home. Surely there was a perfectly good reason for the lie.

Jenn went back to join the girls at the television. Seeing her empty plate, she asked:

"What happened to my pie?"

"Baci ate it," Emily said with a giggle.

Jenn looked at the puppy, who stood looking guilty with light brown pie filling on its mouth.

"Thanks," she said sarcastically and stood up to get herself a new piece.

As she stood at the counter cutting the pie, a movement outside the window caught her attention. For a brief instant, she thought she saw someone standing a few yards from the house, staring at her. A child in a pale-colored, short-sleeved dress—hardly the right clothes for a chilly November night.

"What the hell?" Jenn whispered.

Then the image was gone, so fast that Jenn had to tell herself it was only a trick of the light on the glass.

"Nothing more," she whispered shakily.

In spite of her daughter's protests that she wanted to stay up until everyone came back, Jenn put Emily and Sandy to bed a short time later. She then busied herself preparing the living room for sleeping quarters, pulling out the sofa bed and making it up. The quiet was eerie in a house that had been so full of activity earlier in the day. Every time she passed a window, she avoided looking out into the night, but she never let herself think what it was she was afraid to see.

Jenn was grateful when the front door finally opened and the Dubicki family dragged themselves inside. Meredith's eyes were half closed, and with a weak round of good nights she went to bed. Danny yawned and said:

"This has been one weird experience, man."

With that, he went off to the bathroom. Jenn started to ask her sister for details, but Rosalie's eyes were rimmed with dark circles and her mouth was slack. She seemed half-asleep on her feet, worn out by the night's events. Without a word, Rosalie went to the sofa bed that Jenn had pulled out earlier and laid down.

"What happened, Travis?" Jenn finally asked her brother-in-law.

"I don't know," Travis said, a look of complete bewilderment on his face. "I just don't get it. We brought Merrie to the emergency room, but when the nurse washed away the blood, there was nothing there! The doctor came in and checked her head to foot, but there wasn't even a scratch on her."

"Travis, we saw the bite mark," Jenn reminded. "We saw the blood soaking through those bandages!"

"I know," Travis said. "The doctor thought Merrie might have pulled a trick on us."

He looked his sister-in-law in the eyes, as if she might know the answer.

"But Merrie's a good girl," he said. "She wouldn't pull something like that!"

"Of course she wouldn't," Jenn agreed.

She glanced at her sister, who had fallen asleep in her clothes.

"How's Rosalie?"

Travis looked at his wife. "She was furious, blaming you and everyone else in the world for what happened.

She rattled on the whole ride home—that is, until we reached the road up to this cottage. Then she just clammed up and sat staring at nothing."

Jenn couldn't help a shiver. How many times had her mood—and Emily's—changed when they drove onto the farm?

"I guess the important thing is that Merrie's really okay," Travis said.

"That's right," Jenn agreed, grasping at something positive. "And I'm sure we'll be able to figure this out after a good night's sleep."

Wishful thinking, Jenn. You know damned well there's no answer to this.

Danny came out of the bathroom just then, and his father went in. Jenn helped the teenager unroll a sleeping bag. He would be bedding down on the floor, behind the couch.

"Danny, can I ask you something?"

"Sure, Aunt Jenn."

"Did you notice anything odd when you came here today?" Jenn asked. If Meredith had sensed something, maybe Danny had, too, and hadn't mentioned it.

"Only my sister acting nuts," Danny said. "If you ask me, she started this whole thing. She's just pissed because she wanted to stay home and be with her friends over the holidays. Mom and Dad'll get the real story from her tomorrow."

Jenn was about to ask him how he thought his sister could pull off such an elaborate trick when Travis came into the living room dressed in his robe. She decided it was no time to get into any deep discussions. They were all completely worn out, and their brains were too tired. Instead, she said good night and went into her own room.

Meredith was sound asleep on her side of the bed. Jenn got into a nightgown and climbed in next to her, turning

her back to the young girl. She was glad Meredith slept so
soundly. In spite of anything the doctor, and Danny, had
said, she knew that something *had* happened to her niece.
Something that had to do with this farm.

In the darkness of her room, the bustle of the holiday
behind her, Jenn fell asleep and began to dream.

She was back in Buffalo, married to Evan again. Everything in the apartment was blue—the walls, the furniture,
everything. She held up her hand—it was also blue.

Blue for sadness.

In the background, she could hear the sounds of animals: neighs, honks, moos. A deep and almost demonic
growling made her turn and look behind her. A white dog
stood there, hackles up, teeth bared.

"You're the one," Jenn said to it, her voice strangely de-
tached. "The one who bit Merrie. Where are you now?"

*Where are you now? Where are you now? Where
are . . . ?*

Her voice echoed down the long, blue hall. The dog
stopped growling and spoke to her in Evan's voice:

"Payback is a bitch, Jenn."

"Dogs don't talk," Jenn said dully.

The dog turned and ran away. There was a large circle
of blood where it had been.

"HELP ME! MAMA, HE'S HURTING ME!"

The scream made everything abruptly turn white, and in
the dream her eyes squeezed shut at the brilliance.

Squinting, blinded, Jenn groped through the glare that
surrounded her. She realized it wasn't one singular light,
but a million lights that seemed to emanate from a million
tunnels. Emily had spoken of a "special door." Did these
lights really lead from the land of the dead to the land of
the living?

Am I dead?

Her fingers found a doorknob. The "special door" was

real, she thought with surprise. She could hear Emily crying loudly behind it, begging her father to leave her alone. The voice was a baby's, with a two-year-old's lisp. She tried to open it, this door made of light, but it was locked. The light felt as solid as a real door when she pounded it.

"EVAN! EVAN, YOU BASTARD! LET HER OUT OF THERE!"

She felt a tap on her shoulder and turned.

The while brilliance shut off as if controlled by a switch, and she was looking at Evan through a blood-red mist.

"I'm going to make you pay," Evan growled.

"Go to hell, Evan," Jenn said, her dream voice oddly calm and disconnected.

Behind the locked door, Emily screamed.

Evan roared.

His face began to darken, from the strange red, to a darker purple-red, to black. The colors seemed to carry away pieces of his flesh and hair as they changed, pulling in his skin until it hugged his skull, charring the skull until there was nothing left of his face.

Jenn woke up with a start, her breath caught like a hard lump deep in her lungs. It took a real effort to blow it out, then suck in reviving air. It was just a nightmare, she told herself. A noise in her bed made her gasp, and her heart pounded wildly. There was another pig here, she just knew it . . .

She dared to look, and almost laughed out loud to see Merrie stirring in her sleep. But the smile faded when she heard the frightened whimpers coming from her niece. She reached over and switched on the bedside lamp.

Instantly, Meredith opened her eyes. They were big and shining in the dim light, and spoke of her fear. Jenn knew at once that she'd also had a nightmare.

"Merrie?"

"He's coming," Merrie whispered in a voice without inflection. "Payback is a bitch, Jenn."

Then she rolled over and fell asleep. Jenn wanted to wake her again, but the kid had been through so much that she didn't have the heart. Still, she wanted to know if Merrie had had the same dream.

She started to say that was impossible, but stopped herself. A lot of seemingly impossible things had been happening lately.

There would be no sleep for Jenn that night. The words Emily had cried out in the dream came back to haunt her.

Help me, Mama. He's hurting me!

She'd heard those words long ago, when Emily used to have nightmares after her weekends with Evan.

The child's scream echoed over and over in her mind, until she said something to stop them:

"Something's different."

Her voice seemed loud in the darkness, but Meredith didn't even stir.

"Stop him, Mama," Jenn whispered. *"Mama."*

That was it. Emily never called her "Mama." It had always been "Mommy." Someone else called her mother "Mama."

Tara.

When Emily spoke of Tara, she referred to Tara's mother as "Mama."

"My God, is that little brat haunting my dreams now, too?" she asked in a whisper.

She turned to look at Meredith, sound asleep again. She could almost understand "Tara" entering her dreams. But how had she gotten into Meredith's mind?

Danny's dreams started out in a more pleasant way. He was back home again, celebrating Thanksgiving with his girlfriend Mindy. Dinner was over, he was stretched out on the couch, and she was leaning over him to kiss him. Her breath smelled of turkey, and cranberries, and coffee.

"You don't drink coffee," Danny said in his dream.

"Drink it all the time."

It was a man's voice, and when Danny opened his eyes, he saw a pair of wild, reddened eyes staring down at him from a man's face.

"Who the . . ."

"Get the hell away from here," the man growled. The Thanksgiving smells had left his breath, replaced by something so fetid that Danny tried to turn away.

But he couldn't.

"Get the hell away from my business!"

Danny tried to cry out, but the man clamped a hand over his mouth. He pressed so hard that Danny was terrified his front teeth might be crushed.

Then he woke up. Danny was too old to be afraid of nightmares, especially ones that made no sense. He lay there in the dark, the floor hard beneath his back, and marveled that he could still feel the sensation of a hand over his mouth. He ran his tongue over his teeth, to check that they were okay.

Danny's breath caught in his throat. His teeth felt *strange*. One front tooth overlapped the other at an angle. He could feel spaces where none had existed before. And his teeth were big, huge, twice as large as before.

He tasted blood.

He scrambled out of the sleeping bag. This was crazy. He had to still be dreaming! But he was keenly aware of everything around him as he made his way to the bathroom. His father sleeping on the couch, the dog curled up near the kitchen door, the hum of the furnace. He could also feel things moving in his mouth, as if his teeth had taken on a life of their own. Pushing, crowding, hurting.

He switched on the bathroom light and at once his eyes snapped shut against the brilliance. Pain rumbled in his head for a few moments, joining the pain in his mouth. Blood choked him, and, half blind, he spit it into the sink. Soft clinking made him open his eyes.

Three of his teeth sat in a glob of red.

Danny looked up at the mirror. His T-shirt was stained with blood that had dripped over his lower lip. Slowly, he opened his mouth.

His front teeth had grown as big as a beaver's, crossing each other in an *X*. Some teeth pushed out toward his face, some pointed back into the cavern of his bleeding mouth. Frantic, Danny opened his mouth farther and looked in the back. In several places, there were gaps where his molars should have been.

"Gush a dream," he said, unable to form the words.

But he could hear things, feel things, taste things! This was *real*.

He heard giggling and swung around.

There was a little auburn-haired girl standing in the bathroom. She pointed at his mouth.

"Gee, it didn't take forty-eight hours, did it?"

Danny began to scream.

Sandy was keenly aware that she could suddenly talk, and make sense. But she wasn't surprised. To her dream self, she'd always been talking like that. She was glad, too, because she needed to talk—no, to *yell*—so she could help Emily. Uncle Evan was chasing Emily, and he had a big pizza cutter. He was going to whack off her tongue . . .

"You told! You told that judge lies and now I'm going to punish you!"

Sometimes Uncle Evan was crazy.

"Come on, Emily! RUN!"

Sandy took her cousin by the hand and yanked her

along, toward the woods. They could hide in the trees, be safe from Uncle Evan. He couldn't cut them up in here.

They nearly bumped into Tara.

"Does your Uncle Evan cut things up? My mama does. My mama cut up all the animals and put them in a pit. You wanna see?"

"No!" Emily cried.

"I'll go," Sandy said, because it didn't seem like a scary thing to her.

Emily screamed the whole way, but Sandy wouldn't let go of her hand. They walked until they reached a sunken place in the middle of a clearing. Tara pointed.

"They're under there," she said. "Mama killed them and then she made Peter help her bury them. And pretty soon, Emily's mommy will be in there, too."

It was Emily's cry that woke Sandy up. Both little girls sat up and stared at each other, faces illuminated by the moonlight. Then Emily gave Sandy a hard push.

"You made me go into those woods, you dummy!" Emily accused. "You made me see the place with the dead animals!"

Emily ran to her mother's room. She climbed in between Meredith and Jenn. When her mother asked what was wrong, she whispered, "Dead animals in the woods," and fell asleep.

Danny's screams were so loud that Travis didn't hear his youngest daughter crying. He ran into the bathroom to find his son staring at the mirror, his eyes nearly bulging with fear. He was pawing at his mouth, as if trying to wipe something away. But Travis couldn't see anything wrong at all.

"Danny?"

"My teef!" he screamed. "Sumpin' happen to my teef!"

Travis took his son by the shoulders and turned him away from the mirror.

"Danny, wake up!" he said sharply. "You're dreaming!"

Danny pointed at his mouth. "My teef!"

"Your teeth are fine!" Travis insisted. "Look!"

He swung the boy around to face the mirror. To Danny's relief, his mouth was perfectly normal. He no longer tasted blood, and when he looked down at the sink it was dry and empty.

In a gesture uncharacteristic for this fifteen-year-old, Danny threw his arms around his father. Travis patted him on the back.

"Just a dream, son," he said.

"This is a bad place," Danny whispered.

The brilliant light of the sun found its way into the cottage early the next morning, warming bodies and waking minds. It seemed to wash away not only the darkness but the terrors of the previous night. Standing in the kitchen making pancakes, the sky bright and blue through the window over the sink, it was possible for Jenn to look at Thanksgiving Day from a different perspective. Sunlight brought strength, a willingness to fight whatever it was that haunted her. She still planned to leave the farm, but it would be in her own good time.

Meredith came into the kitchen first. Yesterday she'd been dressed up for the holiday, but this morning she looked more like a typical teenager: sweatshirt, jeans, hair flowing over her shoulders. She had her father's dark hair, but her mother's blue eyes, and the first thing Jenn noticed was how those eyes were shining. As if photons of sunlight had found their way inside, felt comfortable, and refused to leave. Meredith was smiling.

"Good morning, Merrie," Jenn said. "You look happy. Feeling better?"

"I feel great," Meredith said. "Except for feeling like a jerk about yesterday. I don't know what was wrong with me, Aunt Jenn. I'm really sorry for being a dork."

"Getting bit by a dog hardly qualifies you as being a dork," Jenn said. "Can I take a look at your arm, Merrie?"

Her niece frowned. "Dog? Aunt Jenn, Baci didn't bite me."

"We know it wasn't Baci," Jenn agreed. "And I don't care what the doctor said—something happened to you last night."

"Aunt Jenn, you're talking funny," Meredith insisted. "Nothing at all happened to me."

Travis entered the room just then, with Danny at his side.

"How ya feelin', baby?" he asked his daughter.

"See any more weird dogs?" Danny inquired.

Meredith's eyebrows went up. "What is it with you guys? How come everyone thinks something happened to me?"

"She doesn't remember it," Jenn said softly.

Danny grunted. "That figures."

Travis gave his teenaged daughter a kiss on the forehead. "It's all for the best, then. You just gave us a big scare last night, honey, that's all."

"What did I do?"

Jenn set a plate of pancakes on the table and said, "You ran outside after we all had a fight at dinner. We heard you scream a while later, and found you with blood on your arm."

Meredith frowned as she poured herself a glass of juice.

"I remember running outside," she said, "but nothing else."

"Why don't we drop this?" Danny asked. "She's just doing it to bug you guys."

"Be quiet, Daniel," Travis said sternly.

Now the two little girls ran into the room, dressed in their nightgowns. Baci tore around their legs.

"Hi, Mommy," Emily said.

"Where's my hug?" Jenn asked.

Emily ran to her and practically leaped into her arms. She kissed her mother's cheeks, left and right, three times each before pulling away.

"I'm having the best time, Mommy," she said. "Sandy is my most favorite cousin. Can she stay here?"

Relieved that Emily wasn't dwelling on the previous night, Jenn laughed and said:

"I don't know, dollbaby."

Jenn looked over at her brother-in-law. He looked up from the pancakes he was cutting for Sandy and shrugged.

"I don't know how long we're going to stay," he said. "It's up to Sandy's mother."

"We're supposed to stay the whole weekend, aren't we?" Meredith asked.

"Well, after what happened . . ."

"Oh, man," Danny said, "we aren't going to hit the road that fast, are we?"

"Danny, I thought after last night . . ."

"It was just a crazy dream, Dad," Danny insisted. "I'm too old to be scared by nightmares."

The look on Travis's face told Jenn that her brother-in-law didn't believe his son.

Emily ran to her uncle and tugged at his arm.

"Please stay, Uncle Travis!" she cried. "Please! Sandy hardly got any time at all to play with Tara."

"Tara?"

"Emily's friend," Meredith said. She leaned forward and whispered: "Make-believe."

"She is not!"

Jenn could see the possibility of another fight, and came to the rescue with Emily's plate of pancakes.

"Sit down and eat, dollbaby," she said. To everyone in general, she announced: "That's fresh Vermont maple syrup."

"It's great," Danny said.

"Not our syrup," Sandy pouted.

Meredith sighed. "Not again, Sandy, please?"

"Be good, Cassandra," Travis said in a warning tone.

Jenn could see another fight brewing and quickly changed the subject.

"It looks like we have a beautiful fall day," she said. "Maybe we can do something special."

"Hiking?" Danny suggested.

"There's probably lots of sales," Meredith said.

A fight was averted as they discussed possible plans for the day. Jenn was the first to see Rosalie enter the kitchen, the clothes she was still wearing from the day before all rumpled. Her hair hung in strings, and her eyes were even more darkly shadowed than the night before.

"Rosalie," Jenn gasped, shocked at her sister's appearance.

Rosalie stared hard at her. "You knew, didn't you? You knew about the monsters."

"What monsters?" Danny asked.

"Monsters?" Sandy wailed in fear.

Travis stood up and went to his wife. She shook off the hand he tried to put on her shoulder.

"There's something evil in this house, Jenn," Rosalie said darkly. "Something that tried to hurt my children last night!"

"No, Rosalie . . ." Jenn said weakly.

"Rosalie, Meredith's all right," Travis said. "She doesn't even remember what happened."

"Nothing happened!" Meredith cried.

"Yes, it did!" Rosalie screamed. She grabbed Travis's

arm. "We're leaving, now. I want everything packed up within the hour."

"Oh, Mom, no!" Meredith begged. "We just got here! We were going to do something special with Aunt Jenn today."

"Wanna stay!" Sandy cried.

Rosalie ignored them. "I want to leave, Travis. I want to leave!"

She burst into tears. Travis put his arms around her, and said over his shoulder:

"Jenn, she's just worn out. She'll change her mind."

But Rosalie didn't change her mind, and an hour later Travis led three dour children to the car. He gave his sister-in-law a hug and apologized.

"I just don't understand what happened, Jenn," he said.

"I guess . . . I guess it was just all of us crowded in this little house," Jenn lied, grasping at any explanation to give Travis.

She looked into the car, where Rosalie was sitting and staring.

"Rosalie, what can I say?"

Now her sister turned to stare at her. "Say you'll leave, Jennifer. Say you'll find another home, as soon as you can. This place is horribly dangerous for you and for Emily. Something bad is going to happen if you stay. Something terrible!"

nineteen

After her sister's family left, Jenn sat at her table for almost an hour, cradling a cup of coffee and trying to piece together what had happened. When she ended up with more questions and no answers, she pushed the coffee cup away and stood up.

"Emily, we're going out," she announced.

Emily had set up her dolls around the coffee table and was reenacting Thanksgiving dinner. The pink teddy represented Emily, a rabbit stood in for Sandy. Sandy the Rabbit was knocking invisible food into Emily the bear's lap. Emily had the two stuffed animals fighting with each other.

All the more reason to get away from here, Jenn thought, *if only for a little while.*

They wound up at the shopping mall, where Emily found something she wanted for Christmas in almost every store. Jenn was glad Emily hadn't carried the troubles of Thanksgiving Day with her. It amazed her how well the kid could bounce back. If only she could be like that!

After lunch, though, she realized she had to go back home sometime. She delayed the inevitable by stopping at the grocery store. With all the leftovers, she certainly didn't need anything, but made an excuse that they were running low on milk. As she entered, she saw the community bulletin board near the front desk. She wondered why she hadn't noticed it before and stopped to fill out a few blank cards:

WANTED: 2-BEDROOM APARTMENT FOR MOM AND CHILD, NEAR CAMPUS.

She jotted down her phone number and posted the cards in various places. Then she did her shopping and drove home again. After she parked, Emily asked if she could play outside.

"Sure," Jenn said. "Just stay close to the house."

When she found the note Mike Hewlett had left on the door, she was reminded of the stray dog. He said they'd looked more carefully, but it seemed the animal was gone. Jenn went inside the house and put the milk away. She looked out the kitchen window, recalling the child she'd thought she'd seen.

"But she wasn't there," she said, "And I bet the dog wasn't, either."

Not in a way anyone could prove it, she ammended in her thoughts.

Outside, Emily had found a rake leaning against the side of the house and had made a square of leaves. She raked some away from a "doorway," then started to make a connecting square.

She guessed that Tara didn't like Sandy.

"Damn right I don't," she heard her friend say.

"Why?" she asked Tara, not questioning the child's sudden appearance.

"Because she's a stupid dummy."

"Sandy isn't a dummy!"

"She isn't as smart as me," Tara said. She pointed to the ground. "What's that?"

"I'm making a leaf house," Emily said. "Want to play? I can bring out my dolls, and my dishes. And I can bring out Baci for a guard dog, in case Daddy tries to come."

Tara stepped into one of the "rooms," and the leaves on the surrounding walls scattered. There was no wind.

"Don't mess it up!"

Tara ignored her. "I told you there's only one way to be sure your daddy doesn't come get you. You have to let me be inside you, to trick him."

"Mommy likes me this way," Emily said. "I'll be right out."

She was nearly to the door of the house when she suddenly heard a low, feral growling. Was Baci outside? But the puppy had never sounded so *mean* before. Emily turned.

It was the dog she'd seen when she looked out the attic window. Maybe it was the one that had bit Meredith! Its filthy white hackles stood in points, its mouth curled in foaming madness. Emily screamed, backing away.

"Tara! Tara, make it go away!"

But Tara was nowhere to be seen.

A second later, her mother opened the door to see what was wrong. Emily ran to her.

"The dog, Mommy! The ugly dog!"

Her mother lifted her up and hugged her.

"Emily, there's no dog out here," she said.

Emily dared to look back over her shoulder. She could see the vast stretch of farmland between the cottage and the house. Wherever she turned, more open space came into view. No dog could run that quickly, especially not a bent one.

"I . . . I think he went where Tara goes," Emily stammered.

She felt her mother's shoulders stiffen, but Jenn's tone was gentle when she said, "Come in the house, dollbaby. It's getting a little cold out here. Funny how fast the temperature dropped!"

"Okay, Mama."

Jenn put her down inside the door, closed it, then knelt down.

"Why did you call me that?"

"What?"

" 'Mama'," Jenn repeated. "You never call me that."

Emily giggled. "You're silly. I always call you 'Mommy'!"

She ran into the living room to play with Baci. But the dog's tail bent down between her legs, and she began to whine.

"Baci, what's the matter now?"

She reached out toward the dog, who barked a warning at her and ran for the front door.

"I guess she needs to go out," her mother suggested.

Jenn opened the door and the dog shot out as if propelled by a jet engine. Emily sighed. Sometimes, Baci was so *weird*.

She went to her room. Since they'd moved in, her mother had added a few things to the wall: pictures of family members, a painting of a basket of kittens, a dinosaur poster. A poster of the Future Fighter named Tammi, dressed in a silver costume like the one Emily had worn at Halloween, decorated the wall beside her bed.

Right now, though, she thought it was stupid. Tammi was a geek!

She climbed on the bed and started to tear it down. The

ripping noise seemed to snap something inside her. She blinked a few times, stared at the damage she had done, and started to cry.

Jenn came into the room.

"Emily! Why did you tear your poster?"

"I don't know, Mommy," Emily whispered. "I—I thought Tammi was a geek."

"Don't tell me we're going to go through that again," Jenn said wearily.

"But I love Tammi, Mommy!" Emily said, tears in her eyes. "I don't know why I ripped my poster!"

"Well, I'll get the tape and fix it," Jenn said.

In the kitchen, as she searched the junk drawer for tape, Jenn told herself that Emily's behavior was perfectly normal. Calling her "Mama" just once and tearing a favorite poster were just the kinds of impulsive things a typical four-year-old would do.

Except that Emily wasn't a typical four-year-old.

She went back into the room, taped the poster, then offered to play scrabble with her daughter. Even at four, the child had an extensive enough vocabulary to make the game interesting. But Jenn would have played something as simple as Candyland to be with her daughter. Maybe that was the problem. With all the holiday activities, had she really paid enough attention to the child?

"You go first, dollbaby," she said.

Emily's first word was *strange*.

Jenn countered with *train*.

Emily crossed the *e* for *death*.

Then: *stout; trouble; dog; pain; robot; punish.*

"Emily, for heaven's sake," Jenn said. "Can't you think of any nice words?"

"Tara likes these words."

"You tell Tara to butt out," Jenn replied. "This is our

game. And if you don't start putting down some pleasant words, we won't be able to play."

"Then we won't!" Emily cried, knocking the board from the table and scattering pieces in all directions. She got up and ran for the door, grabbing her coat. Tara was waiting for Emily outside, standing in a field of scattered leaves that had once been the little girl's pretend house. Emily stopped short, still holding her jacket. She felt dizzy, as if someone was pulling hard on her head. Her small knees felt weak and shaky. Closing her eyes, she began to cry. It *hurt*.

"Don't do that," Tara said. "It's okay. You just aren't ready yet."

Then the pulling stopped, and her knees were strong once more. She opened her eyes to see Tara smiling.

"What happened?" she whispered.

"Just trying something out on you," Tara said with a smile. "I was inside you, and you didn't even know it."

Emily pulled on her coat. She knew her mother would open the door to yell at her, and she didn't want to go inside. She didn't want to pick up the letter tiles.

"You made me do that, didn't you?"

"Do what?" Tara asked with a smile. Her eyes were big and guileless.

"You aren't very nice sometimes," Emily growled.

"I could leave," Tara threatened. "You know, your daddy almost got to you yesterday. If I hadn't gotten between you . . ."

Emily backed away. "Please, don't!"

Tara looked toward the woods. "He walks around in there. I don't know why, but it's as close as he can get to you. He almost got to your mother a few times, but something protects her. I don't think she has a friend like me, though."

She turned back to Emily, staring down at the smaller

child. "She better get one, if she can. Because there's no way she can stop him once he finds a way through to you. And I'm only strong enough to protect you, not her."

Emily's lower lip began to tremble, and now tears did spill from her blue eyes.

"I don't want Mommy hurt," she said.

"If you become me," Tara suggested, "he'll get all confused and he'll go away. If you don't let me inside of you, then your mommy gets it, too."

"No!" Emily cried. "No! No! Nonononono!!!!"

Screaming it, she ran back into the house. Her mother was on the floor, picking up the last of the scattered tiles. Emily slammed into her, knocking her down. While Jenn lay on the floor, Emily lay on top of her, hugging her, crying.

"I want to go away from here, Mommy! I want to go away!"

Jenn hugged her back.

"We will, dollbaby," she promised. "We will, as soon as I can find a new place. Do you want to tell me what happened?"

Emily shook her head. She closed her eyes and rested against her mother, feeling secure for the moment.

On Saturday, Jenn took Emily to lunch, the video parlor, the movies, and finally to dinner. It was just to stay out of the house. When she got home, she tried to give Noreen a call, just wanting to talk to another adult. Noreen wasn't home, and Jenn couldn't bring herself to relate her worries to an answering machine. She simply stated a holiday greeting and hung up. For a moment, she thought about calling Nick Hasken, but rejected the idea simply because it made her feel uncomfortable to turn to a man.

On Sunday, Jenn was sweeping leaves from her front walk when she saw Laura's car pull up to the big house.

She took a peek around the side of the cottage to see Emily playing happily with Baci. The dog didn't seem to be afraid of her at all today. It was almost like she was an entirely different person.

"I'm going to talk to Laura, Emily," she announced, and trudged up to meet the woman.

Laura emerged from her car laden with shopping bags. She gave Jenn a cheerful greeting.

"How was your Thanksgiving?"

"Interesting," Jenn said in understatement. "How about you?"

"Oh, I had a great time," Laura said. "My friend and I must have hit every store in Boston."

Jenn studied her for a moment. "What's your friend's name? Walter?"

"Walter?" Laura's laugh was a little nervous. "No, her name is Betty. Walter was my husband. You know that."

"I know he isn't dead, Laura," Jenn replied.

She explained what Mike Hewlett had said, and watched the color drain from Laura's face.

"Why don't you come inside, and we'll talk?"

Looking back over her shoulder, Jenn saw that Emily had raked leaves into a pile and was jumping into it with the dog.

"I have to watch Emily," she said.

"You can see her through the kitchen window," Laura said. "Please, I need to explain."

Jenn relented, wanting to get to the truth. Inside the kitchen, Laura told a story of an unhappy marriage. The perfect husband she'd created for Jenn's benefit was a lie. Walter had been cruel, domineering.

"I was so ashamed," she said. "I didn't want to say what really happened."

"Ashamed?" Jenn said. "To talk to someone who's been

there, too? I would have understood, Laura. And I wouldn't have pressed for details. I'm not like that."

Even if I did tell you everything about Evan and me . . .

"Oh, no," Laura said. "We're different. You had the courage to leave your man. But Walter left *me*."

Jenn looked at Emily for a moment, then turned back to Laura. "Why?"

"For another woman, of course! And now Peter had to spend the weekend with the two of them! God only knows what they're exposing him to!"

Jenn was about to reply when she was interrupted by Emily screaming. In a flash, the two women were running to her aid. She met them halfway across the yard, her arms open wide to receive the safety of her mother.

"Emily! Emily, what's wrong?"

"Daddy's back! He's in the woods and he was looking right at me! And he had the pizza cutter!"

"Pizza cutter?" Laura asked.

"No, no, dollbaby," Jenn soothed. "He's not here!"

"Yes, he is! Baci sees him, too!"

One arm slung around her mother's neck, she turned and pointed toward the woods at the back of the cottage. Baci was aimed at the trees, body in a ready-to-strike position, hackles up. She was barking wildly.

"Well, something's got her going," Laura said. "You wait here. I'll get the rifle."

"You have a gun?" Jenn asked. For a moment, her worries about Emily's imagination were overpowered by the realization that her daughter had been wandering around a house where there was a firearm.

"Hunting rifle," Laura said, walking backward. "We keep it locked up, with the ammo in another room. I'll be back!"

Jenn rocked her daughter back and forth, looking from Laura's retreating back to the dog. She wished Baci could talk. The puppy could probably explain a lot more than the humans could.

"Mommy, don't let Baci get hurt," Emily whimpered. "Daddy will hurt her if he comes back!"

"All right," Jenn said. The dog's barking at nothing was getting on her nerves, too. She called to the puppy. At once, the animal swung around and ran to her, tail wagging.

She put Emily down and they both patted the dog.

"What did you see there, Baci?" Jenn asked.

Emily giggled, hiccuped away the last of her tears, then giggled again.

"Mommy, you know Baci can't talk."

"I wish she could," Jenn said.

Laura returned, carrying the rifle. "Be right back," she said, heading into the woods.

Jenn and Emily stood their ground. The day was quiet suddenly, and the wind had died down completely, like the calm before a storm. The stillness around her gave Jenn an uneasy feeling. Emily must have had it, too, because the child moved closer to her and squeezed her hand.

"Something bad's gonna happen, Mommy."

Laura was gone for so long that Jenn began to worry. But she didn't dare investigate, thinking of the loaded shotgun. Laura might be startled into firing at her.

At last, though, the woman returned.

"I didn't see anyone," she announced. "But I think I spotted a buck making his way through the trees. Maybe it got too close to the farm, and Emily mistook its silhouette for a person."

"It was Daddy," Emily mumbled sadly.

"Emily, why don't you come inside?" Jenn suggested. "I'll fix you a hot chocolate, and maybe you can watch a video."

She took her daughter by the hand. Looking back over

her shoulder, she said, "Thanks, Laura. And I'm sorry if I sounded like I was accusing you of something earlier."

Laura's smile was forgiving. "That's okay. I should have been straight with you from the beginning. Just call me if you need anything."

Inside the house, Jenn went into the kitchen to prepare the cocoa. She made some for herself, too, thinking it would calm her nerves. Emily went to her room to retrieve one of her stuffed toys to hug—perhaps the pink teddy from the Trentons.

Her scream nearly caused Jenn to drop the cup she was holding.

She ran into her daughter's room to find Emily wailing, tears pouring down her shock-whitened cheeks. The window hung wide open, curtains flapping in the autumn breeze. Emily was pointing at something in the bed.

"Emily!" Jenn cried. "What . . . ?"

She cut herself off when she noticed something gleaming amidst the dolls and stuffed animals. Carefully, she pulled away a toy lion.

A pizza cutter lay in the middle of the bed, blood spattered on its circular blade.

twenty

The sound of the ringing phone made Emily start screaming again. Jenn had removed the offensive kitchen tool and closed the window fifteen minutes earlier, but in that time she hadn't yet been able to calm her daughter down. She planned to call the police, but right now Emily needed her complete attention.

"It's Daddy! Daddy's calling us!"

Jenn was so tense herself that she half expected to hear Evan on the phone when she said hello.

A male voice responded, "Jenn?"

"Leave me alone!" Jenn cried.

"Mommy!" Emily whined, pulling at her arm. "Hang up! Hang up or he'll come through the phone!"

"Jenn, it's Nick Hasken," the man said. "For God's sake, what's wrong?"

Jenn half choked, half laughed. She looked down at Emily.

"It's only another teacher," she said. She breathed in a deep sigh. "Oh, Nick. Things are crazy around her. I'm so sorry . . ."

"Don't apologize," Nick said, concern in his voice. "Do you want to tell me what's going on?"

Jenn hesitated, still unsure about sharing her problems with a man. Nick would probably think she was hysterical and laugh at her fears.

No, Evan *would think like that. And Nick isn't Evan, is he?*

"Jenn?"

The sound of his voice prompting her jolted her out of her reverie. She found herself talking a mile a minute now. She told him about Emily "seeing" Evan in the woods, then of the pizza cutter left on her bed.

"Have you called the police?"

"I'm going to," Jenn said. "I was just trying to calm Emily down."

"I'll hang up so you can," Nick said. "And I'll be over as soon as possible."

"Nick, that isn't—"

"No, it isn't necessary," Nick interrupted, "but I want to do it. I want to make sure you're safe, Jenn. No arguments, okay?"

"Okay," Jenn replied, because she really did want his company.

She dialed the police as soon as she hung up, and they and Nick arrived only moments apart. Nick held Jenn's hand while an officer questioned both her and Emily. By now, the sheer trauma of the incident had exhausted the child, and she was falling asleep in her mother's lap.

"How long was your landlady in the woods?"

"About twenty minutes," Jenn said.

"Enough time to open the window," the cop said.

"That's ridiculous," Jenn said. "Why would Laura do such a thing? Maybe Emily really did see a man."

"You said her father was dead."

"Yes, but it could have been someone else," Jenn replied. "Are you going to check the woods?"

"We will," the cop replied, but with such little enthusiasm that Jenn knew it wouldn't be much of an investigation. She wished Mike Hewlett had come. *He* wouldn't treat this as just a prank.

When the police left, Nick volunteered to check the locks around the house.

"Thanks," Jenn said. "I'm just going to put Emily down for a nap."

She carried her daughter into her own bedroom and tucked her under the blankets. The child, exhausted by the trauma, fell asleep almost instantly. Jenn found Nick in the kitchen, where he was leaning over the sink to secure that window.

"It's been a long time since Emily took a nap," Jenn said.

"The kid's probably worn out," Nick replied. "How old is she? Four?"

"Almost five," Jenn said. "She has a lot of energy, and she stopped taking naps before she was three. But I think you're right; she's worn out. She's been through so much. Nick, how come you're so insightful when it comes to children?"

Nick smiled at her. "Oldest of eight. My youngest sisters, twins, are thirty years younger than I am."

"Your mother had babies over a thirty-year span?" Jenn asked, shocked.

"Well, they're my half-sisters," Nick replied. "Mom died when I was in my teens and Dad remarried a younger woman. He had five with my mother and three with my stepmother."

Jenn could see that his family position had made him patient and concerned with the welfare of others. She had read once that older children tended to be leaders, bossy like her sister. But it was obvious, just by looking at Nick's sweatshirt, that he'd also managed to develop the sense of humor needed to be diplomatic: the black background bore the legend YOU ARE HERE, with an arrow pointing into the Milky Way.

"I'm glad to see you smile again," Nick said.

Jenn changed her expression, embarrassed. She hadn't realized she was smiling.

"I'm ... I was just imagining you with seven brothers and sisters," she said. "I only had one sister and we fight all the time."

She took a deep sigh. "In fact, Rosalie was here this weekend. The entire holiday was ruined by fights and strange happenings."

Nick moved closer to her when he saw her shivering. She didn't protest when his arms went around her, but rested her head against his shoulder.

"Do you know what she said to me? She said Emily and I were in horrible danger. She said something bad would happen if we don't leave this place."

Jenn looked toward the room where Emily slept.

"Evan—my ex-husband—did something to Emily with that slicer," she said. "Seeing it there, on the bed—it was almost as if he'd come back again."

"There's no such thing as ghosts," Nick insisted.

"I know," Jenn said. "But I just can't explain this. Is there someone pretending to be Evan, just to scare us?"

"Why?" Nick asked. "You told me once that no one here in Vermont even knew Evan. So who would it be?"

"More damned questions," Jenn growled.

Nick held her for a few moments, silent, thinking. Jenn gazed across the room from the couch, her eyes fixed on the antique sideboard that sat against one wall.

"Too bad we don't have any tangible evidence," Nick said.

"The police took the pizza cutter," Jenn replied. "I doubt they'll find it was Evan's fingerprints, or his blood."

Her bedroom door opened, and Emily came out, rubbing her eyes. With a soft whining noise, she climbed back into her mother's lap.

"Bad dream, Mommy," she said.

"Really, dollbaby?" Jenn asked. "You want to talk about it?"

"Tara came to play with me," Emily said. "Only then Tara turned into Daddy, and he was real mad. He's getting closer and closer to us, Mommy!"

Nick leaned toward the little girl. He reached out to pet her hair, but pulled his hand back, obviously afraid she might fear all men after what her father had done to her. Instead, he offered a reassuring smile.

"Do you want me to stay with you a while," he asked, "to protect you?"

"Tara's the only one who can protect me," Emily insisted.

Nick looked up at Jenn. "Who's Tara?"

Jenn explained about Emily's imaginary playmate.

"She's real!" Emily cried.

Nick's expression told Jenn he had something to say. She lifted Emily from her lap.

"Do you think some cookies and milk would help you feel better?"

Emily nodded. She was still young enough to think that simple things, like kisses on boo–boos, made hurts go away.

"Go into the kitchen and help yourself," Jenn said.

Emily ran off. Jenn called after her, "Only two!"

Nick leaned closer and spoke softly. "She could have made up Tara as a sort of bodyguard," he suggested "Maybe you should think harder on counseling, Jenn. You need to get to the bottom of this."

"Counseling wouldn't explain the things that have happened around here," Jenn replied.

"But it's a start," Nick said. "It's just a suggestion . . ."

Jenn smiled at him and leaned her head into his shoulder again. "Thanks."

They listened to the sounds of Emily getting a snack: refrigerator door opening with a soft pop, jangling of the glass lid of the cookie jar, milk pouring into a cup.

"It would be nice," Nick said, "if she really did have some kind of 'guardian angel' standing right behind her."

Jenn nodded, her hair making a soft noise across Nick's shirt. Then she remembered something. The words "right behind her" reminded her of the Halloween picture, where a strange shadow had been behind Emily.

"I've got something I want you to see," Jenn told him, getting up. She went to the sideboard and pulled open a drawer. Removing the envelope of pictures, she carried them back to the couch and sat down next to Nick again.

"Take a look at these," she said. "I took them at the Learning Center on campus, on Halloween."

Nick went through them, actually laughing out loud at one or two.

"She's quite a little actress, isn't she?"

"A ham," Jenn replied. "But those aren't the ones I want you to see. Keep looking."

Nick went through the pack, then went through them again. "Adorable, but they look normal to me. What's your point?"

"How can you say that?" Jenn asked, taking the pack

back from him. "Can't you see the shadow right behind Emily in some of them?"

"No, only a little girl who's standing too close," Nick replied.

Jenn all but grabbed the pack from him. To her surprise, there *was* a girl there, so close that she seemed glued to Emily's back. She was staring at the camera, her eyes solemn, her skin pale.

"Oh, no," Jenn said with a shake of her head. "She wasn't there when I brought these pictures home on Halloween. There was only a shadow—and even the man at the photography store couldn't explain it."

"Let me take a look at the negatives," Nick suggested.

He held them up the light. They could see the image of two children—Emily and one other—in each picture.

"But those were just blobs, too!" Jenn said. "Pictures don't continue developing for a month after they leave the darkroom!"

"I don't—"

Jenn pulled away from him. "Don't you dare suggest that all this stress made me imagine the shadows. I'll take you to the photographer, and he'll vouch for me."

Nick looked surprised at her defensive tone. "I was just going to say I don't know what to think about this. Can I have another look?"

He pulled a small magnifying glass from his pocket and began to study the photographs more closely. Jenn had to laugh.

"Do you always carry one of those?"

Nick gave her a wink and a smile.

"A good scientist is always prepared for research," he said. "I've got a Bunsen burner in my other pocket. The trouble is, the flame keeps burning away any money I tuck in there."

Jenn laughed out loud. She appreciated the way Nick was trying to lighten the mood.

He turned back to the picture. "She does look different, this other kid. More luminous, and paler than the other children."

"Halloween makeup?"

"I can't tell," Nick said. "But it wouldn't explain this slight aura around her."

Emily came into the room, placated by milk and cookies. She climbed across the back of the couch and leaned forward, between the two adults.

"Hey, that's Tara!" she cried, pointing at the photograph. "Mommy, you got a picture of Tara!"

Jenn teetered a little, as if knocked over by the legendary feather. Nick grabbed her.

"Emily, it can't be!"

"It is, too!" Emily insisted. She slid down between them and took the picture in her hand.

"See? She has that pretty red and brown hair."

"Is Tara one of your classmates?" Nick asked.

Emily shook her head. "No, she's my *friend*. She helps keep Daddy away."

Jenn looked at Nick, her face pale. "Oh, God, Nick. Maybe there is such a thing as ghosts."

Nick took Emily's hand, no longer worried the child would shy away from contact with an adult male, since she was cuddled comfortably against him.

"Honey, where does Tara live?" he asked.

"In the light," Emily replied.

"The light?" Nick echoed. "What's that?"

Emily tilted her head and curled her lip impatiently "You know, the *light*. Michelle went there, too. I saw Michelle once, but she didn't come back again."

"But Tara comes back a lot?"

"Sometimes," Emily said. "She knows the way to me."

She frowned. "She says Daddy's trying to find the way to me, too, but he can't. Tara protects me."

Nick nodded, his expression serious. "So, Tara is stronger than your daddy.'

"Yep," Emily said. She looked at her mother. "Only . . . only she says she can't stay strong forever. And she can only help me. She says you have to find someone to help you, too, Mommy."

"I'll take care of your mommy, honey," Nick promised.

Emily squinted. "I don't think you're stronger than my daddy."

"Emily Janine!"

Nick laughed. "You'd be surprised. I've studied a little karate in my day."

"Cool!"

"But we were talking about Tara," Nick turned the subject back again. "This place that you call the 'light,' have you ever seen it?"

"I went there when I was in the hospital," Emily said. "I met Tara there. I got to come back, but she didn't."

Jenn shivered and tightened her sweater. "She went into cardiac arrest in the ICU. She almost . . ."

She couldn't bring herself to say the word "died." Nick gave her a look that said he understood.

"Did you like the light?" he asked gently.

"It was nice, at first," Emily said. "But then it got scary, because I knew I wouldn't see Mommy again. So I wished to come back, and I did. But you know something? Tara wished and wished, she even *screamed* about it, and they wouldn't let her come back."

"Who's they?" Nick asked.

"The other people," Emily explained, "Waiting to go into the light. Lots of people wait their turn. It was Tara's turn, but she didn't want to go."

Jenn and Nick glanced at each other. They knew Emily

was talking about ghosts, but didn't dare say so out loud. It was just too bizarre to believe.

A soft bark alerted them to the dog, standing by the door.

"Baci needs to go out," Jenn said.

"I'll do it," Emily volunteered, running to open the door.

"Stay inside for a while, dollbaby," Jenn suggested.

"Daddy isn't there anymore," Emily insisted.

"No arguments, Emily," Jenn said, more firmly.

Obediently, Emily let the dog out, then shut the door. She went into the kitchen again, found some paper and crayons in a junk drawer, and began to color.

"What do you think, Nick?" Jenn asked softly.

"This might sound crazy," Nick said, "coming from a scientist, but it seems your daughter had a near-death experience. That's what her references to the light mean."

"I thought it was only a dream," Jenn said. "You don't believe that stuff, do you?"

"There have been documented cases," Nick replied. "And the people she was talking about sound like spirits. They say that ghosts are people stuck between this world and the next."

"So you do believe in ghosts, after all."

"No," Nick insisted, "but I can offer a theory. What if Emily really saw this child in the hospital, not in a dream? What if she created Tara from an image she received while fluctuating between a coma and full consciousness?"

"I could buy that," Jenn said. "But how do you explain the photographs? Emily couldn't have changed them!"

Nick picked up the photo again.

"We need to do some research about this kid named Tara," he said. "Emily goes back to school tomorrow, doesn't she?"

"Yes," Jenn said. "I'll ask her teacher about it."

"And I'll take a picture to the hospital," Nick volunteered. "Maybe we can find out if there was a child named Tara in the ICU at the same time as Emily."

Jenn gazed at the photograph for a few moments. Then, impulsively, she leaned over and kissed Nick on the cheek.

"What was that for?"

"For being so sweet," Jenn said. "Thanks for all your help, Nick. You don't know what it means to me."

Later, when they all sat down to dinner, Jenn realized she was feeling better than she had in days. Thanks to Nick, she finally had something concrete to work with. She'd investigate the photographs, and maybe she'd get some answers.

Nick helped her clean up the kitchen. Then, while she prepared for the return to school, he sat at the table with Emily and showed her some simple tricks with various things he found around the kitchen. By attaching them to a strip of paper in a certain way, he made two paper clips connect without touching them. He explained why balloons shoot across a room and made a "volcano" out of a jar filled with baking soda and vinegar.

Jenn looked up from her own work every once in a while and felt content. This was the kind of father Emily should have had.

She shook the thought away. Nick was a friend, nothing more. Maybe he could become a lover, but a husband and father? She was pushing things with that thought!

Before she could dwell on it further, the doorbell rang.

"Let me get that," Nick said.

Jenn looked past him to see Laura at the door. She was holding two plates, each done up with colored plastic wrap, and there was a look of complete surprise on her face. Jenn couldn't help feeling satisfied that Laura might be surprised she had a man in the house.

"Hi, Laura, come on in," Jenn called.

Nick stepped aside.

"I baked a chocolate cake this afternoon," she said, handing the plates to Jenn while keeping her eyes on Nick. "I thought you might like a treat, after what happened."

Jenn realized that Laura had been nowhere in sight when the police were there.

"Thanks," she said, taking the cakes. "You don't know the half of it."

As she set the plates down on the half-wall, she told Laura what happened.

"How awful!" Laura cried. "Poor little Emily must have been terrified. I'm sorry I wasn't here to help, but I'd gone to the grocery."

Jenn recalled the cop's suggestion that Laura might have had time to plant the pizza cutter. Laura wouldn't do a thing like that, she was certain.

She noticed that Laura kept looking at Nick, and Nick was looking at Jenn with questioning eyes.

"Oh!" Jenn cried, as if jumping out of a dream. "Nick Hasken, this is my landlady. She's also my friend . . ."

"Laura Bayless," Nick filled in. "Jenn told me about you. Nice to meet you."

"Likewise," Laura said, taking his hand. She smiled at Jenn, her eyes saying, *Nice guy.* "Well, I didn't come to stay," she said. "I'm sorry I didn't bring a piece for you, Nick. But the piece for Jenn is fairly large. Maybe she can cut it in half."

"I'll do that," Jenn said. "Nick, you have to taste Laura's cake. She bakes for a living."

"Can't wait," Nick said with a smile.

Laura looked around. "Where's Emily?"

Jenn looked into the living room. The television was on,

but Emily wasn't in sight. Then she noticed the bathroom door was closed.

"In the bathroom, I guess," Jenn said.

"Tell her I said hi, okay?"

"Okay."

"I'll bring her more cake tomorrow."

"That would be nice."

Jenn was getting the feeling that Laura was trying to stall, in spite of her insistence that she hadn't come to stay. Was she waiting to see Emily? But why? Maybe she wanted to know more about Nick. Jenn wouldn't give her the satisfaction, the nosy . . .

She stopped herself midthought. She could feel hostility rising in her again, without provocation. It was senseless.

"Good night, Laura," she said, opening the door. Baci shot into the house and tried to jump on Laura.

"Down!" Laura commanded.

The dog ran off and hid behind the couch. Laura said good-bye and left. When she shut the door, Jenn let out a sigh.

Nick laughed.

"What's so funny?"

"The way she kept gawking," Nick said. "You'd think it was still the fifties, and she was shocked you had a gentleman caller in the middle of the night."

"Laura might think I'm a floozy," Jenn said with a shrug. "I'm sure she already thinks I'm a bad mother."

"You?" Nick echoed. "No way. And who cares about Laura's opinion? Look, even the dog is bugged by her."

Jenn picked up the plates and carried them into the kitchen.

"Forget about her," she said. "She can be pretty self-righteous at times. But she bakes a hell of a chocolate cake."

She unwrapped the dishes. Her piece was sizably larger than Emily's. Jenn wondered why—certainly Laura didn't think she'd eat *that* big a piece. Then she concluded that Laura must have seen Nick's car. Three pieces of cake might have made her look like she'd been spying, but a second, larger piece let her cover herself.

She took out a knife and cut the large piece in half, then carried the dishes into the dining room.

"Emily!"

Emily emerged from Jenn's room. She was holding the pink teddy.

"I was showing my teddy a science 'speriment," she said.

"Uh-oh," Nick drawled.

"Not the volcano, I hope," Jenn said.

"The paper clip one," Emily said. She spotted the chocolate cake and jumped into a chair. "Oh, boy!"

"Laura brought it over," Jenn said. "She says hi."

"Hi, Laura," Emily replied.

The adults started laughing. Emily looked up at them, wondering why grown-ups always laughed at the dumbest things. She ate her cake, licked the last of the icing from her fork, and pressed her finger on the plate to get every crumb.

"Yummy!" she said. She looked at her mother. "You let me have chocolate at night," she said in surprise.

"It's a treat," Jenn told her. "Because you had a big scare today."

Emily nodded, then finished her glass of milk before speaking. "I'm tired, Mommy."

Jenn got up, told Nick she'd be right back, and led Emily into her room. She wondered why the child felt safer there. If someone was going to come in, her window was no more secure than Emily's had been. Then again, maybe Emily's window hadn't been locked in the first place. She'd have to be more careful.

"Mommy, you have lines over your nose," Emily said, pointing.

"Lines? Oh! You mean I look worried."

Jenn kissed her forehead.

"It's okay," she said. "We're safe, now that Nick's here."

"I'm safe with Tara," Emily replied.

"Is Tara here now?" Jenn asked.

Emily giggled. "Of course not. You can't see her, can you? But she's close by. I know it. And she's making sure nothing happens."

"Good," Jenn said, humoring the child. "Go to sleep now, dollbaby."

"G'night."

Jenn kissed her daughter again, adjusted the pink teddy bear under the covers, and left.

"She doesn't seem any worse for the wear," Nick commented. "What a great kid."

"Emily's something special, all right," Jenn replied proudly.

"I've never seen a mind like that in such a small child," Nick said. "She's gifted, isn't she?"

Jenn sighed and sat next to him on the couch. She picked up the remote and started to flip through the channels.

"I wonder if it's a blessing or a curse," she said. "Sometimes I think Emily has to take more than a child her age ought to, only because she *does* understand. Then again, she's still very much a baby."

"Sort of caught between two worlds?"

"That's right," Jenn said, once more impressed by Nick's insight. "And I worry that she's going to miss some of her childhood because of it."

She pressed a few more buttons, finally settling on an old movie.

"You like Fred Astaire?" Nick asked.

"Love him," Jenn replied. "I used to be terribly jealous of Ginger Rogers. I wanted to study dance, but I found out I'm too much of a klutz."

"I don't believe that," Nick said. "You probably never had the right partner."

Jenn's eyes widened. "Damn right!"

Evan couldn't walk straight, she thought. *Let alone dance!*

"I'll take you out some time, if you'd like," Nick went on. "I'm pretty good, myself. With all my brothers and sisters, I've had a lot of weddings to practice at."

Now it was Jenn's turn to laugh. She looked at Nick, smiling, wondering what it was about him. He wasn't handsome—she'd established that the first time she'd had lunch with him—but he had a certain charm. Kind of like Fred Astaire—not much to look at, but lovable just the same.

Then again, he *did* have nice eyes . . .

She blinked a few times, realizing she was staring now, and turned her attention to the movie. They watched it silently, appreciating the music and dancing, speaking only during the commercials. Neither one realized they were moving closer and closer to each other until Nick had his arm around Jenn's shoulders. Feeling content and safe, she snuggled close to him.

"Great movie," Nick said when it was finished. "But I'm exhausted."

Jenn knew what was coming next, but she also knew she wasn't ready. Would Nick be upset if she suggested separate rooms tonight?

To her surprise, he said, "Can you get me a pillow and a blanket for this couch?"

His respect for her made her feel all the better. She helped him make up the sofa bed, then said good night. Nick caught her with a gentle kiss, but nothing more. He was a rare gentleman, Jenn thought, in a day of guys who thought of nothing but dragging you into bed almost as soon as they knew your name.

"God, I think I'm falling in love," she said to herself just before she fell asleep.

Sometime in the night, Jenn was awakened by a soft knocking at her door. Disoriented by sleep, she lay frozen for a moment. If Emily was at her side, then who the hell . . . ?

Then she laughed at herself. It was Nick, of course. But why was he waking her at this hour?

As she reached for the robe at the foot of her bed, a pain shot through her stomach that made her cry out. It was like fire, worse than any heartburn she'd ever experienced. She clutched her stomach, bent in half, unable to move. The pain became greater by the moment, so much so that she didn't even move when her door opened and Nick entered her room.

"Something's wrong, Jenn," he whispered. "My stomach . . ."

"Oh, God," Jenn managed to squeak. "Mine, too. What's . . . what's . . . ?"

She couldn't say another word. Pushing Nick aside, she leaped from the bed. She barely made it to the bathroom before she began to vomit.

The sight of blood terrified her, and she knew this was no simple virus. Shaking, pale, she turned to face Nick. He had his back to her, his arms folded around his middle and his head bowed.

"Nick, we'd better get to the hos—"

She choked on the remaining words when he turned around. It wasn't Nick standing there at all. It was Evan, and there was more hate than she'd ever seen before in his eyes.

"How does she do it?" Evan demanded. "How does she keep me away?"

"Go away!" Jenn cried. "Just . . ."

Another pain shot through her, and she turned back to the toilet again. She felt a hand on her shoulder—*Nick, let it be Nick. Let me be dreaming all this*—and shuddered violently.

"Wanna see how I can dance, Jenn? Wanna see me dance with Emily?"

Slowly she stood up. She could see her reflection in the mirror. Her face was pale, her eyes bloodshot.

She could feel Evan's presence thick and evil, but the mirror did not offer his reflection. She tried to turn around, but his grip was as strong as it was invisible.

"NICK! NICK, HELP ME!"

Deranged laughter filled the room.

"Nick! Nick, help me!" she heard Evan mimic. "Nick is dead, Jenn. Dead and sharing a bed with E.J. Bet he's cuddly as a bear . . ."

Jenn tried to run to her room, but a black cloud, like a small tornado, whirled around her feet and tripped her. The fire in her stomach grew even worse, and she became paralyzed with fear and pain.

Emily's scream brought Jenn to her senses. Somehow she had to get help! She knew she was too weak to fight alone. If Nick was dead . . .

"No!" Jenn gasped. "No, it isn't true!"

Then where *was* he?

"MOMMY!"

Jenn grabbed hold of a chair and pulled herself up.

Slowly, with great pain, she made her way into the kitchen. She dialed Laura's number, praying the woman could come and get Emily away from here before it was too late.

The phone rang three times. Halfway through the fourth ring. Jenn fell forward into blackness.

twenty-one

Emily had awakened to find her mother gone. She could hear Daddy outside the room, asking Mommy about dancing. The sound of his voice made her want to scream. He had found them! He sounded mean, crazy. He was going to kill Mommy!

"Don't let him get us!" she whimpered, hugging the pink teddy as tightly as she could.

She tried to call her mother, but no matter how she yelled, Mommy didn't hear her. She needed someone else now.

"Tara? Tara, are you there?" she whispered, her voice hoarse. "Help me!"

But Tara didn't answer. Emily had to help her mother, no matter how scared she was. Shaking all over, she crawled from under the covers. The wood floor was cold beneath her tiny, bare feet, but she hardly felt it. She opened the bedroom door . . .

The living room was bathed in a red glow. Emily thought someone had painted blood on everything, even the air. Slowly, she moved toward the lighted bathroom.

Her father stepped out in front of her, pizza cutter held high, his eyes full of hate.

"I've got you now, E.J.," he hissed. "Time for bad little girls to pay up!"

Emily covered her eyes and began to scream.

Someone was lifting her up. She kicked and struggled, her little mouth finding an ear and biting.

"Emily! Emily, it's only Laura!"

With a wail, Emily opened her eyes to see her mother's friend. Daddy was nowhere in sight. The blood-red "paint" was the light of an ambulance, spraying through the front windows of the house.

"Where's my mommy?" Emily demanded.

"She's very sick, Emily," Laura said. "She has to go to the hospital. She has a terrible, terrible tummyache."

Emily tightened her grip around Laura's neck and rested her head against her shoulder. Daddy wasn't here now. Laura would keep her safe. And Mommy would be okay because tummyaches always went away.

She felt sleepy again, but she didn't want to close her eyes. She wanted to see Mommy.

Instead, she saw Daddy. The men were putting him in one ambulance.

She began to scream.

The man on the stretcher turned slowly, his eyes blinking. Emily saw that it wasn't Daddy at all. It was Nick, and he had blood all over his stomach. Laura had said Mommy had a bad tummyache. Was Mommy's tummy bleeding, too? Terrified, she turned her face away. Laura hugged her tighter and hurried up toward the big house. Once inside, she took Emily into the same bedroom where she'd slept weeks earlier. She lay her on the bed and tucked her in.

"Good night, sweet angel," she whispered, stroking Emily's hair. "You'll be with your mama soon."

"Dollbaby," Emily mumbled, sleep swiftly overtaking her young body. "Mommy calls me dollbaby."

Laura left the room with a smug expression on her face. Things were going well. She'd worried when she saw that man at Jenn's house—*imagine letting a man spend the night with a child in the house!*—but he'd eaten the cake, too. She'd been momentarily worried about the wound in his abdomen but had finally concluded that he must have injured himself in a fall. The wound had looked mortal, but she didn't care whether he lived or died, so long as he didn't come back to ruin things for her. Now that she was rid of both the man and Jenn, her plans could go into effect. She'd hoped to wait until Tara was ready, but Jenn's threat to leave had changed everything. There was no time to waste.

She opened a desk in the den and pulled out a family album. The pictures showed a happy family, with two parents and a brother and sister. A perfect family, decorating Christmas trees, blowing out birthday candles, coloring Easter eggs. Before the father left, before the daughter . . .

Tears spilled onto a family portrait taken just a year earlier. Peter had been twelve, Tara just seven. Pretty Tara, who would never grow up to be the dark-haired beauty everyone predicted she'd be.

"But you will grow up," Laura vowed. "You will grow up, because I deserve to keep you!" She shoved the album back into the desk. "More than *she* deserves to keep Emily!"

She headed upstairs to the attic. There she pushed aside old boxes until she found one marked: TARA: OLD CLOTHES.

Laura smiled to think that she'd soon be able to use these things again. She'd soon have her little girl back, to dress up and fuss over.

. As she went through the box, picking out the things that would fit Emily's body—and it would *only* be Emily's "body" when things were done—she thought of the last day she'd seen Tara alive. She'd been sitting at the child's bedside, in the ICU at St. Michael's, when she overheard a particularly loud nurse talking.

"Two little girls in two days," the nurse had said. "And both such tragic accidents. I heard the father of the one in 135 ran the mother over a cliff. They were lucky to survive."

"His truck blew up," said a man's voice.

And then a frantic beeping had filled the room. Laura had looked up at the monitor to see that Tara's heart rate had gone all wrong. Seconds later, someone was pulling her out of the room. She stood nervously outside while a team fought to save her daughter's life. Somehow, she was also aware of people running into another room. She'd learned later that it had been Emily Galbraith's room. They'd been able to save Emily . . .

Laura twisted a lavender sweater as hard as she could, as if it could bear the brunt of her anger. It wasn't fair! Why had someone else's child been allowed to live? *She* was the good mother! She was the one who bought the prettiest dresses, brushed her daughter's hair a hundred strokes each night, baked all her favorite foods . . .

After a few moments, she managed to collect herself. Things would change, she thought. She'd have her little girl back again, soon. Of all people, it had been Peter who had shown her this was possible. Grouchy, surly Peter, so much like his father. He'd never been as dear to her as Tara, but fate, sick joker that it was, had let *him* live.

Maybe there was a reason for it. Maybe he was a medium of sorts, connecting her world to the one where Tara was held prisoner. He'd told his mother of a dream he'd had about his sister, in which she'd told him she met a little girl named Emily.

"It was crazy," Peter had said. "She told me she was going to find a kid named Emily and get inside of her. Kind of like *The Exorcist*."

Sitting at the breakfast table, a week after Tara had died, he'd shuddered at the thought. Laura tried to assure him it was only a dream, but she knew better. It was a sign that Tara was trying to make contact! Somehow she'd connected to Emily Galbraith. Maybe it was because they both "died" at the same time. The only difference was that Emily had come back.

It wasn't difficult to find Emily. Laura went through back issues of local newspapers and found an account of the crash. The article told her that Jenn Galbraith was going to be teaching trigonometry at Pinebridge College. Laura had hung around the campus until she spotted them. It was no accident that she'd been in the park the day Emily fell off the ladder.

She smiled, stroking a blouse that had been one of Tara's favorites. Had Tara had something to do with that fall? Had Tara helped force a contact between her mother and the Galbraiths? Laura had tried to reach her daughter, but it was no use. Still, she knew Tara was around her. Emily often spoke of her. And those strange things that had been happening—the spiders and bats and snakes— were all signs of Tara's frustration.

She also thought about Emily's visions of her father.

The man had also died about the same time as Tara. If that evil man got hold of Emily before Tara could . . .

"I won't let that happen, sweet angel," she vowed.

She packed the handful of clothes into a small suitcase and carried it downstairs. It was only a few hours until sunrise. She had a lot of work to do . . .

Although she was completely exhausted physically, Emily's mind was working an extra shift, and her dream was as vivid as reality. It was part nightmare, part memory. She was very small, too little to see over the top of the kitchen counter. But Daddy had something he wanted her to see up there, so he picked her up and put her on a chair. Emily screamed to see the little dead starling lying on the counter, its neck bent back in a strange way.

But she went completely silent the moment her father put a finger to his lips. The look in his eyes was the only threat she needed. She felt her heart pounding hard in her small chest and was terrified he'd hear that, too.

"Watch this, E.J.," he said. He opened the kitchen drawer and pulled out a pizza cutter. Emily didn't think much of it. She'd seen her parents use one many times and had even tried it herself. But she'd never imagined it could serve the purpose her father intended for it.

He pressed the blade into the bird's round, fragile chest. Emily gasped. Her father glared at her, and she bit her lip in silence.

"These things are pretty handy, y'know," he said. He pressed harder, and blood spattered on Emily's dress. She bit her lip even harder to keep from crying. "You can slice up all kinds of things with 'em—pizza, sandwiches, little girls' lying tongues . . ."

With an almost theatrical flair, he pushed the blade across the dead bird's body. In her memory, Emily's mind exaggerated the truth. What had been a few drops of blood in reality became gushes now, flowing all over the counter and shooting warm and wet at Emily's pale face.

"Cuts through skin and bone just like that!"

Her father started laughing.

"If I lay your tongue on the counter," Evan said. "I can roll this baby right over it and cut it right off. You'd deserve that if you told about the games we play here, wouldn't you?"

Before Emily could answer, the dream changed, bringing another memory back. Emily was standing in a room with dark walls and a big, dark desk. A woman was sitting behind the desk. She wasn't smiling, and she scared Emily. Some part of the little girl remembered her—the judge from the custody hearing. But now she sat there as still and emotionless as a mannequin.

Then her father was there, too, holding up the pizza cutter.

"You told, you lying brat! Stick out your tongue!"

"I didn't tell, Daddy!" Emily yelled. "They guessed! They just guessed!"

The judge sat, motionless and emotionless.

"Stick out your tongue!"

Emily woke up screaming. In a moment, Laura was in the room, picking her up.

"I want my mommy!" Emily wailed. "I want my mommy!"

"I'm sorry, sweet angel," Laura said. "Mommy is sick in the hospital. I'll take care of you."

"NO! *MOMMY!*"

Laura tried to calm her down, calling her "sweet angel" over and over again, rocking her until at last she began to settle into sleep again. Emily felt herself being lowered into the pillow. She didn't want to sleep again, terrified of the nightmare, but she couldn't stop herself. She barely heard the bedroom door shut as Laura left the room.

A second later, her pillow was jerked out from under her head. Emily was startled awake once more. She gazed in wonder as Tara stood at her bedside, an angry look on her face. With unnatural strength, she ripped the pillow in half.

"Whatja do that for?" Emily demanded.

"She called you sweet angel. But you're not sweet angel. *I am!*" Tara whacked Emily with the half pillow she still held. Feathers flew around the room. Emily batted at them.

"Go away," she said.

"No," Tara replied firmly. "I won't go. You're trying to make Mama love you more than me!"

"That's stupid," Emily growled. "I don't want your mama. I want my own mommy!"

She squinted at the other child.

"Did you make my mommy sick tonight?"

"No way!" Tara tossed the pillow across the room. She stared down at her feet, thinking. "But maybe . . ."

She stopped.

"What?" she asked.

"Maybe it was your daddy," Tara went on. "Maybe he did it. He's getting stronger and stronger, Emily. Can't you feel it?"

Emily nodded. She knew her father was very, very close, as if he was on the other side of a locked door, with a big ring of keys. As soon as he found the right one . . .

"What'm I gonna do?" she asked in a small, frightened voice.

"You hafta listen to everything Laura tells you," Tara said. "Laura knows how to make you safe."

"Really?"

"Really," Tara said. "And . . ."

Tara's eyes squinted, and her mouth set hard in an angry expression She stamped her foot.

"NO!" Tara cried. "I don't wanna go back!"

Emily reached out to grab Tara's hand, but her fist closed on itself. Tara wasn't standing there anymore. Emily was terrified to be without her. She could feel her father's presence even more strongly than a moment ago. She needed Tara to help her.

"TARA! TARA! TAARRAAAAAA!!!!"

Her cries brought Laura running again.

"Emily! Another nightmare?"

"I want Tara to come back!" Emily cried. "Where is she?"

A look of utter disappointment crossed Laura's face.

"She was here? Just now?"

Emily nodded.

"Oh God . . ."

Laura brought her hands to her mouth and began to cry. Confused, Emily watched her. After a moment, she calmed down enough to pull aside Emily's covers.

"Come sleep in my room," she said. "If Tara comes back again, I want you to tell me. I want to . . . to talk to her."

Emily let Laura carry her to her room. Laura tucked her into a huge bed, so big that the blue-green quilt gave Emily the feeling of being lost in the middle of an ocean.

"Are you gonna sleep, too?"

Laura shook her head. "I'm going to sit right here and keep an eye on you. Try to fall asleep, sweet angel. Everything will be all right soon."

"Dollbaby," Emily protested with a yawn. "Tara is sweet angel, not me."

She closed her eyes and settled into the pillow. For the rest of the night, she would be spared of dreams.

Laura stared at her for a long time, trying to imagine

Tara in her bed. Instead of Emily's straight blonde locks, she could see Tara's auburn curls spread over the pillow. She longed to touch her child, to hug her and let her feel all the love she held inside. Soon, it would happen.

Soon, Emily's mind would be Tara's. And Emily Galbraith would vanish forever.

twenty-two

When she woke up in the hospital, Jenn felt as though her stomach had been pummeled repeatedly, but her first thoughts were of Emily. Moving slowly, painfully, she reached for the call button and pressed it.

Just what had happened last night? She recalled waking up with the most horrible stomach pains, like fire inside her. Nick had said the same thing. What had happened to Nick? Where was he now?

She stopped. A chill rushed over her.

Why hadn't he helped her when Evan was there?

"Oh, dear Lord," Jenn whispered, running a shaking hand through her long hair. "That was no dream! Emily was right—Evan has come back!"

Despite all her protests to the contrary, Jenn had to admit now that she was dealing with a ghost. And he was a being more evil than Evan had ever been in real life. He had carried his twisted hatred beyond the grave, and it was directed at both her and Emily. She had to get to her daughter before it was too late!

Jenn tried to get up from the bed, but the beating her stomach muscles had taken knocked her back down again. Her loud moan of pain brought a nurse, probably faster than the call button, she thought.

"Easy, Ms. Galbraith," the nurse said. "You're very sick."

Jenn tried to speak, but couldn't say a word.

"I'll get you something," the nurse said and left.

Jenn lay very still, hoping the pain would flow out of her if she didn't try to fight it. She wondered if Nick was feeling just as bad. And Emily . . . had Emily gotten sick, too?

The nurse returned and helped Jenn drink something. In a few moments, her stomach began to settle.

"Emily . . ."

"Emily's not here," the nurse said.

Jenn allowed herself a sigh of relief. At least that meant that Emily wasn't sick.

"What about Nick Hasken?"

The nurse didn't answer Jenn's question, saying, "Try to get some rest."

Rest was the farthest thing from Jenn's mind.

"Wait," she said. "What time is it?"

"Nearly ten in the morning," the nurse replied.

When the nurse left, Jenn picked up the phone and dialed Laura's number. She let it ring ten times, but no one answered.

A feeling that something was wrong started to grip her, but Jenn forced it away. Breathing deeply to calm herself, she said out loud, "Emily's okay! Laura probably drove her the center, that's all."

She punched in the numbers for the center. When she

got an answering machine, she started to feel nervous again. She told herself that Dee was probably busy with the children. She hung up and called the math department at the campus. She asked for Noreen Kane. When the other teacher came on the line, Jenn explained the situation.

"We won't be in school today, of course," she added speaking for Nick and herself.

"Jenn, this is too weird," Noreen said. "Did you eat something bad last night?"

"I don't really know what happened," Jenn said. "But I need a favor. Noreen, I'm worried about Emily. Could you go to the center and make sure she got there okay? I tried calling both Laura's house and the school, but no one answers."

Noreen promised that she would, and hung up.

Jenn's symptoms sounded like food poisoning to Noreen. And she had a strange feeling that it was no accident. Someone had tried to kill them!

"Laura Bayless," she said out loud.

One of the students walking in the hall stopped and turned. Roy Javier said, "Ms. Kane?"

Noreen looked at him.

"I was just thinking out loud," she said. "I was trying to recall where I heard the name Laura Bayless before."

"Oh, there was an article in the newspaper last summer," Roy said. "Her daughter was killed in a freak accident."

Noreen blinked in surprise. "Daughter? What was her name?"

Roy looked down at his shoes, thoughtful. "I don't really remember. Clara, or Anna ..."

"Tara," Noreen whispered.

"I think that was it," Roy said.

"Shit," Noreen mumbled.

"Ms. Kane?"

But Noreen was already running for the door. She wouldn't take time to call Jenn back at the hospital. There was nothing Jenn could do anyway. But *she* could get to Emily and make sure she was safe. Noreen was pretty certain Jenn had never mentioned that Laura had a daughter. And if Laura had kept that fact a secret, it had to mean trouble.

As it happened, Monday was Noreen's lightest teaching day, with only one morning class. She went directly to the center. Dee Crowley said that Jenn had called her that morning to say Emily was sick and wouldn't be in for a few days. Noreen knew that Laura must have placed the call.

"Call the police," she said. She grabbed a piece of drawing paper and a pencil and wrote down Laura's address. "Send them to this place and tell them a child is in danger."

"Oh, no!" Dee cried. "I don't understand . . ."

"I can't explain now," Noreen said, and was off again.

Noreen's deep concern for Emily's welfare had attracted an unseen presence, but she was unaware of it. Now it switched its attention to Dee, believing she might be the path to Emily.

With no awareness of the evil presence at her side, Dee reached for the phone, her heart pounding. She couldn't bear the thought of one of her precious children being in danger. She heard a strange hissing in the line, but a few seconds later the dial tone came back. Quickly, she dialed the police. She told them of the situation.

"I don't know the details," she admitted. "Only that one of the campus teachers, Noreen Kane, thought that a little girl might be in trouble up there."

"We'll certainly check into it," the cop on the other end promised. "And where did you say the mother was?"

"In the hospital," Dee said. "She became very ill last night. Please, make certain Emily is okay. She's only four."

"She'll be fine," the cop insisted. "We'll get back to you, okay?"

"Okay," Dee said.

When she hung up the phone, she heard one of the children in the classroom crying. As much as she wanted to know more about Emily's situation, there were twelve other kids who needed her, too.

She walked away from the phone without ever realizing she hadn't been speaking to the police at all.

Noreen drove as fast as she could. At the farm, she was surprised to see Laura's station wagon parked in the driveway. She was even more surprised when Laura answered the door, looking prim and pretty in a blue dress with a crisp white Battenburg lace apron. Laura's smile was bright but inquisitive.

"You're Jenn's friend, aren't you?" Laura asked, all politeness.

Noreen wouldn't buy the act. Without waiting for an invitation, she pushed past Laura, into the kitchen. It smelled of spices and honey.

"Where's Emily?" she demanded.

"I made some oatmeal-honey cookies," Laura said, as if she hadn't heard her. "Would you like to try one?"

"Screw the cookies!" Noreen snapped. "Where the hell is Emily?"

Laura reeled as if she'd been slapped. "She's fine. She's watching a video. I have a nice Shirley Temple movie."

"Who'd you buy it for? Your son Peter likes that sort of thing?"

Laura laughed. "Of course not! What business is it of yours?"

"I've made Emily Galbraith's safety my business," Noreen said. "I don't know exactly what you're up to, lady, but I do know that you lied to Jenn. What did you do? Tell Emily about Tara and plant ideas into her head?"

Whether the pleasant smile had been false or not, it fell away now as if melted by a blowtorch. Laura glared at Noreen.

"What the hell do you mean?"

Her voice was dark and threatening.

"I know about Tara," Noreen said. "I know she died. And I think you've got some nutty idea that Emily can take her place. It isn't going to happen. The police are on their way right now . . ."

Laura laughed again, but the sound was more nervous than before.

"What will they find?" she asked. "A woman baking cookies? A child watching an innocent movie?" She grinned and moved forward. Instinctively, Noreen took a step back. "Or a crazy woman making crazy accusations?"

Noreen fixed her glare on Laura's bright eyes. God, she was like an android, programmed to be the perfect mother, always smiling.

Noreen wanted to punch her. Instead, she kept her cool and said, "I want to see Emily."

"Of course," Laura said. "She's right down that hall. Emily!"

Noreen hurried toward the sound of the television. She couldn't see Emily. She moved into the room and looked around, thinking the small child might be half-buried under an afghan. But when she pulled it aside, the chair was empty.

"She isn't . . ."

Noreen's words ended when she saw Laura flying at

her, boning knife swinging. There was no time to move, no time to defend herself as the knife drove sideways through her neck and out at the carotid artery. Noreen's very last image was a flash of red as blood shot up over her face.

She was dead before her body collapsed onto the couch. Laura stared down at her with distaste.

"You got blood all over everything," she scolded the corpse. She sighed deeply. "And on my best apron, too! Oh well, I'll have Peter clean it up later."

She dropped the knife to the floor and stepped around the body. Then she went upstairs, where she had treated Emily to the privilege of listening to music on her personal stereo. With music playing through it headphones, Emily was deaf to any noises that might occur downstairs. Gently, Laura removed them. Emily smiled up at her, but frowned at the sight of blood. Laura spoke quickly to reassure her.

"Oh, that's just red food coloring," she said. "I'm making some cookies shaped like stockings for Christmas, and I accidentally spilled the bottle of coloring. But never mind that. Would you like to see a surprise?"

"Okay!"

Emily protested loudly when Laura picked her up.

"I'm a big girl! I can walk!"

Laura ignored her complaints.

"You'll like the surprise, sweet angel," Laura said, staring straight ahead as she carried Emily down the stairs.

When they passed the den, where Noreen lay in a pool of blood, Laura pressed her hand to Emily's head and turned her so that she couldn't see.

An hour after she'd hung up with Noreen, Jenn took the phone from the stand beside her bed and held it in her hands. In a way, it seemed that holding the phone could make it ring, bringing Noreen's reassuring call that everything was okay.

It was a ten-minute walk from the math building to the center. Why hadn't she called back yet?

Speculation filled Jenn's mind. Maybe she didn't call because she'd found out something. Maybe she'd gone to Laura's house to investigate. If Laura was home, she wasn't answering her phone. But Noreen would see her car, and know she was hiding. Jenn prayed Noreen would find Emily before it was ...

She stopped herself and pressed a hand to her chest. She could feel her heart pounding so hard it hurt. Before it was what? Too late? Too late to save Emily from Evan's evil spirit?

Somehow her husband had come back to seek the vengeance he had not obtained when he drove her car off the road.

"I've got to go home," Jenn said out loud. "I've got to help Emily!"

She pulled herself out of bed and began to dress. She didn't feel as bad as she had earlier, but her knees were weak and her hands shaking. Her clothes were in a blue plastic bag marked "Patient's Belongings." She pulled them out and began to dress.

Jenn was sitting on the edge of the bed, tying her shoelaces, when Dr. Petri walked into the room. Jenn immediately recalled his halo of yellow hair from her previous time in the hospital.

"Where are you going?" he asked.

"Home," Jenn said simply. "I need to get to my daughter."

"You're very sick," Dr. Petri told her. "We found traces of rat poison in your stomach."

Jenn gasped. "Rat poison! But ..."

She stopped, her answer coming to her at once. Somehow, Laura had poisoned the chocolate cake. But Emily had eaten it, too!

Laura had tricked them, giving them the big piece to divide to make certain that Emily got the smaller, untainted piece.

But what if they'd been feeling generous? What if they'd given Emily the big piece, knowing how much she loved chocolate cake?

"How . . . how much poison?" she asked softly, stunned.

"Let's say it's a good thing you weigh as much as you do," Petri said. "We had to pump your stomach. Nicholas Hasken's, too."

Jenn gazed at the doctor with wide blue eyes. Tears lay nascent along the rims, but she wouldn't let them spill. She had to be strong, to help Emily—and Nick.

"What about Nick?" she asked.

"It's a little more complicated with him," Petri said. "We had to call in the police. There was a knife wound to his side. He told Mike Hewlett that he'd fallen on it, but then he passed out. I'm sure Mike will be back to question him further. He wants to know what Nick was doing wandering around in the dead of night with a knife."

He must have seen Evan! He must have been trying to protect me, but Evan got to him first!

She managed to keep her panic inside.

"Ms. Galbraith," the doctor said, "you don't have to worry. We've posted a guard outside Hasken's door. Even if he was well enough to get up and leave this hospital he wouldn't be allowed. Not until he answers some questions."

Jenn could hardly believe it. They thought Nick had poisoned the cake, then tried to kill her with a knife! It was ludicrous—didn't they see that Nick was as sick as she? They'd pumped his stomach, for God's sake!

It was all too crazy. While they were wasting their time

accusing an innocent man, the real culprit might have her
daughter! But she couldn't identify him. What was she going to say? *"My husband came back from the dead and
now he's got my little girl"?*

She gave the doctor a hard stare. "I want to be released."

"Ms. Galbraith . . ."

"I am NOT your prisoner!" Jenn said emphatically, her
panic beginning to show despite her efforts to appear in
control.

Dr. Petri sighed. "Very well. But you must sign a release form."

"Anything."

Even as Jenn was preparing to leave the hospital, Laura
was leading Emily through the woods. Emily held fast to
her hand, her eyes darting here and there, afraid she might
see her father. She tried to concentrate on Laura's promise
of a big surprise, and the excitement took the edge off her
fears.

At last, they reached a clearing in the woods. There was
a little hunting cabin there, run-down and neglected. Emily
frowned in disappointment. What was so great about this
dumpy place?

"I know it doesn't look like much," Laura said. "But
wait until you've seen the inside. I've fixed it up."

Emily gasped in wonder as Laura opened the door and
led her inside. There was a thick purple rug on the floor,
white eyelet curtains in the windows, and toys stacked
neatly on the shelves. The white bed Emily had often
climbed on in the attic was here now, brought down piece
by piece while Emily and Jenn were out. A small round table had been set up with lovely dishes, and a big stuffed
cat sat at one place.

"Wow!" Emily cried, running to investigate the toy shelf.

She picked up a big box of crayons and opened it.

"They're new," she said with delight.

"There's plenty of paper to draw on," Laura said. "And some coloring books. And puzzles and so much more. Do you like it?"

"Yeah!"

Emily put the crayons back. She located a canister of Legos and carried them to the middle of the rug. Settling down, she began to build something.

"I wish mommy could be here," she said.

Laura, sitting in a rocking chair, leaned forward.

"You know," she said, "maybe we shouldn't tell your mommy about this."

Emily froze. Those were just like the words Daddy spoke when he used to hurt her.

"I mean," Laura went on, "she may feel bad. After all, teachers don't make much money. It might bother her that I could buy you all these things, and she couldn't. I know she was upset when I bought you that fancy dress for Thanksgiving."

Emily thought a moment, pushing Legos together. Laura was right. Mommy *had* been kind of mad about the dress.

"I promise we'll tell her later," Laura said. "But not now, while she's too sick, okay?"

"Okay," Emily said. "When's she coming home?"

"I don't know, sweet angel," Laura said.

Emily looked up at her. "Tara doesn't like it when you call me sweet angel."

Although her release seemed to take forever, it was only half an hour before Jenn was on the road. She wished she could have spoken to Nick before leaving, but then she would have had to talk to the cop outside his door. She hoped that Nick was safe where he was. She'd speak up for him later, but right now she had to get to Laura's house.

Emily wasn't at the center, she knew, because if she was, Noreen would have called.

Although the drive to the Bayless farm was confusing, Jenn had gotten so used to it over the past months that she could drive it blindfolded. Today, however, she was so shaky that she took two wrong turns. The delays frustrated her, but the frustration fell away when she finally passed the woods surrounding the farm. Both Laura's and Noreen's cars were there. Noreen would help her get Emily out of here.

Jenn parked her car next to Noreen's, got out, and ran to the door. She didn't even bother to knock, but pushed inside. Looking down the hall leading through the center of the big house, she could see the kitchen light was on, even though it was daytime. The house smelled of oatmeal and spices. She could hear the television set. With a smile and sigh of relief, she hurried to find her daughter. Emily was safe, watching television.

At the sight of Noreen's body, she threw her hands over her mouth to stifle the scream that would alert the killer to her presence.

Then she put her hands down. If Evan's spirit was here, what good would it do to be silent? And If Evan had done this . . .

She turned and ran out of the room. There was no time to grieve for Noreen now. She had to find Emily! Calling to her daughter, Jenn pushed open every room and closet door and turned on every light.

"EMILY! EMILY, IT'S MOMMY!"

Every muscle in her body was tense.

"EMILY!" But she already knew that Laura and Emily were gone.

Had Laura run away with Emily to save her from Evan? Or did she have some plan in mind herself, something that had to do with poison in the chocolate cake?

Jenn stopped short at the end of the upstairs hall, just outside the attic door. She put her hands to her ears to block out the dozens of questions that were forming in her brain. Now was not the time for speculation—now was the time for action!

She pulled open the attic door, turned on the light, and ascended the staircase. The attic was cold and drafty. All she could see was old furniture, broken toys, and boxes. One box lay on its side, as if knocked over.

Jenn turned to leave, resigned to the fact that Emily was not in this house. She was about to go down when the writing on the knocked-over box caught her attention. With a gasp, she could hardly believe she'd almost missed it: TARA — SUMMER CLOTHES.

"Tara?" she said out loud.

Emily's make-believe friend. But, maybe now, not so make-believe.

Laura had lied about her husband. Had she lied about Tara? But, if the child *was* real, where was she? Who was she?

Jenn left the attic. She recalled seeing some pictures on the mantel in the den. She'd never stopped to look at them, but now she hoped there might be a clue, an image of the child named Tara.

She had to pass Noreen's body when she went back into the den. Thankfully, Noreen's eyes were closed. Jenn gave her friend a quick look, and whispered, "I'm sorry, Noreen."

Then she went to the mantel. Sure enough, there were several pictures of a little girl. Jenn took one down to examine it more closely, and nearly cried out. It was the same child who had appeared in the Halloween pictures!

"Put that down!"

The voice made Jenn scream as she swung around, still

clutching the little framed portrait. Laura was standing
there, her eyes wild.

"I said: Put it down!"

"Not until you tell me what you did with Emily!"

"Emily is leaving you! She's going to join with Tara,
and I'll soon have my Sweet Angel back again!"

Jenn made some quick assumptions.

"Tara . . . she was your daughter, wasn't she?"

"IS! IS! IS!"

Laura pounded the back of the couch with each word.

"What happened to her?" Jenn asked softly.

"Nothing happened," Laura insisted. "I'm getting her
back, and you can't stop me!"

Jenn stepped around the couch, approaching Laura with
her arms outstretched.

"Laura, please tell me what—"

Laura must have seen the move as a threat, for she suddenly produced a rolling pin. Flour danced through the air
as she swung it, striking Jenn in the head. The room began
to spin around Jenn, but somehow her mother's instincts to
protect her child came through.

Can't let her . . . get Emily . . .

Jenn tried to take one awkward swing at her opponent.
Laura ducked, then countered with another sweep of the
rolling pin. This time it hit Jenn hard enough to knock her
unconscious.

Laura looked down with distaste at the blood and flour
on her rug.

"Tsk, tsk! My houseguests are so messy!"

Then she proceeded to drag Jenn's body on the couch,
where she tied her up with the corpse.

"If you're such good friends," she sneered, "you can rot
in Hell together!"

twenty-three

Laura had left the cabin because Emily said she was hungry. The moment Laura had closed the door, the box of crayons went flying up into the air as if by its own power. Sixty-four colors sprayed in all directions. Then Tara was there, a mischievous grin on her face.

"Hey!" Emily protested.

Tara ignored her. "I always wanted a playhouse, and now I have one. Hooray! Let's play with my toys, Emily."

"They aren't your toys," Emily insisted. "They're mine. Laura gave them to me!"

She knelt down and started to retrieve the crayons from the rug. They were so pretty and bright, with such nice points, that she wanted to keep them that way. She was reaching for a yellow one when Tara's foot came down on it, hard. Two pieces of crayon lay were one had been before.

"Don't do that!"

"I can if I want," Tara replied. "They're mine."

She stomped on a violet crayon, then a green.

"Tara," Emily wailed, "Stop it! They're MY crayons!"

Tara paused. Emily looked up at her through tears. She was surprised to see that Tara was smiling. Slowly, Emily crawled backward. She didn't like that smile.

"Okay," Tara said with eerie calm. "Then you break them yourself!"

Emily cried out as a strange sensation rushed through her body. She felt dizzy and shaky. She closed her eyes, and when she opened them a moment later things had changed. Tara was gone. The toys looked brighter, bigger. The tabletop loomed a hundred feet above her head. The rug seemed to turn to a purple liquid, the crayons like little boats.

Like a monkey grabbing a piece of fruit before another could get it, Emily snatched at a crayon. She snapped it in two. She grabbed more, breaking them violently, hating, angry, wanting to kill . . .

Then another feeling came over her, a feeling of pure trepidation stronger than any other emotion. Like the time Daddy had chased them in the car, like the time the Trentons' house was on fire . . .

Mommy.

She said it out loud: "Mommy," and the room was back to normal again. She looked down at the broken crayons and began to cry.

"Stay out of my head, Tara," she whined. "Stay out!"

Tara was calmly picking up the undamaged crayons as if nothing had happened at all.

Emily rubbed the cuff of her blouse under her nose. Not her blouse, though. It was too big on her, and it was a shade of pink she didn't like at all. Laura had made her put it on this morning, along with a pair of pink corduroy pants that had to be cinched at the waist with a belt.

"Something's wrong with my mommy," Emily said.

Tara said nothing until the crayons were cleaned up. She put the box on the table.

"Maybe your daddy got her," she said.

"NO!"

Tara giggled. "Only kidding. He's not here now."

"Mommy's hurt," Emily said. "I hafta see her!"

Tara blocked the door. "Don't you dare! Laura wants you to stay here, and so do I!"

"Mommy needs me!"

Tara rolled her eyes. "What a dope you are. How could your mommy need you if she's in the hospital?"

Emily thought a moment. The scary feeling was gone now, but Emily had been certain her mother was very nearby, and in danger. She peered at Tara.

"Did you make me feel like that?" she asked.

Tara shrugged. "Maybe. Maybe not. But if you leave, I'll go away forever. Then who'll protect you from your daddy?"

"How come you find me so easy?" Emily asked.

Tara smiled. "I guess 'cause I'm a kid, like you. But your daddy's getting real strong. He almost made me tell where your door was. If he tries again, I don't think I can keep it a secret."

Emily's eyes rounded, and her knees began to shake.

"That's why I need to get inside you," Tara said. "To trick him. And you hafta pretend Laura is your mama, and you don't even know Jenn."

"Laura isn't my mama!"

Tara's smile was ice cold. "Not yet, she isn't."

Before Emily could say another word, Tara went to the table and sat down. She picked up the little teapot and poured invisible tea into a little china cup. "Now," Tara said, "let's play with *my* toys."

Emily sat down, too, afraid to protest. She looked at the window, praying for Laura to come back. Laura might know if anything had really happened to Mommy . . .

But Laura wasn't coming, not just yet. The time on the grandfather's clock in her living room told her that Peter would soon be out of school. She wanted to meet him as soon as he got off the bus. She made a sloppy peanut-butter-and-jelly sandwich for Emily and stuffed it in a paper bag. Then she left the house and headed up the driveway to the road.

She was so excited she could hardly stand it. Wait until Peter heard the news! Wouldn't he be happy to know his precious little sister was coming back? Peter had been so terribly sad lately, but as soon as Tara was returned to them, things would change. They would be a loving family again. A perfect mother and two beautiful kids.

"And no man," Laura said. "As if I need one!"

She heard the bus before she saw it, a low rumbling that seemed to be answering the voices of the wind. When its yellow top crowned the nearest hill, Laura clapped her hands in anticipation, like a child. A moment later, the bus pulled over. The driver gave her a friendly wave, probably surprised to see her. It was all Laura could do not to shout, "My baby's coming home!"

As the bus pulled away, Laura gave her son a hug. He stiffened in her arms and mumbled a greeting. Laura tousled his hair. He grimaced and backed away.

"Is that the way you greet your mama?" she asked. "After five days away?"

"Sorry," Peter said. "You . . . you didn't have to meet me. I could walk to the house myself."

Laura gazed at him for a moment. There was something different about him.

"I missed you so much," she said.

"Did you?"

Had he grown? Was it a new haircut? Laura couldn't decide. She hooked her arm through his and started walking. "Of course!" she cried. "Wait until you see the hunting cabin. I've set it up nicely, and no one can find us there."

Peter stopped short.

"You've started, then," he said.

"You knew I would," Laura said. "It's meant to be, Peter. Tara wasn't supposed to die that day. That's why she's made contact with this other kid."

"Emily."

"Right," Laura said, starting to walk again. "She's at the cabin right now. I'm hoping Tara will come, too. If she senses the urgency of the situation, she will."

"Why is it any more urgent that before?"

"Jenn's planning to move out," Laura said. "It ruins everything. I don't have time to do things right."

Peter sighed, but his breath was no louder than the wind.

"Where's Jenn now?" he asked.

"Well, that's something you have to help me with," Laura said. "She got sick and had to go to the hospital last night. She came home unexpectedly, started making all sorts of horrible accusations, and when I stopped her, she made a terrible mess in my den."

"I don't get it," Peter said. They had reached the back door of the house.

"You have to help clean it up," Laura said. "I don't want Tara coming home to an untidy house."

When she led her son into the den, he gave a cry of disgust and turned away. He folded his arms across his middle.

"I know, I know," Laura soothed. "I always thought Jenn was a bad housekeeper, but I never imagined she was a pig. I mean, she isn't quite as bad as the first woman who came here looking for Emily. That one got blood on my couch! But she's disgusting enough, isn't she? So do your mama a big favor. Clean it all up, then meet me at the cabin."

Peter closed his eyes.

"Is that where you're going to hide the bodies?" he asked softly.

Laura laughed. "Of course not! There's a much better place. Don't you remember how I took care of the animals? There's still plenty of room in the big pit."

She patted his arm. "Get busy, dear. I expect you to be finished when I get back."

"No."

Laura was a few steps down the hall when she heard the word. She paused, unsure that she really *had* heard it.

"What?"

She turned slowly. And at once she identified the difference in her son. Ever since his father had left, even before Tara was taken away, he'd always stared down at his shoes when he spoke. But today, he was looking her straight in the eye. Something had happened to him at his father's house. Something had given him new confidence. And she couldn't have that.

"No!" he said, more firmly. "I'm not gonna do it, Mom. It's sick!"

She hit him without thinking. Peter reeled back so hard from her slap that even Laura was stunned. She'd never known she had such strength. But it was a mother's power, brought on by her desperate need to get her baby girl back again. No matter that Peter was her boy; she couldn't have him spoiling things!

"Don't ruin this for me," she growled. "You get in there and clean up all that blood! If you don't, I'll tell the police you slaughtered all the farm animals!"

"I never did!" Peter cried, holding a hand to his bleeding lip. "You killed them, and you made me help bury them!"

"They won't believe you," Laura said. "Officer Hewlett knows exactly what you're like. He knows the crowd you hang out with! He'll believe me before he believes you. Now, get to work!"

She turned and stormed from the house. Peter sank to the floor, sick with despair. Why did he have to come back to this hellhole? Why did his father have to go on so damned many business trips that he couldn't take custody of his only living child?

In spite of being thirteen years old, in spite of being as tall as his mother and almost as strong, Peter Bayless tucked his head between his knees and wailed like a baby.

When Laura opened the cabin door, Emily jumped up from her seat at the table and ran to her.

"Did you see my mommy? Is my mommy okay?"

Laura lifted her up. "What's this about, Emily? You know your mommy's in the hospital."

Emily bowed her head and tried not to cry. "I was scared for her. I thought . . . I had a funny feeling she was hurt."

Laura pulled her in for a tight hug. "You dear, sensitive thing! You really do love your mommy, don't you? Well, there's nothing to worry about. I just called your mommy at the hospital."

"That's why you were gone so long?"

"That's right," Laura lied. "She says she's coming home

tonight. But, in the meantime, she wants you to be a good girl and do what you're told."

Emily pulled away from Laura, wiggling until the woman was forced to put her down. Laura's voice was funny, and it scared her.

"I wanna go home," she said softly.

"You can't," Laura said. "Not now. Look! I've brought you a sandwich."

Laura put the sandwich on a little toy plate and instructed Emily to eat. The little girl sat down and pouted. Her own mother would never have made such an ugly sandwich. The jelly was dripping out of the sides, and the bread was soggy and purple.

"I'm not hungry now," Emily said. It was a lie; she was famished, and her stomach really hurt. But this sandwich looked *bad*.

"Don't waste good food, young lady," Laura said, her voice more stern than Emily had ever heard before. "Tara wouldn't do that."

Young as she was, Emily could hear the threatening tone in Laura's voice. Slowly, Emily picked up the sandwich and took a bite. Jelly dripped on her hand. The peanut butter was sticky in her mouth, but at least it tasted okay.

"Can I have some milk?"

"You really are a demanding kid, aren't you?"

Emily coughed. "It's making my mouth stick together."

"I've run out of milk," Laura said impatiently. She walked to the other side of the room and sat in a rocking chair. "God, I can't wait until I have my precious little Tara back again! She never made me work this hard!"

Though she mumbled under her breath, Emily heard. She wished she could ask what Laura meant, but she didn't dare.

twenty-four

The strange noises Jenn heard were like the sounds of little animals to her confused brain. Like squeaking bats . . .

With a cry, she opened her eyes and tried to jump up, away from the offending creatures. It only took her a moment to snap back to reality, and reality was even more horrible than a million rabid, screeching bats. When she tried to move, she felt as if she were pulling a great weight. With a sick feeling, she realized it was true: the weight was the body of her friend, Noreen. She sat side by side with her, tied at one wrist and ankle, as if Laura had wanted to set up a tableau of two friends sharing a couch, watching television.

"Oh, God," she gasped, leaning back. Noreen's arm lifted with hers. She stared up at the ceiling for a moment, too stunned to move.

The strange noises continued. They were coming from the hall, and she recognized them now for what they were: crying.

"Who's out there?" she called. "Please, who is it?"

The crying stopped abruptly.

"Answer me!"

Silence. Jenn looked down at the twine that bound her wrist to Noreen's. The body was already turning a sickly pale color. The sight of the bluish-gray hand flopping away from hers made her already sore stomach hurt even more. She bit her lip and tried to concentrate on getting free. Pulling at the knot with her free hand, she tried to work the twine loose. Every once in a while, she glanced at the doorway, but it remained empty.

"Sorry, Noreen," she whispered.

She fought a battle with tears and won, for now. Sickened as she was by Noreen's murder, she couldn't allow herself the luxury of grief. She heard a snuffling noise, like the deep sigh that racks a person's body after a long cry. It couldn't be Laura—not after the rage she'd witnessed earlier.

"Peter?" she guessed.

He must have gotten home from school. Oh, God—how long had she been unconscious? The thought of time passing brought on new urgency and she pulled even harder at the twine. That Laura had left one of her hands free proved the woman was insane and not thinking right.

"Peter, please!" Jenn called, more urgently. "Help me!"

"Can't."

Jenn's head swung up, but Peter was still out of sight.

"Peter, it's okay," Jenn said. "I don't blame you. Your mother needs help, but I can't get it for her if I'm tied up like this."

She looked down at the knot again. Laura might be mentally unbalanced, but a some point in her life she'd learned how to tie knots. This one was too tight for Jenn. She was trapped without Peter's help.

And that meant Emily was trapped, too.

"Peter, goddamn you! Get in here and help me!"

The boy must have been programmed to obey an angry female voice, for he sprang into the room. He stopped short of the couch, as if suddenly remembering Jenn wasn't his mother.

"Peter, please?" Jenn softened her tone, not wanting to scare him away.

Peter stared at the large red stains that marked the couch and carpet.

"She wants me to clean it up," he said dully.

"I'll help you," Jenn replied, "if you get me out."

Trembling fingers raked through the young boy's long hair. Jenn could see the red rims around his eyes. Peter was terrified—terrified of his own mother.

"Peter, did your mother kill Tara?"

Peter's eyes widened as he jerked his head to glare at her.

"No!" he insisted. "She died . . . she was in an accident early this summer."

Jenn could feel he was telling the truth, and it brought bitter relief. If Laura hadn't killed Tara, she probably wouldn't kill Emily. But Jenn couldn't be sure of that until she knew what Laura wanted with her little girl. The woman's words came back to her:

"Nothing happened. They took her by mistake, instead of your kid. But I'm getting her back, and you can't stop me!"

What the hell did Laura mean?

"Peter, this twine is hurting me."

"So?"

Jenn took a deep breath. Peter obviously didn't care about her, but maybe . . . "Look, kid," she said in a firm but calm voice. "I don't know what your mother has planned. But Emily's in danger, and I have to get to her! Do you want to live with another child's death?"

"I didn't kill Tara!"

"I didn't say you did," Jenn replied. "But if you don't get me out of here, and if something happens to Emily, it will be partly your fault."

"No, it won't!"

Jenn gasped as a little china pig, sitting on the table beside her, flew across the room and shattered against the wall. Peter turned and ran from the room. Something scraped along the wall and hit the floor with a bang and a shattering of glass. Jenn guessed one of the pictures had fallen from the wall.

It was just like the day the bulbs imploded.

When she heard the door slam a moment later, it was all Jenn could do not to burst into hopeless tears. A few drops trickled down her pale cheeks, but she bit her lip and squeezed her eyes shut to stop them. Bowing her head, she whispered, "Not now, not now."

Then she opened her eyes again and dared to look at Noreen. The other woman's head was flopped away from her, but Jenn could see the small wound just under her ear.

Breathing deeply a few times to gather her strength, Jenn wriggled until she was behind Noreen's body. She wrapped her arms around Noreen's waist, one dead arm and leg moving with her own as if Noreen was a life-sized dancing doll. Moving carefully, so the weight of the corpse would not throw her off balance, she got to her feet. Time seemed to pass with excruciating slowness, extra time for something to happen to Emily.

"Stop thinking like that!" she told herself, the force of her breath making Noreen's hair ruffle.

She had to hope that Emily wasn't in danger. Laura

seemed to like the child. If anything, it seemed she wanted to kill Jenn so she could take Emily for her own.

"But I'm getting her back and you can't stop me."

"I don't know . . . what that means," Jenn choked out as she struggled toward the door. "But . . . I will . . . STOP you!"

Painfully, arduously, Jenn made her way down the hall with her bizarre dancing partner, heading for the kitchen and the telephone.

Peter gasped when he opened the door and saw his sister. She was seated at her little table, so much like she'd been months ago when she was . . . alive.

She *looked* alive today. Peter stared at her for a moment, not speaking. The last time he'd seen her, up in the bedroom when Emily came to visit, she'd been as pale as the ghost she was.

Today, however, it was Emily who looked pale and sickly. She was staring at Tara through bloodshot eyes, her hair hanging in lackluster yellow strings. Her lower lip jutted out in a pout. She seemed to be in some kind of trance.

"What . . . ?" Peter said.

Laura cut him off.

"Did you do your chores?" she demanded. She was sitting in the rocking chair, one that had been in their living room only a week ago. She was mending something, as if having her dead daughter in the room with her was the most natural thing in the world.

"Did you do your chores?" she asked again.

Peter let a nod of his head be his lie. Ignoring his mother, he went to the little table and looked down at his sister.

"You're really going to do it, aren't you?"

"It's time," Tara said. "Emily's father is too close. If he gets her, all my hopes are lost."

Peter couldn't say anything. He was far too confused. He wanted his little sister, pest that she'd been, to live again. But Emily was so much smaller, and so innocent. He didn't want her to be hurt. It would be worse than ...

Worse than seeing the animals die.

"Want some tea?" Tara asked, holding up a little cup.

Peter walked away from her.

"Mom?"

The question hung in the air, his mother ignoring him. She held up one of Tara's dresses. "I have to take it in a little," she said. "When Tara comes back, her new body will be too small for all these clothes."

Peter realized his mother wouldn't explain what was happening. Maybe she didn't even know herself. She looked—*weird*, somehow. Not like his mother at all.

Looking back at Emily, Peter saw that the little girl's head had fallen onto the table. Cold fear moved through him, and he walked quickly to touch her.

"Don't worry," Tara said. "She's alive. I don't plan to kill her, you know."

Peter put a hand on the back of Emily's neck. It was so tiny it seemed he could break it in a millisecond. She felt cold to his touch. He took off his jacket and placed it over Emily's frail-looking body.

It took Jenn fifteen minutes to reach the kitchen. When she got there, she was momentarily torn between the phone and a pair of scissors that hung on a cow-shaped metal hook on the wall. She decided it was more important to get help right away. Keeping her captive arm wrapped around Noreen's body, she reached for the telephone. Noreen's body had been dead weight as she'd struggled down the hall, but when Jenn heard the silence of the phone, her burden seemed to grow.

Had she really thought Laura would be so stupid? Of course she had cut the phone lines.

"But maybe not in the cottage," Jenn said hopefully.

Now she yanked the scissors from the wall and cut herself free. Gently, with great respect, she lowered Noreen's body to the floor.

She was opening the back door when she heard a scream.

"Mommy! Mommy, help me!"

Jenn swung around. The voice was thin, as if Emily was calling from behind a door.

"EMILY?"

The sound seemed to be coming from upstairs. Had her daughter been here the whole time? She ran into the hall, calling to her daughter.

"Where are you, Emily?"

"Up here, Mommy! Up in the trees!" The voice was faint, but Jenn managed to trace it to the attic. Taking the steps of both flights of stairs two at a time, she was up there in seconds. She rushed throught he attic, throwing aside boxes as she searched.

The attic was dark and empty.

"EMILY?"

Now she heard her daughter's frantic scream. It was coming from behind her . . .

. . . in front of her . . .

. . . overhead.

Jenn swung around in a wild circle. It seemed that Emily was everywhere.

And nowhere.

"MOMMMEEEEE!!!!!"

Tara stood up abruptly and threw her little teacup at Emily. It struck the child in the head, but Emily didn't react.

"Hey!" Peter cried.

"What's wrong, sweet angel?" Laura asked.

A look of pure anger came over Tara's face.

"She's calling her mother," she said. "She's calling her mother!"

"I don't hear anything," Peter said.

"It's in her mind!"

"Her mother is dead," Laura insisted. "Isn't she, Peter?" She stared at her son.

"Isn't she?"

Peter backed away. "Leave me out of this!" he cried.

The shelf of books crashed to the floor.

"Stop that, Peter!" Tara insisted. "STOP!"

She took Emily by the shoulders and shook her, hard. "You, too! Stop it! Stop doing that!"

Peter lunged for her. "Leave her alone!" He crashed into the table, breaking it, as his hands grabbed nothing.

"You little bastard," he heard his mother say. But it wasn't his mother's voice at all. It was the voice of another woman, the woman who had taken his mother's place after Tara died, the woman who had shot and slaughtered all the animals on the farm in her anger . . .

"Why didn't you tell me she was alive?"

"I didn't know," Peter insisted. "I didn't know!"

He threw his arms over his head, expecting her to strike him.

To his surprise, his mother helped him up and pulled him into her arms.

"She tricked you, didn't she?" Laura said, stroking his hair. "Jenn tricked you. She's evil, you know. That's why she can't have Emily back. She'll be better with me, don't you see? I'll be a better mother to Emily."

Peter didn't dare reply.

* * *

The voice became focused again, and this time it was coming from downstairs.

"Down here, Mommy! She's trying to hurt me! Make her stop!"

Somehow, the voice was different. Instinct told Jenn to be careful, but her mother's love overcame her common sense. She raced downstairs again.

"Emily, what room are you in?"

Running footsteps led her in the direction of the kitchen. The back door stood wide open. As Jenn stepped outside, she saw a child running across the yard. She knew at once it wasn't Emily. She could see the distant trees through the child's retreating form.

"TARA!"

At the unexpected sound of her name, the child stopped short. Jenn moved carefully toward her. She could see a glow around her—the aura Nick had pointed out.

"Are you Tara?"

No response.

"My little girl is Emily," Jenn offered. "She likes you a lot. Can you help me find her?"

Tara turned around. Her face looked more alive, more vibrant than Jenn would ever have expected. She began to giggle.

"Y'know a secret? Mama killed all the animals. She killed them and put them in a big hole in the ground and now you're gonna go there, too!"

Jenn ignored this strange threat. "Please, help me find Emily?"

More giggles. "Just 'cause of the dog and the horse, Mama killed all the animals and made blood go everywhere."

She skipped away, toward the barn.

"Pretty red blood!"

Jenn took after her, but when she got inside the barn

and flipped on the light, she could see the whole place was empty. Instinctively, she looked overhead for bats. There were none—René had done a good job of sealing the place.

Soft, cold prickles moved up her back. Jenn shuddered, terrified the spiders were back again. But there were no arachnids near her. Only a sensation of terrible danger . . .

"TARA? TELL ME WHERE EMILY IS!" Jenn cried.

Deep, feral growling made her turn around ever so slowly. A pit bull stood between her and the door, hunched over, blood showing in its eyes. White saliva dripped from its mouth as it growled at Jenn. She froze, knowing any sudden movement would cause the dog to attack.

And knowing that this was no ordinary dog at all, but the essence of pure evil.

twenty-five

The pain Nick felt in his side was only slightly more disturbing than the sight of a police officer pacing by his door. It took him awhile to gather his thoughts; pieces of information came to him between pain and drowsiness. Everything was clear about last night up to the point where they'd said good night after the Fred Astaire movie. He closed his eyes and smiled, remembering Jenn's kiss.

Then he frowned. He was pretty certain, despite the medication they'd given him, that he hadn't kissed Jenn good night. Had he missed an opportunity? Where was Jenn now—and Emily? Who was taking care of Emily?

Words came back to him that raised gooseflesh over his entire body:

"She's my kid, not yours. I've come to get her back again."

A face, filthy and bearded with wild eyes, appeared in his mind.

Nick remembered it all now. He's awakened with a horrible stomachache, and he'd gone to tell Jenn. Before they could speak, her own pain had sent her running to the bathroom. Nick had stumbled out after her, and a man had stepped into his path. Nick had tried to fight with him, but the man's strength seemed demonic. As they struggled, he kept talking about "E.J."

"She's mine! E.J. is my kid," he had said crazily.

Nick hadn't registered who E.J. was, but this morning he realized the *E* had to stand for *Emily*. Was this the father? Impossible. Evan Parsons had been killed in that car accident! Nick couldn't believe in ghosts, not without hard scientific proof.

The intruder had driven a fist so hard into Nick's midsection that Nick had doubled over. When he managed to stand up again, the man was gone. Nick was sick and dizzy all at once, but somehow he's made it to the kitchen to find a knife. He'd called to Jenn, but she didn't answer. The relief that came over him when he saw her through the bathroom doorway was snuffed out when a hand, so cold it burned, grabbed his wrist. He'd cried out as he was turned around, his arm twisting behind his back.

"I can't find the door!"

"What the . . . hell . . . are you . . . talking about?" Nick had demanded through clenched teeth. The acrid smell of the stranger's breath made him feel sick again, but he put all his strength into breaking free. It seemed impossible— the man's strength was unnatural.

"The door to Emily," the man had said. *"I've got to make her pay for telling lies about me! But I can't find the door to her!"*

And then something sharp had burned into Nick's side.

He knew he'd been stabbed with the knife he'd held. After that, the night was a blank.

He desperately needed to find out what had happened to Jenn and Emily. If the guard was there to protect him, then the woman and little girl he'd grown to love were in danger, too.

He called to the guard. The police officer poked a head in the door, then came inside and asked, "You feel like talking?"

There was no sympathy in the cop's voice, only cold interest. To Nick, it seemed like the way the police would talk to a suspect.

"I feel like asking questions," he said, his voice more choked than he'd wanted. The pain from his stomach and his stab wound were making him sound weak.

"So do we," said the cop. "You wait, I'll get the sheriff."

The nurse came in and tended to him. He tried to ask her about Jenn and Emily, but she only smiled and said the sheriff would arrive soon. There was nothing for Nick to do now but lie back and fight his pain.

The dog moved slowly toward Jenn. She watched it, her heart pounding, trying to find a way to escape.

Laughter filled the air from the loft overhead. Jenn dared to take her eyes from the dog for just a moment to peer up into the shadows.

"Tara?"

How did she get up there so fast?

When she looked down again, the dog was gone. But she felt no relief. The dog represented evil, and evil had been following her ever since Evan had forced her car off the road. Maybe the dog *was* Evan . . .

Jenn shivered violently and rubbed her arms. Looking around, she spotted a pitchfork hanging on a wall. Was it the same pitchfork that had killed René? Was it still spotted with his blood? She didn't take the time to find out. Clumsy a weapon as it might be, she still felt better than if she was completely unarmed.

The barn filled with a horrible cacophony of noises. Screeches, howls, moos, and other racket from countless unseen animals made Jenn squeeze her eyes shut and hunch her shoulders.

But just as abruptly as it began, it stopped. Now she could hear shuffling noises in the dead hay that lay on the dirt floor. Jenn looked toward the sound as she moved backward to the doorway, wary of the dog. As she passed under the loft, something dripped on her shoulder. She touched it and brought back a finger tipped with blood.

"Pretty red blood!"

Tara's voice came from a dark corner, not from overhead.

Jenn swung around.

"Tara, please talk to me!"

Tara stepped out of a shadow, cobwebs flicking the top of her head, her auburn hair wild.

"Tell me where Emily is," Jenn implored.

"You'll never find her," Tara said. "And even if you do, I'll be inside her and she won't be Emily anymore!"

"You little bitch!" Jenn screamed, lunging for the child. Tara vanished at once. Forgetting the dog, Jenn ran outside and called Tara's name. She wasn't surprised by the silence that answered her. Tara could be anywhere, or she could be gone.

"I need help," Jenn said out loud.

The cottage phone! She hurried to the little house to check, but Laura—or someone—had cut that line, too. Jenn realized her only choice was to drive into town to get Mike Hewlett. It meant leaving Emily here, but it was the only way. She couldn't search the thousands of acres of woods herself. And she couldn't even be sure Emily *was* here. It was only Tara's presence that gave her the idea.

There was no time for speculation. She needed a team to help search for her little girl. Her car, parked up at Laura's house, seemed a hundred miles away. She broke into a run, concentrating on her goal, ignoring the strange sounds behind her: horse's hooves pounding the dirt, a goat bawling as if in terror, childish laughter that came from something no longer a child.

The evil was trying to trick her, to make her turn and fall. But she wouldn't listen to it. She would be stronger, and she'd reach the car untouched.

Her determination was so strong that she practically flew the last few feet. She jerked open the car door and jumped in. Fumbling with her keys, she jammed them into the ignition, and turned. Nothing happened.

Jenn allowed herself a quick, ironic laugh.

"Stupid!" she told herself. "Laura's done something to the car, too!"

Laura, or Tara . . . or Evan. Jenn felt sick again, but her pain had nothing to do with her stomach. She prayed Evan didn't have Emily now.

All her options were gone. She would have to look for Emily herself, but where to start? In which direction should she go? The woods seemed endless.

When she got out of the car, she screamed in shock.

The barnyard was littered with the bodies of dead animals. There were two cows, a few goats, countless chickens. A pig lay at her feet, a round black bullet hole between its eyes. Feathers floated in the air, and the stench of decay was everywhere. Jenn fought the urge to retch, closing her eyes. It was all a trick!

"Mama killed them all."

She opened her eyes again. The animals were gone. Tara stood there, a few yards away.

"Mama killed them all," she said again.

Jenn took a step forward. Tara seemed to float above the dirt, her hair blowing in nonexistent wind.

"What happened to you?" Jenn whispered. "Why the hell do you want my daughter?"

Frustration overtook her calm, and she ran for the ghostly child with her arms outstretched and her fingers poised to grab.

"What do you want with my daughter?" she screamed.

Tara burst into tears.

"No, Mommy!"

Taken aback, Jenn stopped short. Tears poured out of Tara's green eyes, and in their shimmer Jenn thought she saw traces of Emily's face. The eyes fluctuated from green to blue, the hair from auburn to golden.

"Please help me, Mommy!" the child begged. "Don't let them hurt me!"

"Emily!" Jenn cried, reaching for the child.

A being that was definitely not her daughter backed away, fists clenched and face screwed up tight.

"NNNNOOOOO!!!!!"

The child vanished into thin air.

In her dream, Emily was running across a field. She could see her mother waiting on the other side with open arms, loving arms that would save her from the bad things. But no matter how long she ran, she stayed in exactly the same place, and the field before her stretched farther and farther away.

Pumping her little legs with determination beyond her years, she forced them to go faster. She had to get to Mommy! If she didn't, Tara was going to make her stay in this place, and Daddy was here somewhere.

She heard her mother scream something, and suddenly she was close enough to touch her. But just as she was reaching out, a horrible noise made her turn around. There was a horse there, bearing down on her, hooves scrambling through the air. Emily threw her arms over her head with a scream. In that moment, Tara possessed her soul once again.

Jenn heard the horse, too. She swung around to see the huge beast heading right for her. There was no time to think, only to react. She raced for shelter, finding it in Noreen's car. Her friend had left it unlocked. The keys were in the ignition, but Jenn knew before she even turned them that Laura had done something to Noreen's car, too. The silence of the engine told her she was right. Sighing, she rubbed her eyes and tried to clear her head. She realized none of this could be real. She saw that there was no mist coming from the horse's nostrils, although the day was chilly. Its feet didn't kick up any dirt as it galloped around the car.

Jenn laid hard on the horn and shouted:

"Go away! I don't see you there!"

The horse reared up, its legs scrambling in the air, but it didn't vanish. Instead, it turned and ran off toward a field.

Her heart pounding, her legs shaking from exertion, Jenn twisted the key again. The only reply was a sickening gasp from the ignition.

"No," Jenn whispered. *"No!"*

The car was useless. Somehow, Laura had found the chance to get out here and do something to it.

"Not Laura, Jennifer," said a sickeningly familiar voice. "Me. I fixed the cars. I want you here, baby. I want us to be one big happy family."

Evan was sitting beside her. Slowly, she turned to look at him.

A scream caught in her throat.

His clothes were nothing but charred tatters. His smile showed all his teeth in a face that was completely burned away, down to the blackened skull. The eyes, although round and lidless, were full of hate.

"I know the door is very nearby, Jenn," he said. "I even saw Emily a moment ago. Won't be long now before I can reach right out and grab her little body. And after I punish her for lying about me, I'm coming back for you!"

"Get away from me!"

Jenn shoved the door open and flung herself out of the car in one smooth motion. Evan reached out to grab her with a charred hand, but she backhanded him with a scream of disgust. The hand broke off and fell to the floor of the car.

Jenn raced away. As she rounded the corner of the house, she tripped over something. Her hands splayed out to stop the fall, slapping the dirt with a force that went right up her arms. Thinking Evan was in pursuit, she jumped to her feet at once, ignoring the pain. She looked down.

Emily was lying on the ground, blood coming from her head.

"Oh, God, no!"

She crouched down, but the child vanished at her touch. It wasn't Emily at all, but a phantom, like the dog and horse.

Unless . . .

"Please, no, dear Lord . . ."

Jenn shook her head as she stood up. Tara was a ghost. Could Emily be . . . ?

She wouldn't let herself believe Emily was dead. The thought of someone stealing Emily's precious young life brought on a great surge of strength. Anger fueled Jenn's tired muscles as she strode toward the woods. The hell with Tara, the hell with Laura!

"The hell with you, Evan!" she shouted.

The rabid dog popped into view before her, white foam dripping from its mouth, blood splotching its strong white head. Jenn didn't pause, didn't back away. She stared down the animal as if she were another dog daring it to fight.

"Go away," she said evenly. "Go away, go away, GO AWAY!"

The dog lunged for her, spittle sailing through the air like tiny white rockets.

"Go away!"

The dog shattered into a million pieces that fluttered away on the wind.

"Stop it, Tara!" Jenn yelled. "No more games! NO MORE!"

Mike Hewlett had a lot of questions for Nick when he arrived. What was he doing with that knife? Did he poison Jenn? Did he want to finish things off with the knife? Why? Why?

"I had the knife because I thought I saw someone in the house," Nick said. "Don't be an idiot, sheriff. I love Jenn! I'd never harm her, or Emily."

"But you were the only one there," Nick said. "There was no sign of forced entry."

"Then someone had a key," Nick replied. "Did you question Laura Bayless? Did you ask her about the chocolate cake she brought for us?"

Mike paused, staring at the sick man. Years of experience as a cop had taught him to know when someone was telling the truth. Nick Hasken seemed desperate to be believed.

"We haven't been able to locate her," he said quietly.

Nick leaned back on his pillow, closing his eyes. "It's her. It has to be!"

"Why?" Mike asked. "What vendetta could she possibly have against you and Jenn? Unless . . ."

The pause made Nick open his eyes again. Mike was staring at him with a new question in his eyes. Nick knew at once what it was.

"Forget it," Nick said. "I never even met Laura until recently. It isn't a jealousy thing."

Mike shook his head. "I hate to make false accusations."

"You've made them against me!"

"But Mrs. Bayless went through so much last year," Mike said. "Her husband leaving her in the spring, her little girl killed in the summer."

Nick sat up straighter.

"Little girl?"

"Her daughter was trampled by a horse," Mike revealed.

"Was her name Tara?"

"Yes, why?"

Wheels spun crazily in Nick's head. Laura's daughter had died. Emily kept talking about a kid named Tara. A child had shown up in the pictures where Jenn said she hadn't been before, a child surrounded by a ghostly aura . . .

"She had red hair?"

"I guess so," Mike said. "Why?"

Jenn had said Laura was paying too much attention to Emily . . .

"We've got to get to the farm!" Nick insisted, trying to move from the bed. Pain shot up his side, and he grimaced to fight it.

"Easy, guy," Mike said. "First, tell me what you're talking about."

Nick took a deep breath. "I'm talking about murder, damn it. Laura's going to kill Jenn and take Emily in as her own daughter."

He didn't dare say out loud what his scientist's mind didn't want to believe: that, somehow, Tara Bayless had come back from the dead. With her mother's help, she was going to take over Emily's body!

"That's crazy . . ."

"Maybe," Nick said, relaxing a bit as the pain slowly went away. "But Laura's up to something, and Jenn and Emily are in terrible danger."

He opened his eyes fully now. "So are you going to sit there like an ass, or are you going to investigate?"

Mike stood up and put his cap on his head.

"I'll get there as fast as I can," he promised.

"I'm coming, too," Nick insisted, struggling from the bed.

"But—the stab wound . . ."

"The hell with it," Nick growled. He set his teeth hard and let Mike help him up. Pain shot through his side, and for a moment he thought he'd hit the floor. But a few deep breaths helped.

"You sure about this?"

"The doctor said the wound didn't hit any vital organs," Nick said.

Mike waited, impatiently, as Nick dressed. He was still buttoning his cuffs when they walked down the hall, past the nurses' station. There was no one on duty to say he hadn't been officially released. Nothing could hold Nick back at that moment. He wanted to be the one to rescue the woman and child he loved.

twenty-six

The effort to get to her mother had brought Emily to complete wakefulness, but she remained still and quiet. Part of it was terror, but part of it was a sense that pretending to be asleep might help. She listened hard, wishing to hear her mother's voice. Why was her mother so far away?

She could hear Peter, Laura, and Tara arguing.

"Why don't you do it now, sweet angel?" Laura was asking.

"It's too soon," Tara replied. "She isn't weak enough yet. She almost got through to her mother! If Jenn finds out where we are . . ."

"This is sick," Peter growled.

"Shut up!" mother and daughter shouted in unison.

"She has to give herself to me willingly," Tara went on.

"I can't force myself on her. She has to say 'yes' to me before I can stay inside her forever."

Emily opened one eye a bit. The trio was across the room, their backs to her, huddled together in conspiracy. Maybe if she ran for the door . . .

She didn't stop to plan things out. Like a typical small child, she moved on impulse, making a mad dash. Her little hand was on the knob when she heard Peter yell:

"Hey!"

Then Tara was there, grabbing her arm, yanking her away from the door.

"You aren't going anywhere," she said grimly.

"You can't make me stay!" Emily cried. "You can't! I want my mommy!"

Hurt, frustrated, and terrified, she threw herself on the floor and began to scream. Why wouldn't Mommy come help her?

Tara leaned down and whispered into her ear. At once, Emily froze in silence.

"No," she squeaked.

"It's true," Tara said. "Your daddy's here. He's been looking for the door to you, and it's right here in this cabin! Your daddy's here and it's all your fault for making so much noise!"

"Not Daddy," Emily whimpered. "Don't let him get me!"

"Too late," Tara said coldly. "I can't stop him."

She turned to walk away. Emily sobbed as she pulled herself to her feet.

"Unless . . ."

"Tara, what's this about Emily's daddy?" Laura asked.

Tara looked back over her shoulder at her mother.

"He's been looking for her," Tara said. "I've been fighting him all along, until she was ready for me. But I don't think I can wait any longer."

To Emily, she said, "We have to trick him."

"How?"

"Let me inside you again," Tara said. "When he looks in here, he won't know you."

"I don't wanna . . ."

"There's no other way. Hurry! Say 'yes'! Let me inside you! Oh, he's here! He's at the door!"

"Yes! Yes! Yes!" Emily screamed.

Tara gave her mother and brother a sly smile, then vanished. A moment later, Emily turned pale white. Her eyes blinked a few times, and she lost her balance. Peter grabbed her before she hit the floor. But his mother took the child away and carried her to the little white bed.

Emily let out a hard gasp, her eyes rolling back into her head. Her face went from white to blue.

"Mom, she can't breathe!"

Laura was oblivious to anything but their daughter's return.

"It's Tara," she said in awe, tears in her eyes. "My sweet angel is coming back again! Emily is going now!"

Jenn went into the cottage to get away from the spirits, both human and animal, that were haunting the farm. She knew they could get in here, too, but somehow having four walls around her gave her a feeling of relative safety. She sat down at the table and buried her head in her arms, wishing there was time for a cup of coffee to revive her. But she knew she only had a few minutes to think, and plan.

Her brain started to work, piecing together what little she knew, trying to come up with logical answers to insane questions. Right now, the biggest and most important question was: Where would Laura take Emily? She wasn't in the big house, or the barn, or in here. She certainly hadn't driven off in her car. It only meant that there had to be some other type of shelter here, something she couldn't see.

Something hidden in the woods.

If only she could get a better look in the trees . . .

Jenn's head snapped up as if pulled by an idea that hit her. She'd thought she'd heard Emily up in the attic. Maybe if she looked out the window up there, she could get a bird's-eye view of the trees.

Jenn ran all the way upstairs and looked out the attic window. The sight of a cabin in a distant clearing gave her newfound strength. Perhaps Laura had taken Emily there to hide! She rushed through the house again, this time stopping to locate the hunting rifle Laura had used the other day. To her surprise, it was still loaded.

"Maybe I can't kill someone who's already dead," she growled, stomping into the yard, "but I can make Laura give Emily back to me!"

And then Evan was there, burned and hideous, hateful. He blocked her path, stepping in time with her as she tried to go around him.

"Get away from me, Evan!" she demanded. "I'm going to get my daughter!"

"*Our* daughter," Evan corrected, his breath coming out in acrid smoke that made Jenn gag. "Our bad, lying bitch of a daughter! Tell me how to get to her, Jennifer! TELL ME!"

"Go back to Hell, Evan," Jenn growled, not shouting it, not screaming it. Her words carried the quiet hatred of a mother protecting her child.

"Come with me," Evan invited.

With a cry, Jenn swung the rifle through the air. It sliced right through him, but it made him vanish.

"God, give me strength," Jenn prayed. "I've got to get to the cabin!"

"The cabin!" Evan's disembodied voice shouted with insane glee. *"I've found the door! She's at the cabin!"*

Heart pounding, adrenaline coursing through her veins, Jenn started to run. Why had she spoken out loud? Why had she given Evan a clue to find Emily? It would be her fault if anything happened now. She had to get to Emily first! She had to find that cabin, somewhere in the woods, before Evan got to her little girl.

Laura took Emily's body into her arms and rocked her back and forth, talking in a soothing way, then singing a soft lullaby. Her eyes were glazed and distant.

Emily was so pale she seemed unreal.

Peter backed slowly away from them, trembling. He'd seen his mother look this way before, on the day Tara died, the day she killed all the barn animals, blaming them for his sister's death.

There was a broom in one corner of the room, left behind after his mother had finished cleaning up the place. Without a moment's thought, he grabbed it and swung. It hit his mother hard across the side of the head, stunning her long enough for him to grab Emily.

"I'm sorry, Mom!" he cried. "I'm sorry, but this is wrong!"

He carried the little girl out of the cabin and into the woods. He didn't know if Emily's mother was still at the house, or if she was even alive, but he had to try. He had to get Emily back to her!

If it was Emily. Peter looked down at the child as he struggled to run with her. Small as she was, she was growing heavier.

Emily was awake. She stared up at him, her face blank.

"Emily?"

"Want Mommy," the child mumbled.

He knew it was Emily. Tara always called their mother "Mama."

Then Emily started to giggle.

"I'm in here, Peter," she said, in Tara's voice.

"Shut up," Peter snapped.

As he ran over Copperhead Hill, the ground became alive with snakes. The part of the child that was still Emily screamed in terror. But Peter wasn't buying the illusion.

"Forget it, Tara," he said. "I'm not scared."

He ran right through them, phantom serpents turning to dust under his boots.

His arms were growing weak, his heart beating too hard. He had to stop to rest. Keeping his arms around Emily, he sat down for a moment, gasping.

"You can't stop me, Peter," Tara said.

"Don't talk to me," Peter said.

Tara turned to look back into the trees, her eyes wide. A moment later, Peter heard his mother calling:

"Peter! Bring her back! Bring her back, or I'll tell the police about the animals!"

Terror coursed through Peter's veins, bringing on visions of life in prison.

"Peter, where's my mommy?"

The sound of Emily's pathetic little voice brought Peter around again. He got up and began to run once more. The child began to struggle in his arms. She made a horrible growling noise and bit him hard on the shoulder. Peter yelled out and stumbled, but his grip was firm. He could see the house now, and Jenn crossing the yard.

"JENN! JENN! OVER HERE!"

He realized from the look on Jenn's face that she thought he was trying to hurt Emily. He cried out as she raised the rifle.

"Let her go!" Jenn demanded.

"No, you don't understand!"

"Emily! Emily, come to Mommy!"

Peter knew it was the only safe thing to do: he let the child go. Jenn saw this and carefully set the rifle on the ground.

"Emily!" she called. "Come here, dollbaby!"

At first, Emily took a few steps toward her mother. But then her whole body seemed to stiffen, and she swung around. As Jenn ran toward her daughter, she saw Laura appear. Emily ran to the other woman, jumping into her arms.

"EMILY!" Jenn shouted.

Somehow, Laura had tricked the little girl into trusting her. Jenn went back and picked up the rifle.

"She isn't Emily," Peter said. "Tara's gotten inside of her. She told Emily that her father was coming for her."

"Keep away from us!" Laura commanded, turning to move into the trees.

"Give her back!" Jenn shouted, raising the rifle. But she knew she couldn't shoot and guarantee missing Emily. Laura and Emily disappeared into the woods.

"It's okay," Peter said. "I know where she's going. We have an old hunting cabin my father built."

"No!" Jenn cried. "She can't take her there! Somehow there's a portal to the other side in that place, a way for Evan to get through to Emily!"

The both ran toward the cabin, as fast as they could, Peter leading the way. They caught up with Laura and Emily in the clearing where the cabin stood.

"No, Laura, stop!" Jenn called. "Please! It's dangerous to go in there! It's Evan's way to get to Emily!"

"She's lying!" Jenn heard her daughter say in Tara's voice.

Laura tightened her grip on the child, her hand pressing Emily's head into her shoulder.

"Tara's come back to me," Laura said. "Your tricks won't take her away again!"

"Laura, look at her!" Jenn cried. "She's Emily! Doll-baby, come to Mommy!"

The child stared hard at her. "Call me 'sweet angel.' "

"Oh, no," Jenn said, moving forward.

Laura took a step back. "Keep away!"

"Mom . . ." Peter said beseechingly.

"Stay out of this, you traitor!" Laura screamed. "You always hated your sister! You'd be glad if she never came back!"

Peter stumbled as if she'd struck him.

"Why Emily?" Jenn asked. "Why my child?"

"Because their spirits were joined once," Laura said. "They were in the ICU at St. Michael's, and they both died at the same time. But Emily came back. It wasn't fair!"

She began to sob.

"It wasn't fair. I'm a better mother than you! I deserved to keep my child, not you!"

She moved toward the cabin door. "GO AWAY!"

Jenn had to stall the woman. She couldn't let Laura take her daughter into that cabin. She set down the rifle.

"Laura, how did Tara die?" she asked gently.

Emily smiled at her, but it wasn't Emily's smile at all. It was Tara who spoke:

"You wanna see? You wanna see?"

Suddenly Jenn was standing in the middle of a huge field of grass and wildflowers. The air was still with summer heat, the sky bright blue. Crickets sang. A dragonfly demonstrated the Doppler effect as it buzzed by her ear: soft, loud, soft.

She spotted Tara a short distance away, crouched down at the side of a pond. She was flicking her fingers on the

surface of the water. Jenn realized this was Tara as she had
been in life.

Jenn looked around. A huge horse stood nearby; she
was certain it was the same horse that had come after her.
Right now, it seemed content to graze in this peaceful, bu-
colic setting.

When she first heard the rumbling noise, it seemed like
the sound of a distant motorboat, or perhaps a lawnmower.
But as it came closer to her, Jenn knew it was the rabid
dog. She looked around, finally spotting it hunkering toward the horse and the child, its killer instinct exacerbated
by its madness. Jenn tried shouting at it, tried throwing a
rock to distract it. It was futile.

Suddenly the dog pounced at the horse, digging its teeth
into the horse's flanks. Its small, muscular body hung on
the horse's brown flesh, whipping back and forth as the
horse screamed and danced in its panic. The hooves came
flying up . . .

It didn't matter that Tara had evil plans for Emily. The
mother in Jenn saw a child about to be hurt, and instinctively called:

"Tara! Look out!"

. . . and came crashing down hard on the little girl's
head just as she swung around in surprise.

The horse ran off, the dog still clamped to it. Before
Jenn could move, she felt a hand on her shoulder.

"I found her," Peter said, a choke in his voice. "The water was filled with her blood. I carried her back to the
house, and Mom took her to the hospital. But it was too
late . . ."

"Oh, Peter," Jenn said, putting her arms around the boy.

She still had her arms around him when they snapped
back to reality.

"Laura, I'm so sorry," Jenn whispered. "I'm so sorry."

"I don't need your sympathy," Laura snapped. "I need my little girl!"

With that, she picked up Emily/Tara once more and moved toward the cabin. Jenn lunged forward to grab her daughter as Laura yanked the door open. A huge wall of flame shot out, filling the air with acrid smoke. Horrible screams rolled out, punctuated by the terrified noises of tortured animals.

It seemed to be the gateway to Hell.

"NO!" Jenn cried. She grabbed for Emily, struggling to pull her away from Laura. A great force sucked them toward the flames, whipping their hair. Emily screamed, then Tara shouted. Jenn held fast to her child, terrified she was going to be inhaled by that gaping mouth of a door.

"Mom! Let her go! *Let her go!*" Peter yelled over and over.

"TRAITOR!" Laura screamed at her son.

Emily found Jenn's ear and bit hard enough to draw blood. Tara said, "You aren't my mother. You leave us alone or I'll take Emily in there and give her to her father!"

Emily's voice cried out desperately, "Mommy, don't! Don't let Daddy get me! PLEASE!"

Jenn knew she had to help her daughter break free, or in a moment of insanity Tara would walk into the flames and give her over to the demon that was once her father.

She could hear him there, calling Emily, his voice full of hate and anger:

"E.J.! Come to Daddy, E.J.! Come to Daddy!"

Tara reached toward the flames, part of her held by Laura, part of her held by Jenn. She smiled.

"I'll give Emily's soul to her daddy," she said. "And I can have her body."

"Yes, Tara! Yes! Make it happen. now!" Laura cried.

Jenn grabbed a fistful of Emily's hair and forced the child

to look at her. Tara growled and snapped, but she wasn't strong enough to resist.

"Emily, listen to me!"

Tara laughed out loud.

"Emily, where are you now? What do you see?"

Tara growled. But Emily's voice said:

"Pink clouds, yellow clouds. I don't want to be in the light, Mommy!"

Jenn took a deep breath.

"Do you see anyone there?"

Emily sighed, her eyes distant. "Pretty angels. People— they're all smiling. I see that nice lady and man who gave me the pink teddy bear."

Simone and Joel! Maybe they could help!

"Do you see Michelle?"

Emily squinted, staring at something no one else could see. Half her face was lit red by the strange roaring fire that never spread beyond the doorway. Her hair blew in a wind that didn't stir the surrounding trees.

She smiled.

"Hi, Michelle!" She frowned. "What's Miss Kane doing there, Mommy? When did Miss Kane go there?"

Jenn felt her heart skip a beat to realize her friend was among the spirits. She collected herself and said, "Emily, listen! Simone and Joel and Michelle are your friends! So is Noreen—Miss Kane! They'd never let you be hurt. Do you see Daddy?"

A pause, then a tentative:

"No . . ."

Tara's voice cut in, and the child's face seemed to change.

"He's here! He's hiding, waiting!"

Jenn ignored her. "Emily, do you think our friends would hurt you?"

"No."

"Do you think the angels would let anyone harm you?"

"I have a guardian angel," Emily said softly.

"There aren't any angels!" Tara cried from Emily's mouth. "Only bad people who want to take me away from my mama!"

"Tara . . ." Laura whispered in a choked voice.

"Emily, do you see Daddy?"

"I don't want to!"

"Look! He's not there, is he? Simone and Michelle and the angels won't let him come near you. Tara is trying to trick you! If you let her stay in you, you'll have to go to where Daddy is! Then none of us can help you. None of us!"

The words were harsh. It sickened Jenn to have to threaten her child. But it worked. Emily gasped, throwing her head back. Her eyes rolled up into her head, and she began to turn blue.

"She's choking!" Laura cried. "You bitch! You're killing her!"

Jenn yanked hard on her daughter and pulled her from Laura's grip. She hurried away from the cabin door. Emily went stiff in Jenn's arms, her little body arching back and her arms curled up in front of her. Jenn lowered her to the ground, helpless as she watched the seizure.

"You don't deserve her!" Laura cried.

Jenn realized Laura had moved away from them. She looked up to see that Laura had picked up the rifle.

Then Jenn heard an unexpected voice:

"DROP IT!"

Oh, God, Evan had broken through . . .

But it wasn't Evan at all. Mike Hewlett stood with his gun aimed at Laura. Nick was at his side, looking from the flaming doorway to Jenn to Laura.

"She's a bad mother! Why did she get to keep her

child? Why?" Laura screeched, and aimed the rifle at Jenn and Emily.

Suddenly a brilliant cloud surrounded the two. The others watched in awe as images of faces appeared and disappeared in the light. Jenn felt arms around her and Emily. The air had grown pleasantly warm.

"What the hell is happening?" Mike shouted. "What is that?"

"Spirits," Nick whispered, for it was all the scientific proof he needed.

The sound of a gunshot snapped the two men out of their reverie. They both turned to look at Laura, who stood with a look of shock and anger on her face. But instead of striking her intended victims, the bullet ricocheted off the almost-solid wall of light. It lodged in a tree just behind the spot where Jenn had been crouched over Emily.

Inside the house, Evan's demon screamed in protest.

The light vanished almost instantly. Jenn was on her knees, holding Emily tightly.

"Mommy . . ."

It was Emily, completely. She knew it. Tara's ghost was gone.

"Mommy, I see Tara," Emily said. "The angels have her now." Then she collapsed.

"I need help!" Jenn cried. "Mike, get me an ambulance!"

Mike was off and running in a second. Nick knelt beside the little girl. Emily let out a scream that was so piercing that it sent birds fluttering out of the trees overhead. Her body arched to an impossible height, then slammed down.

Emily was still and silent.

"Oh, no," Peter wailed.

"You killed her!" Laura cried. "You've killed my little girl!"

Nick pressed his head to Emily's frail chest and heard the faintest heartbeat.

"She isn't dead, Jenn," he said, relief in his voice.

Jenn looked up at Laura. "She isn't dead."

She gathered the child in her arms.

"And she's mine."

She turned toward the doorway.

"DO YOU HEAR, EVAN! SHE'S MINE!"

The flames disappeared and the phantom wind died down. The clearing was peaceful once more.

Peter turned to his mother:

"It's over," he said. "Tara isn't here anymore."

epilogue

Nick took Jenn and Emily home that night. It was cramped in his one-bedroom apartment, but Jenn felt more safe and secure there than she had since childhood. She slept cuddled close to him, her arms wrapped protectively around Emily. When the little girl woke up with a nightmare, they were both there to comfort her.

It took a few days of investigating to piece together what had happened, but at last Mike Hewlett called them to the station.

"According to Walter Bayless," Mike said, "Laura had a history of mental problems."

"Then why did they let her have the children after the divorce?" Jenn asked.

Mike shrugged. "Who knows how the courts decide these things?"

Jenn said, "She certainly gave the impression she was

the perfect mother. Noreen even said she was a throwback to the fifties."

She felt a chill to think how her friend and fellow teacher had died. She and Nick had attended the funeral just a day earlier.

"What sort of problems are you talking about?" Nick asked. "Anything that would indicate she'd resort to murder?"

"When she was eighteen," Mike said, "she broke a cat's neck because it scratched her. And she had a strange habit of showing up at people's doors in the middle of the night, bringing them things she'd baked."

"The cat part is bad," Jenn said. "But other than choosing odd hours, what's wrong with leaving a few baked goods with the neighbors?"

"With rusted nails or dead bugs inside?"

Jenn groaned. "I can't believe she was trusted to bake for that store."

"We questioned the manager at the Mixing Bowl," Mike said. "He knew of Laura Bayless, but she's never worked for him, or anyone else in the area. She's been living off an inheritance for years."

Jenn shook her head, wondering what Laura had done with all the things she'd baked. Probably dumped in the woods somewhere, she guessed.

"I guess Tara's death must have put her over the edge," Nick said.

"Poor Tara," Jenn put in, "it was a horrible way to die. The series of events were one-in-a-million."

"After Tara died," Mike said, "Laura went completely crazy. She transferred her anger at the dog and horse to all the farm animals, and slaughtered each one of them."

Jenn recalled the vision of the dead animals and felt sick. She moved closer to Nick. He took her hand and squeezed it.

"She made Peter help bury them in a pit hidden in the woods," Mike went on. "He never told anyone because she threatened him with jail. Peter had been in some trouble with me before."

"Peter's a hero," Jenn said. "He's part of the reason I have Emily back again. I'm just glad he's going to live with his grandparents, near his father's home. Will you be calling him back as a witness?"

"He's underage," Mike said, "but we might question him further. He can help verify that his mother was mentally insane at the time she committed these crimes."

Jenn bowed her head, thinking of all the people who had been hurt or had died in the past months. How many were victims of spirits, and how many had Laura hurt?

It was possible no one would ever know.

Mike closed his file and shifted in his chair. He leaned forward, folding his hands.

"There are aspects of this case that are ... well, *unusual*," he said. "I want you to know that I've left them out of the report."

Jenn and Nick exchanged glances.

"Why?" Nick asked. "We all saw what happened that day."

"And we'll keep it our secret," Mike added. "Few people will believe us, and those who do will be on the fringe. We'll end up with every tabloid in the country wanting to interview us, asking us about proof of ghosts."

"I don't want Emily to go through that," Jenn agreed. "But what are you going to say?"

"That Laura shot at you, and missed," Mike said. "That I managed to get the gun away from her, at which time she gave up."

"Okay," Jenn said. "If that's the way to end this. It's bad enough that we'll have to go through a trial."

Nick tightened his grip on her hand again.

"I'll be there," he promised.

They spoke a while longer, then finally said good-bye. There would be many more questions to be asked, but not today.

Jenn had left Emily at the center, although she'd been reluctant. She expected Emily to protest against being left, since it was only a few days after her traumatic experience. To her surprise, her daughter ran up to a group of children and started to play as if nothing had ever happened. That afternoon, when she arrived at the center to pick her up, Dee came to the fence with a smile on her face.

"The change is unbelievable," she said. "Emily is so much more sociable now! I'm glad whatever happened with that woman didn't have an adverse effect on the child."

Jenn gazed at Emily, sharing a seesaw with another little girl.

"She's a remarkable child," she said.

Jenn knew the nightmares would last for a while, but she also knew Emily was smart enough to break free of her memories, with the help of her mother's love.

Emily spotted her now and jumped from the seesaw. She ran to the fence, where Dee opened the gate.

"Hi, Mommy! Hi, Nick!"

"Hi, dollbaby," Jenn said, taking Emily into her arms. She hugged and kissed her repeatedly.

"Put me down, Mommy," Emily protested, wiggling. "You hug and kiss too much lately."

Both Jenn and Nick laughed. Jenn *had* been fussing over her daughter a lot.

"I can't help it," she said. "I love you so much."

"I love you, too, Mommy," Emily said, kissing her. "Now put me down!"

"Okay, okay!"

Jenn set the child on her feet. She took one of her small hands, Nick took the other, and they walked to Jenn's car. Emily sang a song to herself, but the adults remained silent for a while. As she drove, Jenn glanced over at Nick every once in a while. He stared out the window with a contemplative look on his face.

"What are you thinking about?" she asked.

"I'm trying to make sense of all that's happened," Nick told her.

"Don't bother," Jenn said. "I don't think any of it will ever make real sense."

Nick sighed. "Sorry, it's the scientist in me. I never believed in ghosts before. But when I saw those spirits around you, and they saved you from that bullet . . ."

He let the sentence trail off, unable to put his thoughts into words. Miracles were not something he could discuss in black-and-white terms, like chemical reactions or the periodic table.

"I keep thinking about that myself," Jenn said. "I'd like to believe that the people we knew only briefly, but grew to love, were there to help us. Simone, Michelle, Noreen . . ."

From the back seat, Emily laughed. She leaned forward to rest her head on the back of the front seat, her safety belt pulling with her.

"Sit straight, dollbaby," Jenn said. "Or the seat belt's no good."

Emily stayed where she was. "You two are so silly. It wasn't ghosts that helped us!"

Jenn kept her hands on the steering wheel, but tilted her head back.

"It wasn't?"

Nick turned a little and started to play with Emily's long blonde hair.

"So what was it, honey?" he asked. "What did you see?"

"Angels!" Emily cried, delight in her voice. "Beautiful angels! Didn't you see their wings, Mommy? Didn't you see their shiny faces?"

Jenn shook her head. She only remembered the soft, beautiful light and the feeling of being held in protective arms. And . . . a warm and wonderful sense of great love.

Nick remembered something now.

"You said that angels had Tara," he said. "You saw her with them?"

Emily nodded, her chin pressed into her arm.

"They took her away from all the sadness," Emily said "She was happy, Mommy. She wasn't afraid anymore."

"I don't understand," Jenn said. "Why didn't the angels come for her before?"

Emily sank back into her seat, folding her arms. Her expression darkened.

"Because of Daddy," she said.

"Oh, no . . ."

Nick gave Jenn's arm an encouraging squeeze.

"Where's your daddy now?" he asked.

Emily shrugged. "He went away. He got scared by all the light and love and he went away."

"Light and love?" Nick echoed.

Jenn took in a deep, shaking breath. A tear spilled down her cheek.

"The light and love of the angels," she said. "Of God. Maybe that's why it was so hard for Evan to get to Emily. Maybe she was just surrounded by too much love."

They had reached the parking lot of Nick's apartment building. Jenn pulled into his space and turned off the ignition.

"No kid can ever have too much love," Nick said.

Together, they turned and smiled at Emily. The little girl smiled back at them, a smile as radiant and innocent as any in her young life. This was one little girl who would always be surrounded by as much love as she ever needed.